D0097665

CAT COMING HOME

ALSO BY SHIRLEY ROUSSEAU MURPHY

CAT COMING HOME

A JOE GREY MYSTERY

Shirley Rousseau Murphy

WILLIAM MORROW

An Imprint of HarperCollins*Publishers*

HarperCollins books may be purchased for educational, business, or sales promotional use. For information please write: Special Markets Department, HarperCollins Publishers, 10 East 53rd Street, New York, NY 10022.

FIRST EDITION

Cat illustration by Beppe Giacobbe

Library of Congress Cataloging-in-Publication Data

Murphy, Shirley Rousseau.
   Cat coming home : a Joe Grey mystery / Shirley Rousseau Murphy.—1st ed.
      p.   cm.
   ISBN 978-0-06-180693-3
   1. Grey, Joe (Fictitious character)—Fiction.
2. California—Fiction. 3. Cats—Fiction. I. Title.

PS3563.U7619C314   2010
813'.54—dc22

2010015336

10 11 12 13 14   OV/RRD   10 9 8 7 6 5 4 3 2 1

For ELT
Joe Cat LeBouef
Lucy
Mousse
Scrappy
Fluffy
And all who went before

Home is where his heart has always lingered, where he
  etched his first kitten paw prints,
Where he sucked in his first lick of milk, smelled his first
  briny scent of the sea,
Tasted, first, the fishy sand and the reek of seagull feathers.
Where he mewed his first word and knew that he was
  different.

—Cat Anonymous

CAT COMING
HOME

1

Fog as soft as a purr drifted among the twisted oaks and tucked down around the weathered roofs of the old hillside neighborhood, blurring their steep angles. On the twisted arm of a sprawling oak, the gray tomcat crouched above the rooftops licking at his fog-dampened fur, his claws kneading idly as he watched the neighborhood below. The old stucco or shingled homes, denizens from an age past, crowded close to one another among their overgrown gardens, descending the hill with dignity, some perhaps still sheltering their original occupants. This early morning, the tomcat was concerned with only one house, with the small, two-story Tudor that, until this week, had stood empty, its tenants long departed.

It was a simple house, and straightforward, its pale plaster walls set within heavy, crisscrossed timbers. A wide bay window at the front revealed a glimpse of the kitchen, and above the kitchen, behind a narrow ledge of dark shingles, opened the wide windows of two upstairs bedrooms topped by a steeply peaked roof. Only the garage roof was flat, out of keeping with the original design as if it had been added on in later years. Replacing, perhaps, the kind of small detached garage common in the age of the first cars, of the little Model A Fords—the kind of shed that would never have held Maudie Toola's big black Town Car.

From the moment, three days earlier, when Maudie's Lincoln parked at the curb and then soon the yellow moving van pulled into the drive, Joe Grey had observed the grandmotherly woman with interest. He knew she had fled L.A., some three hundred miles to the south, after the murder of her son and his wife, but it was even more than the murder that piqued the tomcat's curiosity; it was something about Maudie herself. Something out of keeping, an attitude that didn't seem to fit this gentle person, an occasional gesture or glance that seemed out of character in the soft little woman.

The tomcat had no clue that his interest in Maudie would soon involve a whole tangle of confusing events besides the recent murders, that a stabbing soon to occur at the state prison and the brutal home invasions that had already descended upon the small village would prove all to be connected in some way to Maudie herself. This morning Joe puzzled only over Maudie as he watched for her to appear, watched for an early light to blaze on in her bright kitchen.

The shooting of Maudie's son and daughter-in-law had occurred eight months earlier, east of L.A. on a lonely mountain road as they headed up into the mountains north of Lake Arrowhead. Their destination was Maudie's weekend cabin on the edge of a tiny, man-made lake, where they planned to enjoy the children's Easter vacation. Only Maudie and the three children—her grandson and her son's two small stepchildren—had survived; they were the only witnesses.

THEIRS WAS THE only car on the dark and narrow road, they moved through the night between tall stands of shaggy forest, the scent of pine blowing in through their open windows. Deep within the woods they could hear the occasional booming of a barn owl, solemn and intent. Only where the pines thinned for a moment did light from the low moon flicker into the front seat, catching a gleam of Caroline's honey-colored hair and of Martin's white baseball cap. Caroline's two children and Martin's little boy, Benny, were crowded into the backseat with Maudie, Benny snuggled against his grandma. They were all startled when headlights blazed suddenly into the car from behind them, blasting out of the night as if the overtaking car had snapped out of another dimension. Martin slowed to let the speeding vehicle pass so he could safely make his left-hand turn. Instead of passing, the big pickup cut its speed and pulled alongside, keeping pace with them. Maudie glimpsed the passenger for only a second before she saw the gleam of metal, too, and shoved the children to the floor, crouching down over them as a fiery blast exploded, and another. In the front seat Martin jerked and fell sideways; she could see him between the bucket seats, twisted and slumped beneath the wheel. It all happened in an instant, their car skidding sideways headed for the dense pinewoods. Maudie could see Caroline leaning across Martin's body fighting the wheel, trying to keep them from crashing, trying to reach the emergency brake. A third shot burst from the big pickup and their car spun out of control, skidded off the shoulder, went over on its side, and crashed into a tree. The engine roared, and flooded, and died. The pickup cut out around them screeching tires, kicking up gravel, and was gone. Silence in the car. Neither Caroline nor Martin moved; all was dark and still.

The couple had been married just four months; Caroline was a widow of two years, her husband having been killed in Iraq. Maudie's son, Martin, an airline pilot, had filed for divorce when he learned that his wife, Pearl, during his absences, would go off for days leaving Benny alone in the house to fend for himself, the six-year-old child begging meals and spending many nights up the street with Caroline Reed and her two children. When Martin was home between flights, Pearl had seemed a caring enough mother, though her nature was cold. Certainly the couple had had their problems, but Martin had stayed for Benny's sake—until he learned how much he had ignored of the little boy's life. Only when he pressed Benny for details had Benny confided that, when they were alone, his mother would drive him out of the house or, if she had company, she would lock him in his room.

Benny was always a quiet child, and Martin berated himself for not seeing clearly the little boy's pain. What

4

use was it to provide well for his family if he couldn't take proper care of his neglected child. Stricken and ashamed, he had told Pearl to move out, had gotten a restraining order against her coming anywhere near Benny, had filed for divorce, and had asked Caroline if Benny might stay with her until he found live-in help. Caroline told him the arrangement need not be temporary, that her two kids liked having him there, that that was where Benny felt safe and loved, that was where he wanted to be when he couldn't be with his daddy. Benny, in his loneliness, had drawn Martin and Caroline together, and nearly a year after Martin divorced, they knew they had fallen in love and would marry.

When Maudie returned home to L.A., after a long absence on the East Coast where she'd gone to care for a cousin, when she moved back home and learned the truth about Benny's life, she was devastated. She had thought to take Benny to live with her, but then, on meeting Caroline and learning about their upcoming wedding, she saw there was no need. She was deeply warmed by their newfound happiness, she wept when they said their vows; after the ceremony she held the child and held Caroline and thanked God for the miracle that had brought the two together. Martin's life had turned around—until the evening they headed up to the mountains for that fatal Easter vacation.

It was black night when they reached the mountains. Moving along the narrow back roads, theirs was soon the only car. Moonlight fingered the tips of the pines, and flashed between the trees into the moving vehicle. They met no oncoming lights and they passed no clearing in the forest where any faintest house light flickered, they were alone, content with one another as Benny napped peacefully against Maudie and she herself dozed.

And then the blazing lights. The gunshots. The wreck. Easing up, Maudie caught her breath as pain seared through her shoulder. In the front seat, the newlyweds lay unmoving, a dark huddle; they made no cry, no smallest sound. The children clung to Maudie, Benny's arms so tight that pain shocked through her hurt shoulder, making her vision swim; she clung to the child, dizzy and sick. The night was so black, silent except for the dying ticking of their wrecked car. She cried out to Martin but he didn't answer, nor did Caroline. She tried to wedge her way into the front to find Martin's hand, or Caroline's, to feel for a pulse. She was sick with the terrible, certain knowledge they were dead. They were alone on the deserted mountain road, no one to help them, no one to know what had happened. No one but the killer.

Maudie tried to find her purse, find her cell phone, wondering if, in that desolate mountain area, a 911 call would get through to anyone, wondering if her signal, impeded by the ragged peaks, could possibly reach a tower and be relayed to the local sheriff or the CHP. Or would her call simply die, smothered among the ridges and pinewoods? She thought of a gasoline fire but could see no lick of flame starting among the wreckage. The children clung to her, silent and shivering. As she searched for her purse, for the phone, the pain that surged through her brought tears spurting.

Later she remembered only fragments: the children

6

climbing over into the front seat to their parents even as Maudie tried to stop them. At once, Gracie and Benny started to scream, Gracie's high-pitched little voice screaming, "Mama, Mama, Mama, Mama, Mama . . ." unable to stop. Twice Benny said, "Papa," then he began to retch.

It was so dark, the moon's light blocked now by the mountain of the car itself towering over them. Maudie abandoned the search for her purse, and rummaged through the pockets of the backseat trying to find a flashlight—but she didn't dare shine a light on Martin and Caroline, didn't dare let the children see them torn and bleeding. She prayed they weren't dead, prayed they would live, they were all these children had. Death wouldn't be fair, not for this warm, happy, newly formed family.

But the words "fair" and "right" were arbitrary, they had no connection to real life. Were those concepts applicable in the dimension larger than life, a dimension that neither she nor anyone alive was equipped to understand?

Swallowing back the pain in her shoulder, she reached between the bucket seats, feeling for the children. She felt Gracie huddled down against Caroline, her arm slick with Caroline's blood. Maudie tried to squeeze through between the headrests and the headliner, but Benny swarmed back away from Martin, screaming and crying, pressing her down again. Gracie followed him in a panic, and then Ronnie, the three children clinging and shivering, weeping uncontrollably in their terror and grief.

Later she remembered hugging the children, feeling sick and dizzy with pain. She remembered finding her phone, making the call, but after that the memories became disjointed. She thought a lot of time had passed in pain and blackness until, what seemed hours later, the sound of sirens startled her from half consciousness, and lights blazed in, blinding her, blinding the children . . .

Even now, eight months later, her memories of the shooting and crash were still tangled. She had lucid moments, and long spaces lost in between that she couldn't bring back: waking in a moving vehicle, strapped down to a cot, unable to move or sit up. Not knowing where the children were, crying out for the children. A man's voice, trying to calm her. Waking to a loud insistent thumping that terrified her until the man told her she was in a helicopter. Recognizing, then, the thunder of its propellers, as the white-coated medic leaned over her, telling her the children were right there with her, that they were not badly hurt. Seeing the three children, then, huddled together with blankets around them, and the medic asking her about family, asking who they should call. She tried to tell them where, in her purse, to look for the phone numbers of her older son, David, and of Caroline's sister. Everything happened in torn fragments, ragged and not quite fitting together, a nightmare puzzle that would never, ever leave her. She remembered the loud, slamming wind of the copter's blades above her as the door opened and she was lifted out on the stretcher, uselessly crying out for the children.

She remembered waking in a cage of metal bars, trying to pull herself up, then seeing the tubes sticking out of her arm confining her, holding her down, remembered yanking at them trying to get free until a nurse grabbed her hands. She fought the nurse, screaming for Martin, screaming his name over and over . . .

It had taken her a long time, in the hospital, to face the truth that lay silent and dark within her, to face the fact that Martin and Caroline were dead, to face the grief she didn't want and didn't know how to deal with. A long time to understand that Martin's and Caroline's bodies had been transported to the county morgue to await a coroner's autopsies. A long time to believe what the doctors and police told her, that the three children were safe, that they were in a motel nearby with Caroline's sister, who had flown out from Miami. It took her a while to understand that her older son, David, would arrive from Georgia that evening. Not until Caroline's sister, Maryanne, arrived at the hospital with the children, until Maudie saw for herself that the three children were all right, did that part of the nightmare begin to subside.

Gracie and Ronnie, subdued and pale, clung to Maryanne, needing their aunt, whose golden hair and warm smile so resembled Caroline. Now Maryanne, and David, and Maudie herself, were all the children had left to love and nurture them.

2

IN THE SMALL village of Molena Point, far above L.A. on the central California coast, chief of police Max Harper and his tall, redheaded wife, Charlie, had just returned from an early evening ride up into the hills above the sea cliffs. In their cozy stable, as they unsaddled the horses, their conversation centered around plans for their annual pre-Christmas potluck. Max's buckskin gelding and Charlie's sorrel mare stood in cross ties between the two rows of stalls as Max and Charlie checked their feet for stones and then rubbed them down. At the end of the alleyway beyond the open barn doors, their green pastures spread away between white fences, allowing a glimpse of the sea beyond. The weather was warm for late November, the ocean breeze welcome; though in a few days, the local weather guru had forecast, a cold spell could be expected.

"That would be nice for the Christmas party," Charlie said, "cold weather, and a fire on the hearth." Usually, the

Harpers hosted the casual buffet there at the ranch where they had ample parking for police vehicles and the cars of their civilian friends. This year, because of the rash of home invasions that had descended on the village, their friends and the personnel of Molena Point PD would gather in the heart of the village, at the Damens' house, where officers on patrol could stop by on their dinner breaks, while their wives and families could linger on for a more leisurely visit. The invasions were worrisome, as the department had made no arrests and thus far had no good leads. Max had doubled patrols and extended officers' hours, and many vacations had been canceled, the added costs stretching the department's budget thin enough to cancel Max's order for four new squad cars—and leaving Max short-tempered and abrupt, reining himself in with a far harder hand than he ever controlled his buckskin gelding.

"No one," Charlie said hopefully, "would dare pull a home invasion Christmas week. Not with so many people crowding the village from out of town, for the plays, for the pageant, and a choir singing almost every night, tourists shopping and walking the residential streets, and so much traffic." Although the minute she said it she saw how silly her statement was, that with crowds everywhere, who would notice a few more strangers?

Max gave Bucky a last swipe with the rubdown cloth and looked over at her, his lean, tanned face touched with amusement. "What better time, with doors unlocked to welcome guests, houses full of people going in and out, no one paying attention to who might step inside uninvited, maybe with a weapon at the ready?"

Charlie sighed, and wished the world were different, and then was ashamed of that childish thought. She watched Max lead Bucky into his stall, watched her husband's thrifty movements as he fetched two rations of grain and a handful of carrots from the feed room. The brutal home attacks enraged Max, though he tried to remain low-key. These assaults, all on women at home alone, hadn't so far netted the invaders much of monetary value. Maybe their victims' fear, the enjoyment of their own power over the frightened women, was all the reward they were seeking. As the holidays approached, filled presumably with love and good cheer, these attacks on isolated homeowners seemed far more ugly. It didn't help that the villagers' growing unease was heightened by news coverage that was slanted with the weight all at one end.

The Molena Point *Gazette* had always, in the past, been in harmony with the local law enforcement; the editor had liked Max and was pleased with the job he did, with the stability and low crime rate in the village compared to other nearby towns. Now that the *Gazette* had been sold, and with a new editor at the helm, the little local paper was coming down hard on Max's department. Emerson Ribble, the new editor, and the one new reporter he'd brought with him, seemed intent on smearing MPPD, implying that they should know beforehand the exact time and place of each attack. The paper's cutting editorials didn't suggest how that might be done, how any police department could run surveillance on every house and backyard cottage, on every little twisting street within the crowded square mile of the village, and do it twenty-four/seven. They didn't seem to grasp, or didn't want to point out, that the very basis of home invasions was the element of surprise.

One invasion had occurred just before supper-time when children were still playing in the street. Two homeowners had been attacked first thing in the morning when they went out to get the paper, leaving their doors unlocked behind them, returning to find they were not alone. So far, seven women had been beaten badly enough to be taken to emergency, four of them hospitalized. Max, besides increasing patrols into the quieter, out-of-the-way neighborhoods, had encouraged people to take their own sensible precautions as well. He'd been on TV three times, had done four newspaper interviews laying out the steps that people could take to discourage forced break-ins. It was all commonsense, basic information: Keep doors and easily accessed windows locked when you're inside or out-doors, even when you're right in the yard. Don't answer the door without looking first to see who's there. Don't open the door at all to strangers; speak to them through a window or install a simple intercom. Watch your neigh-bors' houses, note any strange cars in your neighborhood. Call your neighbors if anything looks suspicious—strang-ers hanging around, strange cars showing up repeatedly. Report to the police anything that couldn't be explained, that made you uneasy. He had not suggested Mace or pep-per spray, though anyone with good sense should already have looked into those or other options. The *Gazette* had printed Max's articles as he'd dictated them, but then in their own articles and editorials they'd gone after him viciously, as accusatory as if he were masterminding the invasions himself. The one common denominator among the attacks was that each had occurred at the same time officers were headed for, or on the scene of, some other emergency call, when cars and men were drawn away from neighborhood patrol. Assuming the invaders had a police radio, the department had switched to a new code language, plus more reliance on cell phones.

Leading her sorrel mare into the stall, Charlie removed her halter, shut the stall door, then joined Max in the doorway of the barn; they stood enjoying the evening, watching their two half-Dane mutts out in the pasture, sniffing hopefully around a rabbit hole the rabbit long ago departed. This was the first day in some six weeks that Max hadn't worked long overtime hours. He wasn't twenty anymore, Charlie thought crossly, he needed *some* rest. Max was pushing retirement, and sometimes she wished he'd take early retirement.

But Max loved his work, he loved the department, and she wasn't sure how he'd fare if he were idle. Though the way things were going, it looked like someone was working hard to push him in that direction, to separate him from Molena Point PD before he was ready. That enraged her almost beyond endurance, that someone was trying to destroy Max, that they were beating and injuring innocent civilians in order to hurt her husband.

Not that they would succeed. Whatever these people did, whatever this smear campaign was about, they wouldn't destroy Max Harper, she thought fiercely, or destroy the men and women of the department who were so loyal to him.

But, standing with Max's arm around her as they watched the evening descend, listening to the sea crash beyond the cliffs, Charlie had to smile. Despite the current trouble, there was one aspect of the investigation that even Max didn't imagine, and lent a gleam of hope. Max could have no idea that one gray tomcat might tip the scales, that when Joe Grey and his two lady pals got their claws into the invasions, these cases could begin to open up and the department would start to receive evidence that, by its very nature, was inaccessible to the officers of Molena Point PD.

3

Maudie Toola and her little grandson arrived in Molena Point in early December, eight months after the murder of Benny's daddy and stepmother. They drove up the coast from L.A. with Maudie's older son, David, who refused to let Maudie make the three-hundred-mile trip alone. Maudie seemed to David desperately in need of rest and peace just now, with her painful shoulder from the bullet wound, and after the stress of the murders and of the subsequent investigation. And after the strain of the last eight months as she had worked to sell Martin's house and her own house, and put Martin's and Caroline's affairs in order. Caroline's sister had helped her as long as she could, then had gone on back to Florida with Caroline's two children. Now, Benny was all Maudie had. Except for David, and his first concern, at present, had to be for his wife. Alison wasn't doing at all well in anticipation of her upcoming cancer surgery.

David glanced over at Maudie. Still recovering from her wounded shoulder, and still grieving so deeply for Martin, she needed a hassle-free trip, and he could do that for her. In Molena Point she and Benny could settle quietly into their new home and, hopefully, Maudie could start to make a new life for the two of them.

They had departed L.A. at six on Tuesday morning, planning to arrive in Molena Point that afternoon in plenty of time to meet the moving van, which had loaded up the previous evening. Their Thanksgiving had been quiet, a restaurant meal, the first Thanksgiving dinner Maudie could ever remember not having cooked herself. As they drove north up Highway 101, Maudie and David talked softly while in the backseat the small, pale little boy slept covered with a quilt, clutching his own familiar pillow. Benny's brown hair was just the color of his daddy's at that age, though he wore it longer than Martin ever had. Neither Maudie nor David could look at the child without seeing Martin as a little boy. The memories hurt, but they heartened Maudie, too. Maybe she was overly sentimental, but she took comfort in knowing that something of Martin himself would live on in his little son.

The morning was damp and cold. A thick fog lay along the freeway, staining the crowded neighborhoods the dirty gray-yellow of sour milk. David took the first shift, driving until Paso Robles where they meant to stop for a late breakfast. What worried him, as he pulled into the parking lot of the Paso Robles Inn, easing in between two tall trucks where the car wouldn't be seen so easily from the highway, was that the killer might have followed them. That whoever had shot Martin might think that, despite the dark night, Maudie had glimpsed his face. That she'd seen, if not enough to make a positive identification, enough to give the police a clue. In the months before the shooting, Martin had, on three occasions, reported questionable airport personnel who later turned out to be security risks. Two of them were baggage workers, one the member of a maintenance crew, two with prison records, one with no green card and no passport. David worried that these men might be behind the shooting, and he thought about Martin's ex-wife, as well. Pearl Toola had some questionable contacts, men David suspected she'd remained close to, from her earlier years working in the Las Vegas casinos. Martin and Pearl had married young, when Martin was perhaps wilder, before his responsibility as a pilot had settled him down. Pearl had been so beautiful, Martin hadn't cared that she worked dealing blackjack and ran with a fast crowd.

After the shooting, when the L.A. police interviewed Maudie, she had made no identification, and as far as he knew, they still had no leads. The police told them there were no shell casings found and, on the hardtop road, the sheriff had picked up no tire marks. Maudie told the investigating detective that she had seen only the flashes of gunfire, that she hadn't seen the shooter. When the L.A. detectives queried her about Martin's ex-wife, Maudie told him that considering Pearl had had several affairs while they were still married, and had once asked for a divorce herself, it didn't seem likely, when they did go their separate ways, she'd consider herself a wronged party in need of revenge. She said she thought Pearl was glad to be free of Martin and her little boy, that surely she wouldn't be foolish enough to turn around and put herself in harm's way for no reason. Maudie told the detective she was leaving L.A., and gave him her new address in Molena Point. She said she couldn't continue living in L.A. with the memories of Martin's childhood unavoidably all around her, that she didn't want to live with those painful reminders.

Molena Point, too, was filled with memories, but of a different kind. This was the village of Maudie's childhood, the one place she wanted to be, the one place she thought she and Benny could find peace and begin to heal, as much as they ever could heal. Among the woods and along the seacoast of the small village, she thought Benny's hurt spirit might begin to mend. She wanted only to lose herself again in that perfect place, to return, as well as she could, to those long-ago childhood pleasures, to that early innocence before the world forced her to see life more clearly.

She had kept the two cottages all these years, since her own parents died. She and her husband, Allen, had leased out the larger house, keeping the little guest cottage, four doors up the block, for their vacations. After Allen died, she hadn't had the heart to return to the village, and had rented out the smaller cottage, too. It was then that she had bought the tiny log house nearer to L.A., just north of San Bernardino, the cabin where they had been headed the night Martin and Caroline were killed.

Now she had sold the San Bernardino cabin, and sold the Molena Point cottage. She and Benny would live in her old home, in the two-bedroom Tudor which, with a little addition, would provide room for her quilting studio. She desperately needed that involvement again with color and cloth and stitching, needed to get outside herself. She couldn't hope to heal Benny's broken life without first healing her own—without embracing once more the work that eased her spirit and that she found meaningful.

It had been hard to sell the L.A. home where Martin and David grew up, hard to sell it just after Martin's funeral. But that part of her life was over now. She had put the money from the sale of the house and of the San Bernardino cabin into an additional trust for Benny. When Martin left Pearl he had made sure all his holdings were in trust for the child where Pearl couldn't get at them, and Maudie had done the same. Closing out her bank accounts of her day-to-day funds, she had packed the cashier's checks safely in her luggage among her lingerie, for deposit in a Molena Point bank.

They'd arrived in Molena Point at one, in time for a lunch of hot soup and fresh-baked bread at a small restaurant run by a Persian couple who were among Maudie's favorite people; then they'd headed up the hills to their new home, up the steep, wooded streets above the village. Approaching the dark-timbered Tudor that had been her childhood home, Maudie caught her breath. This was *their* home now, hers and Benny's; they would settle in here, Benny would grow up here. And whatever the outcome of their move might be, maybe the final words of Martin's and Caroline's epitaphs had not yet been written. Maybe, Maudie thought with a cool certainty, the last episode of her son's death was still to be revealed.

4

THE NOTION THAT Maudie's fate and the fate of her small grandson might be guided by a cat would have greatly amused the older woman, the idea that she and Benny would become the subjects of a tomcat's sharp and life-changing attention would have made her laugh. Yet even that first afternoon as Maudie supervised the moving in of her furniture and packing boxes, she was closely observed from the branches of an oak tree just above her, where Joe Grey crouched, his yellow eyes narrowed with interest. There was something about the soft little woman that made the gray tomcat tweak his whiskers and lick a paw reflectively.

She was just a bit pudgy, a pale, round woman with powdery skin, her smile warm, her voice, as she supervised the unloading, gentle even when she was annoyed at a worker's carelessness. She was impeccably groomed, her blond-dyed hair—which was probably gray—styled in an expensive bob, her loose, smocklike jacket well cut, in subtle patterns, over silky, gathered trousers. Expensive, flat-heeled shoes. Tiny gold earrings and a gold choker. A timid-looking woman, well turned out as if to give herself confidence, and with a smile that should draw one to trust her. Yet there was an air about her, too, that didn't seem to fit, a watchful expression that showed itself for only an instant and then was gone again, a look that puzzled the tomcat.

Over the next three days, Joe Grey watched Maudie. He watched her grown son David carry in a fresh Christmas tree, and imagined the three of them busily decorating it among their still unpacked moving boxes. He arrived early each morning with his housemate, Ryan Flannery, as she came to work on the cottage that she and Clyde had bought from Maudie. Ryan and Clyde Damen had been married only since last Valentine's Day, the providential joining of a pair of avid collectors: Clyde of classic cars, which he restored and sold; Ryan, of antique mantels and moldings and stained-glass windows, which she used in the homes she built. Now, perhaps driven by an excess of matrimonial bliss, the couple had combined their creative fervor into restoring old houses.

On this morning, the fourth after Maudie's arrival, Joe sat on the roof of the Damens' remodel venture dividing his attention between Maudie and the construction project under way below him. Peering over, he watched Ryan and her two Latino helpers pulling nails and ripping off strips of weathered siding, in preparation for a new sunroom addition that would look out on the greenbelt behind the backyards: a wild expanse that ran all along this side of the hills, a favorite retreat for deer, raccoons, bobcats, and dog walkers brave enough to face the occasional curious mountain lion. The banging of boards and the screeching of rusty nails was so loud, at this early hour, he expected the neighbors to pour out into the street shaking their fists and shouting, but for the moment, the street remained empty.

Around him, the fog-blanketed rooftops angled so close together that a cat could hop from one roof to the next and not miss a beat; or he could travel above the rooftops, along the aerial highways of twisting oak branches. Later, when the fog lifted, the leafy roof would come alive with sparrows and house finches, a veritable café on the wing if a cat was agile and quick—and the rich supply of small game didn't stop there. Below him among the tangled yards and wandering garden walls and toolsheds lived generations of mice and moles and fat gophers to satisfy a hungry feline.

Between the bouts of noise beneath him, and the rattle of boards being tossed into the weeds of the side yard, Joe listened to the quick Spanish voices of Manuel and Fernando, and to Ryan's softer replies. Her Spanish was so limited that Joe was sure the two men were secretly laughing at her—but in a kind way, the tomcat thought. Both of them liked Ryan, and she seemed to get her message across, enough for the work at hand, enough for her crew to have built some pretty impressive houses. But his new housemate's talents weren't one-sided, Joe was still getting used to the changes in his and Clyde's bachelor life, still happily growing accustomed to Ryan's expertise in the kitchen, which was every bit as impressive as her skills as a carpenter, designer, and building contractor.

What her talents were in bed, he couldn't say. That was none of his business. Ever since the couple arrived home from their honeymoon, Joe spent only short periods of time sharing the king-sized bed before he retreated to his rooftop tower, which Ryan had designed and built for him. The hexagonal little house above the second-floor roof was walled with windows that a clever paw could open for easy access to the village rooftops, and was lined with a bright array of soft cushions. The design had been a collaboration between Ryan and Clyde, before even Ryan learned that Joe could speak. Joe had told Clyde what he had in mind, and Clyde had told Ryan, taking all the design credit for himself. This was long before Ryan and Clyde were married. They had begun seriously dating when she contracted to remodel Clyde's small, dull, one-story summer cottage into a handsome two stories with bold beams, high windows, and a touch of Spanish charm.

It was later that Ryan discovered Joe Grey's secret; she was one of the few humans who shared the knowledge of Joe's talents, and he had to say, the woman had a quick understanding of the feline world—she knew very well how to flatter a tomcat and how to make him smile.

Take this morning. Ryan had made pancakes for his and Clyde's breakfast, confections as light as a fluff of bird down. There she stood in the kitchen flipping pancakes, her short, tousled dark hair dusted with pancake flour, a ruffled apron tied over her work jeans and sweatshirt. And though she hated the smell of fish in the morning, she had generously presented Joe's serving with a half-dozen kippers tastefully arranged on the side—a perfect combination of textures and flavors, the salty fish blending smoothly with the pancakes and maple syrup.

Now, down the block, Maudie's son, David, emerged from the front door heading away for his morning run. He was a tall man, slim and well made, his brown hair trimmed short; he was dressed in navy sweats and dark running shoes. Like his brother, David was an airline pilot—as if, Joe thought, both boys had grown up loving planes, maybe wanting to fly from the time they were toddlers. David had taken time off to get Maudie moved and settled, but soon would be going back to Atlanta, and Joe wondered how Maudie would fare alone, wondered if she was concerned about the unsettling invasions of homes occupied by lone women. But how could she not be, when the *Gazette* kept pushing its hopeless take on the situation to further upset the village.

But, Joe thought, Ryan and her crew would keep an eye on Maudie; Ryan wasn't only remodeling the old cottage, she was at work as well building Maudie's new studio, enclosing the patio that was already walled on two sides where the garage and kitchen met at right angles.

Below Joe's rooftop perch, a jogger raced by, flashing beneath the oak branches. On the next street he glimpsed an old woman walking three elderly beagles, the dogs sniffing high above them in his direction, picking up the smell of tomcat. As the sun rose, a scurrying wind teased the fog and lifted it, ruffling his short fur. Below him, Manuel barked an order to Fernando in rolling Spanish, a song of words that made the tomcat wish he could speak the language—except that all that study would make him crazy, he wasn't the studious type. Joe's ability to speak

English had required no books and studying; the talent had overtaken him without any effort on his part.

One day he was your simple, everyday housecat enjoying a quick tussle in the bushes. The next day, when he found himself not only thinking human thoughts but speaking them aloud, he was shaken right down to his claws. The shock that he was speaking a human language, and was thinking not with sensible feline instincts, but with human logic—with the very turn of mind that so often drove a cat crazy—that revelation nearly undid him. His first awakening to this new experience had scared the hell out of him.

But when at last his terror gave way to this new kind of reason, when he realized what he might do with his new talent, the excitement had lifted Joe to heights he'd never imagined. Somehow, he'd fallen into a new, vast, amazing world. Into a life so different from his old life, so much more detailed and fascinating, that he'd soon had trouble remembering the simple housecat he'd once been—when his greatest challenges were mice, food, and females, when his greatest creative endeavor was thinking up new ways to torment Clyde. And that had been a blast, when Clyde first learned that Joe could speak, when Joe made that first phone call to Clyde and was finally able to convince him it was really his gray tomcat calling. It had taken Clyde a lot of shouting, several violent bursts of temper, before he believed it was Joe at the other end of the line, before he accepted the facts.

Strange, Joe thought. Since Clyde and Ryan married, he never wanted to harass his female housemate the way he liked to torment Clyde. Maybe that was because Ryan didn't get mad the way Clyde did. She didn't swear at him; she refused to indulge in shouting matches. She'd smile at his goading, just as she laughed at his altercations with Clyde that were, after all, only bachelor camaraderie. Instead of arguing, she'd pet him and hug him with an almost embarrassing tenderness.

Now, crouched between the roof's shingled slopes waiting for the fog to lift, for the rising sun to warm his chilly fur, Joe contemplated Ryan and Clyde's new endeavor. The project was meant to be purely for fun, to mentor an occasional forlorn and neglected structure, to see what they could make of houses that would otherwise be torn down. The newlyweds, the tomcat thought, were into creative renovation the way a little kid tackled a new toy.

For this cottage, in its narrow yard, there would be new stone walks and low-maintenance landscaping. In the back, the beams would continue upward to allow for the new, story-and-a-half ceiling of the sunroom. In Joe's opinion, despite his sarcasm regarding Clyde's carpentry skills or lack thereof, the couple was going to make a bright new home of this tired little cabin—and they should make a nice profit, too. Houses along any greenbelt were at a premium; many folk treasured a home where wild land touched the tamed world, where they could watch from their windows an Eden yet untouched by human meddling. For some humans, this strip of wild land would be as close as they ever got to the basics of raw nature, to the tooth-and-claw life familiar to any outdoor feline.

A cat, perhaps more than any other beast, could live most equitably with a paw in each of the two worlds. Cushions and soft comforters by night, a warm fire and a dish of liver or fillet. And in the daytime, when his adversaries were more likely to be asleep—but not always—a spine-tingling foray among the larger predators, a hunt to stalk and kill his own victims, an adrenaline rush that, if a cat was quick and clever, would send him home unscathed, with a belly full of something wild and filling. Joe was watching the greenbelt with an eye for the occasional silent shadow, for, most likely, a silent and marauding coyote, when a harsh scrabble of claws directly above him made him leap aside.

5

A SOFT THUD HIT the shingles as Joe's tabby lady dropped down to the roof beside him from the branches above, her green eyes laughing at his sudden alarm. She flashed him a good-morning smile and snuggled up, her dark, striped fur cold, and as damp as his own, in the chill morning. She smelled of pine where she'd brushed among bushy branches crossing the roofs of the village, leaving her own snug cottage. Her tail twitched against him as they watched Ryan and her two helpers laboring below. Down the street, Scott Flannery's green pickup appeared, heading for Maudie's house to get to work, his red hair and red beard as bright as new rust in the morning light.

Easing on past Maudie's house and past Maudie's black Lincoln that stood on the street, he parked beyond the drive, leaving it empty for deliveries of lumber and materials. A light burned in the kitchen, and the cats could smell fresh coffee brewing. Ever since Ryan started her construction firm, her uncle Scotty had been her foreman; it was Scotty who had taught her the skills of a good carpenter, long before she'd ever studied design. When Maudie had approached her about building the studio, she'd been pleased that the two small jobs were located so close together, shortening their work time and adding to the efficiency of both jobs. Maudie seemed quite content to live among the carpenters' clutter and noise, and she always had coffee for the workers. She even welcomed the cats; Joe and Dulcie and Kit had been in and out of the house ever since Ryan began work, prowling as they pleased. While Joe Grey was curious about Maudie herself, Dulcie and Kit were fascinated with the new studio as it began to take shape. What would a quilter's studio be like? How exactly did Maudie put her lovely quilts together? Ryan had shown them a whole magazine article that listed Maudie's many exhibits, with pictures of Maudie's quilts so bright and intricate that Dulcie had had to stroke them with a soft paw. The studio was dried in now, and Scotty was building cupboards and shelves and drawers, leaving one wall bare for Maudie's big quilting table, with hanging quilts behind it; the two lady cats were fascinated with it all. The problem was, every time they became absorbed in what Scotty was building, they would feel Maudie watching them.

No cat likes to be intently watched, even if it is a friendly gaze. Dulcie grew so irritated that she said maybe Maudie needed a pet of her own. "Then she should go to the pound," Joe snapped. "Get herself a house cat or one of those dinky designer dogs." The tomcat smiled. "A little puff dog that would make one bite for a respectable cat."

Below, Scotty stepped out of his truck and reached in the back for his toolbox. He was a tall man, well over six feet, large boned and broad shouldered, his red hair and beard clearly showing his solid Scots-Irish heritage. As he headed for the house, his long stride seemed better suited to tramping the rocky green hills of the old country. He was dressed this morning in the same faded jeans and dark jogging shoes that he usually wore, and a freshly pressed brown denim work shirt. His profile, against the dark wood of the front door, was craggy and lean, his red eyebrows shaggy, his short, neatly trimmed beard streaked with gray. Maudie opened the door before he rang the bell, her smile showing her delight at his presence—Scotty always seemed to make people feel happy. In the quiet lull from just below, as Ryan laid down her crowbar and hammer, Scotty's and Maudie's voices carried clearly up the hill.

"The windows'll be here this morning," Scotty said, "after all the delay. Then it'll begin to look like home."

"Like a real studio," Maudie replied, a smile in her voice. "There's coffee in the kitchen, and some sweet rolls." As she and Scotty moved inside, up at the top of the hill, an ancient brown pickup came out of the side street and turned down Maudie's street, slowing as it passed the house. The cats saw the driver looking, though the windows were so dirty he was little more than a dark smear, a pale face peering out through the murky glass.

"What's so interesting?" Joe said, bristling. The truck eased past, down the hill, the driver gunned the engine, turned onto the side street, and was gone. A brown pickup, dented and muddy, dark mud spattered heavily on its back

31

wheels, bumper, and license plate. The cats stared after it uneasily. The morning was silent again, and as the sun began to melt away the fog, a cacophony of birdsong made Dulcie look up and lick her whiskers. They heard the Skilsaw start down in the new studio as Scotty got to work. Dulcie yawned, and the two cats stretched out together in a patch of sun, waiting for it to warm them. Dulcie said, "Maudie and Benny will be all alone when David goes back to Atlanta. It has to be hard, grieving for her son, leaving all her friends, and now to be alone, knowing no one in the village."

"She knows Ryan and Clyde, and Scotty," Joe said. "Anyway, she has family here."

Dulcie sneezed with disgust. "Her sister? That prissy Carlene Colletto? And those two nephews? I don't see them lending a lot of support, they didn't even help her move in. Certainly the third one won't be any help, he's cooling his heels in prison."

"The one nephew's all right. Jared. It's the other two you want to steer clear of," Joe said. "The younger one, Kent. What a sleaze." They watched Ryan start down the hill, tool belt slung around her waist and carrying her clipboard, where she always had a tangle of receipts and to-do lists.

Below, Maudie came out of the house and headed down the driveway toward the street where her car was parked. The little boy followed her out, but then sat down on the low front steps as if he was too tired to go farther. He was a frail child, maybe six, thin and pale with light brown hair tucked down over his ears reaching toward his collar. "His face is so drawn," Dulcie said, feeling a deep pity for the little boy who had lost his father, who had seen his father shot and killed right before him.

Hurrying to the car, Maudie looked around with a quick intensity, despite her soft demeanor. She saw the street was empty, but glanced up once at Benny, seeming as wary as a matronly cottontail watching her vulnerable young. Turning to the car, she used her electronic key to pop the trunk open. Beneath the rising lid the cats could see a load of plastic bags stamped with the familiar names of local shops: Molena Point Gourmet Kitchen, Dolly's Linen Den, The Village Christmas Boutique. Maudie didn't yet have her moving boxes unpacked, but she wasn't wasting any time preparing for the holidays. Why had she left all this in the car overnight? Maybe, Dulcie thought, knowing how her own housemate managed such matters, she'd wanted to clean and line cupboards before bringing in new kitchenware and linens. Looked as if she'd bought additional decorations, too, for the big tree that Joe had seen David carrying into the house.

Pulling out half a dozen bulky white bags, most with her right hand and favoring her left arm, she eased the trunk lid closed and turned back toward the house. Loaded with packages, she had paused to peer over them to find her footing on the curb when, up the hill, the same brown pickup appeared again suddenly, racing around the corner, barreling straight down at Maudie, its engine roaring, its sides rattling, the driver only a shadow behind the smeared window.

"Get back!" Ryan shouted as she dove for Maudie,

grabbed her, jerked her from the truck's path onto the curb, Maudie's packages scattering around them, one bag hitting the curb with a crash of broken china. Inches from them, the truck veered out again to avoid the Lincoln, scraping down the car's length as it passed, a violent wrenching of metal, then skidded into a sharp turn onto the side street and vanished.

The two women stood on the sidewalk, the Lincoln between them and the street. Behind them on the porch, little Benny stood frozen, white-faced and seemingly unable to move. The cats' own involuntary cries of warning had been drowned in Ryan's shout. They raced down across the roofs for Maudie's roof as Ryan snatched her cell phone from her belt. She was pressing 911 when Maudie grabbed the phone and hit the end button.

"What are you doing?" Ryan snapped. "We need the police."

Maudie shook her head. She was as pale as Benny.

"He could have killed you," Ryan looked at her, incredulous. "Maybe they can catch him, you need to call in a report."

Maudie looked back at her, shaking her head. Behind them the sound of the Skilsaw had ceased, and Scotty appeared in the open doorway. Benny turned and clung to him. The big, steady man put his arm around the little boy, drawing him close.

"Give me the phone," Ryan said, biting back her temper. The cats expected her to force the phone from Maudie's hand. She didn't, but her voice was low with anger. "You have to report this, Maudie. If only for the insurance claim."

Maudie put her hand on Ryan's arm. "I wouldn't file for insurance. My . . . my deductible's too high." She studied Ryan. "Let it go. Please, just let it be."

Ryan stared at her then turned away and began picking up packages. Maudie took two white plastic bags from her and headed for the house. When the cats, peering over, got a good look at Maudie's face, she looked far more excited than frightened. What was that about? As Maudie and Benny moved inside, the cats scrambled down an oak tree and followed them through the open door into the house where they could watch Maudie and listen.

6

AN HOUR BEFORE the truck came roaring down at Maudie, and a dozen blocks away, the tortoiseshell cat paced the early-morning rooftops looking down from between the peaks and chimneys at the village shops below. Kit's black and brown coat shone dark within the fog, drops of fog clinging to the tips of her long fur like tiny jewels. Below her, the shop windows were bright with a dazzle of small, lavishly decorated Christmas trees, with silver and gold packages which, while only empty inside, were festive and enticing. Several windows featured carefully arranged crèche scenes, and these always drew Kit. In the small hours of the nights before Christmas, when the streets were at last deserted, she and Dulcie would prowl the dark, empty village, standing tall on their hind paws peering in at the baby Jesus and the wise men and the little miniature animals all snuggled in their beds of straw—but there was never a cat, the crèches never had cats. Dulcie said there were no cats in the Bible, but Kit wasn't sure she believed that. Why would there be horses and cows and dogs, wild pigs and weasels, but no cats? Why, when everyone knew that a little cat would have to be God's favorite?

She'd left home this morning before daylight while her human housemates still dozed. Though Lucinda and Pedric Greenlaw, at eighty-some, liked to be up for an early breakfast and an early walk in the hills, they'd been out late last night. They'd been fast asleep as Kit bolted through the dining room, through her cat door that was cut into the window, trotted across the oak branch to her tree house, and took off to the next roof. And the next roof and the next, heading for the village, traveling high above the ground as handily as any squirrel among the leafy canopy.

Now in the center of the village, she listened to the rhythmic thudding as an early jogger fled past, and watched a gray-haired dog walker heading for the shore pulled along by an eager red setter. A young man in sport coat and chinos stepped out from a nearby motel and, two blocks down, turned in at the nearest bakery seeking his morning coffee and, most likely, some delectable and sugary confection. As he disappeared inside the steamy café, two runners came up the hill from the shore, breathing hard, looking smug with their efforts. Humans wore themselves out running from nothing, but too often had no clue when to run from danger. Kit watched the human scene with interest, but she watched the rooftops around her with sharper scrutiny. She was looking for the stranger, for the yellow tomcat.

She'd glimpsed him over the past days only briefly, had

seen him watching her from among shadows, from leafy cover, but had never gotten a close look at him. He was a big cat, his fur as pale yellow as sunshine. He had watched Joe and Dulcie, too, but why was he so shy, why did he keep his distance so stubbornly as he followed them? She knew he was no ordinary cat, the way he watched them, she knew he could have spoken to them if he chose. What did he want, to follow them but then refuse to approach? What was he doing in the village? Where had he come from? The mystery of him sent her heart pounding with excitement and with challenge, sent her imagination rocketing as she searched for the elusive stranger.

A sound startled her. Did she hear a soft yowl, a tomcat's yowl? She leaped to a high peak, listening. But no, what she heard was not a cat at all but the faintest screech of nails being pulled, and then the distant thunk of boards being tossed in a heap, and Kit smiled. That was only Ryan, pulling off the siding, at work renovating that little frame cottage—had to be Ryan, from the direction, and the early hour. What other carpenter or contractor started work so early? Looking around at the empty and silent roofs, Kit licked her cold paws, and then headed across the roofs toward the residential hills where Ryan would be working. If she couldn't find the mysterious tom, she would ease her restlessness among friends, and away she went, racing over the shingles and across the oaks' spanning branches.

She stopped suddenly when three cop cars streamed past along the street below, moving without sirens and in a hell of a hurry. And here came an EMT right behind them, all as quiet as soaring hawks watching for prey.

Spinning around, Kit followed them, praying this wasn't another invasion but, racing over the rooftops, meaning to be there if it was, hoping to get a look at the invaders, this time.

She thought about the women who had been beaten and robbed: a lone woman in her garden picking roses, the front door left unlocked behind her and no one else at home. A lone woman opening her door at night to a stranger because he said his car wouldn't start. He'd pulled her onto her darkened porch, where he'd already unscrewed the lightbulb, had knocked her around, trashed her house breaking furniture, taken a few small items, and left. The third woman was attacked in the dark stairway of her condo, again when the lightbulb had been unscrewed. Why had she gone in there when there was no light?

And the strangest thing was, none of the women had been raped. These men forced themselves into their homes, broke the furniture, stole money and jewelry, and fled. Sometimes two men, sometimes three, their faces covered with stockings in a trite but effective disguise. It was the very absence of further brutality that most puzzled the police, and puzzled the cats, as well. Could the perpetrators, if they got caught, not want to stand trial for the more serious offense of rape? That seemed to the cats the only possible explanation—brutal small-time thugs, wanting to have their fun but still save their own necks.

Racing over the roofs following the silent patrol cars, Kit heard a scream somewhere ahead—but not a human scream. It was an animal: a dog, in terrible pain. A little dog, screaming and screaming, its cries sickening her as she leaped from roof to roof, so upsetting her, she nearly fell off the edge, and scrambled to regain her footing on the damp, slanting shingles.

The cop cars slowed, pulled to the curb. The screams came from directly below her now, from a house she knew well. She pictured the little Skye terrier who lived there, tiny and frail beneath its long silky brown fur. If that little dog was hurt, this, to Kit, was far more upsetting than an attack on a human person. To hear a little animal hurting and helpless tore at her, left her hissing and shivering.

7

B ECKY LAKE'S SHINGLED studio home was shaded by pepper trees, its interior one large room with an alcove for the kitchen, another for the bath and closet. Its steep roof rose like a pyramid, flattened at the very peak into a four-by-four-foot skylight, the thick, clear glass usually dusted with leaves from the pepper trees and decorated with little cat paw prints. Kit had spent many hours lying across the glass looking down into the paneled room with its high rafters and wide stone fireplace, a retreat that might have been built at the edge of a mountain stream or in the Swiss Alps, but that fit right into this casual and wooded village. Peering down through the skylight, she could see Becky's Christmas tree, all hung with little carved wooden toys. On the hearth stood a ceramic pot of holly branches gleaming with clusters of red berries. She didn't see Becky, but she could see the little terrier. Rowdy lay on his side, biting frantically at his shoulder, his cries so loud they made her ears ring.

Had the neighbors heard him, was that what had generated the 911 call? Well, help was here now, but why didn't they hurry? She looked down at the three black-and-whites on the street below and the EMT van in the drive, watched Officer Brennan and Detective Kathleen Ray pile out of a squad car and double-time it up the steps. Kathleen was taller than Brennan and slimmer, her dark hair knotted sleekly beneath her uniform cap. Brennan pounded on the door and then threw it open. Weapons drawn, they eased inside. Behind them, two more uniforms moved up the walk, and Max Harper's pickup pulled to the curb.

The chief sent two additional officers circling around to the back, and then he, too, stepped inside, his hand on his holstered weapon. Where was Becky Lake? How badly was she hurt? Why didn't someone help the little dog, why didn't they help Rowdy?

Becky Lake was only twenty-something, and she and Rob were newly married: Rob was the manager of the little local grocery store. Becky, a slim, pretty girl, always looked so fresh and clean, always smelled of soap and water as if she'd just stepped from a cool shower. Even as Kit watched, Becky appeared in the open door supported by Detective Ray, her ash-blond hair a tangle, her pale blue blouse torn, revealing a white silk bra and various bruises already turning purple or red. Kathleen supported the girl, trying to calm her, but Becky clung to her for only a moment, then pulled away, turning back toward the house. "Rowdy. I have to go back. Oh, please, he needs help, not me."

"Brennan is calling Dr. Firetti," Kathleen said. "He'll come as quick as he can. We don't want to handle the dog and maybe hurt him worse; it's best the doctor take care of him."

Becky fought to free herself. She was shaking, wiping at her tears. "Please, please help Rowdy. Can't I just be with him?"

"It's a crime scene now," Kathleen said. "We'd rather you stayed out here. If we pick Rowdy up or handle him, we could make his injuries worse. We want to wait for the vet." But then, watching the younger woman, Kathleen relented. "Come on," she said, "you can sit with him if you'll stay in one place. Don't pick him up, Becky."

Becky nodded and they moved inside. Above them, Kit slipped down from the roof into the foliage of a pepper tree and then into the bushes beside the open door. She could see where the glass pane beside the door had been broken out, could see Becky inside kneeling beside the fireplace gently stroking the little terrier. Officer Brennan stood by the far glass wall speaking on his cell phone. He had pulled on cloth booties, as had Kathleen and the chief. Kit didn't have cloth booties, and as she slipped inside she hoped to hell that, if they used some electronic gadget to see footprints, they'd miss hers. Shards of glass sparkled everywhere across the dark wood floor; she stepped carefully among them, staying in shadow and close to the walls. The little dog continued to scream. She wasn't sure what she thought she'd see that the sharp-eyed cops would miss. But visual surveillance didn't matter so much, the detective would be on top of that; it was the scents that Kit was after, the elusive smells that no human could detect.

Against a far wall, two armchairs had been overturned and an end table broken. One of Becky's sandals lay beside them. As Kit prowled the room staying out of sight behind the overturned furniture, she could detect no scent but the sharp cinnamon smell of baking that flowed from the kitchen to drown any scent of the invaders. Across the room Brennan was growing nervous, shouting into the phone for Dr. Firetti to hurry.

John Firetti was Kit's own doctor, she knew he'd drop everything and come—if he wasn't in the middle of some other emergency. Beyond the overturned chairs a lamp lay broken, and the phone fallen beside it. By the time Brennan holstered his cell phone and looked up, Kit had abandoned her search and slipped back outside to the porch—that was when she caught another smell, a rank smell, faint but unpleasant. The faint stink of fish so old and ripe it made her pull a face of disgust, flehming and nearly gagging.

Kit liked her seafood fresh, preferred it the day it was caught. This smell was like the rotting fish Lucinda buried under the rosebushes to keep them blooming with such careless abandon. Had one of the attackers come from a fishing boat? Or perhaps from the wharves along the coast where fish might have been cleaned and the offal left to rot? Or maybe from the little fishing wharf at the edge of the village? Kit took a good whiff, gagged again, and backed away. She kept backing, straight into the bushes, as Captain Harper appeared inside the house, coming out of the kitchen. Harper didn't need to catch her snooping, he already had too many questions about cats and crime scenes.

Though the chief had grown used to the three cats wandering in and out of the station, sleeping in an office bookcase or on a desk, enjoying handouts from the dispatcher, being spotted at a crime scene wasn't so smart, they didn't need the officers' puzzled stares. Now, hidden from Harper, Kit stuck her nose out of the bushes and watched as Dr. Firetti pulled up to the drive in his white van.

Parking, he stepped out, and an office nurse with him. The two hurried into the house, and soon the scent of alcohol wafted out. Maybe Firetti was giving the little dog a shot for the pain? Kit listened for several minutes to their mumbled voices, and soon the screaming stopped. Then, Dr. Firetti came out carrying little Rowdy on a dog-size stretcher. Kit watched through the van's open side door as they settled Rowdy in a padded bed with high sides, and the nurse sat down beside him. Sliding the door closed, Firetti stopped to speak with Becky. He'd call her when he'd examined Rowdy. Stepping into the van, he headed for the veterinary hospital. In the bushes, Kit breathed a sigh of relief for the poor little mutt. Rowdy was no bigger than a cat himself—though a hell of a lot louder. Becky stood on the porch clutching Kathleen's hand. Kathleen sat down on the step, drawing Becky down beside her, waiting as the young woman tried to collect herself. Kit, hidden beneath the mock orange bush, crouched only a few feet from them. Kathleen said, "Do you feel like answering a few questions? After that, the medics will take you to the hospital. Is your husband at work?"

Becky wiped her tears. "The questions are fine, but I don't want to go to the hospital. And please don't call

Rob—yes, he's at work, but he'll be so upset. I'll call him myself, in a little while."

"You need someone to be with you. And," Kathleen said gently, "we need to know how badly they hurt you. We need to know exactly what they did."

Becky looked down at her torn clothes, at her bruised arms. The side of her face was red and swelling. When she looked up at Kathleen, her eyes were steady. "They didn't rape me. Thank God they didn't do that."

Kathleen studied her. "If they did, and you press charges . . ."

Becky shook her head. "They didn't. Maybe Rowdy stopped them. He's such a little thing, but he went after them real fierce, screaming and biting them. One of them kicked him. He's hurt so bad. Will he be all right?"

"Dr. Firetti will do the best he can," Kathleen said, then was silent, waiting.

"I'm just bruised," Becky said, seeing her look. "I don't think anything's broken. They beat me, the one did. There were two men, they ran when you drove up. They took money from my purse. Kept trying to make me tell them my PIN number. I don't have a PIN number, Rob and I don't have ATM cards, we've never wanted them. They wouldn't believe me."

"Can you describe them at all?"

"Both tall. One thin, maybe stooped a little. The other square and well built. Black hair, I could see that much under the stocking. A little taller than the thin one." She was silent a moment. "Clean fingernails," she said, frowning. "The bigger man had nice nails, as if he'd had a manicure, and that surprised me. He was the one who kicked the door in, kicked it off the chain, and burst in ahead of the other. I should never have trusted a chain."

Officer Brennan appeared in the doorway. "Dr. Firetti called. He said Rowdy's shoulder is broken, but so far he hasn't found any internal injuries. He wants to put him under anesthetic so he can set the shoulder. He'll go ahead, but he wonders if you'll stop by later to sign the release."

Becky nodded. Kit listened to Becky and Kathleen argue until, under Kathleen's gentle but stubborn urging, Becky agreed to go to the hospital. The minute she had left with the EMTs, Kathleen retrieved a black bag of crime-scene equipment from the squad car, pulled on the cloth booties again, and went inside to photograph and lift prints. Behind her, Kit returned to the little cement porch, took another sniff of the odor of ancient fish, and followed it.

The fishy trail led into the house, but then out again at the other side of the threshold. She followed it to the sidewalk, trying to look casual, like a neighborhood cat out for a stroll. After only a little way, the trail vanished at the curb, most likely transferred into a waiting car.

Unable to find another trace of the scent, she left the scene and headed for Ryan's cottage, hoping to find Joe and Dulcie. Becky's cursory description of the invaders, plus the smell of fishy shoes, had to count for something, and Kit wanted to share what she'd learned. She was high up the hills, below Maudie Toola's and a block over, when Maudie's son David came jogging downhill, his short brown hair tucked under a cap, his tanned face smooth and lean. She peered down from the roof as he passed below her and disappeared down the hill, soon blocked from her view by shaggy, overhanging branches. Kit moved on up, drawn by the screech of nails and the echo of tossed boards.

Trotting along above the side street that would lead to Ryan's cottage, she watched an ancient brown pickup truck pull to the curb beneath her, just before it reached Maudie's street. A rusty, dented old truck with a dirt-smeared windshield. It stood with the engine idling. When the driver didn't get out, but simply sat there, a dark shadow behind the dirty glass, a ripple of unease made her fur twitch, and she settled down to watch. The shingles beneath her paws were rough and damp.

From where she crouched she could see Maudie's Tudor house and the roof of Ryan's cottage. Could see Joe Grey and Dulcie lounging on the cottage roof, glancing idly up at the little birds that flitted among the branches above them—and then everything happened at once. She saw Ryan leave the cottage and head downhill to Maudie's, saw Maudie come out her own front door heading for her car at the curb, her keys jingling in her hand. She watched Maudie step off the curb, pop the trunk open, and begin pulling out packages. At the same moment, the old truck took off fast, heading straight down the hill at Maudie. Ryan shouted. Joe and Dulcie and Kit shouted and damn the consequences as Ryan grabbed Maudie and pulled her out of its path. The truck barely missed her; it swerved around the Lincoln, metal screeching against metal, skidded downhill and around the corner and was gone.

Kit crouched among the branches, shivering. Why would anyone want to hurt Maudie? Why would anyone try to run their truck into a harmless old woman?

48

Down on the sidewalk, Maudie clung to Ryan. On the porch, Benny didn't move, he stood on the step, white and frozen. As Scotty came rushing out, Ryan grabbed her phone and started to dial, but Maudie snatched it from her. Joe and Dulcie had fled to Maudie's roof, Kit watched them scramble down to the garden and slip into the house behind Maudie. Kit remained very still, setting into memory every detail of that strange attack: the vague shadow of the driver's face behind the dirty windshield, a thin face beneath what might have been a dark hood, the rusty scars on the truck, the mud on the back bumper and license plate. Kit's distress at the beating of Becky Lake, and now the attack on Maudie, left her feeling very small and useless. Ears and tail down, she at last made her way from the rooftops down into Maudie's yard, where she crawled under a camellia bush and curled into a little ball among its fallen petals. She didn't understand humans. She thought about all the ugliness among humans that she and Dulcie and Joe had seen, and about the grim photographs and reports of murders that were available to them on the desks of their law-enforcement friends, and the more she thought, the more defeated she felt; all alone, she put her head down on her paws, filled with a terrible remorse for humankind.

8

Aᴛᴛᴇʀ ᴋɪʟʟɪɴɢ Mᴀʀᴛɪɴ and Caroline, the driver and shooter had paused for only an instant to watch the victims' car veer off the road, its headlights swinging crazily through the black night as it rolled onto its side and crashed into a pine tree. The shooter had tucked the .45 Colt revolver behind the seat as the driver floorboarded the pickup. They pulled to the side of the road a quarter mile on, where the driver got out, slipped into a small black sedan, and was gone, speeding away into the night. The shooter slid into the driver's seat and moved on, knowing the narrow two-lane well enough to keep out of the ditch, knowing precisely when to make the turn into the yard of the deserted ranch house. A second turn up the old concrete driveway, and the pickup was out of sight from the country road.

How much had the old woman seen? In the flickering moonlight, before she grabbed the kids and ducked to the floor, had she gotten a look? It was only an instant that she could have seen anything, but it was a loose end, a cause for worry. Over the subsequent months since the shooting, the question had eaten and rankled. If Maudie had seen enough for a tentative ID, what had she done about it? Gone to the cops? Or, fearing for her own life, sensibly kept her mouth shut? Was there a warrant out complete with name and description, or had she seen no more than the blinding flashes of gunfire?

That night, casing around behind the farmhouse, unlocking the machinery barn and easing the pickup inside, sliding closed the heavy door and stepping into the sleek sports car that stood next to where the pickup was always parked, the shooter had waited for more than an hour, listening for any sound from the road, lounging on the soft leather seat but not daring to play the radio even softly. Then jerking suddenly alert at the sound of the sirens.

How could anyone have called the cops? Martin and Caroline had to be dead, at that close range, or too badly wounded to make any kind of call. And as for Maudie, even if she'd had the presence of mind enough to grab a cell phone, reception out there was dicey; usually there was no way to get through.

It was unlikely anyone else had heard the crash; on the little-used back road there'd been no other cars. The scattered houses and what people called ranches were all set back away from the narrow two-lane, and there hadn't been a light anywhere; half those houses were summer places, locked up until the weather grew hot, in June.

But someone had called the cops.

Getting out of the sports car, standing at the door listening, she hadn't heard a sound. The barn seemed

51

safe enough. By the time sheriff's deputies got around to searching the nearby yards and fields, and got warrants to search inside the houses and outbuildings, the pickup would be dead cold, sitting unused as the vacationing owner had left it weeks earlier. The heavy padlock on the sliding shed door would show only the owner's fingerprints.

Listening to the sirens and then to the thumping of a helicopter, the shooter had slid the big door open just a crack, to look out into the night. Lights from the gathered cars a mile away were reflected up into the sky in a milky haze, more cars and a hell of a lot sooner than you'd have thought, way out here in the boonies.

The shooter had waited for a couple hours more after the police lights were gone, and the helicopter gone, before opening the door fully, starting the engine of the sports car and pulling out. Had checked, with a flashlight, the garage floor and wiped away the vague tire marks. Sliding the door closed again and locking it, the shooter had headed sedately away into the night, driving slowly and carefully along the country road, flicking the beams to high when there was no car coming, flicking them low again out of courtesy when another vehicle approached.

Passing two oncoming black-and-whites, the shooter lifted a hand from the wheel in the country way of greeting, though probably that gesture would not be seen in the dark car. And all the while swallowing back a rush of adrenaline, trying to control a heart-pounding panic. The two CHPs must be headed to the scene of the wreck, to join whatever sheriff's units might have remained behind. Maybe looking for shell casings—but they wouldn't find any. That was the good thing about a revolver: the casings remained in the gun, didn't scatter all over. Cops would be checking for tire marks, too, but quite a few cars and trucks, locals, used this road in the daytime.

A lot depended now on the old woman. Maybe she'd seen nothing in the blackness, maybe there was nothing to worry about. She'd answer the cops' questions but have no real information to give them, then go home and mourn for her dead son. The cops would work the case for a while and then, as overloaded as the LAPD was, it would find its way among the cold files and that would be the end of it.

Except, that wasn't the end, there was more to consider. There would be the funeral, the gathering of friends and family around the old woman, and then the disposition of Caroline's personal possessions. That was the complication: What had Caroline done with the papers that must be retrieved before this was finished? Or did the old woman have them? If so, what had she done with them? There was no way to know what Caroline and Martin, and Maudie, might have planned between them. Sure as hell, if Caroline had been a threat while alive, she was no better dead. And the same went for Maudie, for Caroline's soft little mother-in-law.

9

Rising from the bed of crushed petals, Kit peered out at Maudie's front door. It was closed tight. Everyone was inside, she could hear Ryan's voice in the kitchen. Pushing out of the bushes, she hurried around to the back, leaped in through an unglazed window of Maudie's new studio, trotted behind Scotty, who was patching plaster, and in through the open glass slider, onto the pale linoleum.

The kitchen smelled of fresh coffee. Maudie and Ryan sat at the table, and Benny was in Maudie's lap leaning against her, his mouth smeared with icing. A plate of sweet rolls stood on the table, smelling of cinnamon and honey. The little boy looked paler than usual, his dark eyes still reflecting fear from Maudie's encounter with the truck.

Maudie's kitchen was done all in tones of cream and butterscotch. At the far end of the room, pale oak cabinets lined three sides, around a central worktable. Beyond the wide bay windows, a lacy pepper tree framed Maudie's view of the neighboring houses and the street.

The table stood nearest to Kit just opposite the glass slider. Ryan was still arguing gently with Maudie, trying to get her to call the police. Benny seemed uncomfortable with the exchange, fiddling with his sweet roll, tearing it into little bits. He hardly looked up when Kit padded behind Maudie's chair, crossed to the open stairway, and leaped up to the fifth step, where Joe and Dulcie sat as still as a pair of statues, elegant porcelain effigies from some upscale antique shop. Dulcie cut her green eyes at Kit, looking disgusted at Maudie's stubbornness. Kit looked back impatiently, burning to tell them about the invasion and the fish smell, and unable to say a word.

The open stairs faced not only the kitchen but the front entry across a wide tile floor, with the cozy living room to the left. Dulcie twitched her ears at Kit but made no other move as she listened to Ryan's futile arguing. What was wrong with Maudie, why this reluctance?

"If the police can find the truck," Ryan was saying, "and arrest the driver, that would get him off the streets. That might keep you safer, until you know what that was about, and the information would help your insurance company when you make the claim."

"It was an accident," Maudie said. "It could happen to anyone, the driver wasn't looking. I don't intend to make a claim, I don't want to make trouble."

Ryan simply looked at Maudie. She seemed about to form a careful reply when the front door opened and David hurried in, breathing hard from his uphill run, his dark sweats hanging limp and damp on his lean frame.

His crumpled cap stuck out of his jacket pocket; his short-clipped brown hair was damp with sweat. Snatching the cap, he wiped his forehead with it and ran it over his crew cut. "What happened? I was two blocks away when I heard what sounded like a wreck, and an old truck came barreling past me."

He sat down, looking at Maudie. "Didn't you hear it? It must have hit the Lincoln, Mom. There's a long brown scar along the side." He looked at Maudie and at Benny. "Are you two all right? You weren't in the car? What the hell happened?"

Ryan said, "The driver came down the hill straight at Maudie. He swerved, he didn't hit her. He had to be drunk or stoned. Or . . . or it was deliberate," she said softly. "He went racing off, didn't even slow down."

"My God," David said. "Where are the cops? How long does it take? They're only—"

"I didn't call them," Maudie told him.

David looked at her. "Why not? Why the hell not, Mama?"

"Let it go," Maudie said. In her lap, Benny began to squirm. Slipping down from his grandma's embrace, he disappeared through the door that led from the kitchen to the garage. Pulling it closed behind him, he left it barely ajar as if not wanting to cut himself off completely from the adults, as if wanting only to escape the arguing. Or did he leave it open so he could listen to what his grandma might say, once he was out of the room?

But Maudie and David said little more, looking at each other in silence; David's anger had pulled his face into long, stony lines as stern as a Marine general's. It was Maudie who looked away first, glancing out to the studio where Scotty was patching plaster. David watched his mother as if trying to think how to get through to the stubborn woman. "Mom . . ." he began.

Maudie turned a gentle smile on him and put her hand on his arm. "I don't want to make waves, David. Please, just drop it."

On the stairs, the cats glanced at each other and back at Maudie, seeing more than softness in her smile. Seeing, for just an instant, a dark spark of challenge flash out, a steely edge that both heartened and puzzled them. This lady had some backbone. Why did she keep it so hidden?

Maudie had started to speak when they heard a truck stop outside. It shifted gears and then, from the sound of it, began to back down the drive. Ryan rose to look, and the cats stretched up tall. Yes, they could see the top of a truck backing in, could see a load of windows standing upright, securely tied in place. Ryan watched Scotty and the driver for a moment, apparently decided Scotty had everything in hand, and sat down again to finish her coffee.

The dark spark had left Maudie now; she was all smiles and happiness. "It's going to be beautiful, with the big windows, such a bright place to work, with the garden all around me." Her laugh was so happy, but then her look turned sad. "I had such a lovely studio in L.A., with a view of the hills. But I couldn't stay there, not after the shooting."

David rose, muttered something about a shower, and

headed upstairs, stepping carefully around the three cats. In a few minutes they heard the shower pounding in the upstairs bath.

"I read about the shooting," Ryan said. "Of course you wanted to leave the area. I would, too. I'm sure no one can understand what an incredibly hard loss that is, what a terrible emptiness to try to endure."

"I can't seem to get past it," Maudie said. "Over the eight months since Martin was shot, the pain hasn't eased. That moment keeps coming back as if it's just now happening. I thought, during the long sessions with the sheriff and with the L.A. police and the California Bureau of Investigation, that somehow I'd become inured, hardened to what happened, that I'd learn to live with it.

"But I haven't," she said softly. "They were so happy, Martin and Caroline." She looked bleakly at Ryan. "Why was I spared, and those two young ones, who were just into a second chance for happiness . . . Why did they have to die?" She shook her head. "The only good thing was that the children were spared. Except that now two are orphans, and Benny as good as an orphan. How can that be fair?

"But," Maudie said, "life isn't fair. No one ever said life was fair."

Ryan laid her hand over Maudie's. "I'm sorry," she said. "Did you see anything that night? Anything that would help the police?"

"How could I see the killer? If that's what you mean," Maudie said testily. "It was dark." She rose, stepped to the kitchen sink, and ran a glass of water.

Ryan said, "I didn't mean to upset you."

"You didn't upset me, I seem to be in a permanent state of upset." She returned to the table, sipping her water. "Benny and I are having dinner with my sister's family tonight, that will be a nice outing. Carlene and her husband and their two boys. I've hardly had time to visit with her since I arrived. They're just up at the top of the hill," she said, "only about ten blocks. It's that adobe house with the deep veranda, the high wall and jasmine vines in front."

"I know the place," Ryan said. "It's lovely. Your sister is Carlene Colletto? I did a remodel on their kitchen a few years ago."

"Of course." Maudie nodded. "Carlene loves her kitchen, it's so bright with that old dark wall now open to the garden."

On the stairs, Dulcie's ears were pricked, and the tip of her tail began to twitch. Fidgeting, she gave Joe a wild look, leaped off the steps, and disappeared into the garage. Just as swiftly, Kit followed her. Joe stayed where he was. He knew Kit was wired, but what had put the wind up Dulcie's tail? What was so interesting about Maudie's sister, that she and Kit needed to talk about it? And how did they think they could whisper between themselves in the garage, without Benny hearing them? He was puzzling over female cats' erratic behavior when David came down the stairs. He was barefoot, smelling of soap and shampoo, wearing chinos and a clean white T-shirt. He gave Ryan a smile, stepped to the counter to pour a cup of coffee, then picked up the folded newspaper and stood reading the sports page.

At the table, Ryan was saying, "Don't the Colletto boys work here in the village?"

"Jared does," Maudie said. "He was working part-time for a moving service, but I think he changed jobs. I know he takes accounting classes at the college. I think Kent works somewhere up the coast a few miles."

"Jared's a nice young man," Ryan said. "I don't know Kent well, but Jared's helped some of my clients move into their new homes."

Maudie smiled. "I'm hoping, when the studio's completed, he'll help me move my things in. David will be gone, he flies out today," she said, glancing across at her son. "I'm anxious to get my quilting equipment set up, get everything put away so I can prepare for an upcoming exhibit."

"At the Humphrey," Ryan said. "That's a really nice gallery. Will there be a reception?"

"Just after New Year's," Maudie said, seeming pleased that Ryan knew about the show. "You're on my mailing list."

"We should be finished with the studio by this weekend. The cabinets are all in place, we'll have the windows in today, trim them tomorrow, lay the floor, and then a few last-minute details. If Jared can't help you move in, we'll find someone."

"Kent might be able to," Maudie said, "but he works odd hours." She gave Ryan a direct look. "I'm sure you know that the boys' oldest brother is in prison."

Ryan nodded, but said nothing.

"There's no point hiding it," Maudie said, "in such a small village where everyone knows everyone's business. And of course, with your family in law enforcement you hear these things."

"Maybe Victor isn't truly a bad young man," Ryan said. "Maybe just impetuous, slow to grow up?"

The older woman sighed. "Children can turn out so differently. Victor on the wrong side of the law, and Kent no angel, but Jared doing just fine. I guess Allen and I were lucky, to have raised two good boys." She was silent, glancing out to the new studio where the delivery driver, apparently finished unloading, was handing Scotty an invoice.

"I'd best get to work," Ryan said, rising and picking up her gloves. When she had gone, David returned to the table, and spread out the paper. On the stairs, Joe Grey waited, torn between listening to Maudie and David and heading for the garage to see what had so energized Dulcie and Kit, his curiosity pulling at him like two rabbits escaping in opposite directions.

10

THAT MORNING AS Joe Grey eavesdropped in plain sight from Maudie Toola's stairway, forty miles southeast of the village at the California State Prison at Soledad, the warden picked up the phone to dial an inmate's family. This was a mission Walter Deaver seldom had to perform, and one he didn't look forward to, particularly in this case. Jack Reed didn't have any family to notify except his little girl, who was only maybe thirteen. Lori's mother had died of cancer several years before, and Jack was all the child had. At thirteen, a little girl badly needed her father—in Lori's case, even a father in prison was better than no father at all.

Jack Reed wasn't a troublemaker, a long way from it. This was his first offense and, Deaver would be willing to bet, would be his last scrape with the law once he was out. In Deaver's view, Reed shouldn't be in prison at all but should get a medal for what he'd done. But then, he didn't make the laws.

Reluctantly he picked up the phone, not wanting to relay this news. Hoping, in the days to come, not to have to bear worse news, although Reed's condition was critical. If Jack Reed died, the child would have no one.

Except, of course, her guardian, Cora Lee French. Lori was lucky in that respect; Jack had chosen well when he chose the woman who, in his absence, was helping to shape the child's life. He knew that Lori was in a private school, and that she spent much of her free time in an apprentice program working for a local building contractor, a woman who was close friends both with Cora Lee and with Chief Harper.

Deaver generally didn't take this kind of interest in the personal lives of his prisoners; he couldn't, with a population double what the prison had been built to accommodate. Nor did he care to, when most of them were members of prison gangs, vicious, high-maintenance dregs on society. Men so seduced by the criminal culture they were too far gone for anything to be done other than keep them off the streets, keep them from killing anyone else. But because of Harper's special interest in this case, he'd learned a good deal about Jack Reed and his daughter—he just wished the parole board, instead of releasing dangerous prisoners, would release the few men like Jack. But what the hell, who could figure what was in the minds of some state-appointed officials?

It was two hours since Reed had been stabbed in the prison yard outside the mess hall. The shank was a knife made from a length of water pipe that had been removed from the sink in the cell of the would-be killer. The prison was on lockdown, and all cells had been searched for further weapons. Reed had been tended briefly by the prison doctors before a helicopter transported him to Salinas Valley Memorial Hospital where, in the civilian ICU, he would remain under guard, hooked up to life support, closer to death than to life.

The phone rang five times. When a woman answered, Deaver asked for Lori's guardian.

"This is Cora Lee."

Deaver had seen the woman and child on visiting days. Cora Lee was striking, a tall, slim woman with short-clipped, curly black hair streaked with silver. He thought she might be Creole, from her café au lait complexion and her faint accent, as if maybe she'd grown up in New Orleans. Her manner was quiet, self-contained, and she seemed truly fond of Lori.

You got a lot of scum among the visiting crowds, grossly fat women in low-cut T-shirts, women in skin-tight jeans and flip-flops. As if it made no difference, as if no one cared how they looked when they entered the institution, as if his prison were some fourth-rate bordello. But Lori and Cora Lee always arrived well groomed, as neatly dressed and appealing as if they were headed for Sunday church, where they might indeed be judged—by the congregation or the Almighty—for their grooming and cleanliness.

He identified himself to Ms. French, told her as gently as he could that Jack had been stabbed and was in the ICU in Salinas, and that she had his permission to take Lori to visit him. There was a long silence at the other end of the line. Waiting, he wondered idly whether, if Reed died, the guardian would adopt the child. It was none of his business, but he sure didn't like to see any child become a ward of the state. Lori Reed appeared to be a serious and sensible girl, and she'd need that steadiness now, if Reed didn't make it. When these things happened to a prisoner like Reed, someone who wasn't part of a gang, who tried to keep to himself and stay out of trouble, just trying to make it to the end of his sentence, the situation sickened Deaver. At the other end of the line Cora Lee French finally spoke; her voice, which had been light and cheerful, was low and subdued. "How bad is he?"

"He's critical."

"I'll tell Lori. When can we see him?" She was direct, straightforward, but she sounded sick at having to tell the child. They talked for only a few minutes, he gave her instructions for their arrival at the hospital, told her who to ask for, told her how long they would be able to stay. She thanked him in a naked voice that left him feeling like hell.

HALF AN HOUR after the warden's call, Lori and Cora Lee were headed inland to the Salinas hospital. Cora Lee drove in silence, her right hand holding Lori's small, cold hand, offering what comfort she could. Lori huddled down in the seat like a hurt little animal, her school uniform, white shirt and navy skirt, rumpled from the playground where Cora Lee had picked her up, her dark hair tangled, her face pale with fear as she tried to understand how Pa, her pa, could suddenly be so injured that he was fighting for his life. Pa wasn't a bully, he wasn't into prison gangs, he wasn't mean, he had never hurt anyone—no one that didn't need hurting, Lori thought. She couldn't imagine that Pa would die, she wouldn't let herself believe that could happen.

But Ma had died. There was nothing Lori had been able to do, to make her well, to stop her from dying. Certainly her little-girl prayers hadn't turned away the cancer. She'd stood by her mother's bed in that faraway North Carolina town praying and praying, and watched her mother's life drain away.

This hour of the morning, the traffic was heavy with commuters and with trucks: huge, loud, diesel-stinking trucks crowding them, and moving in the other direction, too, along the two-lane, their closed sides marked with bakery and beer logos, or their railed sides penning in cattle headed for some slaughter yard, Lori thought, feeling sad for them. Cora Lee didn't talk, she left Lori to her own thoughts, and for that Lori was grateful. Cora Lee's silence soothed her, she was there for her, but not intrusive. Not since before Mama died, when Lori was little, had anyone understood so well what she was thinking, and known, just by being there, how to make her feel better. In the year and a half since Pa was sent to prison, she and Cora Lee had visited him seven times. Sometimes, at first, she hadn't wanted to go, hadn't wanted to see Pa behind bars. But Cora Lee had urged her.

And then later, she hadn't wanted to go because the other prisoners stared at her. You had to wait in line for hours outside the prison, sitting in a camp chair if you'd brought one, and it seemed like everyone in line stared at you. Then when they finally got inside to see Pa, in the big visiting room at the long table, she and Pa couldn't be alone. Visitors sat lined up along one side of the long table, prisoners on the other, and there was that heavy glass barrier between her and Pa. How could she and Pa even try to be natural, crowded among all those strangers, and talking through a telephone? Each time, as they drove down to Soledad, she'd felt torn between her excitement to see Pa and her disgust at going into the prison.

And then she'd start thinking about the years when she and Pa were together after Mama died, when Pa had locked her in the house and boarded up the windows, and didn't tell her why. She hadn't understood, then, that it was to keep her safe, to save her life. She guessed Pa wasn't comfortable enough with *her* to tell her. If she started thinking about that while they were driving down to see him, by the time they reached the prison she didn't want to go in, she'd want to turn around and go home again.

But now they weren't going to the prison. They were headed for a hospital where she'd see Pa lying helpless in one of those narrow beds with iron sides, like another kind of prison. Pa, so lean and tall, lying limp in a hospital bed hooked up to machines like Ma had been, bandages around his chest where he'd been stabbed. And even with the machines, the oxygen, the IV, maybe Pa wouldn't live, maybe he'd die in the hospital. Die this morning before they ever got there. Or die after she went away again leaving him alone in a strange place. She didn't realize she was squeezing Cora Lee's arm hard until Cora Lee flinched.

"I'm sorry," she said, easing up her grip. The wind through the open windows smelled of onions from the fields, of freshly turned earth and commercial fertilizers, and the early sun slanted sharply into their eyes. She sat nervously telling herself Pa wasn't going to die; she wanted to kill the man who had stabbed him, she thought he should be the one in ICU or in the morgue, not Pa.

She knew when she saw Pa she'd have to be cheerful and positive, try to make him feel better, but she didn't feel positive. She just felt scared. Pa was all she had; sometimes she missed him so bad, missed how he had been when she was just a little girl, before the bad things started to happen. When she'd run away from Pa and hidden for two weeks in the library basement, she hadn't understood then why he'd locked her up. While she was sitting in the dark little concrete hole on the old mattress she'd dragged in, living on peanut butter and canned peaches, sometimes, not knowing why Pa had made a prisoner of her, she really had wanted him dead.

But then later when she'd understood that it was to save her life, then she'd been ashamed. When she'd learned about the children that Pa's own brother, and that other man, had murdered, that Pa was trying to save her from them, she didn't know what to say to him.

And now Pa's own life needed saving. She prayed for him. She wanted to tell him she loved him, she hadn't told him that in a long time. Right now, Cora Lee's presence was the only thing that held her steady. As if, without Cora Lee, she'd fall into some endless dark space with nothing at all to hold on to.

11

Joe was all set to leave the kitchen and slip into the garage with Dulcie and Kit when Maudie set a few crumbs of coffee cake and a saucer of milk before him. Settling down on the step again to enjoy the little treat, he listened with interest as mother and son argued, both so hardheaded that Joe had to hide a smile. That careening truck had worried David far more than it seemed to worry Maudie; he didn't want to leave her and Benny alone, and Maudie refused to go home with him. Nor did she want him to stay; and Joe could tell he really didn't want to stay, that he was too worried about his wife, Alison.

"Think about it, Mama. Whoever killed Martin and Caroline might think you saw him that night. Maybe he followed us here, intending to hurt you, to silence you?"

"Well that's melodramatic. It was dark, how could I have seen anyone?"

"There was a moon, you told me there was a thin

moon. The killer doesn't know you didn't see him." David's smooth face was stern with worry. "Between *whatever* that was this morning and these home invasions, I don't want to leave you two. You're half crippled with that lame shoulder, you can't—"

"I *saw* the truck coming, I was ready to move."

"You didn't have a clue. Benny said you had your back to it, unloading packages."

"I heard it, I heard the truck."

"Come home with me, Mama, just until Alison's through the surgery and on the mend, until I can get a live-in nurse for her, someone reliable. Then I'll take a leave and come on back with you."

"Benny's had enough upset, he needs to be settled in one place, he doesn't need to be shuttled around anymore. No one's going to harm us. I want to get him started in school, maybe that private school where Ryan's young friend Lori Reed goes. He'll be—"

"He'll be what?" David snapped. "*He'll* be sideswiped by a truck on his way to school?"

"No one," she said with certainty, "would want to harm Benny."

"Someone already harmed him deeply when they killed his father." Rising, David stepped to the sink, emptied his coffee cup, and headed for the stairs. "Please go pack, Mama. For the two of you. I'll call and try to get us all on a flight."

"No," Maudie said. "We're staying here. We'll be in our own home for Christmas. And you will be where you belong, with Alison. And that's the end of it."

Apparently it was. David headed up the stairs shaking his head, but saying no more.

"Kids," Maudie said to the tomcat. "Even when they're grown they think their mothers are helpless." Smiling a secret little smile, she sipped her cooling coffee.

"I wish someone could understand how much I dread Christmas," she told Joe. "But Benny has to have Christmas, he's hurting so bad. Benny's daddy was the only stable thing in his life, until Caroline. That little boy idolized his daddy.

"When Allen was alive," she said, "when we were raising the boys, Thanksgiving and Christmas were the most exciting times of the year." She looked bleakly at Joe. "Is a tomcat the only one in the world I can talk to? The only one who won't think me silly and who won't argue with me?" Her blue eyes were flat with hurting. "I miss Martin the same way I missed his dad when he died. Like part of *me* is gone. They say that when a leg has been amputated, the pain in the missing part is still there, you can still feel it there, though there's nothing but empty space."

Joe Grey had such a powerful desire to speak, to answer the poor woman, that he leaped off the stairs with alarm and trotted away into the garage. What was he, a feline shrink? A four-legged therapist for the lonely and grieving? Winding his way among mover's cartons and stacks of banker's boxes, he sniffed a dozen lingering aromas transported three hundred miles from L.A., invisible artifacts boxed and preserved like elusive archeological treasures. The labels were written in a beautiful round cursive, the kind of handwriting Joe saw only among his older human friends: PERSONAL LETTERS, FAMILY PHOTOS, TAX RECEIPTS, OLD SWEATERS. Somewhere ahead among

71

the mountains of cartons, little Benny was talking in a soft monotone, apparently to Dulcie and Kit—unburdening himself to feline sympathy just as Maudie had. What was it about being a cat that made folks so eager to confide, to bare their very souls?

When, ahead in the gloom, he couldn't see the two cats or the child, he leaped to the top of a four-foot carton and reared up for a better look. Nothing. Only when he gave a low hunting cry in his throat did Dulcie rise up out of an open carton, ears and whiskers at half-mast, her green eyes amused. Beside her, Benny peered over, too, but when the child realized the strange sound had come from Joe Grey, he disappeared again, down inside the box.

Leaping across the stacked boxes, Joe looked down into their hideaway. The carton was filled with packets of bright cloth: neatly cut squares of cotton print tied in bundles with hanks of bright yarn. Benny had piled them around the sides, to clear the middle into a little nest. He sat cross-legged, clutching an album open on his lap. The female cats snuggled beside him again, watching the pages as he slowly turned them. His little-boy scent wafted up, as distinctive as the scent of a puppy. Looking innocently up at Joe, Benny clearly expected the tomcat to join them. Quietly Joe dropped down among the little bales of quilting squares and settled beside Dulcie.

There is something sleep-making to a cat about looking at old photographs; the slowly turning pages create a rhythm that makes one give way to jaw-cracking yawns. But these pictures were of Benny's family, each a little window into the child's short past, and the tomcat remained alert. Pictures of Benny and Maudie, of Benny and a boy and girl about his age, who must be Caroline's two children. Of Benny and a tall man resembling David and a pretty woman with tousled hair the color of butterscotch. These were the pictures Benny reached for, stroking their faces. "That's my daddy and that's Caroline, my new mother." He looked seriously and sadly at the cats. "They're in heaven now."

Dulcie rubbed her face against the child, trying to cheer him. Kit nuzzled him, but the tortoiseshell was edgy, too, the tip of her tail twitching with the need to speak, to tell Joe and Dulcie something urgent. What? Joe wondered. What might she have seen, this morning, that was so important?

Well, she'd held her silence this long, and they'd be outside again soon enough—Kit had never been big on patience. Benny was saying, "This is my mother Caroline, she made real sit-down dinners every night, for all of us together. That's Caroline and me and Daddy, and that's . . ." The dry hush of turning pages and the child's droning voice soon had Joe Grey sleepy despite his interest in the dead couple, and despite his curiosity over Kit's unease. He came alert when Benny hugged him too hard and a salty wetness splashed on his nose. "And then we were going to Grandma's cabin and it was dark and the gun was shooting, so loud and bright and Grandma threw us on the floor and I couldn't see anything." He squeezed Joe so hard the tomcat nearly yowled; he was hugging all three of them, gathering them to him like teddy bears, weeping into their fur.

Joe tolerated the child's grief as long as he could, then leaped out of Benny's arms and out of the carton to the top of a wooden crate. Sometimes the burden of understanding humans was more than a cat cared to handle. Looking around him at the mountain of Maudie's possessions, he wondered where she was going to put all this stuff, in the limited space of the four-room Tudor house.

But he could see that much of it was destined for the quilting studio, the long table against the opposite wall, the cartons marked QUILTING FRAME, the two sewing machines and the dozens of boxes stacked next to them. In the far corner, the half-dozen boxes marked DESK had been opened, the tape slit, the flaps standing up, the contents disarranged so that papers and folders stuck out. A box marked CAROLINE had been opened, revealing a woman's clothes neatly folded, layers of sweaters and blouses and among them a half-dozen small, framed pictures. Leaping across the boxes to look, he saw that some were of the two children, some of the children with Caroline and a man in a Marine uniform. Caroline's first husband? Tucked down beside the clothes was a small jewelry chest. When he clawed it open, he found a diary with a leather strap and a little lock. He was tempted to finesse this open, too, but with the child nearby, that might not be wise. Even a seven-year-old boy would have to wonder at a cat snooping into his mother's diary.

The next open carton marked CAROLINE contained nine-by-twelve brown envelopes marked TAXES, LETTERS, PAID BILLS, LEGAL PAPERS. Beneath these, when he clawed them aside, was a sealed, unmarked brown envelope, its flap tightly glued. Again, he was tempted, flexing his claws over the sealed flap, but then sensibly sheathing them again and turning away. The remaining boxes all seemed dull as mud, several were marked as kitchen things, and two boxes contained old tax receipts. Strange that he'd found nothing belonging to Benny's real mother. Had Maudie kept nothing of Pearl's, or had Pearl left nothing at all behind when she left Martin?

And, the tomcat thought, why did he care? Except that Benny's daddy and Caroline had been murdered, the shooter had vanished, and so far neither the San Bernardino sheriff nor the LAPD had a shred of evidence. That was what Maudie had told Ryan, that neither agency had come up with any viable suspect, not enough evidence to hold anyone. Joe supposed the two agencies had done all they could. Killers vanished every day. He supposed, given the pressure in a big-city police department, such cases had to be set aside in deference to the emergencies of the moment.

But that hit-and-run this morning, and Maudie's reaction to it, had prodded the tomcat into a frenzy of curiosity. He was slipping among the last stack of boxes, sniffing at them, when he found Martin's name, written in Maudie's hand. This was the first box he'd found of her son's possessions, and quickly he ripped a claw along the tape until he'd freed the flaps.

Atop a stack of bills and papers lay another photograph album, with pictures of Benny, and Martin in his airline pilot's uniform. There was no mistaking the resemblance between father and son. In some, they were a threesome with a tall, black-haired woman. This must be Pearl. A thin, straight woman with very white skin and sharply carved features, high cheekbones over hollow cheeks, her black eyes keen and penetrating. A severe beauty, stark and cold, in contrast to Caroline's warm features. In nearly every picture Pearl stood between father and son, with Benny shoved nearly out of camera range. In every shot she wore black, a black business suit with a knee-length skirt, black slacks and white blouse, a black dress with a V-neck and long sleeves. Nothing casual, nothing soft or whimsical. In the few pictures where she smiled, her "camera" smile looked patently fake. In only one picture she had pulled Benny against her side as if in sweet companionship, the child looking rigid and uncomfortable.

Joe looked up when Benny crawled out of the big carton and headed for the kitchen door with Dulcie and Kit close behind, Kit fidgeting as if wild to get outdoors where she could talk. With a last look at the open carton, Joe leaped after them, trotting through the kitchen and out to the studio. He paused when the phone rang behind them, looked back as Maudie rose to answer.

There was a long silence, then Maudie said, "Who is this?" Another, longer pause, then very softly she hung up. "No one," she said, shrugging. "Maybe a wrong number." As she turned away, was that a look of concern, perhaps of fear? But then as she sat down again at the table, the hint of a smile touched her soft face, some secret thought that she unknowingly telegraphed to Joe.

He was still staring when he saw Scotty watching him; quickly he slapped his paw at an invisible bug, then raced away as if chasing it, batting at the floor as he followed Dulcie and Kit out through an unglazed window; and the three cats vanished as swiftly as had Maudie's strange little smile.

12

 **IN VALLEY MEMORIAL** Hospital, Jack Reed lay fading in and out of consciousness, sometimes dropping down into deep black sleep, other times alarmed by disjointed dreams where he was back in the prison yard fighting three inmates, was on the ground trying to get hold of Vic Colletto's knife, fighting to grab it from him. Surprised and unbelieving when the knife plunged into him, easy as into butter, seeing his blood spurting out. That would wake him, put him back in the hospital, trapped by metal bars and plastic tubes, surrounded by science fiction machines pumping who-knew-what into his veins. He'd lie burning to tear out the tubes, rip them away and rip away the bed's confining bars. Every waking moment he fought the panic of entrapment. Even the oxygen mask over his face seemed, too often, not to ease his breathing but to constrict it. The doc said that was stress, a residual panic. And then, fully

awake, he'd sink back into a debilitating depression, into the dark futility of his life.

Sometimes he'd wake thinking about Max Harper, about Max walking into Jack's house that day and finding Fenner's body sprawled on the couch, blood sprayed everywhere. Even when he told Max he'd killed Fenner and Max put the cuffs on him, Harper had been more than fair with him. Max had conducted the interview himself, with his two detectives present, the three of them patient and, it seemed to Jack, more in tune with him than he had any right to expect.

Max had booked him and taken him to jail himself, to the little village lockup, and later had talked with the judge privately, in the judge's chambers. Max Harper had testified in Jack's favor; he had Max to thank that he'd gotten off light, with only a conviction of voluntary manslaughter.

He wouldn't have minded too much going to prison, except for Lori. Though Cora Lee French and her housemates had made that easier, taking Lori in, giving her the love and stability she needed. Cora Lee had seen that Lori was able to work when she wanted, for that woman building contractor, had even gotten her into a better school when she was so bored with her public school classes.

Sometimes he thought Lori would be better off without him, that if he were dead, that would put an end to her worry, to her fear for him in prison, and she could get on with her life. Maybe he should have died in this dustup in the prison yard.

Vic Colletto had worked for him when Jack was part-

ners in Vincent and Reed Electrical Contractors. He'd
fired young Colletto for drinking on the job; the kid had
been wiring a house, dead drunk, rolling drunk. Kicked
off the job, Colletto had been angry as hell, and now at
last he was getting back at him. Vic, who was in for breaking and entering and several counts of theft, had been in
Soledad only a few weeks when he challenged him, tried
to make him fight. Jack survived in prison by keeping to
himself; he'd managed to avoid confrontations until Colletto began a steady diet of harassment. Colletto hung out
with several inmates he'd known on the outside, one of
them a con artist whom, Jack was pretty sure, he'd seen in
Molena Point. He couldn't remember the circumstances,
couldn't recall his name. The guy was out now, back on
the street, and good riddance. Strange, though—it was after he left that Victor's bullying grew bolder.

What worried Jack was that Victor's two brothers lived
in the village. If that skuzzy Kent Colletto harassed Lori,
or worse, he'd have to try to escape, to get away while he
was on garden detail, find Kent and kill him. The thought
sickened Jack.

He wanted to talk with Warden Deaver, get him to
call Max Harper with a heads-up on the Collettos, get
Harper's people to keep an eye on Lori. Trouble was, that
could backfire. It was hard to know who to trust, even
within Molena Point PD. If word got back to Vic's brothers that the law was protecting Lori, that would wave a
red flag in their faces. Lori was thirteen, she was growing
up fast and she was probably a lot more savvy than many
kids her age—but savvy wasn't enough by itself to keep
her safe. Vic was in for robbery of a convenience store in

which he'd beaten the clerk so badly he nearly died, and his brother, Kent, was no better, had twice done time in juvenile for battery. Lori was little more than a child, she had no defense against that kind of brutality.

Lori had some childish dream that he'd be pardoned, that he'd soon be home again, but that wasn't going to happen. She talked about his release when she visited, letting her imagination run wild, about how maybe the governor would commute his sentence, let him come home, and they'd get a little house, how she'd cook and keep house for him. Jack dozed, thinking about being home again, in his own home with his little girl.

He jerked awake to see Lori standing by his bed looking down at him, at first thought she was part of his dream. She reached down over the rail, put her hand on his, careful not to move the IV tube. Her small fingers were ice cold, bringing him fully awake. Her long brown hair shone so bright, just like her mother's. He wanted to grab her and hug her, but a guard was standing right there. She was dressed in her school uniform, looking so clean and beautiful. Cora Lee stood behind her, tall and slim, looking beautiful, too, and efficient in tailored white slacks and a cream-colored blazer that set off her warm coloring. Her brown eyes met his, dark with worry.

Holding Lori's hands, he wished he could talk privately with Cora Lee, tell her his own worries about Lori. There was no way they could do that, with the guard standing at the foot of the bed listening to every word, watching their every move, his pale blue eyes never leaving Lori as she held Jack's hand—even though Lori knew she wasn't supposed to touch him—as if a thirteen-year-old child might have smuggled in a gun. She looked up into the man's cold eyes and drew away. Nothing was supposed to pass between them, not even love. When they put you in prison, all your rights were taken from you, and most of the rights of your loved ones. Lori could bring no little gift, Cora Lee had to lock her purse in the car, leave her car keys at the admitting desk, and he knew they'd gone through a body scan.

"Pa? We came as soon as the warden called." She searched his face, trying to see in his eyes how badly he was hurt, trying hard not to cry. He knew he looked like hell, bound up in bandages, and stuck with tubes. He wanted to hug her and hold her and he wasn't allowed. Wanted to tell her how sorry he was that she had to endure this.

Cora Lee said, "I talked with Max." She took a deep breath, glancing at the guard. "The warden called him." She seemed to think the guard might stop her. "Max told me it was Victor Colletto who stabbed you." She put her arm around Lori. "We're doing as he told us. There will be extra patrols along our street, and a grown-up will be with Lori twenty-four/seven, at work with Ryan, at school. And of course up with the horses. Charlie Harper will ride with her." No one said that Charlie Harper rode armed, but Jack knew that.

"I'll be like a prisoner," Lori said in a small voice, and then wished she hadn't said that.

"Can you get her out of the village somewhere?" Jack wanted to say, *Send her to your sister in New Orleans.* But he didn't want to say even that in front of a stranger, not even a prison guard.

Lori shook her head. "I'm not going to run away. That

Kent Colletto's nothing but a punk." And then, at Jack's look, "I'll be careful, Pa. I'll do what Captain Harper tells me." But then she grinned. "Warden Deaver told Cora Lee that Victor's in confinement and will be moved to another prison, that he might have to go back for new sentencing. I hope they hang him."

Jack tried not to laugh, it hurt like hell to laugh. For a long moment they were silent, just looking at each other. He longed to keep her safe, and there was no way he could do that. He felt as useless as he had when, before he was sent to prison, he'd tried to protect her from Fenner, and nearly failed. Felt as useless as when Fenner had found her hiding place and nearly got his hands on her.

He looked at Cora Lee. "Our friend Max, tell him to keep safe. Tell him to take care not just of Lori but of himself." His look held Cora Lee. Her own eyes widened, then she nodded. He wanted to tell her more, but he hestitated to name names since they weren't alone. He said, "Some guy just coming out of prison, that could be bad news." Maybe that was enough, maybe that would give Max a heads-up. Again Cora Lee nodded, and then she grinned at him, gave him a thumbs-up and a look as warm as a hug.

13

T HE THREE CATS had hardly scrambled up to Maudie's roof when Kit blurted out, "*That* was no accident, that truck was parked around the corner up there waiting for her. I saw it, the minute she came out the driver gunned it and took off and—"

"Slow down," Joe said. This tortoise-shell, when something set her off, could be as volatile as bees in a windstorm. "What did you see? Tell it slowly."

"He was waiting for Maudie, parked around the corner where no one could see him from the house, and the truck windows so dirty I couldn't see much of him, only a smear behind the glass." She took a breath, trying to go slower. "When he saw her come out of the house he stepped on the gas and barreled straight for her, you saw him . . ." Again she stopped, her yellow eyes huge with distress, her tortoiseshell ears flat with frustration. "She has to know it wasn't an accident. Why won't she report it? Is she afraid to report it?"

"Or," Dulcie said, "is she protecting someone? You didn't see the driver?"

Kit moved out of the shadows, to sit where the roof was warming. "Only a pale shape with what looked like a dark cap pulled down. The windshield was caked with dirt, and there was dirt on the license plate. And there's something else, too, there was another invasion this morning, I followed the squad cars, it was that house with the glass at the top, Becky Lake's house. I listened when Detective Ray interviewed her, she said two men broke in when she answered the door and she was alone and they beat her and they kicked her little dog and then they ran and . . ."

"Slow down," Joe and Dulcie said impatiently. "Did she describe them?" Joe asked.

"One tall and thin, the other stronger looking, both with dark clothes and stockings over their faces. Chief Harper was really mad when he got there—another invasion where they got away, and maybe mad because of the *Gazette* this morning, too, it was on a newsstand, all about the earlier invasions that aren't even news anymore, smeared all over the front page that there's never a cop when one happens and Harper's not patrolling the village, that he's letting crooks and killers run loose while his officers sit around drinking coffee," she hissed with anger. "Do they think he can have cops lined up on every street waiting for someone to ring a doorbell?"

Dulcie and Joe were quiet. Kit's mood this morning had swung from despondency at the cruelty in the world to flyaway rage—calming for only a moment, for a little snuggle with Benny. Now again she was as volatile as a caged bobcat. "And there was something else, there was a fish smell around Becky's front door, old dead fish, I followed it to the curb and then it was gone, I guess they got in a car, I could still smell a whiff of exhaust."

"Fish," Joe said. "Fine. A dozen wharves up the coast where people fish, hundreds of people coming and going and half of them tourists."

"And our own little fishing dock," Dulcie said. She was quiet, looking at them solemnly. "And there's something else, too. Cora Lee called Wilma early this morning. Jack Reed's in the county hospital in Salinas, they took him from the prison by helicopter. He was stabbed, and he's critical. It isn't fair. Why Jack Reed?" Lori Reed was the cats' friend, she always had time to stop and pet them and find a little snack for them. Though she didn't know they could speak, she talked to them as if they could understand her. It was Dulcie who had found Lori hiding in the library when she ran away from home that one time, when she was just a little girl.

"Jack Reed shouldn't be in prison with those damned gangs," Joe said.

"It wasn't a gang," Dulcie said, licking her paw in consternation. "It was Vic Colletto, it was Maudie's nephew." Sometimes the problems of their human friends were nearly too much; sometimes she wondered if she'd rather *not* know about human troubles, would rather still be an ordinary housecat without a care beyond an elusive mouse or cadging another kitty treat.

Except it really didn't work that way. A nonspeaking cat knew when trouble hit, she could feel the distress of her humans, and could suffer even more because she didn't understand the cause. A nonspeaking cat felt the pain but had no clue as to what had caused it, or how she might help to ease the trouble. No, Dulcie thought, it was better to understand all she could, no matter how terrible. In her little cat heart, she wouldn't want to return to that simpler life. She was lost in her distress for Lori when Joe rose suddenly, his ears laid back, staring away through the tops of the oaks, a growl low in his throat.

High in an oak tree not twenty feet from them, a cat crouched staring down at them, the big yellow tomcat that had been shadowing them. Though he was half hidden among the foliage, they could make out his wide head, broad shoulders, his coat as bright as butter. Boldly, his yellow eyes watched them.

Still growling, Joe was crouched for attack when Kit started toward the cat, her tortoiseshell fur puffed up, but her whiskers curved into a little smile. Her yellow eyes burning with curiosity, she approached the tomcat with her nose out inquisitively, her little dish face showing only fascination. Quickly Joe moved beside her, walking stiffly, ready to fight—but this was no ordinary cat, not the way he was looking at them, not with that wise and knowing expression.

There were no speaking cats like themselves in the village. Only on the empty hills was there a small band, descendants of three pairs brought over from Wales generations ago. That clowder lived now among the ruins of an old mansion, but they knew those cats. There was no big yellow tom among them, this cat was a newcomer. But from where? Even as they approached, Joe still in attack mode, the cat backed deeper among the leaves as if to leap away. The three paused. Joe was about to speak, to challenge him to come down and make himself known, when the cat vanished. He was there one second and then gone among the branches. The leaves shivered where he'd passed, the spaces between the twisting branches revealing empty sky.

They waited, but the yellow tomcat didn't reappear. Kit peered silently up through the treetops, her paw lifted, her ears up, her fluffy tail very still. When at last they turned away, the little birds above them began to chirp again among the canopy of leaves and to flit about, lively and busy once more, now that the stranger had departed—though they kept a wary eye on the three cats who remained prowling the rooftop. Somewhere a door slammed; then once more the only sound was the hush of the sea, and the off-key chirping of the house finches. Kit looked at Dulcie, her eyes wide with interest. A speaking cat, another like themselves. Why was he so shy, why did he melt away, unwilling to speak to them?

They hadn't seen him clearly, hidden among the oak leaves, except his golden eyes. Hadn't caught his scent over the dry smell of the oak itself. They had glimpsed the breadth of his shoulders, but couldn't tell his age, could see for sure only that those knowing golden eyes belonged to no common house cat. And when Dulcie and Joe looked at Kit, they knew they hadn't seen the last of the yellow cat.

"Come on," Dulcie said uneasily, hoping Kit wouldn't race away, following him. "It's nearly noon, maybe Lori and Cora Lee are back from the hospital, maybe they have some news about her pa." Until they knew who this cat was, Dulcie hoped she could distract the tortoiseshell. They never knew where Kit's wild impulses and giddy enthusiasms would take her, but usually it was straight into trouble.

14

THE THREE CATS arrived at the seniors' house panting from their long run up the rising rooftops to the north side of the village. "They're home from the hospital," Dulcie said, seeing Cora Lee's car in the drive. They found the tires still warm, the hood warm when they leaped onto it, approaching the roof beneath Lori's window.

The rambling two-story house had once been a decrepit relic, curling shingles, peeling paint, and a garden full of healthy weeds. Cora Lee and her three senior friends had attacked the neglected house with hammer and nails, new Sheetrock, fresh paint, with the help of Ryan and several handymen. They had built low walls to define new planter beds, where now winter flowers painted an excess of bright colors between the pale stonework. The ladies hadn't known when they moved in that at the back of the deep lot, where it fell away to the canyon below, lay a row of little, hidden graves. Graves undiscovered for years until Jack Reed found his brother standing over an open pit, prepared to bury another murdered child.

It had taken courage for Lori to move here when Jack went to prison. Now she would live nowhere else—until her pa came home. Now the four ladies were her family. She knew the dead children had been exhumed from their anonymous resting places, each sent home for a proper burial, and Lori was okay with that; she could look out at the canyon now and think only that at last those little souls were at rest.

At the back of the house, where the lot sloped down, two small basement apartments looked out to the wild canyon. These were an important part of the senior ladies' retirement plan. Having pooled their savings to buy the old place, they intended to avoid going into rest homes in their declining years. They would remain here together, and later hire live-in help who would stay in the apartments. Trustees would then see to the management. At present they were all four too healthy and strong to need a caretaker, and their only guest was Lori, who shared the upstairs with Cora Lee in a big, sunny room of her own. The cats were crouched to leap to the roof of the garage just outside her window when they heard a choked little sob, and another, from the room above them.

"Oh," Kit whispered, tucking her tail under with dismay. What had happened? Listening to Lori weeping, not wanting to think the worst, she scrambled to the roof, the others behind her, and looked in through the decorative metal grille of the open window.

Lori lay on her bed, her face pressed into her pillow, crying as if her heart would break.

With a reaching paw Dulcie slid the screen open and the cats slipped between the curlicues of metal into the bedroom. Both Dulcie and Kit mewled to announce their presence, but not until Joe gave out a loud tomcat *meowwrrr* did Lori stop crying and look up at them. At once, Kit bounded across the covers and poked her nose at the child's wet cheek. Lori's shudders stopped. She took Kit in her arms, pressing her face against her, then reached to stroke Dulcie and Joe Grey. "How did you know I needed someone?" She looked at the open window. "You heard me crying? Cora Lee was here and the dogs, but I sent them away. I wanted to be alone, and then I was sorry." She looked bleakly at the cats. "I wish you could understand. Pa's hurt so bad. He might die," she said in a small voice. "I wish you could understand, I wish I could tell you about Pa, I wish you could talk to me."

She wiped at her tears. "What will I do if Pa dies? He can't die. He was so still, so white and still, and his voice was just a whisper." She looked forlornly at Kit. "He mustn't die, he can't die alone in that hospital with no one there but some guard, he can't die all alone. That damn prison! Why is he in prison!" she said, echoing almost exactly the cats' own thoughts. "He didn't do anything wrong; maybe he saved a lot of children's lives! He saved my life. If that Fenner had got me alone, I'd be dead too, just like the others." She shoved her face into Kit's fur, her body shaking with hard sobs. It was as if only now, after she had seen her father near death, that all her grief was coming out after nearly two years with her pa in jail, and the years before that when she hadn't understood what was happening to him. She wept uncontrollably, soaking

Kit with tears. She grew still when Mavity Flowers called from downstairs, her gravelly voice reaching Lori with surprising strength.

"Lori, you want lunch?" The little woman must be standing at the foot of the stairs, but very likely she hadn't heard Lori crying, her hearing wasn't that good. Mavity Flowers, one of the four senior ladies, was a small, straightforward woman, her round face prematurely wrinkled from the sun. At well over sixty, she still worked for her living cleaning houses, enjoying a change of pace as she put herself to sleep at night reading her favorite romance novels.

"I made chicken sandwiches," she called. "Charlie's coming by, she has some news, she sounds all excited."

The cats didn't know what news could cheer Lori today, but Lori sat up and wiped her eyes. Slipping off the bed, looking back at the cats to come with her, she headed downstairs. Lori loved Charlie, as she loved Max and all their close circle of friends, and just now, she surely must need them around her.

At the bottom of the stairs, the two big dogs were waiting, staring up. The cats weren't afraid of the family Dalmatian, and Susan Brittain's chocolate poodle, but they descended stiff-legged, their ears back, steeling themselves for the inevitable pummeling and sloppy licks. The minute they hit the bottom step the dogs were all over them, washing and nudging and harrying them until Joe Grey gave them a growl as loud as a tiger, and Kit hissed and raised a paw. Only then did they settle down, their lolling tongues showing doggy laughs as they followed Lori to the kitchen.

The big white and yellow kitchen was bright with sunlight slanting in through its long bank of windows. On the round table sat a platter of quarter-cut sandwiches, a glass of milk for Lori, cups and a pot of tea for the women. Cora Lee and Mavity were already at the table. As Lori pulled out her chair, the cats leaped onto the planning desk tucked beside the refrigerator, out of the way of the dogs. The Dalmatian and poodle stood eyeing the table hungrily—until they heard the front door knocker. Then they raced away with Mavity, only to return the next moment frisking around Charlie Harper.

The tall redhead came striding through, trying not to trip on the dogs as they gamboled around her. She carried a box of books. "For the library sale," she said. "Three more boxes in the car."

Cora Lee nodded and took them from her. Charlie's red hair was twisted into a lopsided knot at the nape of her neck, fiery tendrils framing her freckled face. Lithe and slim in her faded jeans, she wore a faded persimmon T-shirt, and her well-worn boots smelled of horses. She looked more vibrant than the cats had seen her since the *Gazette* began trashing Max and Molena Point PD, her cheeks rosy, her green eyes laughing.

Mavity pushed back her glasses. "You heard from your editor."

"She likes it!" Charlie said. "She likes the new book! She tried all morning to get me on the landline, but I was up in the hills, I took a really long ride and didn't have my phone turned on." She pulled out a chair as Cora Lee poured a cup of tea for her. "She likes it even more than the last book. She . . ."

94

She looked at Kit and went still. She rose at once and moved to the desk, standing in front of Kit, petting her and hiding Kit's incensed, too revealing expression. She'd hurt Kit's feelings. The tortoiseshell's round yellow eyes were wide with hurt, with anger and dismay.

Charlie's first book had been about Kit herself, about an orphaned tortoiseshell kitten trying to survive in the wild on her own. It had been a great success with readers, and in Kit's view it was the best book in the whole world. Now, here was Charlie with another book that was *not* about her, and the editor liked it better. Kit was hot with jealousy. The editor's enthusiasm, and Charlie's joy, seemed a terrible betrayal.

"Editors always like the newest book best," Charlie said, chagrined. "Or they say they do. They think that prods a writer to work harder. But," she said, picking Kit up and cuddling her, "there'll never be another book like *Tattercoat.* I'll never, ever be able to write another story like that one. Everyone who reads it loves it, I get hundreds and hundreds of letters and emails telling me how much they love it." Mavity and Cora Lee had read many of the letters; and of course Kit had read them all, each with a terrible thrill and with a deep and purring satisfaction.

Their friends all knew, of course, that Kit had been the model for *Tattercoat,* for both the story and Charlie's many drawings. But only a few people knew that *Tattercoat* was, in fact, Kit's own true story, much of it told in Kit's own words. So now of course Kit was jealous. Charlie held her close until at last Kit relaxed in her arms, her ears came up again, and she began to purr.

"Still," Charlie said, stroking Kit, "that doesn't mean I

should stop writing. It doesn't mean I should stop trying, even though I know there will never, ever be another adventure as compelling, for me, as *Tattercoat*." With Kit at last purring happily, Charlie sat down at the table, settling the tortoiseshell in her lap.

"Well, your editor's happy," Cora Lee said, and Mavity smiled, as Charlie's two friends, oblivious to the little cat's anger, celebrated Charlie's success.

But Kit wasn't the only one who had bristled. Across the table, Lori watched the three women with her fists clenched on her lap. Charlie and Mavity weren't a bit interested that Pa was in the hospital and might die; neither one seemed to care at all. Charlie was so excited about an old book, so centered on herself. Didn't grown-ups care about anything outside themselves? Didn't *they* ever feel frightened? How come grown-ups were so smug and certain all the time, when it was all Lori could do just to hold herself together?

She didn't realize she was tearing her sandwich into little pieces until she looked up and saw Charlie watching her, saw the eyes of all three women on her. Cora Lee looked at Lori, then turned to Charlie. "I called Wilma this morning, I thought she'd call you. I guess you were riding. And when you called here . . ."

"What?" Charlie said. "What is it? I didn't check my messages, I just put the mare up and jumped in the car." She looked at Lori, at her sullen expression. "What?" she said softly.

"Lori's pa was stabbed this morning," Cora Lee said, "in the prison yard. They flew him to Salinas Valley Hospital, we just got back. He's . . ." She glanced at Lori. "He's not out of danger, but he's stable."

Charlie reached across, took Lori's hand in hers. "I'm so sorry. I didn't know. You were with him this morning?"

Lori nodded.

"Were you able to talk with the doctor?"

Again, a nod. But it was Cora Lee who answered. "The doctor says he's strong, that he's doing as well as he can."

Lori said, "I think they're taking good care of him. He can't . . ." Her voice caught. "He can't die." She turned away from the table, standing with her back to them, petting the three cats with one hand, stroking the two dogs with the other, where they'd come to lean against her, clutching the animals in her need, not bothering to wipe the tears from her face.

Cora Lee watched her, but let her be. "The doctor said if he continues doing well he'll soon be out of danger. He hopes he'll improve enough by the end of the week so they can take him back to Soledad. He thought Jack should heal quickly; he's young and strong, and he has Lori to get well for." She looked up at Charlie, frowning. "It was the Colletto boy, Victor. I've already talked with Max. Until this gets sorted out, he doesn't want Lori to go anywhere alone, not even in the yard, not even outside with the dogs."

Charlie rose and came around the table, putting her arm around Lori. "We can ride together, I'd like that, I'd like the company. Would you feel safe with me?" Lori nodded. Charlie didn't ask about Lori working for Ryan;

she knew Ryan wouldn't let anything happen, knew that everyone would rally around the child. She only wished they could defend the village as handily against these home invaders.

But Max would take care of them, Charlie thought—with a little assist from the feline contingent to hurry things along, hopefully to put these guys behind bars before Christmas.

15

By NOON, THE day after she shot Martin and Caroline, after the cops had come and gone at the small house she'd rented, to tell her Martin was dead, the shooter knew the old woman hadn't seen her. If Maudie had fingered her, the cops would have arrested her on the spot or, at the very least, have labeled her a person of interest and taken her in for questioning. What a laugh, those cops trying to break the news gently, that her ex-husband had been shot and killed, asking if there was someone, a relative or neighbor, who could come in and stay with her. And then at last, asking ever so respectfully where she'd been that night, saying they hadn't been able to reach her.

She had the stubs of her plane ticket, the Visa charge slip, and room receipt from Vegas. Arriving early the day before, she'd seen friends and gambled. If she'd flown out again under another name and ID, no one needed to know that. You could gamble all weekend wherever you chose, at any hour you chose, and very likely no one would remember you. If you lost money and didn't take a big winning, there was no record. A Southwest flight into Ontario International, pick up a rental car, drive back to Vegas and no one the wiser. The cops had nothing to tie her to the shooting or they'd have been all over her—the same way they'd been all over the wrecked car after the shooting, the same way they'd have searched the road and surrounding ranches and fields the next morning looking for tire marks, footprints, shell casings. The news said there were still no leads to the shooter. It didn't mention a second person in the truck, and by now her driver was far away. Though holdbacks by the cops were common, this time she was inclined to believe what the sheriff's department had told the press.

Even if they'd found a casing, which they wouldn't, they wouldn't find a match to this gun on their fancy AFIS network. They might get a warrant to search the nearby houses and farms, but she'd left no trace in the "borrowed" truck; and she'd stayed on the gravel where there wouldn't likely be tire marks. Any gravel in the tire tread would be natural enough, with the truck going in and out across the graveled drives and roads. The truck's owner, Harley Owens, was the brother of a woman who worked where she'd worked. Vera Owens was so talkative that Pearl knew not only Vera's personal habits but Harley's as well—he wouldn't be back there for another three weeks. The Owenses' ranch was a weekend place, the few cattle that were pastured there belonged to a neighbor who cared for them. It had been blind luck that the ranch was located so near to Maudie's cabin, an opportunity too good to let pass. It hadn't taken long, watching the place for a few weekends, driving up in the morning and back at night, cruising the area, to know Vera had described Harley's habits accurately.

Everything had gone so smoothly. Every year at Easter vacation Maudie and Martin and Benny headed for Maudie's cabin; this year was no different except to add Caroline and her brats. She'd left Vegas with ample time to meet her partner, and then to intercept Maudie's arrival. Had timed it so well that once she'd picked the padlock, pulled the rental car into the old barn, and hot-wired the truck, they'd had to wait less than an hour on the dark side road until they saw the pale convertible coming, and had eased in behind it. All had gone as planned, it was the weeks following after the shooting that were tedious, fending off the saccharine sympathy of her new neighbors and coworkers, enduring the funeral—oh, she'd gone, all right. Had even managed to squeeze out a few tears. The reading of the will and trust was a shocker, but she should have known he'd waste no time leaving everything to Caroline, Benny, and the old woman.

Some would say she should contest the will and try to break the trust, that *she* was Benny's mother and should be the trustee of his share. But under the circumstances, that wasn't smart. There were other ways to get what was rightfully hers.

And there was more than the will and trust to worry about. It was no secret that after the funeral Maudie cleared out Martin's and Caroline's house with the assistance of Caroline's sister; then Maudie put her own house on the market, preparing to leave L.A. But taking what with her? Caroline's personal papers? Or did Caroline's sister have them?

With this in mind, and with apparently no follow-up interest from the law, she'd opted to move away just as the old woman was planning to do. She had told the LAPD detectives that staying in the city was too painful, that she was going down to San Diego for a while, to stay with a friend. Lay a trail on to Mexico for them to find, then turn around and head up the coast instead, where Maudie would soon be living. It wasn't likely the old woman would imagine she'd come up there to the village, or that she'd maintained her own contacts in Molena Point so well. With Maudie busy getting herself settled, why would she wonder about her ex-daughter-in-law and those old connections, or what use Pearl might make of them? When, later, she opted to contact Maudie and get back her own, wouldn't that be a nice surprise.

16

JASMINE VINES COVERED the high adobe wall that shielded the Colletto house from the street, the house's pale sides broken by a richly fashioned wrought-iron gate that led to the sheltered garden. The three cats slipped between the curves of hammered metal into a jungle of rosebushes, low and fragrant ground cover, and lavender bushes. A roofed terrace ran the length of the house, its brick expanse graced with wicker chairs and potted geraniums. They could see, above the tiled roof, a second floor rising up, indistinct in the darkness, and to their right a driveway where Maudie's black Lincoln was parked beneath the sheltering oaks before a double garage.

The front door was of heavy oak, hand carved in the Spanish style, secured with wrought-iron hinges and a fancy wrought-iron latch. From somewhere to their left, lights spilled out onto the terrace, and they could hear the murmur of voices and the sounds of silverware on china, as if perhaps glass doors had been left open to the dining room. The air was sultry, the chill of the last few days having left the village until the next change in weather made itself known, the central California weather famous for its notional approach to Christmas.

Mixed with the smell of jasmine, roses, and lavender came a heady scent of roast beef that made the cats lick their whiskers. Silent as shadows they slipped along past the front door, through the garden toward the muted voices and the good smells of supper.

Where the light spilled out, wide glass sliders did indeed stand open, treating the diners to the mild evening breeze. In the dark surround, the lighted dining room seemed as magnified in importance as a stage, the play in progress as quaint as a painting from another era. The room was softly lit, with peach-colored walls and a pastel Kerman rug setting off dark, heavily carved furniture— ornate buffet, high-backed carved chairs—all rich and, in the cats' view, pretentious. The long table was set with white linen, with gleaming white china, and thin crystal. The centerpiece of white candles cast flickering shadows across the faces of the six diners, and illuminated behind them an oversize gold-framed oil painting of red and pink roses that didn't seem to go with the Spanish architecture. Or did it? Dulcie thought about the Spanish families who had settled in California during the hide and tallow days, how they had loved their rosebushes, importing them from Spain to plant around their grand haciendas, training their American Indian servants to care for and nurture the plants.

But the image of a grand Spanish don and a beautiful

Spanish lady at the table, as the setting seemed to demand, didn't apply to these diners. James Colletto, seated at one end of the table, was a small, dull-looking man with short grizzled gray hair and a gray mustache, an everyday, ordinary kind of man dressed in an ill-fitting dark suit, a white shirt, and a satin tie with huge polka dots that might have come straight out of the forties. Carlene Colletto, at the other end of the table, was pudgier than her sister Maudie and seemed even softer. Her gray hair was done in precise waves that clung tight to her head. Her flowered dress and her pink, low-heeled pumps were surely holdovers, too, from the last century. Dulcie imagined her having put them away in a shoe box until they came back in style.

Maudie and Benny sat with their backs to the cats, the Collettos' sons across from them at the far side of the table in front of the oversize painting. The youngest, Kent, looked about eighteen, a tall, lanky young man with rounded shoulders, who sat slouched in his chair as if suffering from perennially weak bones. Or perennial boredom. His shoulder-length black hair was ragged, only hastily combed. All three cats wondered why his mother had let him wear that wrinkled shirt to dinner; they could almost smell the sweat. Beneath the table his blue and white jogging shoes were dirty and worn, his jeans stained with grease. His scowl was so embedded that the cats couldn't imagine him ever looking happy. He pointedly ignored his aunt Maudie, as if he had no use at all for her. When Carlene spoke to him, it was with an expression of helpless acceptance, and Kent's replies were sullen. The boys' father ignored him as if preferring to look anywhere else.

Jared Colletto was maybe twenty. He was taller than his brother, thin and wiry and straight, neatly dressed in tan chinos and a white shirt. His thin, tanned face was clean shaven, his dark brown hair freshly cut. His eyes were a light brown; when he smiled he had dimples at the corners of his mouth, and his teeth shone white and straight. At least he knew how to smile—maybe he should give his brother lessons.

Maudie was dressed in silky beige slacks, stockings and leather sandals, and a smocky patchwork top of pastel swatches in a pattern of partridges in a pear tree, an ode to the coming Yule that made Dulcie and Kit smile. Benny, sitting beside her, was so small that the table came halfway up his chest. Apparently Carlene hadn't thought to offer him a phone book to sit on; he was forced to eat with his elbow straight out in order to reach his plate, an awkward and surely uncomfortable exercise. He was dressed in pale jeans and a clean blue polo shirt, his dangling feet sporting clean white tennis shoes.

Carlene was saying, " . . . and they gave you a very nice interview, Maudie. Of course it's only a local magazine, but still, that was very kind of them."

"The gallery arranged it," Maudie said, "while I was still in L.A. It's such a beautiful magazine, so slick and bright, and they did a lovely spread. So many color photographs of my quilts. Every village shop of importance seems to advertise in it. I feel flattered to be included."

"I'm surprised you arranged for an exhibit, with Martin barely in his grave."

Maudie put her arm around Benny, giving him a hug as she smiled across at Carlene. "This show was scheduled

106

some months before . . . some months before Easter of this year," she said, glancing down at Benny. "The gallery had a contact down there, he took the photographs in February.

"After the shooting, I wasn't sure I could get the show together—or get myself together. But I knew Martin wouldn't want me to cancel. And I knew we'd be moving up here, I knew at once, when Martin died, that we couldn't stay in L.A."

"Aren't you afraid," Carlene asked, "that if that terrible person who shot Martin—that they might see the magazine, even this little local one, and learn where you are? Aren't you afraid this kind of publicity will draw them to you?"

Maudie looked at her sister for some time. "I wasn't the target, Carlene. It was Martin and Caroline who were murdered."

"But you were right there, you must have seen the killer."

"I didn't. It was dark. I didn't see anything, just the flash of the gun and a white empty afterglow as I grabbed the kids and ducked down."

"But you could have seen him. How would he know you didn't? If you—"

"All I saw were split second flashes of gunfire." Maudie laid down her fork. "I did not see the killer's face, Carlene. Don't start imagining what isn't so." Beside her, Benny looked very small, the child sat very still, huddled into himself. Maudie hugged him again and took his hand, but she didn't back off from the discussion; as if, Joe Grey thought, she would not encourage him to hide from this new and ugly turn his life had taken.

"But they don't know what you might have seen," Carlene pressed stubbornly, with, apparently, no notion how her questions might upset the little boy beside Maudie.

Across the table, Jared gave his mother a look of disgust. "She said it was dark, Ma. Let it go."

Next to Jared, Kent lazily stirred his mashed potatoes and gravy into mush, with the manners of a three-year-old. Carlene said automatically, "Don't play with your food," as she must have done for Kent's entire life; she gave Jared a despairing look that he returned with a little smile of understanding. Maudie changed the subject, tossing the conflict back into Carlene's lap.

"How's Victor doing?" she asked innocently. "How much longer does he have to serve, down at Soledad?" Had the two sisters been like this all their lives, at each other with this mean one-upmanship?

At the other end of the table, James said, "It was on the local news, Maudie. You must have seen it. Victor's being transferred out, to another prison." He said it without emotion, his thin, sharply carved features unrevealing. James Colletto had a nose as straight as a new ruler.

"I haven't had the TV on," Maudie told him softly, as if embarrassed that she'd broached something more painful, even, than she'd thought. Beside her, Benny had finished his mashed potatoes. Maudie picked up the serving bowl that sat within her reach, and dished him another helping. Jared reached across the table to pass her the gravy, while James sliced more roast beef for the child. The little boy, apparently paying no attention to the adults, was shoveling in the good hot food—a real sit-down dinner, the cats thought, smiling.

"There was a stabbing in the prison yard," James said quietly. "Three men against one, and Victor among them. Apparently it was Victor who did the stabbing. We don't know much more than that." He laid his fork down. "We're told he'll go back to court, that he could be convicted on a new charge." His voice was flat with resignation.

"Of course they're blaming Victor," Carlene said. "That's what they've done all along. The cops, the judge, everyone. The night that pizza place was robbed, Victor wasn't anywhere near it. Was he, Kent? I'd never have thought we had crooked police, right here in our little village, I never would have guessed that Max Harper . . ." She stopped, staring at Maudie. The cats couldn't see Maudie's face, but in her lap, her left hand was balled into a fist, and beneath the table her sandaled foot tapped silently on the thick rug.

"What's wrong?" Carlene said, staring at her sister. "*You* weren't here. *You* haven't been reading the paper, you don't know half what's going on."

Maudie's foot continued to tap. She made no reply. Jared looked sympathetic, but he, too, remained silent. Kent smirked at Maudie in such a superior way that Dulcie and Kit wanted to claw his contemptuous face. The silence at the table went on for so long that even Benny began to squirm. Carlene let her gaze settle on the child, honing in coldly on the little boy.

"Do you like your new home, Benny? Do you have a nice room? Are you in school yet? Tell us about your new school."

The child looked down at the table.

"Can't you speak to your great-aunt? Tell us what

grade you're in? Do you like your new teacher?" Carlene didn't have the courtesy to gently draw the child out or to wait for a reply; she went after Benny like a bulldog after a little cat. Benny shifted awkwardly, looking up to his grandmother for help, as if silently begging permission to leave the table.

"Doesn't the child talk?" Carlene asked. "Can't you talk to me, Benny?"

Maudie took Benny's hand, shaking her head. His eyes fixed on her, Benny settled down, only the stiffness of his thin back showing his continued discomfort. Carlene's unkindness made the cats wonder how the Colletto boys had managed to survive in this household; it sure explained why Victor might be in prison, and Kent was so sullen. James Colletto didn't seem strong enough, the cats thought, to counter this unfeeling woman.

"Benny hasn't started school yet," Maudie said, putting her arm around the child. "He's been helping Lori Reed, the young girl who works for Ryan Flannery, up at the cottage. Benny—"

"A young girl works for a carpenter? How young?"

"Thirteen," Benny said. "Lori—"

"But that's dangerous, that's against the law."

"She has permission from the school," Maudie said. "She works during certain class hours, and on weekends. Ryan is more than responsible, she sees that Lori's work is safe."

"Ryan can do anything," Benny said as if the change of subject stirred his confidence. "Ryan saved Grandma yesterday when that truck almost hit her, she—"

"*What* happened?" Carlene said, laying down her fork. "Why didn't you tell me this?"

"A car swipe!" Benny said eagerly. "Ryan called it a hit-and-run, a car tried to hit Grandma, he came right at her and tried to hit her. Grandma—"

"It was nothing," Maudie said quickly, trying to hush Benny. "It was an accident, someone looking the other way, driving too fast—"

"Nothing!" Carlene said. "A car nearly hit you, and it was nothing? What did the police say? Did they catch the driver? Crime is completely out of control in this village, the police are doing nothing. An assault on my very own sister, after all your suffering over Martin's murder . . ."

"It was an accident," Maudie repeated. "As to Martin's death, Benny and I are getting on with life just as he would want us to do."

Carlene sniffed with disgust. "And now David's gone back to Atlanta and left you alone in the house with that wall torn out, so anyone can walk in . . ."

"The wall isn't torn out. The glass slider is far more secure now, with the studio built around it, than it was before. Benny and I are just fine," Maudie said, smiling down at the child. Benny looked up at her and nodded.

"I want Jared to stay with you for a while," Carlene said, "until David sees fit to come back." She looked pointedly at Jared. "It isn't safe for Maudie, alone there. I'm surprised David would go on his merry way and—"

Maudie's foot was tapping again as if to deflect some of her anger. "You'd have David leave *Alison* alone, when she's having cancer surgery?"

"Alison has family there, they can take care of her."

"Alison has one sister with five children. You think she wants the confusion of five loud, noisy little kids when she's just out of surgery?"

"Jared, go pack a bag," Carlene said. "You can follow Maudie home, you can stay in that spare bedroom with Benny until David decides to take care of his mother."

"I am not an invalid," Maudie said. "I don't want a caretaker. You are not to come, Jared. If we need you, I'll let you know."

Jared gave her a little grin and nodded. "Between school and work, I'd be gone a lot. But I'd be glad to come, and I'd sure be there at night, if anyone tried to break in."

"You're working where?" Maudie said, as if to retain control of the conversation.

"It's a little used-car lot just up the coast. I do some detailing, painting, cleaning up the cars before he puts a price on them. Mr. Sutter, he liked the way I rebuilt my T-Bird." Jared grinned at her. "He says it looks factory new." He glanced at his brother. "Kent works there some, we like working together."

Outside in the garden, Joe Grey sat very still, his stub tail twitching with interest as he considered the possibilities of Kent's work situation among all those used cars.

"The good thing," Jared said, "he lets me work pretty much the hours I want, depending on school. The accounting classes aren't real demanding, but sometimes there's a lot of history or English homework, and I can choose my work time. When he needs extra help, Kent can get in more hours, too."

"The money helps out," Kent said in a bored tone. As if he really didn't give a damn about the money, or about working anywhere. Joe watched him, and then suddenly rose, flashing Dulcie and Kit a look that had them on their feet, too, and the three took off around the side of the house. Joe was in such a hurry, and the lady cats racing to keep up, that they never once glanced above them into the branches of the overhanging oaks to see the yellow tomcat crouched above, peering down watching them.

17

 Sᴜᴄʜ ᴀ ꜱᴛʀᴏɴɢ hunch drove Joe as he raced for the Collettos' garage. Maybe his idea was off the wall, but who was to say he wouldn't find the old truck in there, the rusted truck that had nearly hit Maudie? The scenario was such a nice fit: angry Kent Colletto—angry at the whole world, it seemed—with access to any number of old vehicles that might later be painted and sold and never found. Those small car lots up the coast, tucked in among the fishing wharfs, had some really decrepit wrecks. He'd often gone with Clyde to look at some rusty "collector's" treasure, a relic that Clyde would end up towing home, give it a pristine restoration, and quadruple its value. Only as he crouched to leap to the windowsill of the closed garage did Dulcie's incredulous look stop him. "You don't really think . . ." she began.

"It's worth a shot," Joe said impatiently.

"No way," Dulcie said. "What could Maudie have

possibly done to make even skuzzy Kent Colletto want to frighten her that way? A joke, a sick joke? I don't think so."

But, convinced he was right, he leaped and peered in, getting cobwebs in his whiskers.

Nothing. No truck. Only Jared's shiny blue T-Bird, and a tan Ford sedan that was probably the family car. Dropping down, he looked at Dulcie, embarrassed. He'd been so sure, such a strong feeling. But she only grinned at him. "Good try," she said, giving him a whisker kiss. And soon the three cats parted, Joe and Dulcie each heading home to their own supper, Kit dawdling along behind, puzzled perhaps by some faint scent, looking back over her shoulder.

Joe's thoughts, as he raced over the rooftops, remained on Kent Colletto. The night was balmy around him, the soft breeze heavy with the smell of the sea; as he neared home, the breeze picked up the heady aroma of spaghetti coming from his own house, making him forget Kent Colletto and race faster, urgently licking his whiskers.

From his own roof, Joe looked down at the drive, surprised to see it crowded with cars. Clyde's yellow roadster and Ryan's red Chevy pickup stood in the carport; Dallas Garza's tan Blazer and Charlie Harper's red Blazer parked behind them; and on the street, Wilma Getz's car parked behind a squad car. Was something wrong? He remembered no talk of everyone getting together for supper. Given the longer shifts the department had been working, there'd been little time for their usual impromptu gatherings.

But emergencies didn't call for spaghetti; and as he hurried up the front steps and through his cat door, he heard only relaxed voices and easy laughter. Trotting through the living room to the big kitchen, he found them all at the table, Max and Charlie, Dallas Garza, Charlie's Aunt Wilma, Ryan and Clyde, and Officers McFarland and Blake, both in uniform. The table wasn't laden with spaghetti and French bread as he'd expected; supper was over, though the spaghetti pot still sat on the stove. The table was cluttered with poker chips, cards, loose change, and dollar bills. He guessed this was just an impromptu supper, Max and Dallas on call, and maybe Officers McFarland and Blake just getting off their extended shifts. He paused in the door to the kitchen listening to the familiar mix of disjointed remarks, aggressive bets, requests for cards, and a few good-natured put-downs; then he padded on in. No one seemed to notice him. In the far corner, the big silver Weimaraner was curled up fast asleep in the flowered easy chair, the little white cat asleep between Rock's front legs, one white paw draped over Rock's shoulder. Turning, Joe fixed his gaze on Ryan.

When she ignored him, her eyes on her cards, he gave a strident mew. Across the table, Dallas watched her, waiting to see whether she would see his raise or fold, his solemn Latino face never changing expression. Wilma Getz folded, laid down her cards, and sat with an amused expression watching Joe as he tried to get Ryan's attention. Wilma wore a red sweatshirt over a white turtleneck, her long gray-white hair done up in a knot at the nape of her neck. She grinned at Joe as he leaped to the kitchen counter, but then she gave him a questioning look—clearly asking where Dulcie was.

Joe blinked and washed his paws and tried to look at

ease, to convey to her that Dulcie had gone on home. He knew Wilma would have left a hearty snack for Dulcie, as she always did. He guessed Kit had headed home, too, where, no matter the hour, her two humans would fix a hot supper for her. Lucinda and Pedric would probably by now be doing up the supper dishes or sitting before the fire reading to each other, the tall, thin octogenarians pleasantly tired after a day's ramble up in the hills or along the coast. Still watching Ryan, Joe shifted from paw to paw. Couldn't she see he was starving?

"Raise two," Ryan said, "and two cards." When still she paid no attention, Joe gave her a series of bloodcurdling yowls that made young McFarland jump and then laugh, made both Max and Dallas scowl at him. Ryan paid no attention. Crowley said, "Ryan, feed your cat. I've won this hand anyway."

Joe stared at Ryan until she won the pot and raked in her money; then at long last she rose. "Deal me out," she said, turning away from the table, fixing her gaze on the tomcat. "You needn't be so bossy."

Unable to reply, he could only glower. Moving to the stove, she dished up a serving of spaghetti and slipped it in the microwave for a few seconds. Setting the warmed plate on the counter before him, she scratched his ear, winked at him, then turned away, returning to the table. Joe was still slurping spaghetti when Charlie raked in the next pot.

"That makes me feel better," Charlie said.

"If you're still stewing about Nancyanne Prewitt," Max said, "forget it. Don't pay any attention to that stuff."

"I can't help it. I'm surprised anyone reads the *Gazette*

117

anymore. It isn't fit to wrap fish." When Ryan looked up questioningly, Charlie said, "She cornered Wilma and me coming out of the plaza, and she really laid it on."

Wilma laughed, and put down her cards. "I had trouble not punching her in the face, right there in front of Tiffany's."

Joe hid a smile, imagining Wilma punching out that overdressed airhead reporter. Wilma could do it, too. Her self-defense skills had been well honed over her twenty-year career as a federal officer. But it was true, the pressure from this new editor and reporter and from a few sour citizens, as well as from two city council members, had to be wearing. Particularly on Max, on everyone in the department. Max Harper had served this town well for his entire career. MPPD had one of the lowest crime rates, and one of the highest rates of arrests for crimes reported, of anywhere in the state. But now suddenly the villagers, goaded by misinformation, seemed to have forgotten the high performance of their police. And the invasions weren't over yet.

So far, the evidence that Detectives Dallas Garza and Kathleen Ray had logged in wasn't adding up to much. Every set of footprints, whether photographed or in the form of a cast or taken by alternate light source, was different: different shoes, different sizes. The threads and fragments of cloth they'd bagged didn't match one another, nor did the few strands of human hairs. They had picked up no fingerprints but the victims' own or those of family members or neighbors. Their canvassing of neighborhoods and the fingerprinting of neighbors were time-consuming and costly. The department had taken men off patrol to help interview, and even the descriptions the victims gave were varied, from two tall men, to a tall man and a blond woman, to a short, stocky man. And to top it all off, the department's three unknown snitches, who normally would have come up with some useful information, hadn't even checked in.

The faint fish scent that Kit had found was the first clue the cats had that the cops didn't. And how could their supposedly human snitch report an elusive smell that no human would easily have discovered? Did a human snitch go around sniffing at doorways?

The invasions hadn't occurred in any geographic pattern, either, that anyone had been able to figure out, though they were all within the city limits. There was no time pattern. No economic or ethnic or gender or age pattern. Detective Ray had tried correlating all the various elements—time of day, day of the week, sex, age, profession, and ethnicity of victims, locations—into various computer charts, attempting to get a fix on some master plan, but so far she'd come up with nothing. Kathleen Ray might sometimes be a bit too empathetic with the victims, but she was sharp and quick, and was a genius at the computer. The tall, dark-haired beauty had, surprisingly, left a promising modeling career, disenchanted with the people she had to work with. She'd gone back to school and, after graduating from the police academy in San Jose, had signed on with the department as a rookie cop and was fast turning into a capable detective. Now, with Detective Juana Davis on vacation, Harper was relieved to have Kathleen on board.

Max Harper had done three interviews for the *Ga-*

zette, urging people to take certain precautions to avoid a forced break-in. But not every villager paid attention to precautions, thinking, "That won't happen to me." In too many households, that seemed to be the operable response. Folks depended on MPPD to protect them, and gave little thought to how they might protect themselves. So many humans, Joe thought, seemed to have forgotten the principles of self-preservation, relying on others for their security—like pampered housecats who, never having learned to hunt, lay around the house waiting for someone to open the cat food. In Joe's case, the fact that he might yowl at Ryan to serve up the spaghetti or make him an omelet didn't mean he couldn't trot on out to the hills and catch his own supper, when he chose to do so.

At the poker table, Ryan was saying, "Maudie worries me, up there alone with that little boy. I don't know what it is about her . . ." Letting the thought drift, she picked up her cards as Dallas dealt, and then looked across at Max. "L.A. still has no lead on the shooter?"

"None." Max frowned. "What is it? What's bothering you?"

"I don't know, something about the way Maudie . . . When we talked about the shooting, I got the feeling she was holding back. I don't know what it is, maybe just one of those feelings. Probably means nothing."

But Joe Grey, watching his housemate, knew exactly the sense of wrongness that bothered Ryan. There *was* something about Maudie, a shadow behind the scenes, visible only in a certain light.

Max glanced at his cards, realized it was his bet, and slid a dollar to the center of the table. "Maudie was the only witness to the shooting," he said, "and she swears she couldn't identify the shooter. The sheriff thinks the three children told the truth, that they saw nothing. Pearl Toola was the only suspect they had. She stayed in L.A. long enough to cooperate in the investigation, then got permission to move down to San Diego. She gave L.A. the address and phone number of a friend there, I guess she didn't think they'd check.

"She never showed up at that address," he continued. "L.A. had no further information on her. Because of their heavy workload and no other leads, they put out an APB on her and temporarily shelved the case."

Dallas dealt the last card of seven-card stud and raised a quarter. Joe was always amused at the high stakes of these friendly games. If a person came out five dollars the winner, that was a big victory, enough to gloat about for days.

Max said, "There's always the chance the shooter will show up here. I've talked with Maudie, suggested she needs to be careful, to report anything that seems strange."

Ryan looked at him, started to speak, then went silent. So, Joe thought, she hadn't told him about the truck—but maybe she would soon if Maudie didn't. Behind them, over in the corner, Rock woke. Lying on his back, he huffed once, staring upside down at the too-noisy humans. Wilma was shuffling the cards when the phone rang.

Ryan rose to answer, listened for a minute, then, "Hang on, I can't hear with everyone talking." Glancing across at Wilma and laying down the phone, she headed for the guest room. "Will you hang up for me?" she said, pushing back a lock of stray hair.

Wilma rose quickly at their little private signal. And Joe Grey dropped to the floor. Whatever the call was about, it surely involved Dulcie—or the call was from Dulcie, and that would have to be an emergency. Yawning, trying to look casual, he followed Ryan into the guest room where he could listen as she took the call on the extension.

18

THE DAMEN GUEST room had once been the master bedroom when the house was a small, one-story cottage. The new second floor with its sprawling master suite included Clyde's office and now a studio-office for Ryan as well; and this downstairs room had been completely changed into a charming guest retreat. The faded and anonymous bachelor furnishings that had suited Clyde and Joe had gone to Goodwill. They had been replaced by wicker and leather furniture and bright, primitive rugs, a far more elegant treatment than Clyde had ever wanted for himself. Slipping in behind Ryan, Joe leaped to the wicker desk where she sat talking softly on the phone.

Putting her arm around him, she drew him close so he could listen. Sitting tall beside her, his ear to the phone, the tomcat tried not to tickle her face with his whiskers. The voice at the other end was Lucinda Greenlaw. "No, Kit's not home yet," she was saying worriedly. "We haven't seen her since early this morning, she's been gone all day. Is Joe home? Is Dulcie? Kit's nearly always home for supper, she's been coming home so regularly, until tonight."

Snuggled next to Ryan, Joe could see down the hall if anyone left the poker table and headed their way; he could see the corner of the kitchen, where the wall phone hung. He watched Wilma step to the extension and pick up. She listened for a moment, then hung up and headed for the guest room. As Wilma joined them, Ryan turned, shielding the sight of Joe from the kitchen, and held the headpiece at an angle so both Joe and Wilma could hear, and so they could speak with Lucinda. The banter out at the poker table was more than enough to hide the tomcat's husky voice.

"Kit was with us," Joe told Lucinda softly. "Maudie Toola went to her sister's for dinner, that's where we were. Not to worry," he said, "we all left together. Maybe she stopped on the roofs to chase bats. She'll be along soon," he said reassuringly. "If she's not home in half an hour, call back and I'll go look for her."

He turned away from the phone wondering why Kit had to be so damned flighty. He hadn't wanted Lucinda to worry, hadn't told her how wired Kit was when they parted, going off by herself stubbornly lashing her tail when Joe and Dulcie headed for home. He was thinking that yellow tomcat had set her off when Wilma said, "If she isn't home, maybe she and Dulcie are together, maybe Kit's at my house."

Joe hissed gently at Wilma. *Just let it be*, he thought. Kit might be foolish enough to race after a strange tomcat, but Dulcie wouldn't. And what was the fuss about?

He and Dulcie and Kit roamed the village at all hours; he'd thought their human families had gotten past this unnecessary worry. Tonight, everyone seemed on edge, too quick to react. That was okay for the law, but it was a different matter for the cats' human housemates.

Lucinda said she felt better after talking with Joe, and she ended the call. Hanging up the phone, Wilma gave Joe a hard look. "It doesn't get any easier, worrying about you three." Picking up the phone again, she dialed her own number and waited for the machine to kick in. "If you're home," she said, not mentioning Dulcie's name on the tape, "please pick up. It's important." They didn't use names over the phone, they kept matters as vague as they could, in case they were ever overheard by the wrong party, or someone else played the tape. She was about to hang up when a small female voice said, "I'm here."

"Are you all right?"

"Fine," Dulcie said. "Just finishing up the shrimp casserole, and about to start on the custard. Lovely," she said, purring into the phone in an excess of carelessness.

"I'll be home soon," Wilma told her, and quickly she hung up. "I didn't tell her that Kit wasn't home, she'd go out looking, and . . ."

"I'll go," Joe said, and at Ryan's worried frown, "Go on back to the poker table, before your luck changes."

Ryan reached to stroke him, trying to look unconcerned about Kit. She'd lived with the tomcat only since February, when she and Clyde were married. She'd known the truth about Joe's extraordinary skills only since Christmas, and she still worried about him, she worried about all three of these special cats with their unsettling talents

125

and their foolhardy forays into human affairs. Three little sleuths out on the streets trying to right the wrongs of the world. If she thought too much about their clandestine activities, she was left with a frightened, sinking feeling in her stomach.

Clyde said it took a person with imagination and courage to accept and to live equitably with a speaking cat. He said a rigid, inflexible mind couldn't wrap itself around the concept, that rigid thinking didn't allow for the wonders that might exist in the world like half-seen shadows around them. As Ryan and Wilma returned to the kitchen, Joe raced for the stairs, meaning to hit the roofs to look for Kit—he paused when he heard Max's cell phone emit its rattlesnake buzz. One of the department's computer gurus had, just recently, changed the signal for Max, and the sound still unnerved the tomcat. When Max said, "Garza's on his way," Joe waited, peering into the kitchen, listening.

"Put the additional patrols on the street," Max said, "and call Detective Ray." The chief looked across at Dallas, who had risen and was pulling on his jacket.

"Two restaurants," Max said. "Blue Bistro and the Flying Galleon. They broke out the front window of the Bistro. A pedestrian saw two dark-clad figures running away, saw no moving car."

Dallas nodded, and he and the two uniforms were out the door. Joe heard the Blazer and the squad car peel away and swing a fast turn up at the corner, their tires squealing. Joe was tempted to race out and follow them across the rooftops, but he was more inclined to wait for what might follow—maybe Max would take another call.

Though the odds were long against such prompt discovery of an accompanying invasion, nevertheless Joe waited, as tense as the chief himself.

So far, all seven invasions had followed this diversionary MO. After the first two forced entries, each preceded by downtown break-ins to distract the police, Max's contingency plan had gone into place. Pulling officers from their homes and beds at the first report of a midtown burglary, they hit the residential streets, doubling neighborhood patrol, watching for any suspicious activity, waiting for the report of a break-in. The village might be only a mile square, but the neighborhoods were dense, the streets crooked and narrow among the wooded hills, the cottages close together, and some of them tucked behind others so they were nearly invisible from the street. And in the questionable interest of "atmosphere," as the city council called it, Molena Point had no streetlights. At night, the crowded residential areas were as dark as the inside of a sealed rat hole, inviting all manner of mischief.

The chief paced, tense and irritable, and in the hall, Joe fidgeted, both the chief and the tomcat willing the inevitable invasion call to come through, though the odds were indeed against such a quick cry for help. It took time for these lone women, who were tied up or beaten, to summon assistance. In all the previous cases, their phone lines had been cut or the phones removed. At one house, the detached phones were found buried in the outdoor garbage can. Now, Max was too impatient to stay in the house. He was headed out the door when the snake rattled again. Max picked up, listened.

"On my way," he said. He nodded to Ryan, planted

a kiss on Charlie's forehead, and was gone. Even as his pickup peeled away, Joe vanished up the stairs, leaped to Clyde's desk, from desk to the heavy beam, out his cat door, through his tower, and out its open window, his paws pounding shingles as he followed the sound of Harper's pickup.

19

THIS INVASION WAS as carefully planned as the others, but this one took just the two of them before joining the others to break up a couple of downtown restaurants. This lone woman was elderly and wasn't close with her neighbors, wouldn't have neighbors checking on her. All the hours they'd watched the place, they'd seen no neighborly visiting back and forth. Only one car in her garage, jammed in among boxes and trash, and there was never a second car in the drive, never any visitors. That first rush was the best, when they forced their way inside—when they rang the bell and the dumb broad opened right up to them. That first rush of the attack, slamming the door open in her face hard enough to knock her down. They'd kicked her a couple of times to keep her quiet and then trampled over her into the house.

They cased these places carefully before they went in, always knew if the mark was alone, always a different neighborhood, one poor, the next one well-to-do, it didn't matter, and always a different time of night or day. Not all the marks lived alone, but each was alone at the time they rang the bell. They'd watched this house all afternoon, watched her pull her car out of the garage, one of them pretending to jog the neighborhood while the other parked out of sight. If they were doing this for the money gained by what they walked away with, it would be a washout, they'd be earning pennies an hour. But they were paid in other ways.

When she left, they'd followed her, driving real slow like she did. Big outing for the old girl, seven blocks to the local grocery. Followed her inside, walked the aisles as she did, making sure she wasn't buying more than usual, wasn't in fact expecting guests.

But she'd been shopping for only one: a quarter pound of hamburger, a small head of lettuce, one tomato. Pitiful, a lone woman, timid and careful in her ways—and stupid enough to open the door in the near dark, to a stranger. You had to laugh, people so trusting they'd let anyone in. Didn't they read the papers? What did they think would happen, what did they expect? Standing over the cowering woman, they'd laughed at her and eased the door closed behind them, shutting out any view from the street. Though it didn't matter much, the entrance really couldn't be seen, the way the house was positioned and the door sheltered by those trellises hung heavy with some flowering vine, thick, dark leaves sprawling up the walls—another example of how foolish people were, inviting anyone to stand hidden in the shadows.

The woman was scared silly even before they gagged her, too scared to do more than croak out a whisper. She lay huddled on the wrinkled-up rug, her hands over her bleeding face, terrified they'd kick her again, begging them not to hurt her anymore. They liked that, they were in control. They took turns, one trashing the house, breaking dishes and furniture and little figurines, while the other fondled and teased her until she was white and shaking, terrified they'd rape her.

Of course they never did, Arlie didn't want that complication. Didn't want any shooting or rape, with the DNA evidence. Didn't want the heavier sentence in case something went wrong—not that it would, not with him running things, Arlie was a master of deception.

They never bothered to steal much, only enough to make it look like a burglary. These diversions had nothing to do with selling stolen goods, that wasn't the intent. Arlie paid his people well enough, and he was, as he put it, in it himself for another kind of payback.

More likely, if he told the truth—which Arlie was never famous for—he was in it for what others paid *him*, which might be considerable. He'd never talk about that, he'd just say, "For the payback," and smile in that way that made a person's spine crawl and leave it to your own imagination: the scenario wasn't hard to figure out, though he'd never admit to doing this stuff for hire.

When they'd left this mark there in her trashed house, the way they'd gagged and tied her, it would take her a long time to call for help, would be hours before she could manage to reach the phone. And then when she did, she'd find it dead, the line to the wall cut and useless. There was an extension in the bedroom, but it would take her a while to make it up the stairs and get it plugged back in.

131

That was fine, they didn't want her *not* to call. The whole point was for her frantic call to the cops to be too late, the damage already done, her attackers long gone, the ensuing publicity enough to keep the village on edge until the next invasion.

After they tied her up, they'd touched base with Arlie there on the street and then headed into the center of the village, taking their time, at last joining the others to trash the two restaurants. What a ball, broken glass, broken furniture everywhere. By the time the cops swarmed in they'd been well away from the shattered windows and trashed interiors; they'd watched from some distance, hidden among the shadows as the black-and-whites came scorching in, their sirens screaming, red lights spinning—only then, still laughing, had they gotten the hell out of there. And the cops had no notion that elsewhere in the village, another invasion had come down. That call shouldn't come in for hours, maybe not until morning.

20

Even after the two darkly dressed figures had left, Nannette Garver couldn't cry out for help. The gag in her injured mouth was so tight it sent pain through her whole face and throat. She felt as if she were suffocating. Her jaw hurt so bad where they'd kicked her, she thought it might be broken. She lay on the living room floor, her legs bent double and bound up to her waist with heavy rope, her hands tied behind her. One big upholstered chair was overturned, her two small side chairs broken almost to kindling. Books had been pulled from the shelves, pages torn out in handfuls. The little porcelain figurines that she so loved, the little rabbits and running children, all were broken into jagged shards.

She didn't think she could stand the pain of the gag much longer. But of course she had no choice. The phone lay across the room, where they'd knocked it off the little writing desk. When she tried to roll to it, she was jerked back—was tethered, like a tied-up dog, to the leg of the heavy armoire. She tried gingerly to pull it along with her, afraid it would fall on top of her. But it was too heavy to move at all, with the big old TV inside. She wondered if, with the receiver off the phone, that would alert 911.

But she knew better. She'd taken the receiver off many times when she didn't want to be bothered with phone calls from salesmen or annoying pollsters. If you took the headset off, the canned voice would come on for a while, then the beeping would start, would go on and on until eventually blessed silence fell. Now she didn't bless the promise of silence, but prayed someone *was* at the other end, someone to help her.

She thought if she could get free of the heavy armoire, even with her legs bent double and her hands tied behind her, she could roll or squirm across the room to the phone, thought that even with her hands tied and useless, she could depress the buttons on the fallen phone somehow, maybe with her chin. She couldn't just give up, she had to do something.

The minute the robbers were out of the house, as soon as she'd heard a car pull away, she'd begun to fight the rope that tied her hands, wriggling and pulling, bending her fingers trying to get a grip on the knots. The harsh hemp fibers tore at her skin, she could feel the blood start. She hated the increasing frailty of her body as she grew older.

She'd be eternally thankful they hadn't raped her. Because of disease, because of injuries, mostly because of the emotional distress, the terrible shame that would never go away. At seventy-two, a widow for ten years, she was sure the distress of such brutality would have been worse than if they killed her.

She wondered why there *had* been no rapes in these invasions. She'd followed the news on TV and in the paper, but she never thought it would happen to her. Only now did she see how stupid that was. She wondered if these people were afraid of the prosecution involved with rape. This county attorney was known for getting maximum sentences when it came to sex offenders; he had been criticized more than once for what some called his one-sided view of the law. And didn't that make a person laugh.

But if these men were so afraid of the law, and, according to the news, they stole no more than a few items, mostly electronics that could be easily sold, why did they bother at all? What was this about, these forced break-ins, this terrifying emotional harassment?

It seemed hours passed as she worked at the knots, her fingers raw and bleeding from the rough hemp rope, blood making the knots so slick that she nearly gave up. But at last, when she was about at the end of her strength, her hands and arms shaking with fatigue, the knot she was working on loosened a little. It was so slippery. She mustn't lose the feel of just where to pull, to untie it all the way. It seemed to take forever, but at last she worked the knot loose, felt the rope ease enough so she could slide her right hand free. Her left hand was bound separately, tied to the rope that went around her waist and legs.

With the one free hand she pulled herself up enough to work loose the rope around the leg of the armoire, tearing two nails to the quick. When the rope fell away, when she was free of the armoire, she rolled painfully to the center of the room. Her own weight on her doubled-up legs, as she rolled over on them, was excruciating.

Pausing to rest, she tried again to remove the gag, pulling and jerking at it. The blood from her hand at last turned it slick enough that she was able to slide it down around her chin, down until it circled her neck. Everything was bloody—her face, her clothes, the carpet were all smeared with blood.

She rested again, then tried once more to free her hand, which had gone to sleep beneath the tight rope that bound her waist and legs. She fought the knots until she was convinced she couldn't loosen them. She looked toward the phone again, and again began to squirm across the carpet, heavy and clumsy and hurting, with her legs and one arm bound. She had gone only a little way, to the edge of the flowered easy chair, when she realized she was whimpering like a hurt puppy, a pitiful, begging sound.

Silencing herself, she wriggled like an injured beast toward the fallen phone, toward the one item in the room that could liberate her, toward her one contact with the world beyond her own walls.

It seemed to take another eternity before she reached the phone. She felt weak and confused. Could feel the double beating of her heart that sometimes happened when she was under stress. Hunching forward, she pressed her face against the fallen headset.

Of course it was dead, having been off the hook for so long. With her bleeding hand she depressed the button, waited with her face to the phone for the dial tone to resume. She waited a long time. When the phone remained silent, she pressed the button again, held it longer this time. Then again, her ear to the fallen phone, listening.

No dial tone, no sound. No little canned voice telling her to hang up and try again. Just a hollow emptiness as vast as eternal space. After a third try she pulled the cord toward her. Watched it snake away from the wall, the cut line slithering to her, the cut wires sharp and useless against her fingers.

The only other phone was upstairs. Bound as she was, she didn't think she could make it up the steps. And had they cut that line, too? Cut both phone lines, intending to lead her on uselessly? Imagining herself hunching and crawling up the stairs only to find that phone dead, too, she lay down with her face against the carpet, tears spurting uncontrollably. She felt destroyed, beaten, beyond trying to think what to do.

All her windows were closed against the chill evening and because, how ironic, she was wary about break-ins. Praying that some neighbor was home and would hear her despite those glass barriers, she tried to shout. She was very hoarse, her voice so weak she didn't think anyone would hear. She wondered if young Bobby West might have his window open upstairs despite his mother's complaints. Beverly said he'd have the house freezing all the time if she didn't make him close that window. Expecting no response, still she tried. Even the effort of shouting hurt so badly, and exhausted her.

Death from thirst and starvation seemed impossible, right here in the little village among the closely crowded cottages, with neighbors all around. She had no relatives living close who might call or come by, wanting to check on her. How long might it be until one of her casual friends tried to reach her, tried so many times they grew impatient and reported her number out of order? And would the phone company actually come out to take a look? Despite her friends' admonitions to get a cell phone, she had never wanted one. Until now.

When her strength returned a little, she thought about the cut phone line, and she hunched toward the wall until she found the other cut end. With one hand, she managed to hold the two cut ends together, hoping they might connect and allow a signal to come through. But she was too clumsy, the wires wouldn't join just right. The blood was so slick, everything slippery and her fingers so stiff, too. Twice she thought she had the wires joined right, but when she bent her face to the handset there was no sound, the phone remained dead. At last, so weak she couldn't think straight, she lay limp on the carpet, defeated, wondering if she would die there—and wondering, inanely, if she could ever get the blood out of the Persian carpet.

21

M**AX'S** **PICKUP** **MOVED** so fast that Joe
Grey lost it only a block from home. He
raced on across the night-dark roofs stubbornly following its sound as it sped south.
He could see, away in the center of the village, a gathering of bright lights and whirl-
ing red lights reflected against the sky and
could hear the distant mutter of police radios—that would
be the restaurant break-ins, but Max wasn't headed there.

The sound of the pickup grew fainter, still bearing
south. Joe had traveled a dozen blocks when, far ahead,
the truck's soft rumble died, faded into silence. Racing on
over slick roof tiles and mossy shingles, and across shadowed tree branches above dark and tangled gardens, he listened for the truck door to open. He heard nothing, only
the hushing of the sea, five blocks away. Ahead against the
night sky rose the spire of the Methodist Church, thrust-
ing above the black silhouettes of surrounding houses.

Leaping from a pine tree onto the church roof, he raced up its highest peak. Had he lost Harper?

Through the trees below him, no car lights reflected, the neighborhood was uniformly dark. At this height, the sea wind hit him full in the face; the balmy evening had grown chill, the shingles cold beneath his paws. In this residential area, even at this early hour, most of the houses were dark, as if the more elderly occupants were already tucked in for the night, while maybe the younger ones were out partying. He was cursing himself for having lost Harper when the scream of a siren blasted nearly below him, flashing red lights stained the sky and an emergency van raced past—he took off after it as if the devil himself were on his tail.

Ahead, the siren whooped and died as the white emergency van swerved into a driveway—and there was Max Harper's pickup, parked and waiting. The van nearly grazed a police unit that was pulling in. Another patrol car drew up across the street from them, in front of the church just beneath where Joe crouched, his claws in the shingles trying not to slide down its steeply angled peak.

The house was a small, two-story Craftsman-style cottage, its wood siding painted off white with a soft blue trim, its front door set deep beneath a sheltering roof and flanked by climbing vines. The front garden was excessively neat, the small, manicured lawn edged with borders of bright impatiens. Joe came down from the peak of the church to its lower roof, pausing with his paws in the metal gutter, watching the emergency unit as its side doors opened and three medics piled out, heading for the shadowed front door. Max pulled shards of jagged glass out of the broken front door, reached through and released the lock. Pushing the door open, he eased through, gun drawn, and soon disappeared inside, where Joe could hear a faint cry. Behind Max, two officers entered, their weapons drawn; the three medics waited for them to clear the house.

A light came on from deep within; Joe heard Max's voice and a woman's faint, hoarse reply. As the EMTs hauled out their emergency medical equipment, Joe watched the street and the dark yards. He saw no movement, no one hidden among the neighborhood's overgrown bushes, no one slipping away. Surely by now the perps were long gone. When the medics moved on inside, Joe dropped onto the roof of their van. There he waited until wiry Officer Reynolds, who stood by the front door, glanced the other way. Quickly Joe dropped to the driveway, slipped into the bushes and inside the house, melting into the shadows beneath a broken end table. He wanted, before the officers' various personal scents compromised the scene, to try to pick up the invader's trail, maybe even find the unlikely scent of old fish that had so intrigued Kit.

The first smell that hit him was a nose-tingling stink of perfume that sure didn't belong to any of the officers present. The second scent was indeed a whiff of aging fish so strong that it prompted an uncomfortable gag reflex. Cats were not dogs, dogs reveled in such stinks. One thing was certain: the two smells together could hide any fainter, personal aroma the perps might have left.

Across the living room, the victim sat on the bloody Persian carpet, speaking in a scratchy, nearly inaudible voice to Harper and the two medics who were crouched beside her. She was as thin and frail as a hungry bird, white-haired, thin-boned, dressed in a peach-toned velvet lounge suit stained liberally with blood. Her birdlike hands were torn and bloody, one side of her thin face swollen, bruised and bleeding. The other officers had disappeared. Slipping out from under the remains of the little table, Joe slid in between an upholstered chair and a broken ottoman, where he could better watch the action.

The pretty, flowered living room was a shambles, side chairs and small tables overturned and broken, the flowered couch and matching chair slashed so deeply that the stuffing spilled out like dirty snow. Books, torn-out pages, and pieces of china littered the bloody carpet, the whole room had been destroyed as if with a pointless and cruel pleasure. Max looked disgusted and grim, as did the two medics, but it was Joe's own reaction that was most worrisome to the tomcat.

He felt terrible for the poor woman. He wanted to pat her poor torn face with a soft paw, wanted to lick her hurt hands, tell her how sorry he was, he wanted to make everything all right again, for her. This wasn't like him, this degree of sympathy was not his style, he thought uneasily. Was he growing soft? Maybe it was the holiday season turning him sentimental, all this Christmas cheer and goodwill muddying his usual detachment, he thought with dismay.

*　*　*

BUT **J**OE **G**REY wasn't the only cat to feel sympathy for the suffering woman, he was not the only cat on the scene. From the roof of the invaded house, tortoiseshell Kit peered over, her black and brown coat blending into the night. She had arrived long before Max Harper's truck pulled to the curb and the emergency van and police cars came racing. It was Kit who first heard the woman's pitiful cries. Though she hadn't been able to get inside, after considerable effort she'd found a phone, had made the call to 911, had seen the law arrive: Harper, the medics, the squad cars. Only when she saw Joe Grey come streaking across the roofs did she slip behind the chimney, not wanting Joe to see her, feeling suddenly too embarrassed by her own preoccupation, inexplicably shy and uncertain.

What a strange night it had been, she was all sparks and fidgets. First that peculiar Colletto family with their prissy habits and their sleazy son, the rude way Kent treated his parents that had left her so angry. Then when the cats left the Colletto house, Joe and Dulcie heading home, Kit caught the lingering scent of the yellow tomcat and she'd hung back. Studying the surrounding roofs, she didn't see him but she knew he was nearby. Then suddenly there he was, a pale shape padding along a branch above the Collettos' garage, looking straight down at her.

He had looked for a long moment, and then had moved away across the oak limb, but glancing back, wanting her to follow. Putting aside her unease, Kit had followed. She'd reminded herself that he was a very big tomcat, that she was alone, that she'd never really seen him clearly, that she didn't have Joe and Dulcie to fight beside her if he turned aggressive. But so far he hadn't bothered them, he'd only watched as if he were curious. And she *was* a strong fighter, she'd thought boldly. She'd followed him because her dreams of a handsome soul mate wouldn't let her do otherwise, because he might be the one mate in all the world she'd waited for and dreamed about. She'd followed through the treetops and across the roofs into the center of the village. There he slowed.

Where the shop roofs crowded close, he'd stayed to the deepest shadows, stopping every little while to look down at the streets and then to look back at her, and there was an urgency in his journey. His route took him across Ocean where the wide street narrowed, to the south part of the village near the steeple of the Methodist Church. Just before he reached it he paused. She heard from below a man's chuckle and a low laugh that seemed to have no gender, that could have come from a man or a woman, she couldn't be sure.

The tomcat backed away into the dark beneath a second-floor balcony, where he could see below and could listen. Kit felt that he wanted her to do the same, though who would care if there was a cat watching? The laughter came not from the small pickup parked on the street before the church, but from a dark sedan that had drawn to the curb behind it, a big four-door vehicle as sleek and daunting as a limousine. A figure stood beside it talking with the driver, their laughter quiet but with overtones that made her fur crawl. As she watched, a third figure got out of the pickup and joined them, slipping into the passenger seat of the sedan, and an elusive whiff of their scents drifted up. Their laughter and voices were as hushed and slithery as a wind stirring beach sand.

The pickup parked in front was old, its dark color undetectable in the night. It appeared badly dented, as beat up as the one that had nearly run down Maudie, and Kit wanted a closer look. She was sniffing for the humans' scents when one of the men said softly, "She can't untie herself, hell, she might never be found." Kit pricked her ears, startled.

"That won't do us any good," the driver of the car said with disgust. Listening, Kit leaned farther. "She can last until tomorrow, can't she? How bad did you hurt her? You remember what I told you!" The man's voice, as low-pitched as it was, seemed somehow familiar. Kit stood with her paws in the damp gutter peering over, trying to get a look at him.

"Of course I remember," the other whispered crossly. "We just roughed her up, is all."

Straining to listen, Kit nearly lost her balance. She backed away, alarmed, still trying to identify the man's cold, superior tones that struck such fear into her heart.

"She'll last," the other said, "so what difference does it make?"

"You want murder on the ticket?" the familiar voice said. "Why do you think we don't rape and kill them! You want to go before a hanging judge? One of you keep watch. If no one finds her by late tomorrow, call the cops yourself—you're an unidentified neighbor—and make sure you use the throwaway phone."

"What do you think? We're stupid?" The tall, thin

man sounded young, though he spoke only in a grainy whisper. Why did he keep looking around into the night, fidgeting and shifting as if he thought they were being watched? That made the tortoiseshell smile. He didn't know half how closely they were observed, who the observer was, or what she'd do with the information.

"The paper has a front-page piece ready to go," the other said, "written, ready to insert, a nice two columns for the villagers to read over breakfast." Still, Kit could see nothing of the figure inside the dark car. She looked away to the blackness where the pale tomcat crouched. Did he know these lowlifes? What exactly was his interest, and why had he led her there? She could just make out the curve of his pale back beneath the balcony's rail.

The moment the pickup left, the tomcat came out from the shadows into a path of moonlight, stood looking after the vehicle. Now, for the first time with the moonlight full on him, Kit got a good look at him.

Oh, my. The surprise that she felt—and the disappointment—rippled through her clear down to her dark little paws.

22

ONE LOOK AT the yellow tomcat and all Kit's grand dreams slid away, crumbled like the walls of a ruined castle; she was as shocked as if the fairy-tale prince had turned into a toad. This was not the fine young tom she'd dreamed of, this was not the mate she'd waited for, whom she'd thought had finally found her. This cat was incredibly old.

She could see that he had once been powerful, even now his bony shoulders were broad beneath his ragged yellow fur. But his tail was thin in the way of an old cat, his muzzle was extended with age, his skin hung slack. Now he was frail and ancient, more in need of tender kindness than a wild romp over the green hills. Now for the first time, with the sea wind blowing in her face, she caught his scent clearly enough to realize it was the *scent* of an old cat, very different from a strapping young tom. And as Kit's heart made the painful adjustment, her eager longing turned away from romantic dreams and she was filled with a shaky sense of desperation at the terrible frailty of old age.

But the tomcat's yellow eyes were clear and intelligent, and when he turned away, following the black sedan, breaking into a gallop, he was surprisingly fast for someone his age. Not lithe or agile, but he kept up with the car and pickup for several blocks before they left him, vanishing down the hill. His interest in this human drama intrigued her. Why did he care? Who was he? Where he had come from, and what had brought him here?

Now that she was aware of his venerable age, she could imagine no aura of evil about him. He was not like the black tom, Azrael, who had once come on to her, rude and bold and demanding, who had helped his drunken human companion rob the village shops.

She'd wanted to follow him, but somewhere nearby an invasion had occurred, and her urgency to find the house, find the victim, and to know how badly those men had hurt her was stronger.

The house had to be nearby, if those men had just come from there. She had studied the dark yards below, willing herself to hear any faintest cry. She'd heard nothing but the distant surf and the sea wind fingering through the treetops. She'd wandered the roofs looking and listening but had heard nothing until the wind slackened, and then she heard a woman's faint, thin cry, a plaintive voice that sent Kit bolting across the shingles and across the gaps between roofs to where an olive tree hugged a modest frame house. When the cry came again she dropped down through the branches and slipped along through the yard through the soft crowns of coral bell bushes. Again the cry, and Kit had looked for a way in, maybe a window open to the cool evening or the front door jimmied. The tomcat had disappeared.

The front door was locked. The high little decorative glass window was broken, but the glass shards stuck up like giant shark's teeth, ready to cut a little cat in two. At the spot along the wall where the cry came loudest, she caught the scent of blood, a metallic whiff seeping even through the wood siding that sent her leaping up at the nearest closed window. Clinging to the sill, pulling and clawing at the casing with one small armored paw, she fought to slide the glass back. When that failed, she tried the other windows, she'd tried all the way around the house, when she heard sirens. Were they coming here? Had someone seen the invasion and called the dispatcher?

But then she heard their wail fade to silence off in the center of the village. That would be the diversionary burglary to distract the cops. Two crimes, committed within minutes of each other. But, she thought, smiling, this time there would be no long delay before the invasion was discovered—provided she could find a phone and alert the department; and off she went, circling the neighbors' houses looking for an unlocked window, peering up, leaping up at closed windows until, doubling back to the invaded house, she heard snores softly from above, from the house next door. She peered up to the second floor, then scrambled up a ragged rosebush, sticking her paw with a thorn.

Yes, an open window, and within, a man's soft snores. Heart thudding, she clawed through the screen with a dry, ripping sound. When the snores faltered, she waited until they steadied again, then pawed the screen out of the way so it wouldn't catch in her fur, and quickly slipped inside.

She'd stood picking out the black shapes of dresser, desk, easy chair. She padded past the bed, watching warily the stout young man who sprawled asleep, the covers thrown back, the cool breeze blowing in on his bare skin. Rearing up to look atop the nightstand, she'd found no phone. She leaped atop the desk, then the dresser. Nothing. Maybe he used a cell phone, though none was in sight. Slipping out the open bedroom door and down the hall, she'd found two unoccupied bedrooms, their doors standing open. She prowled within, her breath coming quick with the need to hurry. Neither room had a phone. The door of the next bedroom was closed. When she sniffed at the crack beneath, she could taste the heavy smell of sleeping humans. Hurrying past, to the end of the hall, she found, tucked beside the descending stairs, a small home office.

Slipping inside, she leaped to the desk, nearly on top of the phone. She hit the speaker button, then scrambled to soften the sound of the dial tone which came in way too loud. When she pawed in 911, June Alpine answered, her young voice high and light, but steady. Kit kept her own voice to a whisper, terrified she'd wake someone in the next room. If the householders heard her and came searching for a prowler, they might be armed. As rigid as the California gun laws were, there was no law against arming oneself at home—with the laughable provision that the gun must be kept unloaded and locked away, separate from the locked-up ammunition. Which, if she heard anyone rise in alarm, would give her plenty of time to escape down the hall, through the far bedroom past the young sleeper, and out the torn screen before they had time to load a weapon and come searching.

She reported the injured woman to June, and gave her street directions. Molena Point cottages had no house numbers. Hitting the speaker button again to break the connection, she padded soundlessly back through the house and across the roofs to the invaded house, where she hid herself at the base of the chimney in the blackest shadows. As she waited for the patrol cars she'd summoned, the words of the invaders echoed in her head . . . *can't untie herself . . . How bad did you hurt her?* She thought about the smooth-talking man who sounded so familiar and so cold, and she hoped the poor woman would be all right. That man was someone from the past, she thought, her ears back and her tail switching. But she couldn't think who, she couldn't give him a name or think when or where she'd seen him, only that he frightened her.

23

Pulled from sound sleep, Dulcie sat straight up on the desk and peered out the front window where sirens cut through the night, echoing from the center of the village. She'd been so deeply asleep, waiting for Wilma to get home from playing poker at the Damens', had fallen asleep after she answered Wilma's phone call. Another blast ripped the night, whooping then dying, and she imagined squad cars gathered around another violent and destructive store break-in.

If that *was* where the cops were gathered, would another kind of crime have occurred as well, blocks away, and in silence? If the pattern ran true to form, there would be no 911 call for help. That victim, unable to reach a phone or cry out, would suffer alone, perhaps for how many hours before someone found her and an alarm went out. Springing off the desk, she fled for her cat door.

Despite the squad cars converged in the center of the

village, she knew that doubled patrols would be searching the dark streets, watching for another, silent crime, shining their spotlights among the cottages and into dark gardens, looking for a running figure. Darkly clad officers would be walking the streets hoping to locate a victim who was unable to alert them, too injured to cry out and be heard. At times like this, Dulcie thought, the village seemed too big, too impersonal and dark; no way one small cat could hope to find a lone victim—but she could try. Scrambling up to the roofs, she raced for the middle of town first, guided by the burst of exploding lights.

The street was filled with cop cars. Across from the roof where she paused, the plate-glass windows of the Blue Bistro Café had been broken out, and two cops were busy stringing crime tape, a bright yellow ribbon above the sidewalk and back between the buildings. Beyond the broken glass, she could see inside where Dallas Garza was taking pictures, photographing broken tables and chairs, the damaged front counter and smashed wine bottles. The smell of spilled wine was so sharp it made her nose twitch. She could see another convergence of lights several blocks away, reflected against the sky—a second break-in. She watched the action for some time, saw Arnold Pence, the restaurant owner, skid his gray VW in among the police cars, pile out and run to the restaurant, his bedroom slippers crunching on broken glass, his heavy leather jacket flapping open over his striped pajamas. As the thin, gray-haired man argued with a young officer, demanding to be allowed inside, Dulcie reared up, looking away over the rooftops to the dark, residential parts of the village. How could anyone find the other, silent crime that was sure to have happened somewhere among the dark houses? She was pacing uncertainly when, over the tangle of police radios and men's voices, came the wail of more sirens, distant sirens somewhere to the south. *Had* a victim called in?

She stood a moment, pinpointing the location, then fled toward Ocean Avenue, coming down only to streak across the two northbound lanes, across the grassy median and then the southbound lanes, and up to the roofs again, guided by her fix on the dying wails. She ran until lights shone ahead reflecting up through the trees, leading her on as surely as an airport beam must summon a lone pilot. Galloping up the last peak, she leaped to the roof of a house stage-lit by the headlamps of squad cars and Harper's truck and an EMT van. Running along the edge of the roof, staring down at them, she nearly plowed into Kit.

"The sirens woke you?" Kit whispered, amused by Dulcie's startled squeak.

"I was waiting for Wilma. They hit a restaurant in the village, maybe two. Cops all over, Dallas is at the scene." She frowned at Kit. "*You* called the dispatcher? How did you know?"

"I was following someone," Kit said shyly.

Dulcie pricked her ears, but said no more. Crouching shoulder to shoulder, they watched two medics emerge from the house carrying a stretcher. The woman beneath the blanket was so frail she hardly made a lump. Her face was bruised and swollen, and caked with blood; even from the roof, they could smell its metallic bitterness. The two white-coated medics eased her into the ambulance, got in behind her and pulled the doors closed. The third

154

member of the team slipped behind the wheel and the van pulled away. As it headed for Molena Point Hospital, another squad car pulled to the curb, and Detective Kathleen Ray got out.

The tall, slim young woman was dressed in navy sweats, her long dark hair rumpled as if she'd just rolled out of bed, pulled on her clothes, and taken off. Stepping to the trunk of the black-and-white, she fetched a brown leather satchel that the cats knew contained evidence bags, some small tools, cameras, and fingerprint equipment. She turned as Max came out the front door, they spoke in low voices, then Max stepped into his truck. As he pulled away, a gray shadow slipped out of the house behind Kathleen and disappeared into the bushes. Not until Kathleen went inside did the leaves of a pittosporum rattle and part. Joe looked up at them and clawed his way up a spindly pine tree to the roof, giving Dulcie a warm nudge.

"The woman lives alone," he said. "Nannette Garver. They beat her up pretty bad. She doesn't know who called it in, her phone is dead, they cut the cord." He looked at Kit. "Did you call the station? From where? How did you know?"

"From the house next door," Kit said. "I found a window open, but before that, I saw them, I saw the men, and maybe a woman, I'm not sure. I heard them talking, I think I recognized one man's voice, and one was driving the same pickup that nearly hit Maudie. There were three darkly dressed men, a black car like a limo. It was the driver who sounded familiar and . . ."

"Slow down, Kit!" they both said.

She tried to go slower. But only at the very last did

she tell them about the yellow tomcat and how he had led her there. "As if he knew there'd be an invasion," she said. "*How* did he know? Oh my, he's like us, but he's very old, so old he's white around the muzzle but when those men left he followed them, chased the black car and all three were wearing stockings over their faces and— "

"Kit!" Dulcie mewed.

"Slow down," Joe snapped.

Kit stopped for breath, staring at the two of them. "Could the thin one have been Kent Colletto? The one who drove the truck? Kent looked so superior at dinner when they talked about the invasions. Could he have left the house after we did, after we looked in the garage? It was so dark I couldn't see his face."

"Kent has a juvenile record," Joe said. "He . . ." He stopped speaking, lifted his head, sniffing the shifting breeze and then scanning the rooftops. Catching the tomcat's lingering scent, he rose and trotted across the shingles, pausing where the scent clung heavily among overhanging leaves, where the tom must have lingered, watching them and listening.

For a moment, Joe paused at the edge of the roof looking down at the officers below, but then he moved on. He supposed they had about all the information they'd get until Kathleen's report lay on Max's desk tomorrow morning and he could read it at his leisure. And off he went, following the tomcat, wanting to know how this newcomer fit into the action. Was he a friend, or was he part of the problem?

He followed the scent to the next roof and the next,

Dulcie and Kit running beside him through the rising sea breeze. Where the trail descended to cross Ocean, they came down, too. For an old cat, he was making good time—heading straight for the center of the village where the sky glowed with the red reflections of police activity. Only as they approached the scene, their noses tickling at the smell of spilled wine, did they lose his trail.

Kit circled the roofs for a while but couldn't pick it up again. Joe and Dulcie crouched at the roof's edge watching the action around the Blue Bistro, the sidewalk beneath them glittering with shards of broken glass. This restaurant had been a fixture in the village long before the cats were born; favored by village residents, it featured locally grown produce, local wines, locally raised lamb. The dining room's oversize fireplace, and the many photographs of famous village residents, offered a cozy aura in which one might happen on a movie star, a famous musician or sports figure. Now, not only had the big front windows been shattered, the portraits had been jerked from the walls and lay smashed on the floor, the frames bent, the glass broken, the pictures ground into the debris. Dallas Garza was lifting fingerprints from the shattered front counter where a smiling hostess should have been welcoming diners. Even the swinging kitchen doors had been ripped off their hinges, and the kitchen beyond torn apart, huge cook pots littering the floor, the counters pulled from the wall and smashed. It was hard to imagine three or four men doing this amount of damage in a short time, but maybe there were more than that. Joe guessed if a person put his mind to it, he could accomplish a lot of destruction pretty fast. Was all this, indeed, simply to divert patrols from the invasion and make the cops look bad? That, coupled with the pleasure of violence just for the hell of it? He'd be willing to bet the officers would find very little missing, maybe the cash box gone and the safe breached—all this to destroy confidence in the police and in Max Harper.

24

BEFORE LEAVING **N**ANNETTE Garver's house, Max had gone through her personal phone list and called her daughter in Sacramento and her son, who lived in Orange County. They both said they'd be there by the next morning, the son arriving as soon as he could get on a plane. Max had called the hospital shortly after Nannette was checked into the ICU. She was suffering severe contusions to her throat and face, but no bones were broken. Her hands and arms were scraped raw; she was shaken, and descended easily into tears. Max had left Kathleen Ray photographing and lifting prints, and taking casts of several shoeprints in the garden beside the front door. An inventory of items missing would have to wait until Nannette was released from the hospital, but he doubted it would amount to much. Neither of the two televisions had been taken, but both were smashed beyond repair. It enraged Max that innocent people were suffering because someone wanted him removed from office. The MO of these attacks, coupled with the newspaper's pressure, could lead to no other conclusion.

He never doubted he'd done a good job over his twenty-five years of service. Molena Point's crime rate was down by thirty percent just in the last four years, while in the surrounding towns, as in much of the country, crime rates had risen as the breakdown in moral restraints increased. Appointed by the mayor, with a two-thirds vote approval by the city council, Max could be removed by the same process. If that was to be the result of this concerted attempt, he would be laying the village open to a new chief he couldn't trust, no doubt backed by the same element that wanted Max out. This was a power grab, and if he could help it, it wasn't going to happen.

He and Dallas had discussed bringing in an FBI profiler. So far, their own take was that the vandals were young, but were working under more experienced direction. The mastermind was very possibly someone their department had arrested with enough evidence to see him prosecuted. Officer Ray had set up a computer program listing all the convictions in their district for the past ten years, with release dates for those who were now out of prison. With access to personal information and fingerprints, they had nine possible suspects so far who had lived in the area or had friends or family here. Two were on probation, four on parole, three out without any restrictions. None was now living close enough to be operating conveniently in the village, but with county probation caseloads so high and its officers spread so thin, cases could slip through the cracks. The man they were looking for might easily be driving down from San Francisco, where three of the parolees were living, or from San Jose, where a fourth resided. Between a parole officer's visits, a parolee would have plenty of time for short and unauthorized forays outside the jurisdiction. This, Max thought, was one situation where he really appreciated the belated help from one of the phantom snitches; the 911 call this evening was the first unidentified tip they'd had. Dispatcher said it was the lady, this time. Despite how edgy the anonymous phone calls left him, he felt remarkably encouraged. This call tonight had put them on the scene hours before Ms. Garver could have summoned help; in fact it might have saved her life. The older woman, weakened from shock and loss of blood, might never have been heard by her neighbors, she might have died in that house alone. How the snitch had found her, had heard her, was a matter he didn't want to pursue.

As for the two restaurant break-ins, they followed the same pattern of extensive vandalism as the others. Dallas had left the Blue Bistro to work the Flying Galleon call, and it was the same MO over there. Lots of damage, nothing much missing, cash still in the cash box at the Galleon. Shoe prints that matched none of the others. What did these guys do, change shoes for every job? He'd had a man checking the Dumpsters for weeks, thinking they might be tossing the shoes after each use. And again no fingerprints. But thanks to the snitch they now had a description of a car and a truck that had fled the invasion scene shortly before the 911 call was made—but no license numbers. Snitch said the plates were smeared with mud. They had Be On the Lookout alerts out on both vehicles. A black four-door Cadillac had been spotted, but it belonged to a new bartender up on Fifth, had been parked in front of the bar, and there was a whole restaurant full of witnesses to vouch for his presence.

Swinging by the Flying Galleon, he found Dallas had finished photographing and dusting for prints, and was trying to rouse a carpenter to board up the windows. He still had to go over the area for trace evidence, but it would take a carpenter a while to show up. "Joe Wood's out of town," Dallas said. "Ditto, Jim Herndon. He and his wife are in Tahoe. I got the restaurant's head chef on the phone, he's over there talking to Brennan. I've called three other carpenters, with no answer. I'm just going to try Ryan, see if she has any plywood. What about the Blue Bistro?"

"Jimmie Chu is on his way," Max said. "He's sending his sons over with plywood, said he didn't need our help. He's mad as hell, says we're not doing our job. I'll swing back by there and talk to them."

He had stepped into his truck and started the engine when a white BMW convertible pulled up, double-parking beside a patrol car. Reporter Nancyanne Prewitt got out carrying a camcorder, which was all the small village paper could supply, no in-your-face camera crew to back her up. Maybe no one had called the local TV station up the coast. Or maybe they were on their way. She was dressed as if for a party in a tight, low-cut black T-shirt, voluminous gold pants, and spike-heeled gold sandals. Talk about professional. Her shoulder-length, square-cut brown hair swung in time with her dangling, gold hoop earrings. Her high heels tap-tapped across the sidewalk, and a little gold purse swung from her shoulder on a long chain as she hurried up to his truck. "Captain Harper, can I have a word?" Her smile was as fake as that of a two-bit public defender sucking up to the judge. When Max didn't respond, she said, "Can you tell me why you had no patrol cars on the streets when these two restaurants were broken into and vandalized?"

Max just looked at her.

"I'll want to photograph both restaurants," she said. "Why weren't there patrols on the street?"

There had in fact been patrols, three of them, the closest five blocks away. They had hit the Flying Galleon moments after the alarm went off, had called in four more cars to cover the area, but the vandals had vanished. No sign of a fleeing car, and no one on the street but a couple of tourists whose IDs had checked out all right. Both said there had been no moving car in the area, that they'd glimpsed two men running away, no description except that they wore black clothes, black caps. Four officers were, at present, canvassing the hotel and motels.

"This is the middle of town, Captain Harper. Why didn't your officers see and arrest these people? They couldn't have missed them. It seems strange that there is never a patrol when one of these shocking—"

Max opened the truck door, gently forcing her hand off the window, and obliging her to step back. "You have my permission to take pictures, Ms. Prewitt. You are not to enter either crime scene. You'll be able to identify the area that's off limits by the yellow police tape that is strung to cordon it off. Now if you'll excuse me . . ." He revved the engine so that she stepped farther back, bristling at his sarcasm. At the intersection he glanced back.

She was mincing along the sidewalk with her camcorder, busily recording the broken windows and broken door. Not only would stills be used for the newspaper, the camcorder footage would be on local TV—maybe for the late news tonight and probably prime-time news tomorrow. So far the TV station, which was short-staffed, had been far more eager to enjoy contributions from the *Gazette* than to cover the crimes themselves. Or to see that they gave the department fair coverage. Heading for the Blue Bistro, Max didn't see, above him, the three snitches watching from the rooftops, nor did he see another small shadow slip stiffly away—didn't see the three snitches turn, catching sight of the yellow tomcat, and hurry to follow him as he left the scene.

25

THE YELLOW TOMCAT seemed to know where he was going, moving swiftly away across the roofs above a street of galleries, little restaurants, a bookstore. At the Kestrel Inn, he headed along one wing of the U-shaped building toward the back, where he stood looking down into the motel patio. The courtyard was lit by ground-level lamps at the edge of the brick paving, their soft glow illuminating beds of geraniums and cyclamens. Where a bougainvillea vine climbed to the roof, he scrambled down it and under a flowering camellia bush beside a sliding glass door. From the shingles above, Joe, Dulcie, and Kit could just make out the pale curve of his back beneath the dark, concealing leaves. He peered in through the open glass slider through open draperies, only the screen barring his entry.

One lamp burned near the windows, where a man stood with his back to them. The rear of the room was in shadow. They could hear a woman talking softly but couldn't see her, couldn't make out what she was saying. Was the cat with these people, traveling with them? Then surely they knew his talents. No one traveling with an ordinary cat would let him go outside in a strange town and expect him not to wander off lured by his own curiosity and become lost. Only a speaking cat could be left to roam responsibly, at his own pleasure.

Deep within the room the woman appeared, moving toward the front where she sat down on the bed. She was tall and thin, her short blond hair fluffed around her face. She wore shapeless black jeans, a black T-shirt, black boots. Their voices were so soft that from the roof, even with the door open, the cats had to listen closely, cocking their ears, peering over. As the man turned to the dresser, a towel in his hand, they could see that he wore gloves, tightly fitting and flesh colored. Picking up a billfold from the dresser, he slipped it in his pocket and then carefully polished the dresser's glass top with the towel.

"That went well," he said. "No delays, no hitches." His voice was so smug it made Dulcie and Kit angrily lash their tails; Kit hung over the edge, intently watching him.

"This is the last one," the woman said. "I don't like this. This isn't why I came here."

"It's them," Kit whispered, scrambling back from the edge. "Two of them. The man in the car, that's his voice. And the woman—I thought she was a thin man, in that long black coat and hard shoes."

The man was saying, "What about the kid? He thinks you're—"

"That's all he is. A kid. He's had a crush on me for

years, ever since he was twelve. He thinks he's a great lover," she said, laughing. "For the moment, he's useful enough."

The man was squarely built. His coal-black hair was collar length but neatly trimmed, his short black beard squarely clipped. Turning away from the dresser, he gripped her shoulders. "If you didn't come to help me out, why did you come? Why did you want to come here, right under her nose? What the hell are you planning?"

"I came to get what's mine," she said sweetly. "And," she said, laughing, "maybe to deal the last hand." Moving away from him, she picked up the black raincoat that lay across the chair, shrugged it on. Pulling a dark cap from the pocket, she occupied herself at the mirror, tucking in her hair until not one blond strand was visible. The man approached the door, slid the screen back. Stepping out to the patio, he stood looking around him. He was only steps from the yellow cat concealed among the shrubs. He glanced up once at the roof, seemingly straight at the cats, but they were still, and their eyes slitted nearly closed—surely, in the dark, they were invisible to human sight. His gaze was compelling, his eyes so familiar that Dulcie eased lower against the shingles and slowly backed away. He glanced several times to the left, to a walkway between the rooms that led from the patio to a small parking area. The cats could see a few cars parked back there, one covered with a tarp. After a long while he turned back into the room. Sliding the glass door closed and clicking the lock, he disappeared into the shadows at the back.

The woman moved to join him, switched on a closet light, and removed a small satchel. When he opened the door to the hall, in the sudden wash of light the cats caught a glimpse of a patterned red carpet and of the closed door across the hall. And then the two were gone, closing the door behind them with a double click of the latch and lock. When the cats looked down again at the bushes there was no hint of the yellow tom, no gleam of pale fur beneath the dark foliage.

Was he slinking through the bushes to the motel's front door, meaning to follow the couple? Or, while the man had stood outside the open screen, had the tom slipped inside and behind a chair, moving so fast that even they, intently watching the bearded man, had missed his stealthy entry?

"Come on," Joe said, spinning around to follow the darkly clad couple—but Kit was already across the roof and nearly to the street. They crowded against her where she crouched above the front entrance looking down. The pair was just leaving the building. The woman was as tall as her companion; she walked with a long stride so that, swathed in her loose black raincoat, shapeless black pants, and flat black boots, her hair tucked under the genderless cap, she could easily pass for a man. Only her slim hands gave her away, and even as the two headed up the street she pulled off what appeared to be rubber gloves, replacing them with heavier, black leather ones. Beyond the motel, they turned into a corner restaurant that opened to both streets, where the bar stayed open late.

In a minute, a car started on the side street, but when they raced across the roof to look, it was only a gray-haired lady pulling her VW Beetle out of the parallel parking.

When they heard another car start, in the motel's back parking lot, again they ran.

There: a white Toyota pulling away between the lines of parked cars. They could see the darkly dressed couple within, the man driving. He moved quickly onto the street and, a block down, turned up the hill, driving fast, heading in the direction of the freeway. And the car was gone, where not the fastest feline could catch it.

Returning to the patio, they backed down the bougainvillea, through the yellow cat's scent, to the brick paving. They checked the bushes, but the tomcat wasn't there. Crowding together before the closed glass, they peered into the darkened room.

Nothing stirred among the shadowed furniture. "The tom's not there, he's gone," Kit said, and before Joe or Dulcie could reply she flicked her fluffy tail and careened away through the bushes, following his scent.

Dulcie gave Joe a questioning stare. He said, "Go on, I'll catch up. I want a look back there, where they parked." He watched her gallop away, and then headed for the small parking lot at the back of the motel, a gray shadow among shadows, only his white markings visible.

Rounding the hedge, Joe came face-to-face with the tarp-covered car, parked in the corner where the hedge met the motel wall. He started toward it, then stopped, his nose to the paving examining the scent of the darkly clad couple. Here, unimpeded by the smell of the garden flowers, he tasted both the man's scent and the woman's. Both led to the tarp.

The tan cover was made of thin, sleazy canvas, fitted

tightly over the big car. The canvas covered the wheels, too, and hugged the ground. Quickly Joe nosed underneath.

It wasn't as dark under there as he'd expected; the sleazy fabric looked like cheesecloth with the light from the motel shining through. Rearing up between the tarp and the shiny black fender, he picked out the wheel insignia of a Cadillac. Nosing along the big black car, he could see that it was a four-door. The car smelled strongly of the departed couple.

The tires were still warm, and a thin warmth radiated from the engine. When he moved to the back and edged up between the tarp and the license plate, he found it covered with mud just as Kit had described. Pawing the mud away, he traced the numbers. "4LTG747," he said softly, wishing his recall were as certain and reliable as Kit's. The tortoiseshell, having all her life memorized folktales, had a memory like a spring-loaded trap. Whatever was caught in it never got away. Had the couple, having used the Cadillac during the invasion, parked it partially out of sight here, and covered it? He had no sure proof to link *this* Cadillac to the invasions—unless Kathleen Ray got lucky and picked up its tire prints at the scene. But thanks to Kit, the department knew there'd been a black Caddy near the scene.

Thinking back, he was sure he'd seen, days earlier, a tarp-covered car parked here, in fact had been seeing the canvas lump for maybe a couple of weeks. Surely the street patrols had taken note, had maybe checked with the motel to make sure the vehicle belonged to a registered guest. Maybe the two cars were switched back and forth, sometimes the Caddy, sometimes the Toyota, so there was always some vehicle filling out the tarp, and it wouldn't lie in a flat heap on the paving, calling attention to a car's absence.

If this car was registered at the desk, they'd have the license number, but he'd bet it wasn't. Right now, he wanted to pass the information along to the department. Maybe the cops could get here while the engine was still warm, take a look, run the plate, maybe dust for prints. And Joe took off fast for Dulcie's house, for the nearest phone; he'd just zip in through Dulcie's cat door onto Wilma's desk and punch in 911, *another tip from the snitch*, he thought, smiling. Racing across the shingles to call the department, he was eager to see what the answering detective would find, and what information he might pick up from the desk clerk, too. Tonight was the first real break they'd had, with the yellow cat leading Kit to the invasion and then to two of the perps and their cars. Thinking about the strange tom's contribution, Joe's curiosity burned brighter even than did Kit's—made him want to be in two places at once: watching a detective go over the Caddy, and finding out more about one old yellow tomcat who, one way or the other, must have a stake in these crimes.

26

KIT FOLLOWED THE scent of the tomcat across the roofs straight into the wooded hills north of the village. Though he didn't look back, she knew he was aware of her by the way he moved, by the way his ears would swivel around, by the way he took shelter occasionally where he could see back across the roofs, watching her. Racing uphill atop the oak-sheltered cottages, he was drawing ever nearer to Maudie's house. But why would he go there?

Or was he headed on past Maudie's, maybe returning to the Colletto house? *Had* one of the invaders tonight been Kent Colletto? If Kent had a part in this, how did the yellow cat know? And did anyone else in the Colletto family know? That would be interesting, she thought, smiling at straitlaced Carlene's stubborn defense of Victor.

Between the few lighted windows, the oak-shrouded roofs were so dark that the yellow tom appeared and then disappeared, vanishing into the deepest pools of blackness, then out again. He had a lot of stamina for an old cat; Kit herself was breathing hard. As he crossed the next roof he stopped suddenly, stood in plain sight in the glow of a lighted window looking back at her. For a long moment he stood looking. He lifted a paw, opened his mouth in a silent meow, and then was gone again, a pale shape racing across the roofs among the dark treetops that sheltered Maudie's street.

Next door to Maudie's he paused again. Maudie's kitchen light was on, and a lamp burned in the upstairs guest room. He was still for a moment, and then leaped to Maudie's roof. He was such a big cat that even now, in his old age, he was an impressive fellow. When he turned and looked at her, his eyes held a world of knowledge, and of pain. How many years had he lived? How many miles had this cat traveled, and what had he seen of the world?

In the guest room, Maudie was making up the empty twin bed. Benny was sound asleep in the other, the covers pulled up around his ears, his face turned away from the lamp's soft light. Padding closer to the yellow cat, Kit sat down near him. He glanced at her, but neither spoke. They watched Maudie tuck the sheets in, making square, neat corners military tight. Had David returned, was she making the bed for him? Had he decided, after all, not to leave Benny and his mother alone in a strange neighborhood and a new house? Though she was filled with questions, Kit found it hard not to stare at the tomcat, too. She felt both shy of him and bold; she wanted to talk to him, ask him questions; but for once in her life, she remained quiet.

He seemed intently fixed on the guest room, ignoring her—until he twitched an ear, in a friendly gesture, inviting her to move closer. She padded right up next to him; they sat in friendly silence watching Maudie shake a pillow into a fresh pillow slip. Kit was so sure David had returned that when she heard a man's footsteps in the hall, she watched for him to appear.

Jared Colletto moved into the doorway, carrying a bulging gym bag atop two folded blankets. "I could have done that, Aunt Maudie," he said softly, glancing at the sleeping child. "I had trouble finding the blankets—that garage is loaded. Where will you put it all?"

"Most of it will go in the new studio," Maudie said. "Except some boxes of Martin's and Caroline's things that I couldn't throw away."

"Mementos?" he asked softly.

"Photographs, letters. Caroline's personal papers. Some things I don't know what to do with. Her sister has her business papers. She and I together dealt with the trust—Martin and Caroline and I had our trusts drawn up by the same attorney at the same time, just after they were married, trusts for Benny and for Caroline's two children."

Entering the room, Jared eased the blankets onto the dresser, set his duffel on the floor, then unfolded the blankets and spread them over the sheets on the freshly made bed. "It's nice to be able to visit. I hope I don't disturb Benny, moving into his space. I guess I'm not disturbing him now," he said, grinning. "Does he always sleep so deeply?"

"Like a rock," Maudie said. "As if this terrible ordeal has produced, instead of sleeplessness, a need to escape into sleep. At any rate," she said, smiling, "it's nice to have you here. Of course no one would have bothered us, but it's nice to have your company. You've grown up a lot since my last trip to the village."

Jared put his arm around her, giving her a hug. "I don't want you to wait on me, I can do for myself." He looked at her almost shyly. "If you don't mind me in your kitchen, don't mind me fixing my own breakfast."

"You're to make yourself at home, Jared. Help yourself to whatever you want. But what is it? Something's bothering you."

"It's just . . . you'll be careful, when I'm out? Now that I'm here, I feel responsible. You won't answer the door until you know who's there? You'll keep your cell phone handy in your pocket?"

"Jared . . ."

"And you won't let Benny play outside alone?" Jared sounded, Kit thought, as bossy as his mother. He said, "I'll play ball with Benny when I get home from work or classes. The car lot isn't far, just around the edge of the bay, a ten-minute drive. I'll be glad when we've moved your things into the studio, when you can get your car in the garage, can come directly into the house."

"Jared, this is silly. I promise I'm in no danger."

He looked at Maudie, frowning. "You were in danger when that truck nearly hit you. And you mentioned to Mother something about boxes being shifted around in the garage? And a silent phone call where the line was open but no one spoke, and no caller ID on the screen?"

"I'm sure that was some glitch in the phone system, maybe one of those electronic political messages that didn't go through. I wish I hadn't told her those things, I should have known better, Carlene can get so excited. I'm sorry Benny mentioned the truck. Well," she said, "you're here and it's nice to have you. I know I must be putting you out, but we'll make it a good visit." She smiled. "There's some lemon pie. Shall I cut us each a slice?"

"Pie would be great, then I'd better get some sleep. My first class is at eight. Go on down, I'll just hang up a couple of shirts."

Maudie left the room, heading for the stairs, and in a minute the kitchen lights brightened as if she'd turned up the dimmer. Kit turned to look at the yellow tom. "Why did you follow us?"

His eyes looked deep into hers. "My name is Misto."

"Are you with them, with those two in the motel who robbed and hurt that woman?"

"Would I tell you if I was?"

"I guess not," she said, half wary, half amused.

"I came with him," Misto said, cocking an ear toward the guest room where Jared was hauling underwear and books out of his duffel.

"With Jared? From Maudie's sister's house? You live with them?" Kit said, amazed.

Misto dropped his ears. "I wouldn't live in that house."

"What do you mean, then, that you came with Jared?"

"I came from the prison at Soledad. I hitched a ride when Jared and Kent visited their brother. I knew they were from this village."

Kit looked at him, puzzled. "Why did you want to come here? What were *you* doing in the prison?" Soledad was where Lori went to visit her pa, where her pa was serving time for murder. "Didn't they see you in their car?"

"It was a hot day. I banked on their putting the top down when they parked, the guards watch the parking lot pretty carefully. They did put it down, and when they returned I was hidden under a blanket behind the seat."

"But what made you want to come here?" she repeated.

Misto smiled. "I knew about you three, I heard some of the prisoners talking."

She felt as if her heart had stopped. "No one in prison would know about us." But then she realized someone would know, there were prisoners in Soledad that she and Dulcie and Joe had helped send there, men they had followed and spied on and snitched on to the cops. Some of those men did know about them, or knew about cats like them.

"You lived there?" she said softly.

"I came there to the prison grounds two years ago. There are fields around Soledad; a lot of cats live there, feral cats, but not like us. There was no other like me, no other cat to talk to."

"Lonely," she said.

"I've lived a lot of places where I was lonely. Only once in a while have I come on another speaking cat. It was there in the prison yard that I heard two men talking about Molena Point and about the strange unnatural cats they'd found there."

She didn't like this, they didn't need anyone talking about unnatural cats, telling where they were.

"The prison ferals live on the grounds and in the surrounding fields, but I hung out with the humans," he said. "I was hungry to hear human talk. I followed the trustees who did the gardening, they talk a lot when they work together. I made friends with some, they liked to bring me food. One morning, two of them started swapping stories about strange cats that were more than cats. The redheaded one said he'd trapped speaking cats near this village. You can bet I hung around to hear more."

"Tommie McCord," she said softly. "The redheaded one. They did trap cats, he and his friends did, but we freed them."

"They laughed about trapping them," Misto said. "The redhead—McCord?—swore he and his partner had had them in a cage and had heard them talking. When he said, 'Those cats are loose somewhere in the village,' I knew I had to come here, I longed to find others like myself. It's been a long time, so many years since I had other cats to talk to, since I parted from my wife and kits."

"There *is* a band of speaking cats, wild in the hills. Those are the ones McCord and his friends trapped, they were going to sell them. That frightens me, that he's telling people about us. But of course he would, wouldn't he? Scum like that," Kit said, hissing.

"Not to worry, the other prisoners didn't believe him, they made jokes about him, called him crazy. Though later," he said more solemnly, "I saw one of the men watching the feral cats in a puzzled way, watching too intently.

"But in a prison there are a lot of tall stories," he said quickly. "No one really believes them." The old cat placed a paw softly on Kit's paw. "That redheaded one's still in prison where he can't hurt us. No one likes him much. Who knows," he said hopefully, "maybe he won't leave Soledad alive."

They both went silent at a rustle of leaves above them. The next instant, Dulcie looked down at them, her dark stripes blending into the dark foliage, only her green eyes sharply defined. She dropped to the roof beside them, looking worriedly from one to the other, having heard enough to be just as upset as Kit by Misto's remarks about the prison.

But the next moment she was even more concerned about what she observed of Maudie.

From the roof of the garage wing, the cats could see not only into the guest room, but also into the kitchen below. As Kit and Misto had talked softly, Maudie had gone downstairs. Now alone in the kitchen, her expression had changed. She was no longer smiling as if with pleasure at having company. Glancing above her toward the guest room, she was scowling as if filled with dismay, as if she did not want Jared there.

"What's that about?" Dulcie said softly, sitting down beside Kit. "She's mad as a caged raccoon."

But Kit's attention, and Misto's, were on Jared, where, within the softly lit guest room, he stood looking down at the little boy who slept so innocently. He looked for a long time; they couldn't read his expression, and then at last he turned away, leaving Benny to his dreams. Reaching into the closet, into the inside pocket of the jacket he had hung there, he removed a lumpy, zippered black folder. Patting it as if to make sure the contents were all in place, he slipped it into the duffel beneath his folded jeans. Zipping the duffel, he snapped a little padlock to secure it and set it in the closet. Whether the folder contained innocent, private business or something more interesting, the cats had no way to know; maybe it was just something he didn't want Benny to play with.

27

HAVING CALLED THE night dispatcher about the canvas-covered car, Joe left Wilma's house and hurried back to the motel through a haze of fog, a mist drifting in from the sea to dampen his fur and blur the rooftops around him. Below him, already parked in front of the motel, was a gratifying response to his phone tip: a squad car stood at the curb, along with Dallas's tan Blazer. From below, from the front office, he heard Officer Crowley and a strange voice, maybe the desk clerk. When he didn't hear Dallas, he trotted across the roof to the small parking lot. Where the hedge met the wall, where he'd reported the black Cadillac covered by the tarp, Dallas stood surveying the scene.

The Cadillac was gone. The corner was empty. No black Caddy, no car at all, no tarp, nothing but blacktop, the area a shade lighter than the surrounding, fog-damp macadam. Well, didn't that tear it. He'd been gone maybe twenty minutes, but enough time, apparently, for the two perps to double back and take the car. Or had they sent one of their pals to retrieve it?

But why? What had alerted them? Had someone seen the cats watching them, and knew what they were, knew they'd alert the cops? But that couldn't happen, that was too far out. Or had the yellow tomcat alerted the man and woman? *Was* he traveling with those no-goods, and not the innocent old fellow that he seemed? Joe watched Dallas kneeling at the edge of the dry parking space, his leather bag by his side, using the department's new, hand-held laser beam to illuminate a tire mark that was, apparently, so faint Joe had missed it. The thin edge of a second, clearer mark was incised into the earth strip that ran along the hedge. Joe looked up when he heard a far door close.

Padding across the roof, he watched Officer Crowley leave the motel office and head across the patio to the parking lot. Joe kept pace with him. Even in uniform, Crowley looked awkward, his thin, stringy six-foot-four body moving as if he were walking behind a plow, his big hands seeming better suited to the plow, too, than to the 9-millimeter he wore at his belt. Approaching Dallas, Crowley stood shifting from foot to foot waiting for the detective to photograph a second tire print that shone as faint as a breath on the dry macadam.

Dallas set his camera aside. "What did you get from the desk clerk?"

"The woman checked out. Name of Karen Birkler. A single, registered for the whole month, special rate. The clerk didn't like that she had two different men in and out at different times; that made him nervous. Maybe he thought they'd run into each other, and there'd be trouble. He was curious enough about her to follow her once, watched her carry a small plastic bag a dozen blocks and drop it in a builder's Dumpster. Said she could just as well have dumped it at the motel. She registered with a Sacramento address." Crowley handed Dallas a piece of paper. "Probably bogus."

Dallas nodded, tucked the paper in a small spiral bound notebook that he returned to his pocket. Crowley said, "I told him to make sure the lock code is changed, that the room remains locked, not to let the maids or maintenance or anyone else go in. Told him we'd cordon off the two entrances."

Dallas removed a clean paintbrush from the satchel and began dusting bits of debris into an evidence bag, maybe loose fibers from the canvas tarp. "Did you put out a BOL on the brown pickup and the Toyota?" Crowley nodded. "Do the same for the Cadillac, do it before you string your tape. When we're finished here, I'm headed back to the Galleon. I hope to hell we don't have another dustup tonight, with three scenes to work. Being this shorthanded makes me edgy."

Crowley grinned. As Joe listened to him call in the Cadillac, he worried over why the couple had bailed out so fast. He followed above Dallas as the detective headed for the motel office, watched him disappear inside. This wing of the building was an old-fashioned brick box, the swinging glass door with a glass transom above it; the other wings were newer. Edging over the roof gutter as far as gravity would allow, he peered in through the open transom.

He couldn't see the clerk, but he could hear his reedy voice, a pale contrast to Dallas Garza's deeper tone. Dallas wanted a look at the motel room, but when he mentioned a warrant the clerk waived that aside. Clerk said if *he* asked the law to have a look, then no warrant was needed. When their voices receded, as if they had headed down the hall behind the office, Joe padded away across the roof. He backed down into the bushes as Dallas entered the room through the inner door from the hall. Through the glass slider, Joe watched the detective fit goggles over his eyes. He squinted as Dallas scanned the room with the laser. Didn't take long to pick up footprints from the carpet, fingerprints from the dresser and headboard. When he'd finished, Dallas turned on the lights, throwing the room into stagelike brilliance, highlighting the shabbiness of the dated, Swedish modern bedroom suite.

Avoiding certain areas of carpet, Dallas began to dust a few selected areas of furniture in the conventional way, to pick up prints the laser had found. Using the laser was a hell of a lot faster than the old drill. If scientists kept coming up with these startling new techniques, they'd put a cat out of business.

When Dallas left the scene, Joe headed for the station, hoping more information might be forthcoming. Maybe a patrol, or the CHP, had already picked up the Cadillac or the Toyota. Or even the old truck, which Kit had reported earlier. All the way to the courthouse unanswered questions rattled around in his head. If Kent Colletto was part of this tangle, could Maudie know that? Did she not want to turn in her own nephew? She hadn't seemed that fond of Kent, but he *was* family, and the woman was harboring some secret. If Kent *was* involved in the invasions and he thought Maudie knew, wouldn't that put her in danger from her own nephew as well as, possibly, from her son's killer?

28

I**T WAS NEARLY** midnight when Maudie and Jared finished their pie and coffee and Jared went up to bed. Maudie, in her robe and slippers, waited a little while to make sure her nephew wouldn't come down again, then headed into the garage, easing the door closed so it wouldn't squeak. Before throwing the switch for the single light, she drew closed the new, dense curtains she'd bought for the garage window. The single bulb cast the stacked cartons into sharp angles and sent long shadows against the garage wall. Pulling her fleece robe tighter, she stood scanning her labeled boxes of quilting supplies. She was so eager to move them into the new studio and to get to work, to lay out patterns for the new designs she had in mind. Christmas themes kept noodging her, though this late in the holidays whatever she began would be for the following Yule. Strange that Christmas could even interest her, this year.

But she needed something to hold on to, she needed

to get involved in her work again. She wanted her studio in order so she could launch into some bright new project; she could heal Benny only when she began to ease her own pain. She imagined the newly furnished studio, the cupboards rich with bright fabric, bolts of yard goods, stacks of cloth squares already cut, the walls alive with her finished quilts. And outside the glass doors the garden blooming with all the bright color California's winter gardens offered: candy-toned cyclamens massed against their background of red toyon berries and yellow acacia.

But before moving and unpacking her studio boxes, she had another mission. Pulling on a pair of thin cotton gloves, in case later some enthusiastic police detective might want to investigate in here, she approached the cartons of her dead daughter-in-law's belongings. The nine boxes were neatly sealed with the same slick brown tape she'd used, but they weren't stacked as she'd left them. And she could see that on the two top cartons the brown tape, which you could buy in any grocery or drugstore, had been slit open and then carefully covered again with a second, matching length.

Benny hadn't done this. Even if he had been into the boxes rummaging wistfully among Caroline's things, he'd have no reason to replace the tape. He knew he was perfectly free to look at Caroline's books and keepsakes, at her hiking clothes, her first husband's U.S. Marine uniforms and the papers regarding his military career, and Caroline's few pieces of costume jewelry that were too nice to give to charity.

Slitting open the two resealed boxes with a small pair of scissors, shifting the boxes around to do the back sides, she found all this activity harder with her painful shoulder. The therapy she'd had in L.A. had helped but had been time-consuming and tedious. She lifted the flaps of the first box, reached in to examine the contents

Yes, the items had been disturbed, the order of the file folders was different, and the large brown envelopes had been rearranged. As far as she could remember, nothing was missing, though she'd never thought to make an inventory. Even if something were missing, there was nothing specific she thought would be of value to a burglar: old letters, recipes, maps to backcountry hiking trails, old tax receipts. She worried for a moment about the Social Security numbers on the tax records, but somehow she didn't think that was what this burglar was after. Only when she selected the carton marked CAROLINE—KITCHEN, sliding aside five stacked boxes with her good arm, did her pulse quicken.

But no, this tape hadn't been slit, she saw with relief, the box was just the way she'd packed it. Cutting the tape, she reached beneath several layers of carefully wrapped kitchen treasures: an old-fashioned pastry blender, Caroline's grandmother's flour sifter and silver pie server, a dozen ornate cookie cutters each wrapped separately, three antique fluted pie pans. Seemed as if, leaving L.A., she'd kept more of Caroline's things than her own. Sentimental, she thought. Though in fact she'd kept much of it for Benny. She and Maryanne had divided up the keepsakes, Maryanne more than generous in sharing. Benny had loved Caroline so. Maryanne had copies, and CDs, of all the family photographs, so those were easy enough to leave behind. Easing the packages of cooking paraphernalia aside, she drew out the brown, sealed envelope that she'd hidden beneath them.

This was what the burglar had come for, she was certain. Someone had been in the house, had stolen her keys, but apparently hadn't had time to find this envelope before being startled, perhaps. Before slipping away, leaving the job unfinished. This, she thought, smiling, was what they wouldn't find now, if they did return. By ten tomorrow morning the envelope would be tucked away in a new safe-deposit box, with a key different from the one that had been stolen, and no one would find the new key.

She'd discovered her extra keys missing the day before, when she'd misplaced her car keys. She'd looked everywhere, then had gone to her desk to get the duplicate set: house key, car keys, safe deposit, and several others which, if she ever lost the originals or her purse were stolen, would supply immediate backup. Opening her big secretary, beside the fireplace in the living room, she'd removed the little stamp drawer to reveal the hidden compartment behind it. Reaching in, she'd drawn her hand back and bent to peer inside. The little compartment was empty. She'd stood there panicked, trying to remember if she'd taken the keys out herself, and knowing she had not. She'd thought, chilled, about someone who now could enter her home any time of day or night, come stealing in when they were sound asleep. It was at that moment that she'd been sure Pearl Toola was in the village, that Pearl had followed her, and had been here in her house. At once Maudie's plan for Pearl had quickened, the cold, precise path that she longed to follow.

Whether she'd have the nerve to carry it through was

in question, but not because she was afraid. She wasn't. Not because she didn't have the means. She did. But because of Benny. No matter how Benny might think he hated his mother, if Maudie took such action, that could be the end of any love between them. Such a terrible betrayal by his grandmother could rob Benny of any hope at all for the years ahead, for any kind of normal life.

She knew she was courting disaster by not reporting the break-in or the hit-and-run. Maybe she should call Molena Point PD now, tonight, and report them both, certainly report the rifled boxes, the missing keys. Maybe an officer would come out, maybe take fingerprints.

But was that what she wanted? And it was the middle of the night, what kind of response would she get? If she did report those things, she didn't want just a cop, she'd want a detective. The person she'd really want to talk to was Max Harper. And before Harper or anyone would take her seriously, she'd have to lay out the whole scenario, explain the significance of what was missing, explain what had gone on in L.A. But even if she did that, what would *her* word be worth? She stood for some time, conflicted and uncertain, shivering in the cold garage, then turned back into the house. In the warm kitchen she made herself a cup of tea and sat at the table warming her hands around the steaming cup, trying to ease her concerns, putting off any discussion with Max Harper, preferring to deal with Pearl in her own way.

29

 JOE LOOKED IN through the bulletproof glass door of Molena Point PD, but hesitated. He didn't demand to be let in, didn't yowl as he always did to attract the daytime dispatcher. Night dispatcher June Alpine might be young and pretty, but she wasn't half as enamored of cats as was their friend Mabel Farthy. Now, instead of drawing June's possible ire, maybe turning her cranky enough to chase him away, he scorched up the oak tree that sheltered the front of the building. Bracing himself on the tiled roof, he pawed open the small window that looked down into the holding cell. With the heavy bars welded across, the glass was usually cracked open—some of these arrestees could smell pretty strong.

This single cell, facing the main entry and the dispatcher's desk, was intended to detain prisoners for only a short time, until they were fingerprinted and their identifying information recorded, before they were taken back to the jail that occupied its own small, fenced building just behind the two-story main building that housed the PD, the court and related offices.

Slipping in between the thick bars, through the open window, Joe dropped down to the cot suspended from the wall below, landing just at the edge to keep the flat springs from squeaking. The thin mattress smelled of throw-up and unwashed human bodies. Padding out through the door's confining bars, he slipped along close to the base of the dispatcher's counter where June might not see him as he headed for the hall. He glanced back twice, but both times she was turned away. Except for the lighted conference room, where three officers sat at the big table with laptops, typing up reports, all the offices were dark, the open doors revealed only blackness. Quickly he vanished through Max's door, into the faint scent of horses that lingered on from years of contact with the chief's western boots.

If Max had been there, Joe might have slipped beneath the credenza, out of sight, until he got a taste of what was going on. Now, with the room to himself, he leaped to Max's desk among the perennial stacks of paperwork, scheduling lists, budget requests, collaterals—enough paper to make the tomcat glad all over again that he wasn't human.

The computer stood dark and lifeless, harboring who knew what secrets, making him wish he were as adept at its use as Dulcie, who'd be able to pull up all kinds of secured information. She'd learned in the library, where she was the official library cat, though an often absent one.

Wilma was a reference librarian, often sharing her office computer with Dulcie. When she worked late at night she would walk Dulcie through some fascinating bits of research, often exploring the cats' own history, tied to Welsh and Irish mythology. Dulcie had learned a good deal about their ancestors in this way, though the subject didn't much interest Joe. He was what he was. A speaking cat with a talent for spying. He didn't give a damn about his ancestral heritage.

Now, looking at the dark monitor, he lifted a tentative paw over the keyboard. If he was to really try, could he learn to bring up police reports? Run fingerprints through AFIS? Access mug shots? Oh, right. And get caught in here alone using Max's computer, and wouldn't that tear it? Turning away from temptation, into Max's bookcase, he curled up in a vacant space between copies of the California Penal Code, hoping the chief or one of the detectives would come dragging back in the small hours with some new information. Snuggled between the heavy books, he was soon warm and yawning; soon sleep eased around him like a huge hand offering comfort and safe harbor, all the security of home.

JOE WAS JERKED awake when the office lights blazed on. He sat up in the bookcase, slitting his eyes against the glare, watched Max toss his Levi's jacket on the couch. The desk phone was flashing red. The chief sat down in his swivel chair, put his feet on the desk, leaning so far back that his brown, short-cropped, thinning hair was right in Joe's face. He picked up the headset, didn't turn on the speaker.

Leaning out from the bookshelf, Joe eased so close to the chief that his whiskers were only inches from Harper's ear. It took him a minute to realize that Max was talking with the LAPD. Detective Sam Lakey's voice was gravelly, he sounded like he had a few years on him, and maybe a bit of extra flesh, as well. "You have our BOL on Pearl Toola?"

"We have," Max said. "So far, no line on her. What's up?"

"You've talked with homicide, here?" Lakey said. "On the murder of her ex-husband and his wife?"

"Several times."

"What we have now might be related, or might not. We're looking at her in an embezzlement, a new case that just came in. Homicide's thinking this might be connected, the thefts a possible motive for the Toola murders in San Bernardino County.

"Beckman Heavy Equipment," Lakey said. "It's a contractor's rental service. Eight hundred thousand dollars missing. Pearl was their bookkeeper, she and Caroline Toola both worked there. They were neighbors, Caroline helped her get the job there some five years ago. Both were still employed there when Caroline died. Pearl left the firm shortly after the murders, told them she needed to get away for a while, too much stress after her ex-husband was shot." There was amusement in his voice.

Max said, "And the company's just now reporting the discrepancy?"

194

"They just now found it," Lakey said. "When Pearl left, they were without a full-time bookkeeper; it was a make-do situation for a while, utilizing other office help. When they finally found a new bookkeeper, she not only uncovered the bogus withdrawals, she's certain it was Pearl. Said most likely Pearl would have kept a second set of books, said you couldn't pull off that kind of manipulation and keep things straight without your own written record. And of course there's no way Pearl would have the second set of figures on the computer. Even if she'd erased it, it would still be on the hard drive, could still be found by a pro."

"So Pearl rips them off," Max said, "Caroline finds out, but in some way tips her hand that she knows."

"Possible," Lakey said.

Then Pearl killed Caroline not only out of jealousy, the tomcat thought, *but to silence her, keep her from blowing the whistle?* Joe was frowning down at Max's notes when he heard Kathleen's voice from up at the front desk, and immediately eased back between the hard volumes. He was curled up again pretending to nap when Kathleen's footsteps came down the hall. She stopped in the doorway, looking in. Max motioned her on in, motioned for her to pull up a chair, and turned the speaker on.

Lakey was saying, "Beckman's new bookkeeper spent several days going over the books, to familiarize herself with how the company operated and to get a jump on tax season. When she began to find the discrepancies, she called in Mr. Beckman. He took one look, and they got in a second accountant to help her. They traced the problem backward, contacted a number of customers to have a look at their statements—which didn't match the copies in the Beckman files. The thefts, and the bogus entries, stopped after the murders. Six weeks later, Pearl left the company.

"She told Homicide she was moving down to San Diego for a while because of the stress, that she'd be staying with a friend. When Jimmie Beckman was sure the books had been doctored, he called us, called in his lawyer, and filed charges.

"San Diego said Pearl never arrived at the address she gave, and didn't contact the friend. That was late June. Then when Maudie moved to Molena Point, homicide thought Pearl might follow her up there. You're the best lead we have," Lakey said. "You have a file on her?"

Max nodded. "Fingerprints. Photographs. Thirty-seven years old. Five ten, about 140 pounds. Jet black, straight hair. Shoulder length, in a forties-style pageboy. Unusually white skin. Lean, bony face. Dark brown eyes, almost black. Some ten years ago, she worked the black-jack tables at Harrah's, in Vegas. California driver's license, no rap sheet."

Listening to the description of Pearl, Joe grew as edgy as if he had ticks in his fur. Tall woman, thin, bony face. How long had that tall blonde been at the motel? How long had she been in the village? In his opinion, if this was Pearl Toola with a bleach job, a short haircut, and a permanent, she hadn't improved her looks much. He thought about the photographs of Benny's lean, sour-looking mother. Why hadn't he recognized her tonight, after having looked at Maudie's album? Why hadn't he known the sharp-faced blonde at once, despite the straw-colored hair?

Max said, "Pearl embezzles nearly a mill, keeps a second set of books, and before she skips she kills the one coworker who might know enough to turn her in. She already hates Caroline, for presumably stealing her husband, so she does a thorough job of it, and kills them both."

When Max and Lakey hung up, Max filled Kathleen in.

"So Pearl," Kathleen said, "thinking Maudie might have seen her the night she shot them, follows Maudie here."

"But why didn't Caroline blow the whistle on Pearl at once?" Max said. "Turn her in when she first found out?"

"Because of the child?" Kathleen said. "Because with the trauma of the divorce, she didn't want that dumped on the kid, too? To know his mother was a criminal and was in jail? Maybe she meant to wait until the missing money was discovered, and then hand over the evidence?"

"Or was Caroline already blackmailing Pearl?" Max said. "And that was why Pearl killed her?"

On the bookshelf, Joe Grey was thinking that the only thing the two hadn't nailed down—and he felt sure they were right on target—was Pearl's connection to the invasions. If that really was Pearl in the motel, if he wasn't imagining the likeness. Had Dallas picked up any prints in the motel? But Pearl had no record, so there'd be nothing on her in AFIS. And why would Pearl, arriving in Molena Point following Maudie, take part in a series of attacks that seemed to have nothing to do with the murders or the embezzlement? What exactly *was* her connection to the invasions?

But that was puzzling only until he remembered that Pearl knew Kent Colletto. That she'd been coming up to the village every summer for years, with Maudie's family, ever since Benny was a baby, that Pearl had known the Colletto boys from the time they were little kids. The tomcat, sandwiched among the volumes of the California Penal Code, sat thinking.

So far, the police had no reason to compare the blonde's prints—provided they'd found any—with the prints on L.A.'s report. No reason to connect the invasions to Pearl, no lead to Pearl in AFIS. The tomcat fidgeted with his need to join the discussion, to suggest to the chief they compare Pearl's prints to the woman in the motel. And the only way he could communicate with the chief was by phone, unseen, unrecognized. He thought about the dark, empty offices opening along the hall, all those unattended phones so quickly accessible. He had only to slip into any office and place a call to Max.

Right. As far as he knew, all these phones were on one central system; he'd never heard an officer mention a private line. The minute he pressed the speaker button, June Alpine would see the light flashing up at the front and, knowing the offices were empty, she'd pick up to see who was there.

No, he'd have to hightail it back to Wilma's house. Or go on home and hope everyone was asleep, that he wouldn't have to listen to one of Clyde's lectures. Sometimes he wished Max *would* discover he could talk, so he could stop breaking his butt trying to find a phone. Yawning, attempting to look bored, he dropped from the bookshelf to the floor. He guessed Max had known he was there, because the chief didn't look surprised. Joe sat lazily washing his paws, trying to calm his pounding heart, then sauntered sleepily past the desk to the door and padded away up the hall.

At the dispatcher's counter, the problem was how to get out of the building. If Mabel Farthy had been on duty, she would have risen from her desk at his first yowl, would have let him out at once, complaining with good-natured amusement. He glanced toward the holding cell, but that ten-foot jump from the bunk across the room up to the high window was different from dropping down; that leap would be a killer. He could imagine himself falling flat on his face on the concrete, splattering like a cartoon cat.

Yowling stridently at June, he fussed and paced until at last she scowled over the counter at him, rose, and let him out. "You keep up that kind of behavior, the chief'll nail your hide to the wall."

No he won't, Joe thought smugly as the petite young dispatcher opened the glass door for him.

"Go catch a mouse," she said flippantly, "cats don't belong in a cop shop." As she locked the bulletproof glass behind him and flounced back to her desk, Joe Grey ran like hell, heading for home and a phone.

30

IN THE DAMEN kitchen, the sun's first light shone through the bay window brightening the granite counter and warming Joe Grey's back, where he sat watching Ryan flip pancakes. She was dressed in work jeans, a yellow sweatshirt, a frilly apron, and fuzzy pink slippers, her heavy boots waiting in the living room by the front door. The smell of pancakes, frying bacon, and warming syrup was so strong it made the tomcat drool. The table was set with three places, two with the conventional mats, napkins, and silverware, one with Joe Grey's plastic place mat printed with a motif of running mice, a gift from Ryan that might be a bit cutesy, but that amused the tomcat. Clyde, in their bachelor days, had never thought to offer him a place mat. Except maybe the want ads, which neither of them ever read. Across the room on the flowered easy chair, little white Snowball lay curled up alone, purring with the warmth of the cushions into which she had burrowed, waiting for her can of gourmet cat food to be served up. Beside her chair Rock waited, too, held in place only by Ryan's earlier command to "Down. Stay." His pale yellow eyes never left the stove, his sighs were frequent and dramatic.

"Don't forget the kippers," Joe told Ryan, licking a front paw. "Pancakes are nothing without kippers."

She turned to look at him. "Pancakes with kippers are as disgusting as it gets. You're lucky Clyde and I put up with the smell of fish first thing in the morning. And what about poor Rock? You know he loves kippers, and you know he can't have them. I think you eat them just to tease him."

"Rock understands," Joe told her.

"He doesn't understand at all. He thinks it's unfair that you get treats that he can't have. It's hard enough for him to deal with a cat giving him orders, without tormenting him with your dietary indulgences. Don't you ever think how he feels?"

"He's happy—he loves obeying my orders," Joe told her smugly. A less intelligent dog might have problems with a speaking cat giving him obedience commands, but Rock had learned early on to accept Joe's strangeness with good will. The big Weimaraner, at first shocked and then curious when the gray cat spoke to him, had come to respect the tomcat's talents, though still he liked to tease Joe, with a keen, doggy humor.

"As to the kippers, you know I need my protein," Joe said, greedily eyeing the browning pancakes and stifling a yawn.

Ryan turned to look at him. "What you need is sleep. I heard you slide open your tower window, coming home. It was after three this morning." Carefully she laid the delicate, salty fishes on his warm pancakes and set his plate on the table.

Leaping to his place mat, Joe tucked into his breakfast, thinking about his phone call to Max last night, wondering what Max would do with the information, with Joe's suggestion that the blonde in the motel could be Maudie's ex-daughter-in-law. The link between Pearl and the Colletto brothers left Joe edgy with unanswered questions, scattered information yet to be sorted out. He'd nearly finished his pancakes and kippers when he heard the morning paper hit the front door. Heard Clyde's feet, coming down the stairs, make a detour out the front to pick up the daily rag. Sounded like he was wearing his heavy boots; that meant a workday at the cottage. He clumped into the kitchen dressed in ragged jeans and a khaki work shirt, sat down at the table generously laying the paper between them so Joe, too, could scan the front page.

LONE WOMAN AT THE MERCY OF UNKNOWN CRIMINALS

When Nannette Garver answered her doorbell yesterday evening the door was shoved in her face, knocking her down. Two men gagged and beat her, robbed her, broke and destroyed everything in her house. There were no police patrols on the street to deter such a crime and Nannette lay tied up for many hours before she was found and released. It is troubling indeed to realize how at the mercy of unknown criminals a lone woman is in our village, without the police protection our taxes pay for . . .

Stifling a rude comment, the tomcat licked his plate clean. Only then did he finish reading the vitriolic article, his ears flattened with rage. "They call this journalism? *This* garbage? I don't even want to see the editorial page."

"This *is* an editorial," Clyde said with equal disgust, and turned to the actual editorial page at the back, where Nancyanne Prewitt's inaccurate interpretation of last night's events occupied two additional columns. Crowded together, Clyde and Joe read with irritated grumbles. Ryan put Clyde's plate down on the table beside the *Gazette*, scanned the article, but made no comment. She sat down at her own place, trying to ignore the smell of kippers, and quietly ate her breakfast, choosing not to comment on the *Gazette*'s vitriol. Talking cats reading the local paper, punctuating the silence with angry comments, was still a bit much, first thing in the morning, she was still trying to get used to these changes in her life. She looked up at a knock from the front door and Charlie's voice through the new electronic speaker, and rose to let her in.

After the third home invasion, Ryan had installed a simple intercom for the front door in the interests of security and peace of mind. No more leaving the door on the latch for drop-ins. Charlie followed her on back, sat down at the table between Ryan's place and Joe, and accepted a cup of coffee. She was dressed in jeans and boots, a leather jacket over her sweatshirt, her red hair tangled from the morning wind. She barely glanced at the paper.

Clyde said, "You've read it?"

She nodded.

"Has Max seen it?"

Again, a nod. "At least the reporter didn't have access to the holdbacks."

"What holdbacks?" Clyde asked.

Joe said, "There were two cars parked near the scene. A black Cadillac and an old, junky pickup."

All three looked at Joe. Clyde said, "Did you see the drivers?"

"I didn't, Kit did. She called it in. A black-haired, middle-aged man was driving the Cadillac. Black shirt, short black beard neatly clipped. The other two were tall, darkly dressed. We think one was a woman; she showed up later at the Kestrel Inn, a blonde." He told them what they'd seen at the motel, the couple switching the cars under the tarp. He left out the part about the yellow tomcat. "By the time I called the department and got back to the motel, Dallas was there and both cars were gone. He got a nice plaster cast of a partial tread mark; we'll see where that leads."

"A cast complete with gray cat hairs," Charlie said dryly.

Joe felt his breakfast turn sour.

"Not to worry," Charlie said, stroking him. "I told Max I've seen a gray and white cat around that motel, that I thought she lived there, or nearby." Motel cats were common in the village. Often guests inquired, when making reservations, if there was an in-house cat, and then upon arrival they would seek out the little four-legged PR executive for a pet and a cuddle. Some guests liked to share supper in their rooms with the resident cat. If the manager knew them from past visits, this was often

204

allowed, and a special meal was served for the feline host or hostess.

"So what else do they have?" Clyde said. "One tire cast, with cat hairs. Fingerprints? Footprints?"

"They have footprints," Charlie said. "Max didn't go into a lot of detail, he only got a couple of hours' sleep. He was so preoccupied with his own thoughts that I have to think this is coming together. He mentioned something about a connection to someone in Soledad, someone with ties to the village or to some parolee."

"If there's a parolee mixed in," Clyde said, "maybe his parole officer will come up with some information."

Ryan shrugged. "Probation and parole is stretched pretty thin. State parole is running caseloads of three to four hundred." Ryan's dad had recently retired as chief of the federal probation office in San Francisco, and she'd followed with interest the increasing strains on the various state and federal departments.

Clyde glanced again at the front page. "What about the two restaurant break-ins? Anything there?"

"Same as the others," Charlie said with disgust. "Lots of damage, not much taken. Obviously diversionary, but a terrible thing for the owners."

Ryan finished her pancakes and reached for the front page. She glanced at the first few lines, about the invasion, scowled at the tone of the article, folded the paper, and laid it facedown on the table. "Street patrol should have been right there on the spot. Oh, right. Should have been sitting right there waiting for someone to come along and break the door in." She looked at Joe. "I'm with you, I don't want to even *see* what Nancyanne Prewitt has to say. One good thing," she said, "the thicker these new people at the *Gazette* lay it on, the less likely people are to buy their garbage."

"I hope," Charlie said. She reached to scratch Joe's ears. "The information you cats picked up last night—the descriptions, the tire track, the motel . . . that's a huge help. Between you cats and the department," she said, stroking his back, "you'll get these SOBs sorted out."

Joe seldom heard Charlie swear. But then, it wasn't every day someone came after Max like this—and Joe had no doubt that was the scenario. He just hoped she was right, and that the case would be resolved before anything worse happened.

Joe wasn't sure why he hadn't mentioned the yellow tomcat, why he hadn't shared with them this strange cat's part in last night's surveillance. Maybe, he thought ashamedly, he wanted all the glory for himself, and for Dulcie and Kit? Or maybe it was because he knew no more about the yellow cat than he did about the invaders, didn't have a clue what the cat really wanted or why he was here in the village. Until he had a handle on that, maybe he didn't want to get into a long and pointless discussion.

Ryan said, "This Arlie Risso? This newcomer in the village who's been complaining about the invasions?"

Charlie nodded. "I've heard the name."

"He moved here about a month ago," Ryan said. "I think he bought a house; he was in Haller's Building Supply a couple of days ago when I picked up a lumber order, he was buying some replacement hardware. He's been here less than a month, he said. He was complaining loudly about the invasions, going on to George Haller. When I heard him bitching, I moved away among the aisles where I could listen. He said he meant to be at the city council meeting, see what excuse the police have for 'this rash of crimes,' as he calls it." She looked at Joe. "Black hair, neat little black beard. Well built, maybe in his sixties. Sounds like he's going to raise hell at the meeting."

"We'll be there," Clyde said with interest.

Charlie said, "Not me, I don't want it to look as if the chief needs his wife for backup. But I'd sure like to be a fly on the wall."

"The meeting is when?" Joe said in an offhand manner.

They all looked at him. Clyde said, "No way," and helped himself to the last pancake.

"Why shouldn't he go?" Ryan said. "He goes everywhere else."

Clyde scowled at her. "Have you ever been to a council meeting?"

Ryan shook her head.

"The room's too open, there's nowhere for a cat to hide. Space under the pews is open, and only a bare wall at the back. I can just see the mayor dragging Joe out by his furry neck."

"You don't have to be so graphic," Joe snapped. Though he knew the room didn't lend itself well to feline surveillance. He thought about the windowsills, but those skinny strips were way too narrow even for a cat to cling to. He could perch on a branch outside with his ear to the glass, except that the meetings started at four-thirty, and it would still be light out. He'd be seen from within like one of those paper cutout cats decorating grade-school windows for Halloween. He was wondering how to bring this off when Ryan caught his eye as she reached for the bacon, gave him a quick look of complicity.

Joe licked a last smear of kippers from his whiskers, hiding a smile, and before the discussion could go further he dropped to the floor and headed for the living room and his well-clawed easy chair. Ryan would smuggle him in, and not by his furry neck. Yawning, Joe curled up on the ragged chair, thankful once again that Clyde had married a woman of such keen imagination and sly complicity, a woman more than willing to bend the rules for a deserving accomplice.

31

IT WAS LATER that morning that Joe dropped to the roof of Ryan and Clyde's little cottage amid the drumbeat of hammering from the yard below—and landed facing the yellow tomcat. They hissed at each other and bristled, but without much ferocity, only with the usual rush of tomcat one-upmanship, that sudden and heady surge of adrenaline that made the yellow cat lash his tail and give Joe a ritual snarl. Below them, Ryan and Clyde were building wooden forms, getting ready to pour the foundation for the new sunroom. When Joe padded around onto the small wing that extended behind the cottage, he could see that they had the big header in for the glass sliders. A roll of heavy plastic lay nearby, ready to cover the new opening against unexpected gusts of passing rain. He didn't see the two Latino laborers; he thought they were working another job, preparing for yet another remodel. Ryan was right, this would be a busy month for her, the joys of the holidays sandwiched in between bouts of heavy labor; and that was the way she liked it. She never complained, so Joe guessed the construction work must be for Ryan as heady as restoring rusty old cars was for Clyde or, for Joe, offering up to MPPD a nice piece of evidence to fit into their investigation.

When he looked over at Kit and Dulcie, he had to laugh at the feathers stuck to Kit's mottled face where she'd just finished off an unwary starling. Beside him, the yellow cat had relaxed his wary stance, and the four of them lounged companionably, watching Clyde drive stakes for the forms. They watched Lori Reed came out the side door, hauling pieces of carpet taller than she was. Dragging her burden into the narrow side yard, she heaved the heavy bundles into a green metal Dumpster that seemed nearly as big as the house. Her brown hair was tucked up under a baseball cap. She wore shorts, boots, a faded T-shirt, leather work gloves, and a cloth mask tied over her nose and mouth against the dust from the ancient rug.

"Her pa's going back to prison tomorrow," Dulcie said softly as Joe rolled over, close beside her. "To the prison infirmary." Her fur, baked from the sun, smelled clean and sweet. Over the noise of the hammers, the three talked in little cat whispers. "That's a visiting day," Dulcie said. "Lori and Cora Lee will leave at midnight tonight, to be in line in the morning."

The yellow tom flicked an ear. "A long wait for tired families, wives and kids in line for hours, and then only a few short minutes for their visit. And a long wait, too," he said dryly, "for the prisoners' scuzzy partners, on the outside, to pass on their coded information. Their plans for whatever's coming down out here, beyond the prison walls."

From within the house, Benny appeared, also wearing a mask. He went straight to Rock, to lean companionably against the patient Weimaraner. Lori, having apparently hauled out the last of the carpet, went to kneel beside them, putting her arm around Benny. "You can help me sweep, if you like. There are two brooms." Looking pleased, Benny nodded and rose, and the two disappeared inside again. In a moment the cats could hear their brooms swishing across the bare wood subfloor. Joe looked at the yellow tomcat.

"There was a man in prison," Joe said. "Kit said his name was Arlie something? What did he look like?"

"He's been out a couple of months," Misto said. "A handsome man, maybe in his fifties, close as I could tell. Square build, very white hair. Clean shaven, soft-spoken, and—*urbane* is the word. The others laughed at him, called him 'the gentleman.' But not to his face; he could be mean, you could see the rage surge up in him. They didn't mess with Arlie, even the prison gangs left him alone."

"And the man you were watching in the motel," Joe said, "could he be the same?"

Misto flicked his whiskers. "*His* hair was black, and a black beard. I couldn't pick up his scent, nothing but shaving lotion, and her perfume. He's built the same, voice the same. Not hard to grow a beard, then dye his hair and beard."

"Did you follow him here," Dulcie said. "Is that why you came?"

The yellow cat smiled. "Not exactly. It's what he said that brought me here. Arlie and Tommie McCord talked about the village. Prison talk, McCord going on about the burglaries he'd pulled here. And Arlie describing the fine house he'd once owned on the shore when he lived here. Bragging talk. But I thought I'd seen that house, a vague memory of concrete slabs with glass in between. 'Modern,' he called it. The memory of that house was like a dream, I didn't know then where I'd seen it.

"He talked about beautiful women sunbathing on the beach, and then about cats, said there were too many cats on the shore around his house, cats hiding in caves in the cliffs. Said they were disgusting, that the village should get rid of them. That had McCord listening, all right, and laughing, a strange, mean laugh. But it sounded so like the muddy shore I remembered, that house, and the shore where the sea will come up to cover all the sand, and there's a little fishing dock. When he told about a man who came to feed the cats, that was a jolt. I was sure I remembered him." Misto looked at them with excitement. "I was a kitten in that place, I'm sure of it. I think I was born there."

"That could be Dr. Firetti," Dulcie said. "The man who fed the cats, he's fed them for years. He's *our* doctor. He feeds the strays and traps and, pardon the expression, neuters them, gives them their shots and turns them loose again."

"He didn't neuter me," Misto said. "He couldn't trap *me*. I remember the traps, like wire cages. When he set them, I always hid from him. I was only small when a woman began to feed me, she came every day until we were friends. And then she took me away; I made my

212

home with her until she died. She died very young, she was fine one day, and then an ambulance was there, it took her away and I never saw her again. And then I was on my own," Misto said sadly.

"And you came here because you remembered this village, and because those prisoners talked about us," Kit said, her ears sharply forward.

Misto's ears and whiskers were down, his thin tail curled around him. "It's hard to get old among strangers. Hard, when there's no one else like you, no other speaking cat, no one who understands."

"And your family?" Dulcie said. The hammering below and the scurries of wind among the dry oaks masked their whispers.

"My mate and I were happy, we had three fine, half-grown kits when she disappeared. I searched for her for a year, I found tufts of her fur near some spent bullets. If she was dead, I never found her body, and at last I gave up.

"I raised the kits, they were good hunters. But then in a garden near our den they took up with a family of children, and all three decided to stay. I didn't want another human family, I wasn't done roaming. They were grown and on their own, and I left them."

"You've traveled all over?" Joe said, wondering how that would be, to live that vagabond life.

"I traveled for months, but then returned there, I was lonely for my young ones. But they were gone, the family was gone. I looked for a long time but I never found them. At last I moved on again, and I kept moving, always traveling. I didn't find my children, and I met no more of our own kind."

Misto looked from one to the other. "Do you know how it feels to think you're the only cat within hundreds of miles like you, the only cat who can understand human speech, who could speak to a person if you chose?"

They all three knew how that felt, they knew that frightened loneliness. That was how Dulcie and Joe had met, when each thought there was no other cat like them. They remembered well the wild thrill, when they discovered each other.

Only Kit had never experienced that particular kind of loneliness, for she had grown up among a band of speaking cats. Kit knew loneliness of a different kind, shunned by the others like herself, an orphaned kitten, an outsider, tagging along behind a feral band that didn't want her, eating the few scraps they left, trying not to starve. She wasn't born of their group, she was a speaking cat but she wasn't one of *them*, and she was driven off again and again, a little kitten who did indeed understand loneliness.

"And then," Misto said, "there at the prison when I learned there were other speaking cats nearby? Of course I came to find you." He smiled, such an open, delighted smile that Joe had to trust the old cat. "When I saw that blue vintage T-Bird pull into the prison yard on visiting day, I guessed that had to be Jared Colletto's car, and I took a chance. Victor was always bragging about that car, how his brother kept it in factory-new condition, how Jared was okay in most ways but he was real prissy when it came to that T-Bird. When I saw that car, I thought, how many vintage blue T-Birds could there be? And here I am."

"Did you live inside the prison?" Dulcie said. "How could . . . ?"

214

Misto shook his head. "I lived in the open fields among a band of ferals—or at least people called them feral. Many were dumped cats who'd once had homes. Others were truly feral, born wild and their ancestors wild before them. I was the only speaking cat, though I never spoke to them." The old cat licked his paw. "One of the guards put out food for us, at a side entrance. He'd pet us and talk to us. I wanted badly to talk to him, but of course I didn't. He was a kind man, he was my friend.

"Some of the prisoners were kind, too. Some saved food for us, leftovers from their meals, they'd slip food to us in the prison yard. We could get into the fenced exercise yard, and even into the prison itself if we were quick, but you had to be wary, we weren't allowed in there."

"Weren't you afraid?" Kit said. "Won't those men hurt cats?"

"Most of them liked us, they liked having an animal around, to pet and talk to. We stayed away from the threatening ones, the reaching, hard-eyed, cold or spacey guys. Or the guys who were too gentle and smarmy and tried too hard to lure us close."

Below them, Benny and Lori emerged from the cottage carrying a big trash can between them. Misto said, "Lori's pa was nice, we were friends. As much as you can be friends, when you can't talk together. He talked about Lori, he described her so well that I knew her at once. Long shiny brown hair, big brown eyes and little tilted nose. He said she worked for a contractor, and he was proud of that." Misto twitched a whisker. "There's a lot of regret in that man, the kind of regret and hindsight that traps a human, that can eat on a person and make him miserable."

Lori and Benny emptied the trash can, tipping it high into the Dumpster, the carpet scraps and dust cascading out. After they put the can on the back porch, Benny continued to follow Lori, as clingy as a puppy. As if, Joe thought, the kid hadn't had many young friends in his short life. He thought about the hit-and-run, about the danger to Benny, and about the stabbing of Jack Reed and the possible threat to Lori, and he was glad Rock was there watching the two of them with that keen, proprietary gaze. He just hoped Rock's attention, and the vigilance of the people around the children, would be enough to protect these two from harm.

32

FIVE DAYS BEFORE Christmas, Jack Reed was transferred from Salinas Valley Hospital back to the state prison at Soledad, riding in a prison car accompanied by two guards. He was settled, not in the open infirmary, but by himself in a secure room until Victor Colletto and the other two inmates who'd attacked him had been transferred out. The room was plain, with bland beige walls and a locked, barred door. He welcomed the isolation; it beat the open infirmary, crowded among complaining, bad-tempered men with their own ills and medicines and body functions, and no nicety of canvas curtains between them as in a civilian hospital. He was processed and checked in, and the prison doc looked him over. Dr. Ralph Flaggan was a tall, meaty man with a round, baby-smooth face and a closed, superior attitude that could have put Jack off, until he thought about the men this guy had to deal with on a day-to-day basis.

"Your wounds are healing well, Jack. You're out of danger, provided there are no setbacks. Another two weeks, you should be ready to return to the general population. I don't want you out there until you can hold your own. We'll transfer you to the ward once Colletto is gone."

"Tomorrow's a visiting day," Jack said. "If my little girl wants to come, can I see her?"

"You'll go to the secure visiting room in a wheelchair," Flaggan said. "The warden has notified her guardian that you're back in the prison." This would not be the family visiting room, but a secure cubicle, again with a glass between them, where they could speak only by phone, every word subject to prison monitoring. Now, within the confining metal bars of his narrow bed he had nothing to do but think. He didn't feel like reading any of the dog-eared magazines the prison supplied; instead he lay worrying about Lori, increasingly afraid someone would try to hurt her as Vic Colletto had hurt him. Colletto was mean, his angry attack just a small indication of his vindictiveness. Jack thought Vic hadn't been put with more violent men because he was young, wasn't a gang member, and this was his first time in prison. Colletto's hatred of Jack stemmed from two years ago, when Jack had fired him.

When, that morning crossing the prison yard on his way to breakfast, Jack overheard Colletto and his two pals talking about Molena Point and Max Harper, he'd caught the name Dorriss and paused. When Colletto glanced around and saw Jack listening, he'd come at Jack. Colletto had been thick with Marlin Dorriss in prison, before Dorriss was released. Dorriss, too, was a vindictive man, and he had no love for Harper, who'd ruined his smooth thieving operation.

Jack didn't know what Dorriss and Colletto might be planning, but the conversation ate at him. Dorriss, on the outside and with moneyed friends, could set up any number of ugly operations to get back at Harper.

And if Colletto was in some way part of it, Lori might become a victim just to entertain him. Colletto, already hating Jack and blaming Jack because he was now in trouble with prison authorities, would sure as hell encourage Dorriss to rough her up, or worse.

He knew Molena Point PD would watch out for Lori, he had to count on that. But with Harper, Dorriss's agenda could be anything. The man was a cool, manipulative liar, liked to think of himself as a high roller, a charming fellow who knew how to pull strings, how to get things done and be well paid for it. He'd hire someone to do any dirty work involved, though he might enjoy roughing up a few people, too. Seemed strange he was close with the Collettos; they had no high-toned connections, no power. He was probably paying them to do the grunt work; Victor's younger brother, Kent, would be good for that. If Dorriss did plan some retribution against Max Harper, that bothered him. Max had been a good friend, he was a good man, Jack didn't want to see some scum try to take him down.

And they'd better leave Lori alone. She'd had enough ugliness in her life. She was fearful and worried about him in prison, and before that, before he was sent up, even then he'd caused her pain, he hadn't really been there for her. Then, *he'd* been the one who was afraid, afraid for Lori, terrified for her. What kind of example was that? Her mother dead, and only a weak, fearful father. No one strong enough to understand and support her. That was hard on a young girl, he understood that now. And here, in prison, he was less than useless.

The night Jack found his brother, Hal, standing over those children's graves, holding a dead child carelessly under his arm like a bag of flour, and a shovel in his other hand, the rage that hit him hadn't abated until he'd killed Hal. Until long after he'd buried him beside those pitiful little graves and shoved weeds and overgrown geraniums back over the raw earth. Nothing in the world could shake him as he'd been shaken the night he killed his brother.

That was when the battles at home began, when he and Natalie began to argue over Lori's safety. Natalie thought he was being overprotective. He never had told her the truth of it, hadn't wanted to make her a party to Hal's murder.

Then when he realized his brother's partner, Irving Fenner, was still out there killing other children, he was wild with fear again. That was when he began to lock Lori in the house, wouldn't let her go out even in the daytime, not even to school. He wouldn't tell Natalie why, he didn't want to terrify her, too, and that was his biggest mistake; their fighting grew worse until Natalie took Lori and left him, managed to get away to the East Coast where he could never find them. Since he didn't have the money for a private detective nor was he sure he could trust one, he decided it was best for Lori if he didn't know where she was, if he made no contact that could be traced. Lori was six when Natalie ran off with her, and Jack didn't see her again for five years. After Natalie died, Lori was flown back from North Carolina in the care of a social worker. And the nightmare started all over again; Jack, filled with fear for her because the killer was still out there, hid her away, boarded up the windows, locked her in the house. He'd known no other way, he couldn't go to the law. As much as he respected Max Harper, Harper would have to bring Children's Services into it, and that was all Fenner would need. He'd find Lori before the cops had enough on him to arrest him and take him off the streets, and Fenner would kill her.

But by then, Lori was older and she soon figured a way to get out of the house. She ran, found a cavelike hiding place that no one knew about. Even so, Fenner at last spotted her on the street, when the child ventured out for a few moments like a little animal coming up for food and air. Fenner followed her, Jack discovered him stalking her, and in a rictor of renewed fear he hadn't waited for the cops, he'd killed Fenner just as he'd killed Hal. Only this time, he didn't hide the body. He was too tired, he had ended the nightmare that threatened Lori, it was over, he was willing to take the lumps. When Max Harper found him with Fenner's body and arrested him, no other cop could have been more fair, could have treated him straighter than Max did. It was Max who helped him through the legalities of placing Lori with Cora Lee French and the senior ladies, and in selecting an attorney to draw up a trust for Lori that included the income from the sale of their house and of his half of the electrical company that he and his partner had established before Lori was born.

Now, Harper himself could be facing trouble, and Jack would like to give him a heads-up. In the hospital, with the guard right there in his face, he hadn't been able to say anything to Cora Lee or Lori. But now that he was back in prison, all he needed was a few seconds in the visiting room, with the guards' attention diverted. If a guard overheard him talking about criminal plans on the outside, and told the warden, Warden Deaver would be required to pass that on to Molena Point PD. That was too many people knowing. As much as Jack respected the warden, he didn't trust all the guards or every cop, not even among Harper's own officers.

How was he going to give Lori or Cora Lee any message for Harper, in a secure visiting cubicle, able to speak only through a monitored phone? He lay there worrying until he wore himself out. And then, drifting off, he got to thinking for some reason about that stray cat. Prison cat. Wondering if, when he got out of this bed and back among the prison population, back to his gardening job, he'd see that cat again. Strange he'd think about that.

He hadn't had a pet since he was a kid, hadn't had time when he was grown. And he'd never paid much attention to the cats that hung around outside the prison. Living on mice and gophers, he guessed, and on handouts from the inmates and some of the guards. He'd paid little attention except for the big yellow tomcat that had followed him and made up with him. Came trotting over every time it saw him working outside, hung around the whole time he was digging weeds and trimming bushes. He'd liked stroking it and scratching its ears. Tomcat could purr like a buzz saw. There was something about the simple honesty of an animal, unlike the deceptive layers of most humans, that eased him. When he imagined a world without animals in it, without Lori's beloved horses, without the birds that scavenged the prison yard, the friendly dogs all over Molena Point, the rabbits around the prison he saw leaping across the fields, the shy cats slipping away, he thought that such a world would be cold, and one-dimensional, that a world made up only of humans would be far more discouraging, even, than the prison that was now his home.

LORI COULDN'T STAY awake as she and Cora Lee drove through the dark midnight hours. Tired from a long morning's work at the cottage, then school, and then riding Smokey with Charlie Harper, she fell asleep before they were out of the village onto the highway. She slept all the way to Soledad, woke when Cora Lee pulled off the freeway to park in a long line of cars beside the six-lane. She imagined, inside the cars in front of them, unseen people dozing cramped and uncomfortable, waiting for morning to enter the prison, each with his own sad story. The night was still except for an occasional bump or click from within another car. She knew the noises were only sleepers shifting position, but they sounded stealthy, made her uneasy. The dark emptiness of the night, among so many strangers who could be convicts themselves, made her glad the doors were locked and that Cora Lee had her phone and her pepper spray. The night had turned cold, the wind from the freeway forcing icy fingers in around the closed windows, the glass cold against her hand. She yawned, pulled her coat collar up, and despite her fear she curled up against the door, dropping once more into sleep.

She dreamed that Benny was trapped underneath a whole stack of Maudie's quilts. Maudie kept frantically pulling off quilts, trying to free him—but then the quilts were pale hands, thin, white hands reaching for him, Maudie throwing quilts over the hands to try to smother them.

She woke at first light, cold and cramped, and startled that she was in the parked car. Some time during the night she had crawled over into the backseat and lay twisted up in the blanket Cora Lee had thrown over her. Rising up, she looked into the front.

Cora Lee was asleep behind the wheel, her head resting against the side window. Her dark curly hair was so short it was never out of place. She had pulled her creamy down jacket over her legs. Her hand lay inches from her cell phone, and from the can of pepper spray half concealed beneath the edge of her jacket. Looking out across the freeway, Lori studied the huge, pale box that was the prison, a cold, impersonal building. She hated this place, it made her feel as small and helpless as a bug. Pa shouldn't be here, he should have gotten a medal for killing those two men, not be locked up. She hated the powers in the world that you couldn't reason with, powers that sucked the life out of a person.

Cora Lee didn't wake until the cars around them began to start up, their engines grumbling in the cold morning. At once Cora Lee was awake, starting their own car, nosing along in the slow line to the 101 freeway and crossing over, above it, then into the prison yard. Through the gate and into the parking lot, where everyone piled out of their cars and made a dash to get in line, or for the Porta Pottis. They got in line, and in a little while Cora Lee turned to the lady behind them, a short, square, black-haired woman, and asked her to hold their place. They couldn't take turns standing in line to use the Porta Pottis, if a guard saw a child standing there alone he'd come to investigate, tell them that was against the rules. It was so cold they were both shivering. Coming back, they washed their hands with the wipes Cora Lee had brought; then Cora Lee unwrapped their sandwiches, to eat standing in line. Cream cheese and ham, from their paper bag. Milk for Lori, which they'd kept cold in an ice chest in the car. Orange juice for Cora Lee. Around them, the lawn was neatly cut, the bushes trimmed so perfectly they looked artificial. As if the trustees who cared for them had all the time in the world, and she guessed they did.

It seemed hours until they reached the gate, dumped their trash in a receptacle, and went inside. People ahead of them had to empty their pockets, hand over their purses, go through a body scan. Like at the airport. At least they weren't patted down, she'd hate that, a stranger's hands all over her. Cora Lee had locked her purse in the trunk. She dropped her car keys on the table. A guard pulled Pa's file, their picture IDs were checked, and they signed in. They moved on through the narrow entrance building, a few people at a time, and through a barred gate into a prison yard, then into the prison itself. Down a hall, this time not to the visitors' big, open room with its long table and vending machines, but to a small room where they sat down at a little square table, in hard chairs, but again facing a clear glass barrier, with a phone on either side of the glass. "Why is it different?"

"Security," Cora Lee said.

"Why? Pa didn't do anything."

"The other guy did. They're protecting your pa." Cora Lee looked down at her, her brown eyes concerned for her. They watched the prisoners march in, glimpses of them between the pillars as they moved down the table to take their seats facing their visitors. Pa arrived in a wheelchair pushed by a nurse. It shocked her to see a woman in the men's prison, though she knew women worked there. Pa's legs were covered by a brown blanket. He looked so frail. But as he was wheeled up to the table, he grinned at her through the glass. She hated that glass, she hated the phone that filtered their every word, their whole visit wasted on meaningless questions and canned answers: "How are you feeling?" "Much better, it doesn't hurt so much. How're you doing in school?" "Fine." "How's your pony?" "He's fine. I've been riding with Charlie Harper." So stiff and unreal, eating up their precious time. She could see Pa wanted to tell them something, something he couldn't say with the phone monitored. Was this another message for Max Harper? She wanted to crawl through the glass so they could talk—like Alice stepping through the looking glass—so she could hug him and tell him she loved him. She wanted to tell him Harper had gotten his first message all right, Cora Lee had seen to that.

"Thanks from our friend," Lori said, "from Charlie's husband."

226

Pa smiled and nodded, and looked relieved. Whatever more he wanted to say, he kept to himself, until, Lori thought, they could be back in the family visitors' room again, where they might not be monitored. She hoped that wouldn't be long, she hated this, hated being listened to, with no privacy; she hated it more for Pa, even, than for herself.

THE LAST JACK saw of Lori was her rigid, angry back, angry at the rules, he thought as she and Cora Lee filed out of the visiting room, Lori's long brown hair shining in the overhead lights. On his side of the glass the line of prisoners marched out, too, and he was wheeled away to the infirmary, his message for Max Harper unspoken. He knew Harper would figure it out when the pieces started coming together, but meantime who knew how much damage Arlie Risso would do? He felt worn out, even with only that short time in the visiting room. With the stress of being unable to talk freely, to let Max know about Risso—about Marlin Dorriss. The doc said it was normal to tire out easily while his body was healing. Well, he didn't have to like it, he was done in. Not since he'd tried to protect Lori when she was just a little girl had he felt so damned useless.

33

Cats weren't officially barred from city council meetings but only because no one had ever imagined that a cat would want to attend. It was Ryan who'd insisted they bring Joe. She'd hung tough until she won the argument, and just for an instant Joe was chagrined to be the cause of the new-lyweds' heated conflict. But if the two had to battle, what more urgent subject was there than the happiness of the family cat?

"He'll be good," she'd told Clyde, fixing Joe with a threatening gaze that made his fur twitch. He'd tried to look innocent, but they all three knew his behavior would depend on the situation of the moment, on his anger as a few biased citizens rose to criticize Max Harper and make trouble for the chief.

The city hall had begun life, early in the last century, as a village church. The peak of the handsome red-wood building rose steeply between two lower wings that now housed a variety of city offices, from administrator to public works and zoning. The gnarled branches of a twisted oak sheltered the deep porch, which was reached by a sturdy ramp to accommodate the occasional wheelchair. Beside the front door stood two ceramic pots of holly bushes heavy with red berries. Taped to the rail were paper cutout Santas and reindeer, hand-colored by the local schoolchildren. Within the wide entry foyer stood a six-foot Christmas tree, thick and dense, decorated with silver and white bells. Deeper in, against a long expanse of wall, the crèche had been arranged, the wise men as tall as six-year-old children, the little Christ child snuggled in his crib. The wooden figures, carved by hand nearly a hundred years before, were still celebrating the traditional spirit of Christmas despite a few hard-nosed citizens who didn't approve of such sentiments.

Joe, concealed within the leather tote that Ryan carried, could see only the high, raftered ceiling as they entered the meeting room. Ryan tucked the bag on the seat of the wooden pew beside her, where he listened to the reading of the minutes; he yawned and dozed off during a tedious discussion of city business. He came wide awake when members of the audience began to file up, one at a time, to the little side podium that featured its own microphone. Each citizen speaker stood at the side of the room facing both the audience and the council that sat behind the polished wood barrier: a council of three men and one woman, and the woman mayor, her white hair knotted at the nape of her neck, her navy blazer well cut over a white silk blouse. Each citizen to come forward talked about the home invasions, venting considerable anger toward the police. It was amazing to Joe that the speakers would rant so vehemently about the department's incompetence when Chief Harper sat not three feet from them, just beside their small podium.

Max wasn't there to make a rebuttal, this was a traditional part of the chief's job. The city charter required his presence to keep order, though there'd never been a fistfight in a Molena Point meeting. Max, in uniform and wearing a sidearm, listened without expression, an enforcer of the law, a guardian against some outbreak of unbridled rage. Hard to imagine, Joe thought, in this small village. In San Francisco or Detroit, matters might deteriorate as had indeed happened in several large cities, one even evolving into a near-fatal shooting. In most Molena Point council meetings, the tomcat suspected, one was more likely to die from boredom.

But not this afternoon. Despite Max's disinterested expression, the tomcat would give a year's supply of deli takeout to know what the chief was thinking as a dozen misinformed and angry diatribes were laid on the council members and audience, and on the chief. Peering discreetly over the top of the bag, he watched the tiny crease at the side of Max's mouth, just the ghost of a smile. As each speaker questioned the competence of MPPD, the male council members maintained suitably blank expressions; only Pansy Nitonski, her thin face framed by straight, chin-length brown hair, smirked with ill-concealed pleasure at the insults, making Joe want to slash her smug face.

Well, but nothing would be decided at this meeting, no decision would be made here about whether Max was competent in his job. That issue would be resolved in private session; this display was all smoke and mirrors, because the city council had no final authority in the matter. They were advisors; they couldn't directly fire Max though they certainly had input with the city manager. He was the one responsible for hiring and firing the chief, often advised by a board of experts that could include police chiefs from other central coast cities—but these accusations were so trumped up they were laughable. Joe burned to leap to the podium and have his own say, tell these airheads just how wrong they were.

He also would have liked to see how the audience was responding, he could see nothing from the bottom of the damned bag. He'd like to know whether Phelps Leibert was in the crowd, too. Leibert was head of security at the local college and was the man the *Gazette* was pushing, in its editorials, as a replacement for Harper: a harsh, controlling, egocentric man who would be bad news indeed for MPPD, for the whole village. Most likely, Leibert had had the good sense to stay away from the meeting, not telegraph his punches, not let anyone think he cared what happened. How would it look for him to be there watching Max and the department deliberately trashed, when everyone knew he hoped to replace Max in the near future.

Natty Bowen had come to the podium, and she sounded nervous as hell. Joe eased up out of the bag for a quick look. The thin, worn woman had dressed for the occasion in a lavender velvet jogging suit that she'd accessorized with enough gold jewelry to serve her as workout weights—gold necklaces, gold choker, gold earrings.

Her slim feet were encased in lavender and pink glitter-encrusted sports shoes that looked as if they'd never been out of the box before this very afternoon. Her delivery was nervous but pushy, and she stuck closely to an apparently rehearsed agenda, as did the other speakers: The invasions were terrifying, people were being injured, traumatized, no telling what the lasting effects would be on these poor women, and many thousands of dollars' worth of property had been damaged. Why were the police looking the other way, not putting a stop to these atrocities? And though Natty might have stammered through her presentation, the next speaker did not.

Having returned to the bottom of the bag, Joe slipped up again when he heard Arlie Risso introduced. He was straining to see over the top of the seat in front of them when Ryan's hand forced him back down. Holding him out of sight, she gave him the faintest headshake, as if someone were watching. Subsiding irritably under Ryan's confining hand, he listened to Risso explain that, being a new resident, he'd been shocked and disappointed when, after buying a home in the village, these terrible invasions began, even right there in his own neighborhood. So disappointed he'd almost decided to sell and move on, find a more amenable environment in which to enjoy his retirement—his tone, and his expensive cashmere sport coat, white silk shirt, and silk tie implied a more amenable environment in which to spend his considerable retirement income. His polished delivery was as fake as that of a telephone solicitor asking for your Social Security number. Peering up again when Ryan glanced away, Joe watched Risso make eye contact with each council member, his penetrating look bringing color to Pansy's cheeks. Risso ended his two minutes with a plea for the law to "Step in and lock up the miscreants and save our lovely village," making Joe want to upchuck his breakfast. When Risso left the podium, and Ryan let go of Joe's neck, he slid up for another quick look. Yes, Arlie Risso was the guy in the motel room, slick black hair, neatly trimmed black beard. Before Joe ducked down again, he caught a glimpse of Max Harper's face, too. Max's flash of surprised recognition, quickly hidden, made the tomcat smile. The chief had quickly stripped away the black hair and black beard, replaced them with handsomely styled silver hair. This man's skin was tanned to a darker shade, and even his black-dyed eyebrows sharply changed his appearance. But both Joe and Max knew him as Dorriss: con artist, master chameleon, the slick investor and thief whom Joe had helped Max put in prison a couple of years back. He'd be willing to bet this was the first time Max had seen Dorriss since Dorriss arrived in the village. Dorriss had probably taken great pains to stay out of the way of the cops, either remaining indoors or hiding behind the tinted glass of the Caddy or the Toyota, keeping a low profile, avoiding anyone who might know him. Joe wondered if Dulcie and Kit had gotten a look at Risso/Dorriss from where they crouched outside among the limbs of the oak that overhung the main entry. Risso, standing at the side podium with its auxiliary microphone, appeared totally unaware of Max, as if the chief might be just any rookie cop, even though Risso had had extensive dealings with Max.

Only after Risso had his say and took his seat again did two speakers point out that if citizens weren't prepared, if

they had no alarm system or did not call 911, then patrol
units *could* only arrive after the fact, after the harm was
done. While Joe was grateful for these sensible folks, what
he wondered was, after the meeting, would Max Harper
arrest Risso? Did he have enough evidence to hold him?
Or would he put a tail on the man, wait to apprehend him
at the next invasion attempt and, in Risso's words, *Step in
and lock up the miscreants?*

She left the city council meeting never looking in
Arlie's direction. She had debated whether to come, had
waited in the shadows of a shop across the street, and then
had slipped in among the crowd of locals, taken a seat way
in the back. She'd almost turned and left again when she
saw the police chief sitting up front in some kind of official
capacity. Why would a cop be at a city council meeting?
In this little burg? This wasn't L.A. or New York. Nervously she'd sat down behind a tall man, hoping to be out
of Harper's sight. Though he couldn't know her, couldn't
have any interest in her, he made her nervous. The speakers from the audience had been entertaining—angry, ac-
cusing, just what Arlie wanted. It had come off very well,
and she knew he'd be in a good mood later.

When that part of the meeting was finished and the
council moved on to other city business, she'd wanted
to leave, but couldn't without attracting attention. She'd
wasted an excruciatingly boring hour before she could
vanish within the crowd. The streets were growing dark,
and the sea wind was cold. Walking up the street, turn-

ing right at the first side street, and then left, she headed up the eight blocks to the new motel room she'd checked into—it was a drag to move, but something about the first place had made Arlie nervous. Hurrying through the little lobby and down the hall, into the darkening room, she sat down to wait for him. It had been a successful meeting from his standpoint, a waste of time for her. This had nothing to do with her, except that she enjoyed the drama, she liked seeing Arlie at work.

Her involvement with the invasions had started as a favor, a trade-off that had ended up entangling her more than she liked. Now she was sorry she'd connected up with Arlie; she wouldn't have if she'd known that he and the Colletto boys knew each other, that Arlie had been in prison with Victor. Talk about coincidence—this was an ugly one.

She'd thought she could spend some time with Arlie in San Francisco, now that he was out on parole, that she could bring back some of the excitement of their weekends in Vegas, and then come on down here alone to the village, take care of her business. But it hadn't worked that way. Well, she was moving toward what she wanted. But she was being sucked in deeper than she liked by Arlie's affairs, and away from her own objective. It angered her that he was paying out hard cash for these break-ins but wasn't paying her, that he figured her help was for old times' sake.

Whatever compensation she got would be from Maudie. Meanwhile, she had to admit, she liked the excitement of the invasions, getting in and out fast, the quick violence, terrifying those soft little women. The invaders were always the winners, and that was how she liked to play. And now, with David Toola gone, Maudie was just as easy a mark. She'd soon have the papers and, when she was done with Maudie, she'd have the money that was rightfully hers, would be out of California headed wherever she chose.

34

THE OAK TREES outside Maudie's bedroom windows were barely visible when she woke, the sky deep gray, just beginning to lighten. Rising, she pulled on her warm robe and slippers and headed downstairs, glancing into Benny and Jared's room to make sure the two slept soundly. She liked her early mornings alone, she liked the solitude. Today she would move into her new studio and she could hardly wait to get started; she wanted to do what she could before Jared came down to help her, wanted to do it her way. She felt like a kid at the prospect of her new work space, was nearly giddy with excitement.

In the kitchen she made a pot of coffee, and while it brewed she stepped into the dark studio, enjoying the clean smell of new lumber and fresh paint. Beyond the bare glass of the floor-to-ceiling windows the twisted oak branches loomed black and remote against the predawn sky. It was still too dark to see if anyone stood among the trees, looking in—but Pearl wouldn't be prowling this early in the morning, she needn't be prepared for her at this hour, Pearl was a late sleeper.

She was so anxious to get settled, to stack her bolts of bright fabric neatly on the shelves, to arrange her quilting frames, quilting table, and cutting table, to have them all in place beside her computer and sewing machines. Once she got to work, she'd feel that she was really home.

Working here would be like working right in the garden, she thought, in her own small Eden where her invented patterns would vie in color with cascades of garden flowers. Martin would have liked the new studio, she told herself, trying to put away the heaviness that surrounded every thought of him; he would have approved of their moving back to the village.

Quickly she returned to the kitchen, poured a cup of coffee, and carried it into the chill garage, propping the door open behind her. Setting her cup down on a carton, she pulled the lightweight office cart over to a stack of boxes and began sliding the smaller ones onto it, using her good arm. Jared and Scotty would help later with the heavy ones, and the furniture. She worked for nearly an hour, trying not to think about Martin. Thinking about Benny, and about Pearl, her emotions swinging from sadness to rage, to a cold need to see Pearl punished, to make right this one terrible wrong in the world. Wheeling her loaded cart into the studio, she opened the boxes, began to stack fabric neatly on the shelves, to arrange her spools of thread and small equipment in the new drawers that Scotty had built. When she had put away all she could, she returned the empty boxes to the garage, stacking them in one corner. That was when she realized that some of the packed boxes were missing: two bankers' boxes containing Caroline's personal papers and the mementos and photographs that she was saving for Benny. They had been right here just days ago, when she removed the sealed envelope from the kitchen box.

She wondered if Benny might have taken the boxes up to his room. But no, she'd cleaned in there late yesterday, had dusted under the beds and in the closet. Would the child hide them somewhere? Did he think she might throw them out when she moved everything else, that she'd decide she didn't want to store them? She *had* said she'd be glad when the garage was cleared out, when she could pull the car in. Did Benny think she'd give Caroline's things away, after she'd gone to the trouble of packing and moving them three hundred miles from L.A.? But who knew what scenario might occur to a child whose first seven years had been filled broken promises?

No, she thought. Pearl *had* returned, but when? Had she, not finding the ledger pages, taken the boxes to allow time for a more leisurely search? Maybe she thought Caroline had secreted the papers among her tax files or medical records, where one would have to go through everything to find them? Anger filled her that Caroline's family photos were gone, and the mementos of Benny's few short months with his stepmother that the child so valued, as well as Caroline's marriage certificates, Benny's father's enlistment papers, and the official notice of his death. She didn't like losing Caroline's tax records, either, which she'd agreed to send on to Caroline's sister along with a clutter of old family recipes and letters, and copies of a family genealogy that Caroline had saved for her own children, too many heavy items to take on the plane when she had the two children and their suitcases. The bigger cartons, containing the rest of the children's clothes and books and toys, seemed undisturbed, nearly hidden beneath Maudie's own cartons. She stood in the cold garage sipping her cooling coffee, feeling both frightened and energized, her hand straying once to the comforting weight hidden in her robe pocket. Now, with the whole village edgy over the invasions, who could fault her if she was prepared to defend herself and protect her grandchild?

It was six-thirty when she heard Jared getting up, heard the shower running. Rousing herself, she hurried back into the kitchen to heat the waffle iron, to get out the big pitcher of waffle batter she'd made the day before, the butter and syrup, and to put bacon on the grill. In the downstairs bath she washed her face, gargled some mouthwash, and ran a comb through her hair. When Jared came down, she said nothing about the missing boxes. Just as, days earlier, she hadn't mentioned the missing keys. Jared appeared in the kitchen showered and scrubbed, dressed in a fresh blue sport shirt and Dockers. Benny straggled down behind him yawning, still in his sailboat pajamas. They ate in comfortable silence, Jared reading the sports page, Maudie scanning another ugly editorial about the invasions, then turning to the home section, while Benny carefully distributed the butter and syrup evenly into each well of his waffle. He ate each quarter with equal concentration, as if even homemade waffles were a special treat. It was seven-thirty and they'd finished breakfast when

Scotty arrived, parking his truck at the curb. Coming in, accepting a quick cup of coffee, he stood at the counter to drink it, avoiding the syrupy mess at the table, which made Maudie smile. Scotty's bright blue work shirt made his red hair and beard blaze like flame. "Wanted to get in an hour's work or so, before we begin pouring cement up at the cottage," he said.

Jared grinned and rose, and the two men headed into the garage, Benny following. During the next hour, the child insisted on carrying heavy loads for such a little boy, but Maudie didn't caution or scold, she knew the one thing Benny needed was to feel useful. The two of them had spent the previous afternoon, as Scotty finished up the painting and hardware and locks, baking cherry pies and apple tarts for the Damens' potluck afternoon and evening that this year fell on the same Sunday as the village pageant. Benny was so excited about dinner at Ryan and Clyde's house and all the events to follow: the reenactment, in the park, of the journey of Joseph and Mary; the choirs in the village streets; and, most of all, the wagon rides put on by half a dozen village horsemen, who would trailer their horses and haul the wagons into town for the event. The usually silent child had chattered nonstop as together they prepared the cherry filling and peeled the apples. In the warm, spice-scented kitchen, Benny had seemed almost to forget the nightmares that made him wake up screaming and continue shivering as she held and cuddled him.

In L.A., friends had told her she should take Benny to a therapist, but she didn't want to do that; she didn't like

241

the idea of a stranger manipulating the child's emotions. She would provide all the therapy she could, holding and loving Benny, getting him to join her in household tasks and encouraging new interests. Providing real sit-down meals and as much companionship as an old woman could give a little boy. Benny loved being in the kitchen with her; Pearl's kitchen had been a cold, neglected place where the child had to make his own sandwiches and hope the milk wasn't sour. Benny liked being with Ryan and Scotty, too, liked watching them at work. Under the watchful eye of Scotty and of Lori Reed, he was learning the proper use of the simpler carpentry tools, to drive a nail without smashing his thumb, to saw a board straight and easy.

Jared's presence in the house was a help, too, and her nephew seemed to have taken a real interest in Benny. That morning, after they'd moved everything into the studio, Jared made sandwiches, packed a lunch, and took Benny with him to run errands, and for an impromptu picnic. She was sorry Jared couldn't join them at the Damens'. He'd said, making a face, that his mother made it clear she had special plans.

Maudie, enjoying a little break and a moment of solitude, was sitting at the kitchen table with her own lunch and a cup of tea when Ryan came down the hill, pulling her truck into the drive. She had to smile as Ryan stepped out, and not only the big silver Weimaraner jumped out, but the gray tomcat, too, behaving almost like a small dog. She didn't know what it was about that particular cat and his two friends, but Benny surely had taken to them.

Benny had never had a pet. Pearl didn't like animals; she said they were dirty and that people simply wasted their money on useless beasts. Caroline and Martin had planned to get the three children a puppy for Christmas—another simple joy taken from them. She rose to let Ryan in. "Have you had lunch? Jared made chicken sandwiches, and there's a pot of tea."

"That sounds wonderful." Ryan laid the final bill and the studio keys on the table. "I meant to go home and warm up a bowl of soup, but this is much nicer. You sure you want company?"

"I'd love the company. Bring Rock in, please." She needn't invite Joe Grey in, the tomcat was already stretched out on the stairs. "Rock's such a lovely dog," she said, stroking his sleek head. "We had Dobermans when the boys were growing up. Martin . . ." Her voice caught. "Martin was very good at training them, they had lovely manners. As does Rock," she added. "Would you prefer coffee to tea?"

"The tea smells good," Ryan said, glancing at the steaming ceramic teapot. "You *are* coming for dinner tomorrow? It will be casual, and there'll be other children in and out, the younger officers' children. Just a potluck buffet, and we'll eat in relays when officers take their breaks or go off duty. The Harpers usually have it at the ranch, but with everyone on extra patrol, it makes more sense to have it at our place, where the men can move out faster." She watched Maudie pour the tea. "You're moving into the studio today?"

Maudie smiled. "The cartons are all moved. I've sent Jared and Benny on errands. Sometimes it's easier to work alone, for unpacking and organizing."

"And more satisfying," Ryan said. "Organizing a creative work space *should* be a solitary occupation." She studied Maudie, her green eyes questioning. "You're upset about something?"

"I didn't think it showed," Maudie said. "This morning, I found a couple of boxes missing from the garage, Caroline's things that I'd saved for Benny. I thought he might have taken them up to his room, but I'd already been through the room, cleaning. I expect they'll turn up, but it's puzzling. I . . . didn't mention this to Jared," she cautioned. She didn't know why she'd mentioned it to Ryan. The moment she did, she was sorry. "Nothing else is missing," she said quickly.

Ryan looked at her sternly. "You haven't reported it to the police?"

"I would have," she said quickly, "if I'd found anything else missing, or found where someone had broken in. I examined the garage door, all the doors and windows. There's no sign of damage."

"The police wouldn't have to send out a patrol car. If you reported it, it would be on record. That would help in case anything more happens." Ryan tried not to scold, but this was worrisome. Why this distaste for the police? "The department does have its hands full," she said, "with these invasions, but certainly they'd take a report."

"You're not thinking there's some connection?"

"Probably not," Ryan said shortly. On the floor by her feet, Rock rolled over, sighing. But on the third step, Joe Grey watched Maudie with such keen interest that Ryan gave him a warning scowl.

Maudie said, "That's why I didn't call the police, because they *are* busy. I saw this morning's *Gazette* . . . I wouldn't have started taking it if I'd realized just how one-sided the paper is." She passed the sandwich plate, seemed pleased when Ryan took another quarter-cut morsel. "I don't remember this newspaper being that way, all the summers our family spent in the village when the boys were small."

"The paper was sold recently. No one I know likes this new approach—though I haven't heard of anyone canceling their subscription," Ryan said wryly. Glancing around the big kitchen with its glass door into the studio, she was acutely aware of how open the house was, kitchen, living room, and entry open to one another with no way to shut any room off, open stairway leading to the bedrooms, no way to secure the second floor. "You haven't considered an alarm system?"

"I thought about it, but they're such a bother, always having to remember to arm and disarm them, and then sometimes they go off for no reason, throwing everyone into a panic. I keep the doors locked, the windows locked except when I'm right in the room. Unfortunately," she said, "I've misplaced my second set of keys, and that's worrisome, but they'll show up."

Ryan remained quiet. She couldn't understand, as vulnerable as Maudie was here alone, and with the shooting so recent and raw in her emotions, how she could be so unconcerned. She had started to speak, to ask more about the missing keys, when she caught Joe Grey's eye, the tomcat's look so intense that she had to look away.

What was he telling her? But then almost as if he'd spoken, Ryan knew. It was the one question Joe had asked her about the shooting, the one element of that double murder that Maudie had never made clear, that she seemed to have carefully skirted, the few times the subject was mentioned.

On that black night, on that dark mountain road, with only the thin flicker of moonlight Maudie had described, *had* she seen the face of the killer?

If she'd seen the shooter and had told the police, wouldn't she have been encouraged to stay in L.A., maybe with a guard, until the shooter was arrested and she could identify him? If she was the only witness, surely the LAPD wouldn't have wanted her to move away. Ryan could conclude only that, most likely, Maudie hadn't seen the shooter. And yet the woman's unease when she talked about the shooting, something apart from the horror and pain of the murder, made both Ryan and Joe Grey wonder.

"That night," Ryan said, "the night of the shooting— *did* you see the killer? See anything you could tell the police?"

"Nothing," Maudie said quickly. "The sheriff questioned me while I was in the hospital. Later when I got out, when David took me home, the L.A. police questioned me. I guess they were doing some kind of . . ." Maudie paused, searching for the word.

"Collateral investigation?" Ryan asked.

Maudie nodded. "But no, that night—so black . . . Hardly any moon at all. It had been a hot day, was still hot and we had the top down. Suddenly the pickup loomed beside us, seemed to come out of nowhere, racing along next to us, and the next instant the gunshots, the noise, and those three explosions of light blinding me, the car spinning out of control and going over . . ." Maudie said, telling more than she'd been asked, more than was needed.

Ryan said no more. She glanced at Joe Grey, feeling the same uncertainty that gleamed in the tomcat's eyes. At that moment, woman and cat were caught in the same sure sense that Maudie wanted only to divert Ryan, that she was surely holding something back.

Had she lied to the L.A. detectives? Maybe lied so she'd be free to leave L.A., so the police wouldn't press her to stay in the city, under their protection? Or if Maudie was the only one who could identify the killer, would she lie to protect herself, so the killer wouldn't come after her?

But this was all conjecture. Probably in the dark night, Ryan thought, Maudie had seen nothing more than the flashes of the gun, she was most likely telling the truth, had told L.A. everything she knew. After all, who more than Maudie would want to see the killer pay for those brutal murders?

35

 IT WAS HARDLY light when the first good smells of party food filtered up to Joe's tower from the kitchen below. The tomcat woke, yawning, drinking in the scents of frying meat and onions. Ryan and Clyde would be putting together the tamale pie, and probably the taco fillings, for the Christmas party. Out across the roofs, long streaks of sunrise bloomed beneath a cover of heavy gray clouds. But it wouldn't rain, he couldn't smell rain in the offing. No matter what the weather gurus might think, Joe knew better; he knew the sky would clear before the day's festivities. Rising from among his pillows, his mind on the feast to come, he headed in through his cat door onto the heavy rafter. Dropping down to Clyde's desk, he hit the floor and galloped down the stairs.

Clyde was just setting the last of five huge casseroles on the counter, to be baked later. Joe reared up, looking. "You leave any for my breakfast? I'd be happy to lick the pot."

"It isn't fully cooked yet," Clyde said, glancing at the casseroles.

"It's cooked enough for me." He leaped up to the counter as Clyde, having indeed saved some back, set down a small plate of the half-cooked delicacy for him. Besides the tamale pie and tacos, there would be all manner of food for the buffet, a ham, chicken pies from Jolly's Deli, and a variety of salads and casseroles that their friends would bring, all carefully packed in Styrofoam coolers. Dinner would go on all afternoon in a marathon buffet as officers came and went, taking their hasty breaks. Every available officer would be on duty. With all the events scheduled, this could be a perfect time for an invasion—not a pleasant end to a happy holiday celebration, to return home in a happy mood and find unwelcome visitors offering a dark side to the usual Christmas greetings.

As soon as Ryan and Clyde had opened up the big round table in the kitchen and laid out the napkins and plates and silverware, Ryan disappeared into the guest room. Joe followed her, leaping up onto the wicker desk among boxes of Christmas cards and unwrapped gifts. Though their tree was up, filling a corner of the living room, and Clyde had mailed his cards to favorite clients, Ryan hadn't started her own cards or wrapped her gifts. "Why the hurry?" Joe said. "Christmas is a whole week away."

"I don't need the sarcasm," she said, scratching his ear. The bed was covered with boxes and bags from her favorite village shops, and with rolls of red and green Christmas paper. Beneath the wide windows, the wicker game table held boxes of Christmas cards, stamps, and sheets of computer-printed address labels. She had set up a fold-ing table nearby, where her scissors and tape and fancy tags were lined up awaiting a frenzy of gift wrapping. A box of tall red Christmas candles stood on the nightstand, scenting the room with bayberry. "I was supposed to start the new house up on Third next week," she said. "I put them off until after New Year's. Between it and our own remodels, I'm lucky to have even a start on Christmas. I hate being stressed during the holidays."

Joe looked at the organized start she'd already made, and thought about the nine houses she'd remodeled just this last year, and could only admire Ryan's efficiency. If she'd been a cat, she'd be a skilled mouser, every move keenly planned—the little beasts wouldn't have a prayer. Rubbing against her hand, he said, "Thanks for loaning us the phone. And for not asking questions."

"What's the point in asking? You'll tell me only what you want me to hear."

What he'd told her was that he needed to borrow a cell phone, just for today. She'd looked at him for a long time. He'd be around the house today, so why would he need a phone? He could use the house phone, could find privacy upstairs if he needed to make a call. And who would he call? Dulcie and Kit would be right there, as well as half the department, the chief, the detectives. But now, too cu-rious to remain polite, she did ask.

"Is the phone for that yellow tomcat?"

Silently Joe looked at her.

"I've seen him on the roofs. I thought . . . the way he acted . . ." Her eyes widened, then she laughed. "So he *is* like you!" And then she couldn't help it, that one question burst into multiple questions. "Where did he come from? He has to be new to the village. He's not part of the wild clowder from up in the hills?" She shook her head. "I said I wouldn't ask, but . . ." She looked down at the table, feeling shy suddenly, and spread out the first sheet of bright wrapping paper.

Joe watched her with a crooked smile. Ryan was as curious as a cat herself, no wonder they were friends. Sitting on the desk watching her wrap Christmas gifts, he told her what he knew about the yellow tomcat, about Misto's journey from Soledad prison hiding in Jared's T-Bird. Told her what Misto had learned in prison about Maudie's nephew, Kent, and about Marlin Dorriss. "Right now," Joe said, "Misto's watching Maudie's house, that's why he needs the phone. She's had one mysterious burglary, and her keys have vanished. If a burglar has them, he need only unlock the door and step in." He couldn't understand why Maudie hadn't changed the locks, he didn't think that was an oversight. Made him wonder if Maudie *wanted* someone to enter, perhaps when the house was empty or in the small hours, unbidden. "I don't know what this is about," he said uneasily, "but with no one home, with Maudie and Benny here for dinner, and Jared with his family, it can't hurt to watch the place."

The phone Ryan had stashed on the cottage roof was an old, discarded model that the local electronics shop had taken in trade, to pass on to old folks in home care facilities. The shop owner was a friend of hers, she'd done some carpentry work for him. The phone had a new battery and was in good working order, and she'd set up a temporary account for it under an assumed name. She'd added to its convenience by keying in one-digit operation for the Damens' house, Wilma and Dulcie, Max's and Dallas's cell numbers, and her own cell. And now, to cheer the old cat while he was on watch alone in the branches of Maudie's oak tree, she said she'd take him a plate of selections from the buffet, leave it on the cottage roof.

"Where did that cat come from before the prison?" Ryan said. "Is he all alone?"

Hopping from the desk to the table among the tangle of bright Christmas wrappings, Joe sat down on the gold paper she was folding around a box. "I don't know the whole story, but you can bet Kit will find out." He went silent when he heard Max's voice just out in the hall, and then Dallas. They were talking about day patrol, the voices coming from the alcove just beside the stairs. Other voices, from the front door, cut in as more guests arrived, and then Max was saying, " . . . to know why she checked out of the motel. Maybe you made her nervous."

Dallas laughed. "I'll check the other motels. Long shot, though, that she's registered under her own name."

"I had a call from L.A.," Max said, "just as we were leaving the house. Detective Lakey. He said they went over the Beckman offices again, found a false compartment under the center drawer of Pearl's desk. Pearl's prints were on the metal plate that holds the false bottom in place—and so were Caroline Toola's."

"Say Caroline knew Pearl was keeping a double set of books," Dallas said, "she made a copy, put the original back."

"But she didn't report the thefts," Max said. "As if she meant to blackmail Pearl?"

"Or she didn't have time?" Dallas said. "Say Pearl booby-trapped the drawer, slipped a hair across the opening, something so she knew it had been tampered with. She figures it was Caroline, maybe Caroline had been nosing around before that. Pearl kills Martin and Caroline not only out of jealousy, but to stop Caroline from turning over the copies to Beckman or to the law."

Ryan was embarrassed to be inadvertently eavesdropping, though she hadn't heard anything the two men wouldn't have told her. But Joe Grey smiled with satisfaction as the officers fitted the pieces together—with no clue that they were helping to inform their prime snitch as well.

Not until Max and Dallas moved away did Joe and Ryan leave their hideaway and return to join their guests. The crowd had doubled, the front door stood open, and the street was lined with cars—not much chance of robbers here, with half the guests in uniform and armed, sitting down only long enough to enjoy the pre-Christmas treats. Sunlight slanted in through the open front door, warming the living room where happy diners sat with their loaded plates on their laps. There was a crowd in the kitchen around the buffet, too, and outside on the back patio where the sun's heat bounced off the high plaster wall, guests sat elbow to elbow at four long tables enjoying the feast. Joe was winding between pant legs and bare ankles, heading for the living room, when Lucinda and Pedric Greenlaw arrived, Pedric carrying Kit on his shoulder. As the tortoiseshell leaped to the mantel, out of the way of hard shoes, the tall, slim, gray-haired couple stood talking with Clyde. Behind them, Wilma and Dulcie came in, Wilma dressed in jeans and a red blazer with a sprig of holly on her lapel, her white hair done in a braid that circled her head. Dulcie jumped to the mantel, too, beside Kit, and Joe made a flying leap to join them. Clyde headed for the kitchen and soon returned with three small, cat-sized plates loaded with delicacies, which he set before them. Around the cats, there were scattered moments of silence as newcomers bowed their heads in prayers of thanks before they settled down to enjoy their meal. Maybe law enforcement families, Joe thought, were more aware than most of the preciousness of life, more thankful for what they had. When he looked up, Maudie and Benny were just coming in.

Maudie was dressed in one of her soft-toned quilted smocks over neatly creased slacks. Benny wore his tan chinos and a blue V-necked sweater over a white shirt. The moment they entered, the little boy pressed against his grandmother, staring up at the crowd—but then he saw Rock sitting beside the couch with his head on Kathleen Ray's lap, and the little boy went straight to the big Weimaraner.

Rock let Benny grab him in a bear hug that would have angered many dogs, but the Weimaraner only licked Benny's ear and wagged his short tail. Kathleen moved over on the couch to make room for Maudie; the detective was dressed for surveillance in faded jeans, an old faded T-shirt, and worn jogging shoes. Joe had seen her arrive in an older Ford sedan, one of the unobtrusive cars Max sometimes obtained from Rent-a-Wreck when he wanted his officers to move about the village unnoticed.

"Are you getting moved in?" Kathleen asked Maudie. "That's not a job I like."

"Actually," Maudie said, "I'm doing pretty well. Our tree is up, I have most everything put away, and I'm moved into the new studio."

"That wasn't easy, with your hurt shoulder. It's been, what, eight months since you were shot? That's another thing that seems to take forever, to recover from a wound like that."

"I've been using a rolling cart," Maudie said. "One of those lightweight office models that I can shove the boxes onto." She smiled. "That's given my other arm a workout. I'm just glad it wasn't my right shoulder that was hit." She looked up when Lori and Cora Lee arrived, along with Mavity Flowers. The other two senior ladies were gone for the holidays, Susan Brittain to her daughter in San Francisco, Gabrielle, always looking for a new beau, off on a cruise to Greece. Lori took Benny's hand and they headed straight for the kitchen buffet table, Cora Lee following the hungry pair.

Ryan came to join Maudie and Juana Davis, sitting cross-legged on the floor. "That little boy idolizes Lori. He told me he didn't know girls could hammer and saw so straight."

Maudie laughed. "Benny loves having someone besides an old woman for company, and Lori's good with him. He's enamored of Rock, too . . . I thought, for his birthday—it's just two days before Christmas—I'd go out to the pound, see if they have a really nice young dog. What do you think?"

"I think that's a great idea," Ryan said. "Your backyard's already fenced, with a lawn where a boy and a dog can play. Or you might decide to take Benny with you, let him pick out his own dog?" She went silent as Benny, Lori, and Cora Lee returned with loaded plates. All three sat down on the floor beside Ryan to enjoy their supper, Cora Lee nearly as supple as the children.

"The nativity pageant starts at four," Cora Lee said. She looked up at Maudie. "You are coming, you won't mind the crowd?"

"I'm a bit under the weather," Maudie said. "My shoulder's hurting, but nothing to worry about."

"We can take Benny," Cora Lee offered. "See the pageant, take a wagon ride, then I'll bring him home." She reached to pat Maudie's hand. "No one would dare bother him with us, in that crowd."

"I could pick him up here," Maudie said, glancing at Ryan. "If that would be all right? It would be closer for Cora Lee."

"That's fine," Ryan said. "Rock will be happy of the company." Her glance said, No one will bother him here, either, in front of half the department. Soon Maudie had risen and hurried away, down the street to her car. Padding out to the porch, Joe watched her with interest, thinking about her returning to her empty house alone. He had turned back inside when Kit streaked past him out the front door and up the nearest pine and took off, heading for Maudie's. As if *she* didn't want to see Maudie go home alone, with so much activity in the village inviting mischief in the quieter neighborhoods.

Or did Kit not want Misto to face an emergency alone? Or, fascinated as she was by the grandfatherly cat, was she simply using Maudie's departure as an excuse to share Misto's vigil and perhaps learn more about him?

36

MAUDIE'S CAR STOOD in the drive and a soft light burned in her upstairs bedroom, but from up the street where Kit and Misto crouched on the Damen cottage roof, they couldn't see the front door of the Tudor bungalow. The cell phone lay beside them, next to Misto's plate, which he had licked sparkling clean. Above the mottled oak branches, heavy gray clouds were blowing in, leaving only patches of darkening blue as evening closed around them—but it wouldn't rain for the Nativity play, the air didn't smell of rain.

Lights would be bright down in the village, every house sparkling with decorations, the shopping plaza ablaze with hundreds of tiny lights for the pageant. Kit imagined folk crowded along the plaza's upstairs balconies, against the shop windows below, and lined up all around the big, enclosed garden where the Nativity drama would be played out. She imagined Benny and Lori afterward, riding all over the village in a horse-drawn buggy. Kit had ridden on the back of a horse once, sitting in front of Charlie, but never in a wagon with a driver snapping his whip.

Beside her, Misto yawned. "Don't go to sleep," she told him. "You were asleep when I got here." He'd been tucked beneath the overhanging branches in a bed of fallen leaves, had pawed the oak leaves up around himself to keep warm, and had been snoring.

"I wasn't asleep, I was resting, I didn't miss a thing. House has been silent as a deserted rat hole, no one there but Maudie. All the windows dark until she got home, nothing moving in the yard, no one on the street, no cars cruising." As they watched, the bedroom light went out, and in a few minutes a faint light came on in the kitchen.

"If there had been someone," Kit said, "would you have used the phone?"

He laid his ears back. "Of course I would. Why wouldn't I?"

"Have you ever talked to a human?"

Misto gave her a devilish smile. "Not so they knew. When I was a kitten, I liked to sneak up behind someone, say something rude, then run like hell. I'd be gone when they swung around, I'd watch from up a tree. They'd look and look, but saw no one." The yellow cat licked his paw, laughing. "I thought that was funny until I got older and saw what a chance I was taking—not just for me, but for all of us. After that, I didn't play those games anymore."

Down the hill, a second, brighter light came on in the kitchen and they could smell coffee brewing. The windows were still bare of shades, but from this angle they couldn't see directly in, could only see Maudie when she moved close to the glass. When the brighter light went out again, and a light blazed on in the studio, they trotted over the roofs to the house next door to Maudie, where they could look down directly inside.

The new room was a storm of color, the shelves stacked with squares of rainbow bright cloth. On the far wall hung three quilts, their patterns so intricate and vivid they took Kit's breath away. One in autumn colors, one a winter pattern in shades of gray and soft blues, with twiggy branches woven across; and the third quilt shouted of Christmas. Its many shades of red and green and brown picked out partridges, pear trees, maids a-singing—such a happy scene it made Kit laugh.

"She invents the pictures," Kit said. "Then cuts out little pieces of cloth and sews them together, to bring her dream alive." Kit knew about dreams. "Quilts like music," she said. "Quilts that tell stories."

The tomcat looked and looked, then turned to Kit, his thin tail twitching. "That's what it means to be human," he said softly. "A cat might dream, but without human hands, what can we do? Not even a speaking cat could bring to life a work of art or an invention. We can never make our dreams into something that will please others."

Kit considered Misto, his scarred ears and shoulder, his big, scarred paws with the one crooked claw that must have been torn and healed wrong. She imagined how he must have looked as a little yellow kitten there on the shore, and then how he'd looked grown-up and handsome, his wide shoulders hard with muscle, a fine young tomcat—but now he was frail and old, old enough to be her great-great-great-grandfather. What had he seen in his long life, this cat who had, clearly, once been a muscled brawler and bold adventurer, but who was a dreamer, too?

Below, Maudie took something from her pocket and laid it on the worktable beneath a fold of cloth, then began to select squares of fabric and lay them out into a pattern. Though she was working in the lighted room with no shades or draperies at the windows she didn't seem nervous. When shadows stirred outside she glanced up briefly, saw only tree shadows blowing in the wind, and turned back to laying out quilting pieces in an intricate Christmas tree design.

But soon something did startle her, jerking her gaze up to the garden. Her hands stilled; then she slipped one hand beneath the fold of cloth, revealing for an instant, a dark revolver.

She was still for a long time, looking out into the night. At last she slid the gun back into her pocket, picked up her empty coffee cup, and moved away into the kitchen.

"Well," Kit said with surprise. "Maybe Maudie doesn't need so much protection, after all."

Misto smiled. "That soft little grandmother. She isn't as helpless as everyone thought. Maybe," he said, "if we need to use the cell phone, it'll be to help some unfortunate burglar."

S TANDING IN THE doorway to the kitchen, Maudie looked back through the darkened studio and out to the garden. She'd be glad when the shades had arrived and been put up; she knew she was vulnerable in the lighted room where anyone could look in, anyone could fire through the glass, killing her as easily as they'd killed Martin and Caroline. Though she didn't think that would happen; she thought the shooter had another agenda. She thought she wouldn't be in danger until Pearl had what she wanted.

Moving into the kitchen, she turned that light off and stood at the sink, looking out toward the street. The sky was heavy with clouds blending into night. As she moved on through the kitchen and up the dark stairs, a belated shiver of fear made her pull her smock closer. As if someone was here, in the house with her. As if now, this night, was the moment. Only at the top did she flip on a light. She circled through the two bedrooms and bath, but there was no one, the upstairs rooms were empty. Going back downstairs to the kitchen, she sat at the table, in the dark, waiting. If Pearl let herself in with the stolen key, Maudie was trusting her instincts to take over, trusting that Pearl's own actions would tell her what to do.

She waited nearly an hour, listening, watching the dark glass. There was no sound outside, and nothing stirred in the house. When at last, both relieved and disappointed, she turned the kitchen lights back on, she turned the TV on in the dark living room, too, to make the house seem occupied while she was gone, while she went to pick up Benny.

She had so hoped Pearl would slip in unannounced, would come while she was alone. Once Benny was home again, and maybe Jared, it would be too late for what she planned. Picking up her coat that she'd dropped on a kitchen chair, moving to the sink to make sure she'd unplugged the coffeepot, she pulled the coat on and transferred the .38 Special to its deep pocket. As she headed for the front door she heard a car pull into the drive. She paused, listening.

PEARL HAD LET herself into the house unseen before Maudie and the boy left. They'd been all dressed up, Maudie carrying a huge cooler out to her car, awkward with her lame arm. She'd heard, the last time she slipped into the house, enough to know where they were headed. Supper with a bunch of cops. Wasn't that just like Maudie.

In the empty house she'd searched at her leisure, searched as thoroughly as she had the other times, but she hadn't found the ledger pages. Later, she'd watched Maudie return alone, apparently leaving the kid at the holiday party. She had stood in the hall closet listening while Maudie moved around upstairs, then came down to the kitchen, where she made coffee and carried a cup into the studio. As Maudie busied herself there, Pearl had slipped through the house behind her meaning to enter the studio and confront her. But, crossing the softly lit kitchen, she'd heard voices from somewhere out in the night, someone too near the house, and a thrill of danger had held her still, listening.

Earlier, even before she'd entered the house, even as she'd approached the property coming up the hill from behind, through the neighbors' backyards, tearing her windbreaker on a tangle of thorny holly bushes, she'd felt watched. A strange sensation, a feeling she'd seldom experienced. Arlie said she had nerves of steel. Arlie would be along soon, on his own mission, but now, unsuccessful in her search, she was beginning to feel pushed. She wondered again if she'd been foolish to link up with Arlie. It wasn't smart to let herself be sidetracked by his agenda, all for the little bit of help he'd given her—and maybe because she'd wanted to recapture those Vegas weekends, she thought, smiling.

The voice came again, an old man. The other was a woman, soft and indistinct, not loud enough to make out the words. The voices seemed to be coming from above, some trick of the wind, she supposed. She stood trying to think where she hadn't searched, what she'd missed—if Maudie did have the ledger pages. If she did, did she mean to give them to the cops? Or would the old woman try to blackmail her? But for what? To stop her in case she tried to take custody of Benny? Who would want the kid?

That had been a shocker, going into the office that morning to find the ledger had been disturbed, finding proof it had been copied. No one could have done that but Caroline, she was sure that only Caroline had any suspicions about the way she did her work.

Not only had she rigged the lock to the hidden compartment each night before she left work, fixing two hairs across it, she'd sprinkled talcum powder in the seams of the ledger pages, too. The day she found the lock disturbed and found traces of talc in the seam of the office copier between the glass and the metal rim, she'd almost panicked. Had stuffed the ledger in her carryall and was nervous the rest of the day. Weeks later, after the funeral, she'd told Mr. Beckman she was leaving, that a month's leave wasn't enough, that she needed to get away from the city. With the office shorthanded, the quarterly taxes already paid, and the way she'd juggled the expenses from one client's account to another, she'd gambled that no one would find the discrepancies for many months.

But Beckman Equipment couldn't remain ignorant forever of the glitches in their cash flow. Paying one client's bill in arrears with part of a subsequent client's payment, and in the process skimming off cash for herself, left balances owing that did not bear close scrutiny. The minute Beckman hired a full-time bookkeeper again, the missing money would come to light and they'd go to the cops. And LAPD would pull the file on her and talk to the homicide division, follow up on the connection between her and Maudie. She still wasn't sure what Maudie had told them about the night of the shooting. Wasn't sure what the woman *had* seen, or what the kid had seen. Though who would believe a kid testifying against his own mother?

But now she'd get it sorted out. Having taken her time going through the rooms, using a small flashlight as the late afternoon light dimmed, she was puzzled as to what hiding places she could have missed. Convinced the pages weren't among Caroline's other things that she'd left in the garage, she'd searched all the rooms, under chair cushions, under and between mattresses, had gone through every drawer and cupboard, had rifled Maudie's desk again thoroughly. She had even examined the Christmas tree and searched beneath its quilted skirting. There were no wrapped packages, yet. No doubt Maudie would pile gifts on the kid later. Upstairs there were just the two bedrooms, the bath, a small storeroom, and a narrow linen closet. She'd gone through them all with care. The kid's bed was littered with sissy toys, that ratty teddy bear and other stuffed animals the boy had clung to since he was a baby, girly toys unbecoming to a boy.

If she'd *had* to have a child—and this child hadn't been planned, it was Martin who insisted on keeping it—then why couldn't she have had a boy like Kent? From the time the Colletto kids were little they'd been as bold as brass, she'd gotten along with them just fine. Though Kent was her favorite, Kent was the pusher, even more than Victor, taking what he wanted when he wanted, and exactly how he wanted, she thought, smiling.

Despite its two stories, the house was small, it didn't take long to search. But it didn't offer much space to conceal herself, either. The best place was the coat closet beneath the stairs. With the door cracked open, she could see into the living room, the kitchen, and through the kitchen's glass door to the studio. The attached garage would have been an adequate place to wait for Maudie, but the outside pedestrian door was blocked with a stack of heavy crates, leaving no way to escape except through the noisy overhead door. By staying in the house she had access to the front door, the outside studio doors, or the low living room windows, one of which she'd unlocked earlier. She'd also unlocked an upstairs window. Later, when Maudie came up to search that floor, she'd been standing just outside on the roof that sheltered the front door below.

Earlier, at the bottom of the stairs, looking across the kitchen to the studio, watching Maudie at her worktable, she'd had no idea what instinct held her back, but she'd

paid attention. She *was* nervous at the faint voices she'd heard from outside. That couldn't be Arlie and Kent, they wouldn't talk out loud, though they were probably already nearby, watching the target house. Maybe she'd heard some neighbors' voices contorted by the wind, floating on the night.

As Pearl was waiting for Maudie to leave again to go pick up the child, as she seemed to be preparing to do, the sound of a car in the drive and then footsteps on the porch made her back deeper into the closet. Pulling the door to, she pushed in behind the line of hanging coats, into the smell of old wool. She heard the front door open, heard Jared call out to Maudie, heard Maudie's step as she came out of the kitchen.

"I was just leaving to go get Benny," Maudie said. "You missed a good dinner."

"I'll get him if you like. Maybe there'll be some left-overs," he said hopefully.

"I never saw so much food," Maudie said. "But you'd better hurry, those cops wolf it down like it's their last meal."

"I'll go get Benny, and then, early as it is, I'm hitting the hay. I've had a ton of homework this week, feel like I'll never catch up on my sleep."

Pearl heard the front door open and close, heard Maudie move away across the tile floor toward the living room, heard Jared's car start and back out of the drive. Now, again, she and Maudie were alone. Slipping out of the closet, meaning to trap Maudie in the living room, she heard the voices again, closer. Someone *was* out there, and a sense of wrongness tingled through her, the feeling she

got sometimes at the poker table when, despite how the cards were falling, she knew to stop betting. That instinct was at work now. If she was smart she'd go with it.

Easing open the closet door to peer out, she saw Maudie in the kitchen, sitting at the table with her back to her. Silently she slipped to the front door, cracked it open, but drew back when the voices came again, the soft grainy voice of the man and the faint laugh of the young woman. Quietly pulling the door closed, she left the house, not through the front or side door, but out the low living room window into the bushes, where she was sure no neighbor would glimpse her. Moving along close to the side of the house and then into the neighbor's wooded backyard, she waited for her companions. She would return in a while, this time to do more than confront Maudie, this time to force Maudie's hand.

37

FOUR HOUSES DOWN from Maudie's stood a wood-sided Craftsman cottage, its ivory tones picked out by four decorative lamps standing among beds of pale alstroemerias that were nearly finished blooming for the winter. Grass clippings from the little lawn were scattered along the stone walk, where Alfreda Meiers or her gardener had apparently neglected to sweep. The walk was sheltered by a Japanese maple, bare now in the winter cold. Three steps led up to the cream-colored wooden porch and the pale front door that was carved with fern patterns and without any panes of decorative glass. The walls flanking the door were solid, too, and unbroken, there was only the peephole in the door itself through which to view whoever might ring the bell. A widow of twenty years, a shy, fearful woman, Alfreda kept her windows and front and back doors double-locked. She had no dog to provide protection or warning barks; she didn't want dog hair on her furniture. She didn't have a weapon for protection, she was afraid of guns, and she felt that even pepper spray was far too dangerous. She carried her cell phone in her pocket so that if she ever did have an intruder, she could summon help. She had two grown daughters, both married and living in Southern California. She had no desire to live with either of them, nor they with her. The girls visited their mother infrequently, and with restraint.

Alfreda's dinner had consisted of a broiled chicken breast, a small salad, and for dessert a sliced pear with a square of white cheese. After dinner she allowed herself a cheerful gas fire in the fireplace, and curled up on the couch to read the latest in a series of gentle mysteries that wouldn't keep her awake. She heard several cars pass on the street, saw their lights bleeding in arcs through her living room draperies. She was only vaguely aware of a car pulling into a drive four doors up, and then soon departing again; she knew it was at the Tudor house, by the heavy sound of the front door closing. She hadn't met her new neighbor, not formally, but they waved to each other on the street. At nine-thirty Alfreda closed her book, turned off the gas logs, turned down the furnace thermostat, and switched off the lights. By ten o'clock she had washed her face, brushed her teeth, slipped on her flannel nightgown, and was in bed, already drifting off, willing her dreams to be happy. This time of year, she tried to fix her thoughts on the happy holidays of her childhood, not on those later on in her life. She woke again at ten-forty, rudely pulled from sleep by the door chimes ringing, accompanied by frantic pounding on the door itself, as if someone were in trouble.

* * *

Up the hill from Alfreda Meier's house and Maudie's, atop the Damens' little cottage, Kit and Misto sat at the edge of the roof watching the street below. They had watched Maudie in her studio, had seen Jared arrive home and leave again, then later seen him return with Benny, the child stumbling into the house half asleep, leaning against Jared. Had seen the guest room light go on and shadows move about as if both Benny and Jared were getting ready for bed, and in a few minutes the light went off again. Soon Maudie's light went out, too, the house was dark, and Kit imagined the three drifting off into sleep. Only the cats were wakeful, alert to every smallest sound, to that of a passing car along the surrounding streets, to the distant bark of a dog, to a door closing blocks away. To the tiny scratching from above as a flying squirrel landed on the rough bark of a nearby pine. He looked down at them with huge, dark eyes, and sailed away again into the night.

Kit had, with a thoughtfulness that surprised even Kit herself, used the cell phone to ease Lucinda's and Pedric's worries when she didn't come home; they had gone to the party early and, wanting to see the pageant, had also left early. They were home now, and they did worry when she was out in the night. As Kit and Misto held their vigil, he told stories from ancient Wales that she had never heard, she had committed each to memory, making it forever a part of her hoard of mysterious tales.

Below, they heard a car park four or five blocks down, the reflection of its lights suddenly extinguished. Footsteps cut the night and then silence, as if perhaps the driver had gained his own front door, silently opened it and closed it, not wanting to wake those within; and again the neighborhood was still. Kit was reciting to herself one of Misto's stories when they heard the faintest echo of a doorbell just down the street, and then loud, insistent banging—maybe half a block down? Kit scanned the houses below. The banging continued and the bell kept on ringing, and they could see a dark shadow on the porch of the cream-colored house four doors down from Maudie's. As they watched, the porch light blazed on revealing a thin man pounding, his back to them. He wore a black jacket, dark jeans, a dark cap. The questioning voice from within, a woman's voice, was as thin as a whisper. Was she peering out through the peephole? How much of him could she see of him?

"There's been a wreck," the man said tremulously, "I need help. Please . . ."

The cats looked at the empty, silent street, the silent neighborhood. *They'd* heard no wreck, there *was* no wreck. Alarmed, they dove among the oak leaves, pawed the phone out, and Kit punched in 911, trying not to shout. "Man pounding on a door, a lone woman lives there. He says there was a wreck, but there was no wreck, there's no car on the street . . . Could it be another invasion?" She ended the call before June Alpine could ask any questions. The new dispatcher hadn't been sufficiently indoctrinated yet, in how to respond to these particular snitches, she hadn't learned not to ask, but to call the chief pronto. Kit hit the disconnect, and they fled down across the roofs, two small, silent shadows. Kit would have carried the phone but it was too clumsy and heavy. Even as they approached the pale house two patrol cars came slipping along the street without lights, their radios silent, one from downhill, one from uphill behind them. Each pulled to the curb several doors away from where the man stood talking through the door.

Two uniforms slipped out of each car, keeping to the dark edges of the yard beyond the glow of Alfreda's lights. They watched silently the figure at the door with his back to them. He seemed unaware of anything but the little click as Alfreda turned the dead bolt from within, possibly leaving the security chain in place—not that a chain would do any good, Kit thought. The cats watched the front door cautiously open a few inches—and everything happened at once. The invader hit the door with all his weight, jerking the chain loose and ramming the door back. He grabbed Alfreda, hit her when she struggled. Two cops charged up the steps and grabbed him, breaking his grip on the victim. And three figures exploded from the bushes, streaking into the backyard, heading for the wooded greenbelt beyond; the other two officers were after them, crashing down the hill.

Officer Crowley held the invader jammed against the house, pressing his face into the wood siding. Crowley was half a foot taller, thin but big boned, his large hands jerking the invader's arms behind him. As Crowley snapped on the cuffs, securing them through the guy's belt, Officer Brennan pushed inside to clear the house, his overweight frame blocking the lamplight as he passed. And as Crowley marched the prisoner to the patrol car, the cats got their first good look at the man.

It was Arlie Risso, black beard, black hair. He stood

straight and stiff beside the car, his expression affronted as Crowley snapped on leg irons. More than one officer leading a handcuffed prisoner whose legs were free had been unpleasantly surprised by a sudden attack and escape. Crowley didn't mean to risk that embarrassment.

"I was trying to warn her," Risso was arguing. "I was at the door to warn her, why are you arresting me? You'd better call your captain."

Crowley just looked at him, his big hands gripping Risso's shoulders, hands strong enough, Kit thought, to easily rip a bale of hay in two. His look said he'd like to do that to Risso. Risso said, "You'd better go after the thieves, Officer. You'd better arrest *them*. You'd better get your commander over here, pronto, to straighten this out."

"We'll just make you comfortable in the patrol car," Crowley told Risso dryly, "until we can arrange an appointment with the chief." Towering over Risso's six feet, Crowley turned the handsome, bearded man around as easily as spinning a doll, so he faced the patrol car. Opening the back door, he enthusiastically pressed Risso's head down, making sure he cleared the opening without a concussion and an ensuing lawsuit. Above on the neighboring house's roof, Kit and Misto grinned and switched their tails, laughing.

Officer Brennan came outside with Alfreda, where she sat down on the little low wall that flanked the porch. Three more squad cars arrived, their radios spewing canned voices, their spotlights washing across the neighbors' yards and even up across the rooftops, forcing the cats to flatten themselves in order to stay out of sight. Leaving the black-and-whites, four officers ran for the

274

greenbelt, their torch lights cutting through the bushes. The blare of a bullhorn thundered, telling the escapees to stop. It was pitch-dark back there, the swinging lights blinding as they swept into the tangled woods cutting pale swaths across the tree trunks.

In the Tudor house a light came on in Maudie's bed-room, the cats could see her silhouette at the window, looking out. The guest room windows remained dark. Were Benny and Jared still sound asleep, unaware of the crashing and running, of breaking bushes and even of the bullhorn?

"Maybe the cops can make Risso talk," Kit said. "Maybe he'll ID the others."

"Would he? Risso—Marlin Dorriss—he's a cold one."

"To save his own skin, he might." She turned to look at Misto. "I never thought of Dorriss doing strong-arm stuff, like hitting a woman. Thought of him as the gentle-man thief, the con artist, the slick crook who gets others to do his dirty work."

"Maybe so, but they were afraid of him in prison. All the men were. And why do *you* care so much?" he said with interest.

Her yellow eyes widened. "I hate that man. These in-vasions are for one purpose. To discredit Max Harper, dis-credit the department, to hurt our friends. The cops are our friends. I hope Risso rots in jail for the rest of his life, that those men burn in hell forever."

"I've never had a human friend I cared so much about." Misto licked his paw. "What must that be like, to love a human friend?"

"That's why you came here," Kit said, "to find friends,

cat *and* human. We're your friends now," she said softly. She went silent as a big pickup came up the hill and pulled to the curb. Max Harper got out, looking pleased that Crowley had nailed Dorriss. He wasn't wearing his usual Western boots tonight, but soft black running shoes, more than ready for a chase. Up the street, Maudie had disappeared from her upstairs window, and in a moment she came out the front door. Standing quietly on the porch, she watched the scene below. Behind her, Jared came out of the front door, yawning, his hair tousled from sleep. He had pulled on a striped robe over the sweatpants he must have slept in, had pulled on his running shoes, the laces still untied. He yawned again, stood on the porch staring down the street toward the police cars.

"What's happened? Not another invasion? Not here!"

"Where's Benny?" Maudie asked with alarm.

"Sound asleep, he didn't stir." He didn't take his eyes from the street. "It's a robbery of some kind, the way they're searching the yards. The lights and bullhorn woke me, their torches shining up." He started down the steps toward the dark yards as if he meant to help search, but Maudie caught his arm. "Don't, Jared. Don't go out there, let the police handle it."

He looked at her, and pulled away.

"Stay here," she said boldly, almost angrily. "If you get into the tangle, they could mistake you for one of the burglars. In the dark they might shoot you."

He hesitated. "I suppose you're right, but . . . I'll just go look in the backyard," he said edgily, "while they're searching down there. Maybe—"

"No," Maudie began, "you—"

"Stay where you are," Max Harper said, stepping out of the shadows beside the house. As Jared spun around, Harper grabbed him, threw him against the doorjamb, and jerked his arms behind him. Maudie caught her breath as Harper snapped handcuffs on him.

"What is this? Jared didn't . . . He isn't . . ." Then Maudie looked down, where Max Harper was looking.

The two cats, peering over the edge of the roof, could see it, too. A faint trail of grass clippings led across the porch from within the house. When Maudie turned on the inside light, two trails of clippings led up the stairs for as far as the cats could see, one on each side of the steps. In the entry, one trail turned away toward the kitchen, one followed Jared out onto the porch where he now stood. And when the cats looked back at Jared, they saw bits of grass clinging to the elastic cuffs of his sweatpants, to his damp running shoes and to his dangling shoestrings.

An officer came up from Alfreda's house, and together he and Harper loaded Jared into a squad car. Same drill with the leg irons, same ducking of Jared's head to clear the door. Maudie stood very still in the doorway, simply watching. As the two squad cars took off with their prisoners, heading for the station followed by another black-and-white, Detective Ray's old rental Ford pulled up in front of Maudie's house. Kathleen, dressed in jeans and sweatshirt, was carrying an evidence bag. She spoke with Maudie and Max Harper briefly and then began taking photographs of the two trails of grass, one coming down the stairs and out to the porch, the other leading away to the studio. On the roof, Kit gave Misto a quizzical look.

"That's one we were wrong about," she said. "Jared

Colletto. Well, he was quick on his feet, you have to give him that. Slipped out of the house after Maudie went to bed? Was down there, closing in on Alfreda's house, when the cops grabbed Risso?"

"He had to be one of the three the cops chased," Misto said. "He veered away behind Maudie's house, where we couldn't see him, into the studio and upstairs again."

"Threw on his robe," Kit said, "and came down yawning, with not a thought to the grass clippings. Jared Colletto," she repeated, and she felt sad that someone she'd almost trusted had turned out to be all deception and lies.

38

FROM MAUDIE'S ROOF, Kit and Misto continued to watch Alfreda's house, where Detective Garza was lifting prints from the front door and surround. It was nearly an hour since Marlin Dorriss and Jared had been taken away in a patrol car, Jared wearing his robe and sweatpants and a pair of bedroom slippers, his grass-covered jogging shoes having been bagged as evidence. They'd watched Dallas collect and bag fibers caught on the Meier house's door molding, and photograph and make casts of five footprints incised in the garden earth along the edge of the lawn. They'd watched Maudie go down the hill and disappear within Alfreda's house, apparently to commiserate with the frightened woman.

Most of the officers had departed, leaving behind a barrier of yellow crime-scene tape surrounding the house and yard. Detective Ray had finished photographing the grassy trails that entered Maudie's house and out again, and had gone upstairs to the guest room. They could see her through the window, examining Jared's clothes and duffel and photographing with sharp flashes of strobe light. Kit didn't know what Kathleen could take into possession without a court order, but she guessed Maudie's house was part of the scene now, too, and she could confiscate any evidence. Ever curious, Kit padded along the narrow lip of roof beneath the window to look in, squeezing her eyes closed when the light flashed. Benny was sound asleep, as deep under as a kitten tucked against its mama. The little boy had burrowed beneath the covers, head and all, cutting out the noise and the painful flashes; all one could really see was a lump of quilt and blanket. Had he slept like this all through the chase, even through the bellow of the bullhorn? He didn't stir at Kathleen's intrusion, though Kit herself squeezed her eyes closed at each lift of the camera to avoid the fierce blazes of the strobe light. Kit returned to the garage roof squinting and shaking her head.

Out on the street, before Alfreda's house, Officer Brennan had settled down in his patrol car as if to stay and keep watch; Kit could smell the coffee from his thermos and the faint scent of cinnamon as he unwrapped what was probably a sweet roll. Dallas was packing up to leave, putting his equipment in the trunk, when his cell phone buzzed. When he flipped on the speaker, Max's voice crackled with a tinny sound. "Arlie's all tucked away—one more alias to add to Dorriss's file. That tip made all the difference, put us right on the scene."

Dallas laughed. "Not just to mop up, this time." Kit guessed it must have been frustrating, one invasion after another and not one fingerprint except the victim's own, or that of a neighbor or service person, and no match to the fibers and debris they'd bagged and logged in. "Now," Dallas said, "with Jared and Dorriss off the street and a BOL out on Kent, we're getting somewhere. Maybe the two in jail will ID the fourth guy—or maybe that will turn out to be the woman."

Kit thought it might. The figure that had vanished so fast, even before Arlie was arrested, was tall and thin and might indeed have been the woman.

Kit had already phoned and awakened Clyde to tell Joe the news. And to brag a little, to say that it was their call, hers and Misto's, that had brought the cops on time. From the brightness of Misto's eyes and the way he lashed his tail, it was clear he liked this new twist to his life. She bet he'd never dreamed of working alongside a bunch of cops, that he'd never imagined such an exciting interaction with humans. Now he looked almost like a young cat, his smile as excited as that of a frolicking kitten.

ALFREDA MEIERS WAS so upset after the attempted invasion and all the fuss with the police, so nervous that two men had escaped and might return, that after Detective Garza took her statement, she wanted only to lock herself in the house and rest. But even before Detective Garza departed, Maudie Toola came down the hill and invited her up to her house for a cup of tea and a slice of pie, offering to make up the couch in her living room, on this night when both women needed company. Alfreda went back with her for the tea and pie, carefully locking the doors behind her. She felt almost comfortable, with Officer Brennan on guard, sitting there in his squad car. She told Maudie she would visit for a little while, try to calm her nerves, then would go on home. Not that she could sleep, but she could lie down, prop a chair against the bedroom door, get a little rest. She didn't know what those men would have done to her; she didn't want to think about that. She and Maudie hurried up the street and into Maudie's house, looking back to see Brennan nod and wave to them.

Maudie settled Alfreda at the kitchen table and put the kettle on, then went to make doubly sure the studio door was properly locked. She found the grass trail through the studio disturbed as if someone had walked through it. But Detective Kathleen Ray had photographed the damp lawn clippings, so maybe she'd scattered the grassy trail, hadn't been careful—though that did seem odd. Detective Ray seemed exceptionally careful in how she went about her work.

In the kitchen she laid out cups and plates, sugar and silverware on a tray. Neither of them took milk. She left Alfreda cutting the pecan pie that she and Benny had made, and went to light the gas log in the living room and draw up the little tea table she liked to use, opening out its two small leaves. She didn't remember leaving the table standing out so far from the cupboard door; she preferred it snugged against the closet that was meant for the storage of firewood, and which she didn't use. She'd thought of asking Ryan to convert the space into bookshelves, and maybe she'd do that. Maybe Benny had been playing in there, she thought as she hurried upstairs to check on the child.

In the dark bedroom, she wanted to whisper to Benny, wanted tell him everything was all right, in case he had awakened at some point, after the commotion was over. But apparently not, he was sound asleep, snuggled down with the covers pulled up, and she moved away and let him be. She stood a moment enjoying the little-boy scent of him, smiling because he slept as deeply as had his daddy. Martin had never awakened to sounds in the house; he could have slept through an alien attack. At last she turned away, went back downstairs to her guest.

Alfreda had cut the pie and poured the tea. "I'm better off doing something," the frail woman said as Maudie carried the tray in before the fire. "Tomorrow I'll be steadier, I'll be better in the daylight."

"You're more than welcome to stay here for a few days," Maudie said, though in truth she hoped Alfreda would refuse. The woman was so frail, seemed so in need of nurturing. But in fact, Maudie's own scenario called for solitude, she would prefer the house empty; she was relieved when Alfreda shook her head.

"Thanks, Maudie, but I'll be fine. Tomorrow I'm to help with the Christmas bazaar, and that's good, that I keep busy." She smiled wanly at Maudie. "I should feel relieved the police arrested two of those men. Detective Garza said there was little chance the other two would go on with these invasions now.

"He said there could be more than four of them, but from the information they have, they don't think so." Alfreda seemed to be talking to ease herself, to calm her fears. Maudie listened and nodded and let her go on, though Alfreda's rambling certainly didn't calm her own fears. When she heard Benny cry out in his sleep, she hushed Alfreda to listen, but then there was nothing more. If he were having one of his nightmares, he'd make more noise than that, would be crying for Grandma, over and over. They talked for nearly an hour, about Benny and the new school, about Maudie's son David. If Alfreda knew about the shooting, about Martin and Caroline, she didn't ask questions, didn't pry. Maudie avoided talking about her quilting, too, she didn't want to have to drag a neighbor whom she hardly knew through her new studio. When Alfreda headed home, Maudie watched her hurry down the block past the squad car, where she waved to Officer Brennan, then disappear into her own house. Maudie pictured her carefully locking her door; she locked her own door, rinsed their cups and plates and put them in the dishwasher, and headed upstairs. She'd left the light on in her room, but before she got ready for bed she stepped into the dark guest room one last time, to check on Benny.

She hadn't admitted to Alfreda how nervous she was. In a way, she wished Alfreda had stayed, even wished she had put fresh sheets on the guest bed and made Alfreda comfortable there. Not that the frail woman would be any protection. *Do I just want the company?* Maudie thought, annoyed at herself. *Want to circle the wagons, even decrepit wagons, because I don't know who or what will appear out of the night, out of the empty dark?*

Benny was still cocooned down among the covers. Amazing how soundly he slept. She thought she shouldn't be calling this room the guest room, it was Benny's room now. But it didn't fit a child; this wasn't a child's room, with its grown-up, too formal furniture. Benny needed a child's furniture: toy chests, a sturdy desk, maybe one of those bunk sets with a built-in ladder, something a boy could *use*, not just tolerate.

Benny seemed drawn to the little sewing room down at the end of the hall, which Maudie was using for storage as she unpacked boxes. The room was tiny, maybe eight by nine; Benny like to slip in between the boxes and curl up on the deep bay window seat. Maybe for a few years he'd prefer that room, at least until he outgrew the space. She glanced at her watch. It was just past midnight. Guided by the night-light, she reached to straighten Benny's covers.

As she took hold of the covers, they gave too much under her hand. She felt the little mound, but didn't feel the solid form of the child, only the soft give of pillows. She snatched the covers away.

The bed was empty. Nothing but wadded-up blankets under the quilt. Flipping on the lamp, she stared at the empty bed, at the pile of blankets. She whirled to look around the room. Jerked open the closet doors. Nothing. Benny's clothes, hanging on the lowered rod. A heap of toys lying in one corner of the closet. She knelt to look under the bed, thinking he might be hiding—as a joke, or because the commotion of police cars and lights had frightened him.

Nothing under the bed but a toy car and dust. Hurrying down the hall she looked in the bathroom, the linen closet, then searched in her own room. She searched the entire house, up and down, the firewood cupboard, the garage and studio, everywhere a child could hide. Had he gone outdoors, in the middle of the night?

Thinking of the two invaders who had escaped the police, she snatched up her coat from where she'd dropped it on the arm of a chair, made sure the gun was safe in her pocket. Turning on the yard lights, she locked the door behind her and hurried to her car, praying the little boy was there, curled down under the lap robe, asleep.

The car was empty. She popped the trunk lid, looked in. She searched the yard among the dark bushes, calling for him, yet certain that he wouldn't be hiding out here in the cold, in the middle of the night. When she looked down the hill at Officer Brennan, he'd left his car, was headed up the sidewalk, looking around into the shadows, looking up at her, frowning.

It was Brennan who called the station to report the little boy missing.

39

Hᴏᴡ ᴄᴏᴜʟᴅ ʜᴇ be gone?" Kit said, looking down from the garage roof to where
Maudie wandered the yard calling Benny.
"He was in bed, asleep. Has she searched
the whole house?" They watched Maudie
hurry down the street and Brennan hurry
to meet her. Their voices were faint, and
Maudie sounded nearly breathless. They listened to Brennan call the dispatcher.

Kit said, "Could he be playing games, hiding from her?"

"After there were cops all over?" Misto said. "Everyone running, lights swinging everywhere? Not likely. And
if he woke scared and is hiding from those men, he'd have
found a place in the house, not gone outside in the dark,
alone."

Kit began to shiver, looking down into the bushes
and along the street, hopefully listening. There was no
sound but Brennan's voice, talking to the dispatcher, and
the whisper of the far sea. "You don't think someone *took*

Benny?" Kit said in a small voice. "*Kidnapped* him? But how could they get him out of the house, how could anyone get him away, and we didn't see them?"

"We can't see the studio door from here," Misto pointed out. "Only from the other side of the garage."

"We'd have heard him," Kit said. "We'd have heard Benny yelling."

"Not if he was gagged," the yellow cat said. "And we don't know when he disappeared. Was it while the cops were still chasing those men? Or," he said, "did *they* double back and take him?" Misto rose. "If they took him out through the studio, we can pick up their trail, we can follow them," and he headed for the nearest oak, meaning to scramble down its broad trunk.

Kit started to follow him, then spun around and raced up across the roofs for the cottage, for the cell phone. Pawing the phone out from among the leaves, she hit the single button for the Damen house. Rock could track Benny faster, he was bigger, and she had to admit the Weimaraner could outrun even her, over long distances.

Wilma answered, sleepily, on the first ring.

"What are you doing at Clyde's?" Kit said. "What . . . ?"

"I'm not at Clyde's, I'm at home," Wilma said hesitantly. "You dialed wrong. What's happened, what is it? You sound—"

"Benny's missing, we think he's been kidnapped," Kit hissed. "I have to call—" and she broke off before Wilma could ask even one question.

* * *

Dragged out of a deep sleep, Clyde stared at the ring-ing phone and then at the bedside clock. Twelve-thirty, and this was the second call since they'd tucked up for the night. He'd just drifted off after the last frantic ringing, so what the hell was this call about? Snatching the head-set off the cradle to silence it, he lay staring at it, saying nothing.

Leaning across him, Ryan grabbed the headset. "What?" she said softly, looking at the caller ID. "What's happened?"

At the other end, Kit said shyly, "I . . . I need to talk to Joe again."

"Clyde will get him," Ryan said, nudging Clyde. "Hang on."

Grumbling, Clyde swung out of bed, padded barefoot into the study, and shouted up at the cat door. "Get the hell down here! It's Kit again. What am I, your damned answering service?"

Joe appeared on the rafter above, pushing in through his cat door. He paused, peering down over the rafter at Clyde.

"Get your tail down here."

Dropping from the rafter to Clyde's desk, Joe hit the speaker button on the office extension. Kit had already called him about the arrests, not more than an hour ago . . . *"Another invasion,"* she'd said, *". . . arrested Marlin Dorriss . . ."* It'd been hard to believe that slick con was in jail, behind bars. As Kit described the action, all he could think was that somehow Dorriss was going to slip out of this. That by morning he would have lawyered up, would have brought in half a dozen slick attorneys, posted bail, and vanished, maybe never to be seen again. "It was Dorriss who kicked the door in," Kit had said. "Dorriss and Jared are in jail, and—"

"*Jared* Colletto?"

"Jared. And they have a BOL out on Kent. Harper and two squad cars are headed for his house, and . . ." Despite Kit's giddy excitement, he'd gotten most of the story, and then had scrambled back up to his tower, where he'd sat staring into the night debating what to do. Whether to hightail it down to the station and pick up the latest as officers and detectives began to return—maybe slip back into the jail and hear what the two prisoners, once they were alone, had to say to each other about the night's adventure.

Except the two would be detained as far apart as possible, in the department's small jail, so they couldn't get their stories straight; maybe one would even be left up front, in the holding cell. And, at the scene, the action was over. The cops had left. Whatever had come down, Kit had witnessed. At last, yawning, he'd opted to wait until morning when more information would be at hand, when he could catch an early briefing in the chief's office, if he timed it right. Curling up among his pillows, he'd gone back to sleep, had been deep under when the phone rang again, in the study, echoing in the bedroom inches from Clyde's indignant ear, and then Clyde had shouted at him.

Now, as he crouched on the desk listening to Kit, she sounded so scared that she scared him. "Benny Toola's missing, Maudie came running outside all frantic looking for him, searched her car and all around the yard call-

290

ing him and then started down to Brennan where he was parked at Alfreda's house and . . ." She paused, was silent for so long Joe thought the phone had cut out. "Here comes Kathleen's car," she said, "and two squad cars, they . . ."

By this time, Ryan and Clyde were crowded around Joe at the desk listening to Kit over the speaker, and Rock had piled off the love seat to push against them, wanting to be in on the action. When Kit paused, Ryan nearly shouted into the speaker. "Rock," she said, "Rock can track him."

"Yes," Kit said. "That's why I called. We—"

From the bedroom, Ryan's cell phone rang, belting out a Dixieland beat. "Wait a minute," Ryan said. "Hold on." Hurrying into the bedroom, she snatched up her phone from the dresser. She was silent for a moment, listening. "Benny Toola?" she said, trying to sound surprised. "Oh, not Benny. What? Rock? Of course we can, we'll be right there."

Hanging up, she looked at Joe and Clyde. "Dallas," she said. "He's afraid Kent Colletto might have Benny—they only caught his brother Jared and that Dorriss person."

As she headed for the closet to throw on her jeans and a sweater, Rock followed her, caught up in their excitement, shivering with anticipation for whatever adventure the night offered.

It had been nearly a year since Rock learned the protocol and honed his skills to track a human victim or criminal. A Weimaraner hunts by both sight and scent, he's bred for many jobs, and a good Weimaraner is hungry to work. But without proper training, even the best dog is of no use. Ordinarily, such training is started when a dog is very young, and takes many months, or years, to perfect.

But not Rock, not with Joe Grey running the show. In one amazing lesson, in one afternoon, Joe had taught Rock to track as skillfully as a seasoned bloodhound and with equal determination.

Joe's nose was as keen as Rock's and, using a technique impossible for a human trainer, Joe had hurried along with his own nose to the trail, while at the same time giving Rock voice commands. Rock saw, he smelled, he followed the scent that Joe followed, while absorbing Joe's voice command words. He learned all at once what he must do, and the command to do it, bonding with Joe's single-minded passion as the tomcat pursued the scent. By the end of that afternoon, Rock was hooked. He knew what to do, he would stay on any given scent undiverted, would not veer off after rabbits or a deer or even a rare sirloin steak emitting its charbroiled aroma. Since that memorable day of training, Rock and Ryan had assisted Dallas in three cases, with results that left Dallas deeply puzzled, and as deeply impressed. Dallas Garza was a dog man, he knew what it took to train a good tracking hound. Rock's sudden metamorphosis from undisciplined natural talent to honed professional was impossible—but at last Dallas had accepted what he saw, sensibly laying aside his uneasy questions. The fact that their efforts had put three separate offenders in jail was proof enough, for the moment. One man was still awaiting trial, and two were already convicted, one for armed robbery, the other for burglary and grand theft auto, for stealing the high school principal's vintage Austin-Healey. Rock had nailed the three, and the big dog was now an unofficial volunteer for MPPD. At this very moment he was gearing up for work, pacing and pushing at Ryan to hurry, his short tail vibrating with excitement.

Within minutes the four of them were down the stairs, Rock and Joe Grey leading at a gallop, and into Ryan's truck, heading for Maudie's house. Only little Snowball was left behind in the upstairs study, sitting up in her blanket on the love seat, listening to her family depart. The little white cat didn't offer to follow, didn't consider for a minute leaving the warm house in the middle of a cold winter night.

40

WHEN BENNY'S MOTHER woke him in the dark room, he'd yelled once before she slapped a hand over his mouth, hurting him, pressing so hard he tasted blood. He tried to scramble out of bed on the opposite side from her, to get away, maybe crawl under the bed, but she twisted his arm, jerked him off the bed, and pulled him against her, squeezing his shoulder hard. In the glow of the night-light he couldn't see Jared, Jared's bed was flat and empty. He stared at the woman's curly blond hair, not his mother's sleek black pageboy, but it was his mother's face scowling down at him.

The last time he'd seen her, a slant of moonlight had lit her face—then there'd been the blaze of gunshot, the white light blinding him as Grandma jerked him down to the floor of the car, into the smell of dust. In the blackness after, he could still see his mother's face, cold with anger. He'd told no one he saw her, not even Grandma.

Now, panicked to have his mother's hand across his mouth so he couldn't yell for help, he bit her. She hit him so hard it made his ears ring. "You do that again, or make a sound, I'll send you where I sent your daddy." She smelled of the tingly perfume that made him sneeze. Bending his arm painfully behind him, she'd managed with her other hand to stuff a pillow and a blanket under the covers, patting them into a shape that, he guessed, would look like him sleeping, with his head tucked under. Then she pushed him ahead of her, gripping his shoulder like a metal claw, forced him out of the room and down the hall to the stairs. She paused at the top of the dark steps, listening.

Below, the front door stood open, the porch light was on, and Grandma stood on the porch, her back to them, talking to someone. His mother forced him down the stairs behind Grandma, keeping to the edge of the steps so they wouldn't squeak. Why was there grass on the stairs? Grandma wouldn't like that. With her hand hard over his mouth, his mother jerked him past the front door into the kitchen and through the glass door to Grandma's studio. He could smell cut grass in there, mingled with the new-room smell. Pushing and dragging him through the studio, she shoved him outside, slid the door closed behind them. The bricks were cold under his bare feet as she dragged and pushed him up the hill through the neighbors' backyard and the next yard, through the scratching bushes. Up and up the hill, behind Ryan's cottage and up through the thorny tangles. He wanted to yell for help but was afraid she'd hurt him worse. He could still see that explosion of gunfire and her cold face as she killed his daddy and Caroline. At the top of the hill they came out of the bushes to a sidewalk. Turned right up a side street to a white, sleek car. When she tried to push him in the backseat he fought her, jerked away, ducked under the car against the tire. He clung to the tire but she loosened his arms, twisting his left arm, she pulled him out again. When he hit and kicked at her she held his hands behind him, shoved him in the car on the floor of the backseat.

He hurt bad, but he didn't dare move as she got in the front. She closed the door softly so no one would hear from one of the houses that loomed dark all around them. He could see her between the bucket seats, he kept his eyes slitted closed so she wouldn't see him looking. Her white thin hands on the wheel were shaking. He watched her warily, clutching his arms around himself, shivering in his pajamas. His bare feet were cold, and stinging from the thorny bushes. When he tried to see out the window, she turned to look at him. "You keep down. I don't want your head above the glass. Don't bother trying the doors, they have safety locks, you can't open them. Be quiet and keep down." She didn't call him by his name, not once. Starting the car, she pulled out real slow and quiet. She turned down Grandma's street, he could see the paler sky above black trees, could see the high roof of Grandma's house slip by, the familiar stone chimney. Maybe he could slide between the bucket seats fast into the front, unlock the passenger door, jump out, and run—except he knew he wouldn't be fast enough, he knew she'd catch him.

When they were past Grandma's house she hit the gas so hard she sent him sliding, and she sped down the hill toward the village. There were no streetlights, only a few house lights swinging across the glass above him. They must have crossed the village, for soon they were among bigger, taller houses, where he could see upstairs lights burning. She slowed and pulled to the curb.

Killing the engine, she put the window down. A blast of cold air sucked in. It was lighter here, house lights and some shops. Slowly he eased up to look. She was watching the tall house down at the corner, across the street. His heart pounded with excitement when he heard the metallic sound of a police radio. When he eased up, he could see a black-and-white parked just past the tall house.

"Get down. I told you to stay down," she snapped. She started the car and pulled away, around the corner and up the hill.

When she parked again, she was angrier than ever. Opening the driver's door, she slipped out, closed it without even a click. Opened his door and pulled him out. "Come on. Not a sound." He could almost smell her meanness and hate. She dragged him along the sidewalk, down the hill again, two blocks, and in among some bushes where she could watch the house on the corner and watch the cop car, its radio like talking into a tin can. Her hand on his arm was sweating, he'd never seen her sweat before. Somehow that made him feel better.

Never taking her eyes from the cop car, with her left hand she pulled her cell phone from her pocket, flipped it open. She started to dial one-handed but then, backing deeper into the bushes, she closed it again. The uniformed cop had stepped out of his black-and-white and stood looking across the street toward them.

Benny didn't think he could see them there in the dark

bushes, but his mother was as still as a scared rabbit. They stood there a long time. The cop did too, but then he got back in his car. He sat there, with his radio turned down but still tinny. Benny had to pee. He thought of asking if he could pee in the bushes, but he decided to hold it. They stood there with her hand scrunching the bones of his shoulder until another cop car came around the corner and parked behind the first one. When that cop got out, she dragged him away through the bushes and up the dark street again, to the car. Shoved him in the back, told him to stay down, swung into the driver's seat and eased the car away, heading up into the hills. She drove slowly until a siren whooped behind them. She took off fast, careened up the hill watching in her rearview mirror so she nearly hit a parked car.

Were the cops looking for her? Had Grandma found him gone, and called them? But she was his mother, maybe she could take him wherever she liked, and what could the cops do? He wanted to look out the back window, but she kept watching in the rearview mirror as she skidded around corners, up the dark streets. Not many house lights up here, and those were far back among the trees. Suddenly she slammed on the brakes in a squealing skid, metal rammed into metal and he was thrown against the door; the car tilted sideways and went over, he fell hard onto the door and window that were now under him.

He could hear clicking and something dripping. In blackness he tried to find the door handle. His face was wet, and he could smell blood, the same as the night his daddy and Caroline died. He began to shake. His stomach heaved and without warning he threw up on himself.

Throw-up on his legs and bare feet, soaking his pajamas. He couldn't crawl away from it. In the front seat, he heard her moan and then swear. She began to struggle, rocking the car. There was a clicking, and then thuds; then he heard the driver's door swing open, bouncing as it fell, bouncing on its hinges. He heard cloth slide across cloth. She grunted; then his own door fell open under him with a screeching complaint and he fell out onto dirt and sharp rocks.

She dragged him out from under the door, didn't ask if he was hurt. "Get up. Get up now!" Dragging him up, she jerked him away from the wrecked car. It was tilted against a tree where the road fell away, and tangled with a big pickup truck. The lights of both threw yellow rivers up into the night. In the truck, someone moaned. The air smelled of gasoline and of whiskey. She dragged him down the hill away from the wrecked vehicles, maybe before anyone saw them. "Run, damn it! Run!"

He tried to run. His feet were so cold, and his right leg hurt. Her hard shoes made running sounds on the pavement, pulling him along, running down the hill. When he stumbled and fell, she grabbed his shoulder, heaving him up and carrying him, running awkwardly. He went limp, tried to make himself heavy.

"Come on, Benny. Hold on, put your arm around my neck. I can't leave you here."

He didn't see why not. He didn't want to be with her. "I can't hold on," he lied. "My arm hurts. My leg hurts, it won't work right."

They were passing dark houses, all dark, no lights that he could run to if he could get away. But he tried pulling away and fighting her anyway. She carried him a ways as he fought her, then at last put him down. She was standing over him staring angrily down at him when voices broke the night. A man's slurred voice and then a woman's. Benny thought they sounded drunk, he knew about drunk. Pearl pushed him into the bushes. "Stay there and keep quiet. I'll come back for you." She ran, fled down the hill away from him, didn't look back.

He knew she wouldn't come back, she didn't care what happened to him, all she cared about was herself. The sound of her running grew fainter until it was gone in the scuffling wind. He huddled shivering in the scratchy bushes, his leg hurting but not so bad as he'd said. The tears that squeezed out weren't because of his hurting leg. He lay in the bushy shelter hugging himself. Which way was Grandma's house? Could he find home? This road sloped up, and their house was in the hills, so maybe he should go that way. Rising, limping on his hurt leg, he moved up the dark road. The trees crowded black above him, branches over the road hiding the sky. Ahead, he could still hear the drunk couple arguing. He didn't want to go near them. He was cold. He hurt, his leg hurt. His arm hurt bad where she'd jerked and pulled him. Among the trees that lined the road, there were no house lights at all now. *Were* there houses back in there, or was it all just woods? Should he go to those people, take a chance and trust a drunk man? Or go into the black woods and circle around the arguing couple? He moved on at last, away from them, up the narrow road, then through the woods, on up the hill through the night.

41

"THIS WON'T WORK," Dulcie said as Wilma hurriedly pulled on a pair of jeans and a sweatshirt. "From the car, we won't see anything, won't have a clue where they've taken Benny. What, you want to just drive the streets clueless?"

"But you can find him, running the roofs clueless?" Wilma gave her a skeptical look and bent down to tie her jogging shoes.

"I can scan the streets faster from up there. I can see on four sides of a block in seconds. And sound rises, Wilma. I can hear more, too. If you try to follow me in the car, how will you see me? And what if I lose you among other car lights? It isn't like we carry walkie-talkies." That wasn't a bad idea, Dulcie thought, except for the weight, except for having to wear a collar, which in itself terrified her. "I can look for him better alone," she repeated stubbornly.

"Go," Wilma said at last, exasperated. She had never, in all her working career, let her parolees rag her the way the little tabby bossed her around. She watched Dulcie streak away through the house, heard her cat door slap open and back as she bolted through. She imagined Dulcie scrambling up the oak tree, leaping to the neighbors' shingles and vanishing across the rooftops. Where would she go, how would *she* know where to look? And yet, having lived with Dulcie a long time, she suspected the tabby would find a way.

She debated whether to call Ryan and Clyde, find out if they'd gone to help search for Benny. Maybe she could help them? Kit must . . . *Oh*, she thought, *it's Rock! Kit wanted Rock, she wanted him to track the child.*

But then Dulcie's on a wild-goose chase, she thought, looking away toward the windy rooftops. *Will Dulcie think of Rock? Will she try to find and join them, instead of searching blindly by herself for Benny?* She imagined Dulcie alone in the night searching uselessly, then imagined the ragtag midnight procession as Rock pulled Ryan through the dark streets, Clyde and Joe running to keep up, joined perhaps by a detective or two, a strange parade racing through the night. *Will Dulcie find them? Or will she just go on searching all alone?*

RACING OVER THE roofs toward the hills, Dulcie didn't think about Rock, she was obsessed with the notion that the kidnappers, unless they had a safe house in which to hide, would escape among the hills above the village, among the twisting and narrow lanes. Maybe they had a cabin back in the woods somewhere. Parts of Molena Point, wild enough for deer and coyotes and the occasional cougar, were surely remote enough to hide a kidnapper. A thin fog was beginning to drift down over the village. She paused frequently to rear up and listen, though chances were slim the child would be able to cry out. The village seemed huge tonight; one little boy could easily be swallowed up in the dark. An owl swooped low over her head, but she was too big for its supper. Ahead, a car passed on a cross street; she followed for only a block before it turned into a driveway.

A lone woman got out, a teenager who really shouldn't be out this late. This was crazy, searching with no clue, running after every car. Though this time of night the cars were few, their tires singing a lonely song on the paving. Dulcie was maybe ten blocks from home, above the village, when she saw a red light undulating up through the pine trees some blocks ahead. A cop car? Faintly she heard a car door open, and the squawk of metal grating on metal, heard a distant police radio kick in. The sounds came from higher up the hill and, hearing no other commotion in the silent village, she headed there. She had raced three blocks when a patrol car came slipping along below her heading in that direction. She was racing to keep up when it turned on its siren, and she burned up the rooftops running, her paws pounding like rain above the heads of the sleeping village.

IN MAUDIE'S GUEST room, Ryan picked one of Benny's dirty socks from the hamper, using a pencil to lift it into a plastic sandwich bag. She didn't open the bag until Clyde had brought Rock in, on his lead; then she presented the scent to him, letting him take a long sniff. Rock knew what this was for, he knew the drill. His short tail wagging fast, he sniffed the lure, then sniffed thoroughly along the length of Benny's unmade bed. Clyde and Dallas stood in the bedroom doorway, watching—and Clyde looking smug. Dallas was still perplexed at the big dog's sudden expertise, with no long regimen of training. Rock peered under the bed for only a second, then backed out again.

From beneath the bed, Joe Grey watched his protégé, but made no move to join him. When Rock peered hard at him, Joe closed his eyes in a gesture that Rock knew meant, *Don't mess with me now, ignore me.* At once Rock backed away, staring up at Ryan for direction, huffing with impatience.

"Find," she said softly.

Rock put his nose to the floor, drank in Benny's scent, and sped out of the room, nearly knocking Clyde and Dallas down, flew down the stairs pulling Ryan along so she had to grab at the rail to keep her balance. Racing through the house with his nose to the floor, through the studio, he pressed his body against the glass slider, pawing at it until Ryan could shove it open. Bolting through into the backyard, his nose to the ground, he headed up the hill crashing through bushes, jerking Ryan along as fast as she could run. This wasn't obedience time when the big dog had to walk at heel on a loose leash, this was work time, Rock was in charge now. As he dragged Ryan up through the neighbors' backyards, Clyde and Dallas following, the detective didn't see Joe Grey following behind them, nor did he see, racing across the roofs above them, Kit and the yellow tomcat leaping in fast pursuit. Didn't see Kit nipping and shouldering at Misto until he stopped and turned on her. With all the crashing through the bushes, no one heard them arguing in soft cat voices, Kit saying they should go back, should watch Maudie, not leave her alone, the tortoiseshell so adamant that finally Misto did turn reluctantly to go back with her, to peer down through the windows at Maudie.

MAUDIE WATCHED THE trackers from her studio doorway as long as she could see them, listened to them crashing up the black hill. She'd wanted to follow in her car, to be there when they found Benny, but Dallas had other ideas. "You'd be in the way of the dog," he'd told her, his square Latino face serious with concern. "Driving along after him, your headlights behind him, you'd distract him, make him lose the trail."

Maudie wasn't sure this was true, but she didn't want to impede the search. "I can keep up, on foot," she'd argued.

"That could confuse him, too. You have Benny's scent on you. You'd have him doubling back sniffing at you. We want him to follow fresh scent."

Maudie didn't know whether Dallas was speaking the truth at all, or simply wanted her out of their way. But she couldn't argue with him, she surely couldn't jeopardize the search. The police thought Kent might have kidnapped Benny, but she was certain it was Pearl. And if Pearl had him, she was terrified for the child.

"You'll help most by staying here," Dallas had said, "in case Benny somehow manages to escape and find his way home. You need to be here for him, Maudie. To comfort him, and to let us know he's been found."

She prayed to God he'd be found. She thought about Jared being part of that gang, and she felt sick. Could you trust no one? Soft-spoken, clean-cut Jared. Sleeping in the guest room alone with Benny. Had Jared had a hand in this, had he helped get Benny out of the house? And exactly when had they taken him? Behind her back as she stood on the porch watching the police? Or when she'd left the house to go down to Alfreda's? This all had to be connected, the invasions, the theft of her keys, the rifled and stolen storage boxes, the invasions. All linked together with Benny's kidnapping. But for what purpose?

Standing at the kitchen sink wrapped in her woolen robe, she watched the dark yard, praying Benny would appear out of the night, that somehow he would break free and find his way home. Praying to see his small shadow slipping along through the neighbors' dark yards, making his way home. Praying to see him free of Pearl, and safe. Turning to the stove to pour the rest of the cocoa into her cup, she caught her breath at a sound behind her. Turning, she spilled hot cocoa on her hand. Pearl stood by the table, her thin face smeared with blood, her windbreaker torn and bloody, her expression smug. A bloody gash ran up her face into her kinky, bleached hair. She held a small automatic, aimed at Maudie.

"Where's Benny?" Maudie whispered. "What have you done with him?" She dabbed at her hand with the dish towel, edging the towel toward her pocket.

"Give me the ledger pages Caroline had," Pearl said. "And your bonds. You'll sign them over to me. Then I'll bring Benny here."

Maudie just looked at her.

"I want the pages now, or you won't see Benny again. You're alone in the house, David's gone, there's no one here to help you." She glanced at the dish towel. "If anything happens to me, you'll never get Benny. No one will ever find him."

"You wouldn't kill your own child." But Maudie wasn't sure that was true.

"No woman has ever killed her own kid? I never wanted Benny. All these years, he's only been in my way. Why would I want him now? Except to use in trade," Pearl said, smiling.

"And Jared was in it all along," Maudie said. "You and Jared and Kent did those cruel invasions together. And that man with the black beard. But why? Who is he?"

"Get the pages."

"You've already been through Caroline's things. If you didn't find what you wanted, then it isn't here."

"Do you want me to bring your grandson back to you, dead?"

"It's too late to trade," Maudie said. "The LAPD has a copy of what you're looking for, and there's a warrant out on you."

"I'm losing patience. I want the pages. Without them the boy's dead."

"What makes you think there isn't more than one set of copies?"

"If there is and I find out, I'll come back and kill him."

"From behind bars?" Maudie said, laughing.

Pearl clicked off the safety. Her dark eyes were cold, her face as pale and hard as stone. Was this how she looked across the blackjack table, dealing out a crooked hand, taking the players' money? Pearl glanced down at the gun, lifting it slightly so it was aimed at Maudie's throat.

"There's only one set of copies," Maudie said, resigned. "In my safe-deposit box."

"And the bonds?"

"And the bonds." It was the middle of the night, they'd have hours to wait before the bank opened. Maybe this would give the searchers time to find Benny, maybe time to find and arrest Pearl? In that moment, she knew she should have made another copy. She'd thought about it, but had decided the pages would be safe enough, locked in the bank vault.

"We'll be at the bank when it opens," Pearl said. "You'll give me the pages plus whatever cash you keep in the box, and sign over the bonds. You always kept cash in your safe-deposit box." She smiled. "You didn't know I knew that."

All Maudie could think was, she wanted Pearl dead. Beneath the dish towel, her hand was so close to her pocket. Could she be quick enough? Shove her hand in, shoot through her pocket, never revealing the gun? But Pearl stood so close to her, still with the safety off the automatic. She was trying to think how to do this and not die herself when she heard a man's voice from some-

308

where above them. Startled, she glanced toward the ceiling. Pearl stiffened but didn't look up, didn't take her eyes from Maudie.

There was no one upstairs, Maudie knew that. Unless that officer down the street had seen Pearl slip in and had followed her? Maybe he'd come to the kitchen window and seen Pearl holding a gun on her? Maybe he'd somehow gotten in upstairs. Not likely, that portly cop climbing on the fence or up a tree. She wondered if the construction ladder was still outside, lying beside the garage wall. Maybe he'd called a second cop and they were ready to come down the stairs behind Pearl? Except, they wouldn't be talking, knowing they'd be heard in the kitchen below.

But then, when the voice spoke again, it seemed to come not from the rooms above at all, but from over the garage. Or maybe from someone out on the street, maybe it was one of her neighbors, his voice deflected by the house walls. She shifted the towel, rubbing her hand with it as she eased toward her pocket.

But what if she killed Pearl, and Benny *was* badly hurt somewhere, and the tracking dog didn't find him? What if help didn't come in time, if they found him too late because she'd killed the only person who knew where he was?

How badly *had* Pearl hurt him? Pearl's face and hand were bleeding; what was that about? Had Benny fought hard enough to injure her like that, to make that deep wound down Pearl's cheek? What would Pearl have done to him in retribution? Maudie's heart pounded with fear for her grandson, far more fear, even, than the storm of hatred that she felt for Pearl. As Pearl gestured with the gun, quietly Maudie laid down the dish towel and slid into a chair at the table. Prepared to wait for morning, to wait for the bank to open. Prepared to do as Pearl ordered—praying that, one way or another, Benny would be safe and unhurt.

42

PEARL WATCHED MAUDIE sitting so patiently at the table, snuggled cozily in her robe as if she weren't afraid of the gun, as if Maudie didn't believe she'd kill her. Certainly she wouldn't kill her until morning, until she had the ledger copies and the bonds and hopefully some cash. Then she'd decide what to do.

Getting rid of Maudie's body would take time. It might be easier just to leave her tied up somewhere and give herself the chance to get away, change her looks again so she could travel unnoticed. Maybe she'd dye her hair red this time, straighten it to a sleek bob. Her distinctive bone structure was a hindrance. Even her long, pale hands were too easily recognizable—a dealer's hands, swift and clever. But ruined now, her hands bleeding and ugly from the cuts and bruises. She winced, looking at her pretty hands so cut up; she'd always taken care of her hands, babied them, had regular manicures, carefully selected polish. Hands were important, men watched your hands at the card table, trying to catch you up or thinking how those silky hands would feel on their bodies.

It would take the abrasions a long time to heal, the ugly, broken nails a long time to grow out and be perfect again. There was blood on her face, too, she could feel it pulling as the wound began to dry. That frightened her. She didn't want a scar marring her face, her smooth white skin; she didn't want to come out of this ugly, she depended on her looks.

Well, the damned car was a loss, that was sure. It was while she was climbing out that she'd cut her hands so badly. And all the while, the driver of the other car wailing and carrying on, loud enough to be heard blocks away. He'd been drunk, she could smell the liquor, the whole thing was his fault. There'd been no witness to report the crash, but she supposed by now someone had come along the road and called the cops and the place would be crawling with them. Maybe they wouldn't find the kid, though, the way he was hidden.

Him whining and crawling into the bushes, that had bought her some time. She'd dragged him a long way but at last had left him, making her way back to Arlie's place. She knew that was foolish, but cops or not, she had to have a car. Why were the cops there? Had they caught Arlie, arrested him? She'd fled the house the minute she spotted a second cop car coming up the street, had gotten out of there fast, but she knew they had Arlie, he couldn't have gotten away. Were they now watching for her? Or for Kent? They wouldn't be looking for Jared, she thought, smiling. He'd been safe with Maudie, pretending to have

312

just awakened. Though he'd planned to leave Maudie's before she found the kid gone. He didn't want to be pressed into searching for him, didn't want any part of that.

After the wreck, she'd wanted to clean up at Arlie's and change her clothes. She'd already checked out of the motel, of course, but could check into another, the town was crawling with motels. But going in looking the way she did, bloody and her clothes torn and without luggage, and in the middle of the night, even the dumbest desk clerk would call the cops.

When she'd gotten back to Arlie's place, staying in the shadows, the cop cars were gone. Easing around a corner, she'd stood in the blackness across the street beside a sheltered porch, watching and fingering the keys in her pocket, keys to the house and to his car. She'd stood there a long time, but saw no dark uniform standing in the bushes or in a doorway, even as far as several blocks away. When she felt sure the cops had given up and moved on, she'd slipped into the house, easing quietly through the dark rooms, calling out softly to Arlie so if he *was* there, maybe sitting in the dark, she wouldn't surprise him. The house seemed strange, didn't seem right. He hadn't lived there long, but had taken great care with the placement of every piece of furniture, he was so damned picky. A living room chair was out of place so she nearly fell over it, a window shade crooked, a closet door had been left open. Prowling with her gun drawn, she'd found Arlie's flashlight in the kitchen drawer and had gone through the place again shielding the light. Several pieces of furniture had been moved, papers on the desk were in disarray, not the way he kept them. The cops had been there, all right.

Or someone had. Quickly she'd retrieved her bag, didn't look to see if someone had rummaged through her clothes but had headed for the garage.

She could have gone back for the Cadillac, which Arlie had left parked four blocks from Maudie's, but by now the cops had probably found it. Sliding into the leased Jaguar, she was glad now that he was such a damned high roller he had to have a second car. She'd started the Jag, liking its faint but deep-throated rumble. The garage door made hardly any sound. She'd backed out, closed it with the remote, and driven sedately away—thinking Arlie wasn't such a high roller now, with his ass cooling in the local tank. As for her, her next stop would either gain her the ledger copies and bonds or drop her straight into the cops' laps with Arlie.

Leaving the car on a tiny side street, she'd walked the three blocks to Maudie's. The yard lights were still on. One cop car was still parked in front of the invasion house four doors down, and she'd drawn back against an oak tree. Stayed still, then, as car lights came up the street and that contractor's pickup pulled up in front of Maudie's. What was this about? Ryan Flannery and her husband got out, they had that big gray dog with them. They took the dog inside, and in only a little while they came out again through the studio, the dog on a leash and moving fast, jerking Flannery up the hill following the route along which she'd dragged Benny—the dog was tracking Benny. A chill had iced her, she'd wanted to turn and run.

She wasn't sure a tracking dog could follow a moving car. Unless there was scent on the outside of the car, she thought, remembering Benny clinging so desperately to the tire. If the dog picked that up and got to the wreck, where they'd been on foot again, he'd find their trail. Likely he'd find the kid. But would he keep on, then, tracking her? She'd watched until they disappeared, then looked to where Maudie stood at the kitchen window, looking out. Pearl could picture her twisting a dish towel, worrying over the kid. Using the key she'd taken, she'd slipped inside, and into the kitchen—and here she was, she and Maudie having a nice little chat, Maudie whining about the boy.

But now it was time to move on, she'd been here long enough, she wanted to get away before they found the kid and came back. "Get dressed," she told Maudie. "You can't go in the bank looking like that."

"We can't go to the bank, it's the middle of the night."

"Move it," she said, gesturing with her gun toward the stairs.

Silently Maudie went up. Pearl followed, checked all the rooms, then watched while she dressed. When the man's voice came again it sounded almost like he was right there in the other bedroom, but that wasn't possible.

"Get a move on," she told Maudie. "Hand me the belt from that robe." She was reaching for the belt to tie Maudie's hands when the man shouted an urgent, panicked cry accompanied by a muffled banging on a window.

"Stay here, get your shoes on. You leave this room, you're dead." She moved toward the hall, glanced back to see Maudie hanging up the robe and reaching for a jacket.

Slipping into the guest room, she found it empty. And no one at the windows. No one could be, there was only a thin lip of roof running along outside beneath the glass.

Could the man have been at the front door and some trick of the wind made him sound like he was inside the house? Returning to the bedroom, she bound Maudie's hands behind her, forced her out of the room and down the stairs. Hurrying past the front door, she pushed Maudie on out through the studio, through the yard, and up the street, staying to the darkest shadows, heading three blocks up where, beyond a curve, the maroon Jaguar waited out of sight.

PEARL DIDN'T SEE, on the roof behind them, the two cats watching, nor would she have paid any attention, she certainly wouldn't have looked closely enough to see that one of the cats, a dark tortoiseshell, was placing a call on a cell phone. Hurrying away from the house, she didn't hear the soft female voice that set in motion a BOL on the Jaguar, bringing into action the cruising street patrols—nor did she see the yellow cat stifle a laugh.

The old cat had found it wildly liberating to shout at Pearl; and when his shouts and paw-pounding on the guest room window distracted and unnerved her long enough for Maudie to slip the gun from her robe into her jacket pocket, that was a fine example of feline/human teamwork—even if Maudie didn't know she'd had help. Now, both cats, following along the roofs above, wanted to whisper a word of encouragement to Maudie as she was forced up the street. All they could do was race after them over the shingles following the dark, sleek car, determined not to lose Maudie.

* * *

PUSHING MAUDIE INTO the backseat, Pearl engaged the safety switches and locked the doors. Her eyes felt gritty, she longed to clean up and tend to the wound on her face, try to prevent a disfiguring infection, but she didn't dare return to Arlie's house. As she headed up into the hills, she could see a convergence of lights near where the wreck would be, the lights of cop cars reflected up through the trees; when she cracked the window she could hear their radios. She hoped the driver wasn't dead, that would complicate matters. Hoped they hadn't found Benny, she didn't want the kid blabbing. Maybe she shouldn't have left him, should have gotten him away, hidden him somewhere they'd never find him even with the dog.

But maybe he'd stay away from the cops, maybe he was trying to find his way home, wandering lost up through the black woods. When she was above the wreck, heading higher into the tangle of hills, she watched for a place to park unseen among the darkened houses, maybe near where that canyon ran down. If the cops came nosing around up there, if she had to get away from the car, the canyon could be useful, even though she hated getting torn and scratched again by fallen trees and bushes. Once she had the papers and money, she'd decide what to do with Maudie. Pulling onto a twisting side street, she heard dogs barking somewhere to her right, as if she had disturbed them. But then in a moment someone must have shut them up, the night was still again, and she settled down to wait.

43

ONCE PEARL LEFT him and Benny had come out from his hiding place and hobbled up into the woods, hurrying away from the direction his mother had gone, his leg didn't hurt so bad. Not as bad as he'd let on, he'd wanted her to think he couldn't walk much. Circling through the woods, past the metal heap of the white Toyota and the truck, he could see a porch light burning, in the house just above. Avoiding the man and woman who stood by the truck arguing, slipping around them, he couldn't help the brushy sounds of his bare feet in the wet leaves. He thought they didn't hear, because they didn't stop arguing. Twice he stepped on sharp rocks and had to swallow back a yelp, and then a twig poked into his ankle. The woman's voice was mean, as scratchy as a nail scraping the sidewalk. "Why the hell didn't you look when you backed out of the damn drive?"

"I *did* look, dammit. Car came around the corner so

fast I couldn't even shift gears, and you know damn well my horn don't work."

"First person sees this mess in the morning, first car comes down the road, the cops'll be all over it, and you with no insurance. I told you this would happen."

When he was past them, Benny ran, up through the woods, trying to remember the way he and Grandma took driving down to the village and home again. He thought Grandma's house was away to the right; he wanted to go that way but the woods were so tangled and black. Who knew what was in there, hidden among the trees? When the road made a sharp bend to the right, the voices grew fainter behind him, but still he hurried uphill, his leg hurting worse. Once, he saw strings of little Christmas lights back in the woods. He guessed they were Christmas lights, hoped they weren't something else, ghosts or something creepy. He was getting warm from walking, but he was out of breath. Sitting down on a long mound of earth at the side of the road, he yawned, and rubbed his hurting leg. He wasn't lost, he told himself. The sudden sound of men's voices made him look up. Had that drunk man followed him? He could see lights moving behind him, now, reflecting up among the trees. Frightened, he slipped behind the berm, out of sight from the road. A man was calling him, calling, "Benny? Benny?" How could he know his name?

The calling went on for a long time, but he was afraid to answer. He could see the light approaching uphill toward him. If he ran, the man would hear him. Quickly he dug down against the berm and pulled some fallen pine branches over himself. As he huddled there, again tears came, but these were tears of fear and of exhaustion and from the pain in his leg. He wouldn't cry again for his mother, he didn't have a mother, his connection to Pearl had been torn away, that woman who had hurt him wasn't his mother. Yawning, he snuggled down beneath the branches, wanting help, but not from a stranger. Curling up trying to stay warm, he closed his eyes just for a minute.

He woke to a soft *meow*. He opened his eyes to see a cat crouched on the berm looking down at him. He came fully awake. He could see the darker blackness of familiar stripes, the wide, curved stripes across her shoulders, the stripe that blackened half her left ear. "Dulcie?"

She mewed at him and leaped down, and snuggled against his neck, purring. She was warm, cuddled against him; even her purr seemed to warm him. He petted her and talked to her and wished she could tell him how to get home, wished she could lead him home. But she was just a cat, she didn't know he was lost. He lay there cuddling her, wondering if she was lost, too? Why would she be so far from home, from where he usually saw her? When she rose and moved away, he was afraid she'd leave him, he didn't want her to go away to hunt and leave him all alone.

WHEN DULCIE HAD arrived at the wreck, there were two patrol cars nosed in facing it, their headlights picking out the tangle of the white Toyota crumpled half on its side against a badly dented king cab pickup. Rearing up until she could see the license plate where it was jammed against a tree, she discovered it was the Toyota from the motel. The tangle of wrecked vehicles spilled across the road and up into the driveway of a dark brown, shingled house, a grim, depressing place crowded on three sides by the dense pine woods. Looking at the wreck, she imagined the truck backing down the drive, the Toyota coming fast up around the curve from below, hitting it broadside; imagined the car spinning the truck around in a lethal dance before it lost its footing, skidded over, and tilted into the tree. She could see no one inside either vehicle. If the three officers on the scene had found anyone, they'd have an ambulance there by now. Or they'd have the coroner. She didn't want to think about that, hadn't wanted to think about Benny hurt or dead.

Had an ambulance already come and gone, maybe taking the little boy away? She watched one of the officers move up the stairs to the front door, his flashlight beam raking the face of the house, and Dulcie circled behind the other two uniforms, through the dark to nose around the Toyota.

She found the woman's scent, mixed with the smell of blood. And yes, the little boy's scent where he'd eased or been pulled out of the backseat through the broken door. Both trails led downhill along the narrow road. She'd followed to where the two trails parted, the woman's scent going on down, toward the village.

Benny's scent led into the bushes, and she'd found where he had lain beneath a rhododendron bush, curled up long enough to leave a little puddle of blood that was now beginning to congeal. When he'd moved on again alone, back up the road toward the wreck, he had circled wide around it, staying among the bushes as if avoiding the cops. Why would he do that when he needed help? Or had he passed before the cops arrived? But, thinking back to what Maudie had said when Benny's daddy was shot, the sheriff's spotlights shining suddenly into the car onto the torn bodies, the voices of men Benny didn't know, the harsh police radio, the child staring at his murdered father's torn body, maybe she understood his fear of cop cars and harsh spotlights.

Leaving the scene, she had followed Benny's scent on uphill through the woods and back onto the dark road until she'd discovered him asleep behind the berm, huddled up like a little hurt animal. She'd snuggled with him, wondering how best to summon help, wondering if she could get him to follow her. Though she didn't think he'd follow her back to the police units. She'd lain against him worrying until she lost patience and had padded away waving her tail, looking back at him—and it had been as easy as enticing a young kitten. Benny, distressed that she was leaving, reached out to her. When she didn't stop, he scrambled up, ignoring his hurt leg, and limped after her, unwilling to be left behind.

BUT DULCIE WASN'T the only cat who'd raced out into the night on a search against all odds. Down in the village Misto and Kit chased across the rooftops, running as fast as they could, but soon losing the lights of the faster moving Jaguar, which had far outdistanced them. "Go on," Misto said, panting. "Catch up, don't lose them."

"I'm winded, too." But Kit fled on, her heart pounding so hard it shook her. She was thankful for the stoplights that slowed the Jaguar, she didn't dare lose Maudie. She hoped this chase didn't do Misto in, but she mustn't wait for him. Such a dear old cat, so frail in his aging. Once when the maroon Jaguar passed some lighted houses she got a flash of Maudie in the backseat struggling to get loose from her bonds. Where was Pearl taking her? Fear sent Kit pelting headlong, running so fast her back and front legs crossed in deep Xs, a flying ball of fur sailing across tree branches, above alleys yawning black below her. When she lost sight of the Jaguar she followed its receding rumble. She was nearly done for, she had raced farther and harder than she had ever run chasing some terrified and willful rabbit.

Pearl's lights flashed between houses and woods as the car moved higher into the hills, forcing Kit to leave the last accessible rooftop and race up a narrow road, led only by the sound of the Jaguar. Pearl was headed high above the village where the houses were closer together again, crowded along the wild ravine, where she'd be able to see the streets below but could park out of sight. It was a logical place to take cover. If she was pressed, she might escape down into the canyon, just as she must have escaped behind Alfreda's house earlier that night. Escape, and leave Maudie bound in the Jaguar? That would mess up her plans to hit the bank first thing in the morning. But it might save Pearl's own neck, if she could dodge the cops.

But maybe you won't dodge them, Kit thought, smiling.

High above her, Pearl's lights stopped, then were extinguished. Yes, she had gone to ground in a secluded neighborhood just above the canyon where it would be easy to stay hidden—except that this was the canyon behind the senior ladies' house. Pearl wouldn't know that, Kit thought, smiling. She would know nothing about the seniors. Her choice of hiding places made Kit laugh out loud and lick her paw with satisfaction. This was the kind of good fortune where, when you'd slipped up on a mouse hole, you found a discarded cheese sandwich and the mice already gathered, too busy to notice their silent visitor.

Kit turned when she heard Misto panting behind her; he came flying, as if he'd gained his second wind. They raced on, not speaking, up the road among the woods toward the houses above. If Pearl was holed up for good, they had only to slip up on her, one of them keep her in sight, and the other race away to the seniors', where Kit knew how to get in through Lori's window. She'd just slip in past the sleeping girl, steal downstairs and use the kitchen phone, and she'd have the law up there pronto. As they approached the crest of the hill they heard a dog bark, his voice deep and melodic, and then a second dog: Lamb, the seniors' big chocolate poodle, and their Dalmatian. Both knew something was out there, maybe they'd heard the Jaguar pull up the hill and park.

But what now? If she slipped into the house to use the phone, the dogs would be all over her. Even now, their barking might scare Pearl away, prompt her to run again. Rearing up looking through the trees trying to make out the dark shape of Pearl's car, Kit was uncertain what to do. Uncertain how to play this game, maybe a far more dangerous game, with Maudie's life at stake, than any she'd ever tackled.

At last, shivering, she headed for Lori's second-floor window. Leaping to the hood of Cora Lee's car, scrambling up, she found the window shut against the cold night, shut and locked. When she tried Cora Lee's windows, they were locked, too. Both rooms were dark. As she crouched, peering in, she saw the reflection of a soft light come on at the back of the house, the kitchen. She could hear soft voices there, too, and could smell chocolate; maybe the ladies were having a little before-bed cocoa. She had to find a phone without alerting these ladies who had no idea she could speak, had to call the department, tell them that Pearl had Maudie. Looking up at the high little bathroom window, seeing it open a crack, she made a flying leap, clinging and clawing at the sliding glass.

44

EAGERLY BENNY FOLLOWED Dulcie. He wanted to go home, he wanted his grandma, and apparently he had perfect faith that she would take him there, that she would save him, she thought, smiling. Little kids were like that, they believed in the wisdom of animals, the magic of animals. Well, she might not have all the magic skills the child found in a favorite fairy tale, but she could sure as hell lead him to where he could get help.

What she didn't understand was why Pearl had kidnapped her own child. For money? For some kind of ransom? And if she'd wanted him bad enough to snatch him, why had she left him again so soon? Had he turned out to be too much of a burden? Benny would have slowed her down after the wreck, which Pearl must have feared would draw the cops to her. Whatever the cause, in her need to escape she had abandoned him, and Dulcie was glad for that.

But where were Kit and Joe? Kit had been there at Maudie's when Benny vanished, but where was she now? She supposed Joe was somewhere out in the night with Rock and Ryan, following Benny's trail. It was hard when they weren't together, couldn't talk, couldn't help one another. She had no way to tell them that Benny was safe, they weren't cops with their sophisticated electronic devices, able to talk to each other over long distances. Humans' inventions were marvels of ingenuity; she wondered if humans realized how very special they were, that they could not only visualize such wonders but had worked out how to build them, how to make them real.

Hurrying uphill with the child close beside her, she headed not for Maudie's house, which lay far to the right, but for the crest of the hill that towered above them. Benny might be lost, but she wasn't, she knew where to find help. She left the road when it turned away to the left, leading Benny straight up through the woods, a hard climb for the tired, injured child through dense trees and tangled vines. Heading straight for the seniors' house, she mewed her encouragement, wanting him to move faster as she leaped over fallen branches. Benny didn't like pushing through the black, clutching woods, she could see that he was afraid, but still he followed her. Only once did he pause and whimper, but then he pushed on again bravely, trusting her, trusting that she would take him safely through the night to where help waited, where someone friendly waited.

* * *

THE TRACKING TEAM did indeed form a strange procession through the dark and empty streets, the silver-colored dog with his nose to the paving jerking Ryan along, Clyde and Dallas jogging behind her, the hurrying gray tomcat taking up the rear. An untidy line of runners tracking Benny's scent, which clung to the long-since-vanished white Toyota. Sometimes Rock lost the scent in the wake of a passing vehicle and had to cast around to find it again. Twice he lost it so completely he had to double back, his nose lifting and then down to the macadam until he picked up the trail, alternately following airborne scent and sucking up the faintest odor that lay along the street. Joe wondered that Benny's scent had remained so strong—almost as if the child had rubbed against the tires or maybe clung to the fender or bumper trying to keep from being forced inside the car. Joe had, some time back, given up dodging into the shadows whenever Dallas glanced back at him. The detective knew he was there, and though his remarks amused Joe, they were unsettling, too.

"Why the hell is the cat still following us?" Dallas grumbled, scowling at Clyde. "He's like a dog out for a run, I never saw a cat that acts so much like a dog."

Clyde laughed. "He *thinks* he's part dog, always been like that. He liked to run the beach with Rube and Barney. Remember how they'd race? Now, with both the old dogs gone, he's grown pretty close to Rock."

"He thinks he's part cop," Dallas said, "the way he hangs around the station."

"It's the food he likes," Ryan said, sucking in breath, pulled along by Rock. "Mabel spoils him, you all do, he's really getting too fat."

Joe gave her a look as he moved along at a gallop beside Clyde. Ryan shook her head imperceptibly as Dallas glanced down at him, frowning. "Part dog," Ryan said, laughing. "Thinks he can do whatever Rock can do." She was about done in, was beginning to think she wasn't as young as she used to be, not a pleasant revelation. They'd been tracking for nearly an hour when Rock swerved suddenly up a hillside street, leaped ahead so violently he nearly jerking Ryan off her feet.

"The wreck," Dallas said, watching the light reflection among the treetops. With a BOL out on the white Toyota, the responding officers at the crash scene had called through to Dallas as soon as they ID'd the wrecked car.

"Neither driver on the scene," Officer McFarland had said. "Some blood on the seat of the Toyota, shoe prints over the skid marks, a woman's shoes and the boy's, but no one here now."

"See if you can find Benny," Dallas had said. "The woman's wanted on several charges." Dallas could have pulled Rock off the scent, taken him directly there, put him back on Benny's scent at the scene of the wreck. He'd opted, instead, to let Rock find his way without interference. If they took the big dog off the trail, they might miss something. Maybe the kidnapper had stopped somewhere, maybe pulled the child out of the car, locked him up somewhere. This, plus the fact that he didn't want to screw up the dog's training by taking him off fresh scent—not when he was ramping ahead on the lead nearly choking himself.

They arrived at the wreck to find Kathleen Ray photographing the car and truck and taking blood samples.

Neither driver nor passengers had been found. Before they reached the wrecked vehicles Rock brightened on Benny's scent so powerfully that he nearly flew off the road, jerking Ryan downhill for a long way, and then into a tangle of bushes, sniffing at an indentation of crushed leaves, a little bed matted down into a child-sized nest. Huffing, drinking in the scent, he'd circled wide around it, his nose to the ground, and then headed uphill again, veering back and forth between two trails.

At the wreck again he gave a yip and tried to climb into the turned-over Toyota, sucking at the scent from within and around the hanging door that gaped open. Proudly Joe Grey watched his protégé, smiling at the success of his training.

But there was one thing Joe and Rock knew that their human companions did not.

They had now picked up not only Benny's scent, but Dulcie's, and a thrill of apprehension touched Joe. Dulcie, too, was tracking Benny, alone through the black night.

Or maybe Dulcie had already found him, Joe thought hopefully. Maybe by now the child was no longer alone. And though Joe wasn't given to prayer, tonight he made an exception as he worried for his tabby lady.

Leaving the wreck behind, Rock took them straight up the steep road until it dead-ended, and there the silver dog plunged into the woods again, dragging Ryan crashing up through vines and heavy undergrowth. Rock's human followers were soon fighting blackberry thorns that snatched at their jeans and windbreakers, swearing with a creativity that amused the tomcat. When, above them, two dogs began to bark, Rock paused, listening. But their voices were familiar and welcome, and he wagged his short tail.

"Benny can't be headed for the seniors' house?" Dallas said. "How the hell could he find their place in the dark? How would he even know the direction? What kind of blind luck is that?"

Not blind luck, Joe Grey thought, this was Dulcie's doing, she had led Benny there.

They came out of the woods at the top of the hill, the three humans scratched and cranky from the blackberries' embrace. They were half a block from the seniors' rambling frame house. No lights burned in the flat-roofed, two-story structure, except for a faint light at the back, apparently from the kitchen. The seniors' dogs were still barking, but now with pleased little woofs. They knew who approached, and were excited to have midnight company. Rock wasn't distracted by them, he hurried along sucking Benny's fresh scent from the air. Only when Dallas put a hand on Ryan's arm did she speak to Rock and pull him to a halt. The good dog looked up at her reproachfully. He'd run for nearly two hours tracking Benny, he wanted the satisfaction of the find, he wanted a joyous reunion. "Just for a minute," she told him, stroking his muscled shoulder.

As Dallas and Clyde stood surveying the house and street, Joe moved on up beside Rock, to reassure him that this pause was all right, that this was part of the job. Ryan waited as Dallas and Clyde walked the street, checking the interiors of the seven cars parked at intervals before they turned their backs on them. Though Joe hadn't caught any fresh scent that could indicate someone waited concealed there. When at last Dallas nodded to Ryan and she released Rock, the big dog bolted not for the front door but around the side to the back deck.

Above the daylight basement, where a light burned in the kitchen, they could hear the murmur of voices. Benny's voice? Rock leaped up the stairs to the deck and across it, yipping at the door with impatience. Before Ryan could knock or call out Cora Lee opened it, releasing the smell of hot cocoa—and releasing the Dalmatian and the standard poodle. They rushed at Rock, excited and ready to play. But Rock plunged past them through the open door and raced across the kitchen, heading straight for Benny.

The child sat at the kitchen table with a blanket wrapped around him. Lori had pulled her chair close beside him, and there was a big mug of cocoa on the table in front of him. There was a fresh bandage on his face, and one on his right arm. Rock reared up, softly keening and licking Benny's face; and when the big dog cut a look at Ryan, his yellow eyes were filled with such pride that Ryan pressed her fist to her mouth and couldn't speak; Rock's doggy excitement at his accomplishment was so great that Clyde and Dallas, too, seemed choked with emotion.

From atop the little planning desk tucked beside the refrigerator, Dulcie looked on, purring extravagantly, her own triumph nearly as great as Rock's. Joe didn't know the details, but from the look on his lady's face, Benny Toola had enjoyed two miracles tonight. One when an "untrained" dog successfully tracked and found him. The other when he must have been led through the cold night to safety by an "ordinary house cat," a miracle that most humans would find impossible to believe. A rescue that, even to the hard-nosed tomcat, proved there might, indeed, be a touch of magic in the world. A special Christmas blessing, perhaps, that Dulcie had found Benny in the dark night, searching all alone, and that the child, lost and afraid, had been willing to follow her.

But Joe wasn't the only one focused on Dulcie. When he looked at Dallas, the detective was frowning at the purring tabby, as if puzzled that Wilma's cat was up there so far from home. Benny saw him looking. "Dulcie brought me," he blurted out. "She was in the woods, a man was calling me and I saw lights and I didn't know who that was. I ran, and then Dulcie was there, and she brought me here."

"She must have been hunting," Ryan said. "I've seen her over there on that road. Maybe she heard the police, saw the lights, and that frightened her just as it scared Benny."

Dallas watched Ryan, puzzled and silent—maybe not really wanting to know what this was about.

"A miracle that they met up," Ryan said. "Maybe, since she knows the seniors' house, maybe she thought of this as a place of safety . . ." Ryan knew she was talking too much, but she couldn't seem to stop. She didn't like the skeptical look on Dallas's face. He'd started to reply, his scowl stern, when his cell phone rang.

Picking up, the detective listened, then turned and stepped into the entry hall where he could talk in private. Silently Joe followed him, slipping into the shadows to listen.

"She's where?" Dallas said. "How could you know that? Who is this? Where are you? Are you certain she has Maudie?"

* * *

I'M SURE," KIT said. "She pushed Maudie in the backseat of a maroon Jaguar, her hands tied behind her. I followed them up where you are. I saw you with that dog. She didn't stop anywhere, she couldn't have let Maudie out. She's parked up in those trees, in the darkest shadows."

Kit's heart was pounding when she clicked off the speaker on the phone by Lori's empty bed, after calling Dallas's cell phone. She listened to Lori's voice and Dallas's voice from the kitchen below, heard him ask a question, heard Ryan answer. There was silence for a few minutes, then she heard the front door open. When she peered out through Lori's window, Dallas and Rock were on the porch, Rock straining at the leash, staring up the dark hill, his ears up, his whole body quivering. Soon they would head up there. Kit didn't know whether to follow them as they closed in on Pearl, or go down to poor Misto, who was crouched beneath the back deck, waiting for her.

Having clawed through the bathroom window, then slipped into Lori's room, having found Lori's bed empty and heard her voice downstairs, she'd made the call to Dallas, all the while worried about Misto. The old cat was worn out from running, tired and sore, and he'd been breathing hard when she left him. Now, still hearing Lori's and Cora Lee's voices from the kitchen, she fought the lock on Lori's window, pawed it open, and slipped out onto the roof. Peering down, she listened as Dallas spoke on his cell phone, talking with Max. She watched Rock pull on the lead, staring up into the night, fixed intently on Pearl's hidden car. She knew Dallas was waiting for backup. She wanted badly to follow when they closed in on Pearl's car. Instead she dropped off the roof onto Cora Lee's hood, then to the drive, and streaked around to the back and beneath the deck, where Misto lay curled up, breathing raggedly.

45

The maroon Jaguar sat high up the hill sheltered among a dark overhang of cypress branches, well hidden from the houses below. Weeks ago, Pearl had driven up here with Arlie when he was looking for a house. He'd taken one look at the neighborhood and pronounced it a wilderness, too far from the amenities as he called them, too removed from his lifestyle. Didn't that make her laugh. What about his lifestyle while he was in prison? Though the area *was* so out of the way she wondered if the cops even bothered to patrol here.

The street ended in a cul-de-sac, but a narrower road led away down the far side of the hill, and she had parked facing that for a quick exit. The night around her was clear, but a fog was creeping up from the scrubby canyon, making it look like a pale river. She could escape down in there if she needed to, though the idea of climbing down among that tangle of weeds and trees didn't really appeal; she'd done enough of that, earlier in the night.

Down the hill, despite fingers of fog, light from a thin moon picked out faintly the shapes of the large old houses. All were dark except for a faint glow from behind one, maybe a low-watt security light. The time was two forty-five. In the rearview mirror she watched Maudie, ready to stop her if she struggled with her bonds again; she'd already slapped her once for doing that. Maudie kept glancing down at the street below as if imagining that someone in one of those houses would wake and come to rescue her. When a couple of dogs started barking, Pearl studied the yards, but it was too dark to see where they were or what they were barking at. Only when a brighter light came on from behind one of the houses did she reach to switch on the ignition.

But then she paused. Maybe it was nothing, maybe the barking dogs had awakened someone, maybe they'd shut up and the light would go out again. This was too good a shelter to leave, she didn't want to move. Settling back, she thought about where she'd go once she had the bonds and ledger pages and with no loose ends left behind. No good to get involved with a casino anywhere, too easy for the cops to track her through the gambling industry. Unless she left the country, worked a casino in the Bahamas or maybe the West Indies. Behind her, Maudie had settled down, too, as if giving up her hopeful vigil. When the dogs barked again, Pearl thought shadows moved in the yard before the lighted house and she strained to see—but maybe the dogs were loose or tied out there, surely it was just the dogs, milling around.

It was maybe ten minutes later when lights blazed in the front windows and the front door opened, emitting a river of light. A man stepped out with a big dog on a leash. Was that the detective? Garza? With the light at his back she couldn't be sure. His build was the same as the Latino: square shoulders, short-clipped hair that looked dark. But what would he be doing here? He'd gone off with that Ryan Flannery and the cursed tracking dog—tracking Benny. Was *that* the tracking dog? But Benny wouldn't be up here, the dog couldn't have tracked him here, the kid couldn't climb all the way up here from the wreck, that whiny, limping kid. If he'd gone anywhere it would be downhill toward the village, if he could walk even that far. He'd be scared silly to climb up here alone, through the black woods.

The man turned, and the light caught his face. When she saw him clearly, again her hand slipped to the ignition, ready to ease the car away down the far side of the hill. It was Garza.

Could he have given up trailing Benny, and started tracking her car? But how could he even know Maudie was gone? When the detective and Flannery and her husband left to search for Benny, Maudie had been safe in the house. Or so they thought. And once she had gotten Maudie away, who was going to come to the door in the middle of the night and discover Maudie wasn't there? Not Jared, she thought, smiling. He'd be long gone, headed up the coast somewhere, maybe had hit some bar until closing time, to establish an alibi. She and the Colletto boys had escaped into the greenbelt together, Kent turning away downhill, she and Jared swinging back toward Maudie's house. Jared had slipped in through the studio while she waited among the trees in the dark yard, then had gone in later to get the kid. Now, watching Garza, she glanced again toward the escape road, but if she moved the car, even without lights he'd hear her. Or the dog would, and make a fuss that would bring the damned cop straight to her.

Maybe they'd be gone soon, maybe the dog had lost Benny's scent somewhere and the cop was just nosing around among the houses up here. Maybe he thought that, from above the woods, he might hear Benny crying for help. She had six hours until the bank opened, she could wait him out until he left. After the bank, she'd decide what to do with Maudie. She couldn't turn her loose to run to the cops; she'd have to dispose of her or, as much of a drag as it would be, she'd have to take Maudie with her, kill her somewhere far away, dump her where no one would find her.

M AUDIE, FROM THE moment Pearl parked at the top of the hill under the trees, had known where she was. Below, fog lay thick along the ravine, the black line of roofs softly silhouetted against it. They were just above the senior ladies' house. Even in the dark she knew the old established neighborhood, knew it from when she was a child and it had seemed so very far from the village. And knew it from more recently when she'd brought Benny up here to spend some time with Lori while she visited with Cora Lee, getting to know the four ladies, wanting to make friends her own age, establish some connections. Now, with the house so close, there had to be some way to reach them, to tell them she needed help.

She looked longingly at the soft light that burned around the back, most likely from the kitchen, and imagined the four women in their robes, sharing late-night cocoa. For her, they were worlds away; they might never know she'd been there. If she cried out for help, Pearl would hit her again or would drive off down the hill again. Even if she tried to cry out, she doubted they'd hear her since the dogs had started barking. She yearned to be down there safe in their kitchen. The thought of escape, of safety, brought tears of frustration that, with her hands tied behind her, she couldn't even wipe away. She didn't want Pearl to see how weak she was.

Whenever Pearl looked away from the rearview mirror, Maudie worked at the knots that bound her hands, picking and pulling at the soft belt, bending her fingers awkwardly. Pearl hadn't found the gun in her pocket. Hadn't felt it, hadn't even looked. Apparently she didn't think Maudie would have a gun or know how to use it. There were advantages in looking soft and helpless. And in not sharing all your personal information, even with your daughter-in-law. It hadn't been any of Pearl's business that she and Allen, on their weekend trips, had often included several hours at a county pistol range. They had kept several guns locked away, not only from Benny, but from any visitor who might enjoy snooping.

When one of the knots gave, a shock of excitement made her heart pound. It was almost loose. She tried to keep her upper body still as her cramped fingers fought to undo it. She was startled when, below at the seniors' house, lights suddenly blazed on in the front windows, the front door opened, and Detective Garza emerged with Ryan's tracking dog. She couldn't believe he was there, not a hundred yards from her.

Had they found Benny? Had they brought him here? Was he all right? She jerked her hand loose from the last knot, tearing her skin in a long burn. Then she remained still again, not daring to divert Pearl's attention from the scene that held them both riveted. And now with help so near, she was jolted to action. Slowly, watching Pearl, she reached toward her coat pocket.

HOLDING ROCK ON a short lead, moving along the porch away from the lighted doorway, Dallas stood against the wall of the house surveying the dark neighborhood. Beside him Rock was tense, predatory, his attention fixed on the wooded hill above. Light from the thin moon faintly defined the rising street, the big square houses and overgrown trees. Dallas couldn't see into the woods at the top of the hill, but the big dog was alerting him in every way, straining to move out, wanting to have a look. Slowly Dallas edged toward the hill, keeping Rock close, knowing better than to approach the car alone.

Earlier, in the seniors' kitchen, after he got the snitch's call, Dallas had tried to call Maudie at home. He had gotten no answer, though she'd promised to stay near the phone. He'd alerted Brennan, but the officer, watching both houses, hadn't seen or heard any disturbance. Brennan had seen Maudie's bedroom light go on, and in a little while go off again, and had assumed that in spite of the missing child, she might be lying down, preparing herself for whatever came next.

The dog was tense with nerves, and so was Dallas. Where was Max? Too risky to move up on that car without cover and blow the whole thing, if Maudie was up there, maybe get her killed. Staying to the darkest part of the yard as Rock tried to pull him up toward the woods, he paused when he heard a vehicle coming up the hill. Rock stopped and looked expectantly in that direction, knowing the sound of Max's truck. They heard it park somewhere in the dark below, and Dallas's phone vibrated.

"Rock's fixed on the top of the hill," he told Max. "Something's there, all right. We're just at the base of the hill, and he's hyped to have a look."

In a minute Max's shadow moved toward him through the dark. Rock wagged his tail and licked Max's hand, but then again he fixed his attention on the hill above, his ears sharply forward, his pale yellow eyes never wavering from the black tangle of woods.

Max looked at the eager dog, looked up the hill. "Let's go with it," he said, and the three headed silently up through the dark, Rock straining at the leash, the officers' hands close to their holstered weapons. Neither officer saw Joe Grey behind them slipping from the shadows. Moving swiftly, Joe picked up Pearl's scent from the damp air, just as Rock was doing, a scent that made the fur along his back bristle. The instant they glimpsed the car the two men separated, circling around to come at it from the back, and Joe moved unseen into the woods. When Dallas was deep among the trees he gave Rock the command to "down, stay."

Rock obeyed, but so grudgingly Joe thought he'd soon break position. Shivering, Rock stared at the car, the rumble in his throat so faint only Joe could hear it.

As Max moved along beside the car hunkered down, keeping below the windows approaching the driver's door, Joe saw movement behind the glass that made him want to yell, to warn the chief. Pearl had turned in the driver's seat, watching Max. Joe saw the gleam of a gun as she swung on Harper—and he did yell, yelled a warning, he couldn't help himself. Dallas appeared on the far side of the car, his flashlight blazing in on Pearl, her gun pointed at Max. At the same moment, Maudie rose up in the back-seat, a dark silhouette.

Two shots blasted the night: Maudie's gun and Max's. Dallas didn't fire for fear of hitting Max. Two shots were enough. Pearl jerked and fell against the door. Max flung the door open, his gun on her as he pulled her out of the car to sprawl facedown in the dirt.

Pearl didn't move. In the beams of the officers' lights a thin finger of blood began to pool from the back of her neck, and blood stained the ground beneath her. Joe could see where one bullet had exited, tearing through her throat. When Dallas shone his light around inside the car, Joe could see through the open door that two of the dashboard dials were shattered where a bullet must have passed through Pearl. Easing back out of the way, Joe lay down beside Rock, wanting to comfort the big dog. Rock was shaking—from the stress? From the smell of human blood? Or from the loud explosion of gunshots?

Lying close together, cat and dog watched Max slip into the backseat of the Jaguar beside Maudie and put his arm around her, saw the older woman lean against him.

Who had killed Pearl was a toss. But did it matter? Pearl wouldn't kill anyone else, Joe thought with satisfaction. And she wouldn't torment Benny or his grandma anymore.

And the tomcat had to wonder, what would happen to Pearl if indeed she now faced some divine retribution? This was a matter of conjecture, but Joe Grey had his own version.

46

Benny Toola's birthday, two days after his mother's death, could have been a grim affair for the little boy, and Maudie did her best to provide a gentle celebration. The child needed a party, needed folks around him who cared, who might herald a new stage in his life, help him deal with his fear and conflicted feelings. Benny had hated his mother, had mourned her lack of love for him. His shock when she murdered his father could have turned the child inward with a hatred and fear that might never leave him. But Pearl was his mother, after all, and he'd surely grieve for her, if only for what she'd denied him.

But Maudie's emotions were conflicted, too, her guilt at having shot Pearl battling with her sense of strength and closure. She didn't want to know the autopsy results, didn't want to know whether her shot or Max Harper's had killed Pearl. It was enough that she had taken a stand, though at that moment she could have done nothing less.

Max said she had saved his life. Maybe she had, or maybe he'd saved his own. Whatever the truth, she had set out to kill Pearl, to see that Pearl paid for Martin's death; she had never deceived herself about that. Now it was done, and she and Benny were free, now her concern was for Benny.

There would be no funeral until the coroner released the body. Most likely, he said, some time between Christmas and the New Year. Maudie hoped Benny could start the New Year with the funeral, too, behind him.

The day after Pearl died, Maudie made a trip down to the station to give her statement to Chief Harper and Detective Garza; then she fetched Benny from Ryan and Clyde's remodel, where he was happily scrubbing the bathroom tiles alongside Lori, and together Maudie and the little boy went shopping to pick out the makings of a special birthday gift.

They found a set of furniture Benny liked, bright oak with brass fittings, and they consulted paint samples, taking home dozens of little colored swatches which Maudie held up to the wall while Benny chose the one that pleased him. Returning to the store, they bought the paint, and the next morning they were up before dawn, Maudie making pancakes as Benny set the table. Then, together, they painted the walls of the little sewing room. When the paint was dry they washed the windows and polished the hardwood floor. The next morning, the furniture was delivered: a twin-sized bed with drawers underneath, a small desk and bookshelves and a soft pad to fit the window seat, which Maudie covered with a bright quilt. They hung the big bulletin board they had bought and a trio of framed airplane prints they had found in a hobby shop. Benny moved his clothes and his few possessions into his new room, and he slept there the night before his birthday, at first curled up on the window seat under Maudie's quilt, looking out over the rooftops and away across the greenbelt that ran behind the house.

"I looked for the yellow cat," he told Maudie the next morning. "The yellow cat on the roofs, and for Dulcie and Joe Grey and Kit, but they didn't come, no cat came. They haven't gone away?"

"They're not gone," Maudie told him. "Ryan and Clyde wouldn't let them go away. I'm sure that at least Ryan's gray tomcat will be here later, for your birthday party."

Neither Joe nor Dulcie nor Kit meant to miss Benny's birthday, though Misto was otherwise occupied. The night that Pearl was shot, Misto, who was curled up beneath the seniors' deck with Kit, felt lame and was hurting all over from his long run up the hills. Ryan had enticed him to come out, and she took him home with them, holding him on her lap as Clyde drove. Misto investigated the Damen house only briefly before he followed Snowball upstairs and curled up on the couch between the little white cat and Joe Grey. Next morning, the Damens and Joe crowded into Clyde's yellow roadster to take Misto to see Dr. Firetti.

Even after all the passing years, John Firetti remembered the little yellow tom kitten who, he'd suspected even then, would one day realize that he could speak. When the kitten disappeared from the shore where Firetti fed the strays, he had searched for weeks for him. "I put ads in the paper for a lost yellow kitten," he told Misto, "but they came to nothing. I hoped someone had adopted you, but I worried, wondered if you were with someone kind, if they were treating you well. I thought whoever took you might be strangers, tourists. I watched in case you should find your way back, and fretted about you for a very long time."

"I did find my way back," Misto said, laughing. "Though it took a while. I've wandered a long way and lived many places." He looked at John Firetti eagerly, as if he might like to share his adventures with the doctor, as if he might enjoy settling in with a human friend for a little while; and John looked back at him with such excitement and wonder that both Ryan and Clyde had to hide a grin. Joe Grey watched the two of them with interest. Maybe, he thought, Misto's tales might be worth a listen. Who knew what wild scenes the old cat could paint of close calls, of adventures and escapes among the human world.

There in the clinic, Dr. Firetti checked Misto over, then invited them across the way to his cottage, Clyde and Ryan for a cup of coffee. Mary Firetti settled Misto on a blanket on the flowered couch while Joe prowled the house, forever nosy, and John Firetti laid another log on the fire. Mary Firetti was a slim woman, her soft brown hair done up in a bun at the back, her denim jumper, over a white T-shirt, loose and comfortable, her leather sandals low-heeled and sensible. When she carried in the coffee tray, she set down a bowl of cream for Misto and one for Joe Grey. "Will you stay with us a while?" she asked Misto. Her direct address to him startled the yellow cat; he looked at her with alarm, then looked up at John.

"It's all right," John said. "Mary's kept the secret just as I have."

Misto looked at Mary for a long time, then stuck his nose in the cream. Yes, he would like to stay for a while. Mary seemed a warm, comfortable person, the Firetti cottage smelled of lavender and of cats, and he thought he quite liked the cozy household.

BENNY'S BIRTHDAY SUPPER featured an array of potluck casseroles and salads, many brought by their guests, and the chocolate birthday cake Maudie had made the night before, after Benny slept. Chocolate icing with Benny's name and HAPPY BIRTHDAY in red and green writing as fancy as Maudie's quilts. Around the cake was piled a mountain of gifts which, soon after supper, Benny tore open, scattering the wrappers and revealing bright and intriguing books he'd yet to read, board games he'd never played, more gifts than he could ever remember receiving, though Martin had done his best to please his little boy. Dulcie and Kit curled up beside him on the floor as he pored over the books, the lady cats snuggling close; around them the conversation swung comfortably from Christmas Day plans, to the depositions of Marlin Dorriss and Jared Colletto and the warrant out on Kent Colletto, to Pearl's embezzlement. Her ledger had not been found, but the copies of her alternate set of books had been sent to the LAPD. Though she would never face a judge in this life, the information would help Beckman Heavy Equipment straighten out their clients' accounts. The stolen money, if LAPD could uncover any hidden bank accounts in Pearl's name, might help make up the funds that the firm had refunded to their wronged clients.

As a fresh pot of coffee brewed, and second pieces of birthday cake were cut, a heated discussion ensued as to who would bring what dishes for Christmas Day at the Harpers' ranch. Soon that morphed into the last two church concerts and the Christmas play at Lori's school where she had wanted to play Mary, but yet was relieved that she hadn't been chosen; Lori and Cora Lee planned another visit to her pa at Soledad, the morning of Christmas Eve; and no one mentioned Benny's soon-to-be Christmas present, not a word, this was a gift Benny knew nothing about. The rescued German shepherd was, at that moment, playing with the Harpers' two dogs up at the ranch, an eight-month-old pup that his owner couldn't afford to keep, who needed training and patience but needed, most of all, a little boy to love him.

The day after Pearl was shot, when Dallas and Kathleen searched the Colletto garage, they found a bag of three pairs of fish-scented running shoes. Having presented Carlene Colletto with a warrant and searched the house, they found, hidden among Jared's last-semester school papers, ticket stubs for a round-trip flight to the Ontario airport in Southern California, under another name, but on the date that Martin and Caroline Toola were shot. The Orange County Sheriff's Office was still checking rental cars out of Ontario in that name, though it was unlikely Jared's prints would have remained in the car undisturbed all these months. The fake ID and credit card did not turn up, Jared had hidden them well or destroyed them.

Carlene Colletto had at first refused to let the detectives in. She read the warrant with the judge's signature twice, scowling, then had called the judge. When Judge Bryant's secretary assured her there was a legitimate warrant and she was obliged to honor it, Carlene had followed the detectives closely as they searched, crowding them, peering over their shoulders. "The boys can't have been part of those invasions. Jared was furious that they were happening right here in our little village, he was as disgusted with you police as everyone else." Carlene didn't seem to get it, didn't want to get it; her comments netted her a smile from Dallas, a haughty but amused look from Kathleen Ray.

It was the morning after Benny's birthday that Dallas, taking a run up to the fishing wharves, to the used-car lot where Jared and Kent had worked, found the dented brown pickup. The lot was tucked between a seafood restaurant and a tool repair, next to the wharves. There were three corrugated-tin storage sheds at the back, and the truck was in the center shed. The prints of both young men were on the dash, the door handles, and the steering wheel. The scent of long-dead fish was ground into the floor mats. A long scrape of black paint decorated the truck's left front and back fenders. Dallas photographed the vehicle inside and out, made casts of the tires, locked the shed, and strung crime-scene tape around it, effectively impounding the truck until the case was resolved.

As for Misto, he might have missed Benny's party but he wasted no time settling in with the Firettis, enjoying a welcome rest and Mary's succulent meals. The Firettis couldn't get enough of his stories, of his life among the coastal fishermen, of his travels with a long-haul trucker—of passing friendships that had all been conducted in silence on Misto's part except for an array of meows as he passed himself off as just another friendly, stray tomcat.

But soon after Christmas, the yellow cat would begin to remember other adventures, events he couldn't account for. He would wake from a nap experiencing a moment as bright as if it had just occurred, but a scene that did not come from his wanderings. He would remember running down cobbled streets that smelled of open sewers, remember hunting birds on rooftops made of straw thatch, times and places he was sure he'd never known, not in this life. The dreams frightened him, but they needled his curiosity, too, and opened a whole new world for Misto. He didn't know where the tales would lead but surely they fascinated his new human family—and they fired Dulcie and Kit to a frenzy of questions. Only Joe Grey scoffed. The tales of Misto's travels might be fine, but the gray tomcat didn't hold with this kind of story, with a cat remembering earlier lives, if indeed there was such a phenomenon. Dulcie laughed and cut her green eyes at him, and held to her own view of what Misto's dreams revealed about feline pasts.

On Christmas morning, as Misto basked contentedly beneath the Firetti Christmas tree, up in the hills at the Harper ranch an impromptu Christmas breakfast was under way. The invasions were ended—two of the invaders behind bars, one dead, and San Francisco PD was pursuing a solid lead on Kent Colletto. MPPD was back on regular hours, and every officer was in a mood to celebrate. As cars pulled into the ranch yard, and officers and their families and civilian friends carried covered dishes into the house, out in the fenced pasture Benny and his new pup ran, played ball, fell on the ground wrestling, took turns chasing each other. Lessons and training would come later; this was getting-acquainted time, bonding time.

From atop Ryan's truck, Joe and Dulcie and Kit watched the two young ones, their smiles indulgent and a bit smug. Benny was safe, and they had helped to put away the no-goods. Peace reigned over the small village, their friends were gathered close around them, the air was scented with breakfast delicacies. Turkeys would soon be cooking for Christmas dinner, and all was well in their small portion of the world. Only Kit seemed restless.

She thought about Christmas parties all over the village, about happy, laughing families, about the lavishly decorated trees and beautiful music. Thought about her gift from Lucinda and Pedric that she had found under their tree this morning: a present that Kit would treasure always. She thought about the satisfying pastiche of holiday joys, and knew she should envision nothing more— and yet Kit dreamed of more. There was an empty space in her little cat soul; even with all the riches she had, still something was missing. Thinking about the new year to come, she was so filled with restless longing that she began to pace atop the truck between Dulcie and Joe, paced back and forth, looking out to the wild fields and the vast and rolling sea. She had no clue to what lay ahead, no clue to the magic that waited for her in the coming year; she could only dream her impatient dreams, could only hope and wonder what was there, waiting for her, within the bright new year.